SHAPERS
of WORLDS
Volume IV

SHAPERS
of WORLDS
Volume IV

Science fiction and fantasy by authors who were guests on the
Aurora Award-winning podcast **The Worldshapers**

Edited by
EDWARD WILLETT

Illustrated by
WENDI NORDELL

SHADOWPAW
PRESS

SHAPERS OF WORLDS VOLUME IV
*Science fiction and fantasy by authors featured on
the Aurora Award-winning podcast* The Worldshapers

Published by
Shadowpaw Press
Regina, Saskatchewan, Canada
www.shadowpawpress.com

Trade Paperback ISBN: 978-1-989398-88-3
Hardcover ISBN: 978-1-989398-90-6
Ebook ISBN: 978-1-989398-89-0

Edited by Edward Willett
Cover art by Tithi Luadthong

Shadowpaw Press is grateful for the financial support of Creative Saskatchewan.

CREATIVE
SASKATCHEWAN

COPYRIGHTS

CONTENTS

INTRODUCTION

So, here I am, writing another introduction to another volume of short fiction by authors I've interviewed on my podcast, *The World-shapers*.

It is still amazing to me I've done this four times now. Back in 2019, when the podcast was new, and so was Shadowpaw Press, I was inspired to consider Kickstarting an anthology by a presenter at the SaskBooks (the organization of Saskatchewan publishers) annual conference in Saskatoon. She, a publisher based in Winnipeg, had successfully Kickstarted an anthology to the tune of $100,000, and I thought, *Hey, I know some authors! I could do that.*

And so I have, beginning in 2020 with the first *Shapers of Worlds*. (Although not, alas, to the tune of $100,000. But, hey, the *Shapers of Worlds Volume V* Kickstarter will be coming up in the spring of 2024, so it could still happen . . . hint, hint.)

Volume II followed in 2021, Volume III in 2022, and now, here comes Volume IV, featuring new fiction (and a few reprints) from another amazing group of authors, each of whom I got to know at least a little bit through an hour-long conversation about their creative processes: David Boop, Michaelbrent Collings, Roy M. Griffis, Sarah A. Hoyt, Sherrilyn Kenyon, Noah Lemelson, Edward M. Lerner, David Liss, Gail Z. Martin, Joshua Palmatier, Richard Paolinelli, Jean-Louis Trudel, James van Pelt, Garon Whited, James Kennedy, Mark Leslie, R.S. Mellette, and Lavie Tidhar. In addition, for the first time, every story is accompanied by an original black-and-white illustration from artist Wendi Nordell.

In the introduction to the last volume, I talked about the challenge of finding a new metaphor for this kind of anthology, which is, after all, quite different from the far more common themed anthology.

Rather than every story being based on the idea of, say, long-forgotten technological devices finding a new purpose or exploring what ancient gods might be up to in the modern world (two themes I've written stories for in anthologies Kickstarted by Zombies Need Brains LLC, the company founded by my fellow DAW author Joshua Palmatier—who, by the way, has a story in this anthology), the *Shapers of Worlds* anthologies are eclectic showcases for stories that have nothing in common except they're all fantastical and they're all written by authors I've interviewed.

In the introduction to the first volume, I rather self-servingly compared authors to potters, shaping worlds out of the clay of their own reading, thoughts, and experiences—self-servingly because I had a new series called Worldshapers launching at the same time that was kind of based on that metaphor (the cover of the first book even featured a potter shaping a world on the wheel).

The second year, I compared the anthology to a "cabinet of curiousities," the personal collections of oddments assembled by individuals in past centuries, the precursors to museums of natural history (and other sorts).

Last year, I was inspired by a walk in the prairie to compare the anthology to that kind of landscape, one that appears uniform (and rather uninspiring) on the surface that in fact contains fascinating ecological depth when you look closer, a rich variety of flora and fauna.

This year, for some reason—and maybe it's just because it's almost lunchtime as I write this—I keep thinking of food.

There are a number of directions such a metaphor could be taken. Do I call this anthology a smorgasbord, a buffet, or even dim sum? I could, but those are typically planned by a single chef, so they are more like a themed anthology.

How about tapas, small dishes that, eaten together, make a satisfying meal? That could work—though again, in a tapas restaurant, the dishes are likely all created by the same chef.

Maybe a charcuterie board? As it happens, my daughter recently ate with a friend at an Ottawa restaurant famed for its charcuterie and reported it was, indeed, sublime: the best she'd ever had. In book terms, that would make some stories rich cheeses, others thinly sliced but savoury meats, still others solid slabs of bread or crisp bits of toast; others pickled vegetables; and still others piquant bits of mustard or other condiments whose presence enhances the effect of the rest of the selection.

That could work, but maybe it's a bit overwrought.

No, in the end, I've settled on the most prosaic and yet (in dining terms) one of the most satisfying of bountiful spreads of food: the potluck.

There were a lot of potlucks in my upbringing, most of them associated with church. At a potluck, everyone brings something different to the table. Someone might offer a light, crispy, simple salad of lettuce, tomatoes, and a bit of vinaigrette or a delicious concoction combining watermelon, onions, feta cheese, and black olives; someone else, a heavier but fabulous potato salad from their German grandmother's book of recipes. Round, savoury meatballs steeped in homemade barbecue sauce sit next to sliced, glazed, and clove-studded ham, crisp-skinned fried chicken (again usually a family recipe), macaroni and cheese, scalloped potatoes, and a bewildering variety of casseroles, from tuna to vegetarian, with perhaps a lasagna for variety.

There are fresh-baked rolls and store-bought chips and dip, and on a separate table, the desserts await: fruit salad, perhaps, or chocolate cake; pecan pie or apple pie or rhubarb pie or any of half a dozen other kinds of pie; Nanaimo bars (invariably, if you're in Canada); possibly homemade ice cream; and, always, cookies.

Every potluck is unique, and yet, every potluck is satisfying. It's almost impossible to leave a potluck feeling you haven't dined sufficiently. Indeed, you'll generally leave feeling pleasantly stuffed or even a little overstuffed—but happy.

And that's why, after my highfalutin "this anthology is like a collection of beautiful pottery" and "this anthology is like a cabinet of curiosities" and "this collection is like a patch of prairie" metaphors, I've come down to earth with "this anthology is like a meal assembled by the ladies of the church on the first Sunday of the month and eaten in the fellowship hall."

Which, metaphor-wise, makes the authors into church ladies, the first Sunday of the month into the annual release of the *Shapers of Worlds* anthologies, and the book the potluck dinner itself.

That just leaves the fellowship hall to be assigned a metaphorical meaning, and that, dear reader, is where I hope you feel you are as you read these stories: inside a warm, welcoming, and cozy room filled with fellowship, the hum of conversation, laughter, and even, occasionally, tears (for some potlucks follow funerals), where you and your fellow readers partake of a fabulous meal of stories, served potluck-style by some of the most talented authors of science fiction and fantasy working today.

May you leave the fellowship hall pleasantly stuffed with vivid characters, memorable prose, and thought-provoking ideas: or maybe, even, a little overstuffed—but happy.

It's all on the table. Come and get it!

Edward Willett
Regina, Saskatchewan, Canada
September 8, 2023

MATTER OF LIFE AND DEATH

By Sherrilyn Kenyon

"Ding dong, the bitch is dead."

Elliot Lawson looked up from her email to laugh at her assistant, Lesley Dane. "And there is much rejoicing."

Dressed in a pink sweater and floral skirt, Lesley flounced around Elliot's tiny office with a wide smile before she added yet another bulging manuscript to the top of the mountain of manuscripts in Elliot's inbox. Was it just her, or did that thing grow higher by the heartbeat? It was like some bad horror movie.

The Stack That Wouldn't Die.

"Just think," Lesley continued, "no more emails with her calling us names and complaining about everything from title to synopsis to . . . you know, everything."

That was the upside.

The downside? "And no more selling three million copies the opening day, either." While Helga East had been the biggest pain in the ass to ever write a book, her thrillers had set so many records for sales that her unexpected death left a huge hole in their publishing program. One that would take twenty or more authors to fill.

Elliot's stomach cramped at that reality and at the fact that she'd just lost her star pony in the publishing race. "What are we going to do?"

"We'll build another blockbuster."

She scoffed at her assistant. "You say that like it's an easy thing. Trust me, if it was, every book we published would be one." And that didn't happen by a long shot. They didn't even break even on ninety percent of them.

"Yeah, but still, the bitch *is* dead."

It was probably wrong to be happy about that, but like Lesley, she couldn't help feeling a little relief. Helga had been a handful.

Oh, who was she fooling? Helga had been the biggest bitch on the planet, a chronic thorn who had given Elliot two ulcers and a permanent migraine for four solid months around the release of any of Helga's books. In fact, Helga had been screaming at her over the phone when she'd had a heart attack and keeled over. It was creepy, really. One second, she'd been calling Elliot's intelligence and parentage into question and the next . . .

Dead.

Life was so fragile, and tragedies like this rammed that home.

Lesley's phone rang. She left to answer it while Elliot stared out her tiny window at the red brick building next door where another drone like her worked a sixty-hour-a-week job at the bank. She didn't know his name, and yet she knew a lot about him. He brought his lunch to work, preferred a brown tweed jacket, and tugged at his hair whenever he was frustrated. It made her wonder what unconscious habits she had that he'd pegged about her. They'd never waved or acknowledged each other in any way, yet she could see enough personal details about him that she'd know him anywhere.

Not wanting to think about that depressing fact, she returned her attention to the cover proofs piled in front of her. One was for Helga's next book—the one she'd been working on when she'd died.

Her phone dinged, letting her know she had a new email.

Sighing, she picked up her phone and looked at it.

For a full minute, she couldn't breathe as she saw the last name she'd ever expected to see again.

Helga East.

Relax. It's just an old email that was forwarded by someone else or one that got lost in cyberspace for a couple of days. No need to panic or be concerned in the least. It was nothing.

Still, her stomach habitually knotted as she opened it.

Tell me honestly, Elliot, does it hurt to be that stupid? Really? What part of that heinous, godawful cover did you think I'd approve of? I hate green. How many times do we have to have this argument? Get that bimbo off the cover and take that stupid font and tell Creative to stick it on the cover of someone too moronic to know better.

H.

P.S. The title, Nymphos Abroad, *is disgusting, demeaning, and insulting. Change it, or I'll have another talk with your boss about how incompetent you are.*

She sucked her breath in sharply as she realized the email pertained to the cover on her desk.

A cover Helga had never seen. It'd only arrived that morning. Two days after Helga's funeral.

Yeah, there was no way it was Helga. Anger whipped through her as she replied to the email. "Okay, Les, stop messing with me. I'm not in the mood." She hit SEND.

A second later, a response came back.

Les? Are you on drugs? Surely you can't afford them on your measly salary. I've seen the cheap shoes you wear and that sorry excuse for a designer handbag that you think no one will know you bought in Times Square for five dollars. Now quit stalling, stop reading your email, and call down to art and get me a cover worthy of my status.

She looked out her door to see Lesley on the phone, her back to her computer. Definitely not her pretending to be Helga.

But someone was. And they were doing a good job of it, too. They sounded *just* like her.

Who is this? she typed.

Helga, you nincompoop. Who did you think it was? Your mother? I swear, is there no one up there with a single brain cell in their head?

It couldn't be. Yet the return address in the header was Helga's. It was an email addy she knew all too well: numberonewriter @heast.com.

Maybe one of Helga's heirs was messing with her. But why would they do such a thing? Surely they wouldn't be as cruel as Helga had been?

Then again, maybe it was genetic. Meanness like Helga's had

to be hardwired into her DNA. Venomous cruelty was what the lonely old woman had lived and breathed.

Her heirs wouldn't be able to see that cover. They'd have no way of knowing what was on it.

There was that. No one outside of their publishing house had seen it.

Another email appeared.

Why are you still sitting at your desk, staring into space? I told you what to do. Get me a decent cover, you twit.

A chill went down her spine. One so deep that she actually jumped when her cell phone went off, signalling her that she had a new voicemail message. Weird, she hadn't heard it ring.

Reaching down, she pulled it up and accessed her box.

"I will not stand for that tawdry, disgusting cover. Do you hear me, Elliot? I want it gone, right now. Hit delete."

Her heart pounded at a voice she'd know anywhere.

Helga.

"You all right?"

She looked up at Lesley, who was staring at her from the doorway. "I . . . I . . . ." Pulling up her voicemail screen on her phone, she tapped the message. "Tell me what you hear?"

Lesley put the phone up to her ear. After a few seconds, she scowled. "Man, I hate those pocket dials where all you get is background noise. What kind of imbecile doesn't lock their phone?" She handed it back.

Baffled, Elliot replayed it and held it up to her ear to listen. It was still Helga, plain as the desk in front of her. "It's not a butt dial. Can't you hear her?" She held it back out to Lesley.

Again, Lesley listened. "There's no voice, El. Just a lot of background sounds, like trucks on the highway or something, and someone laughing. You okay?"

Apparently not. How could they listen to the same thing and yet hear such radically different messages?

She swiped back to the home screen, and gave Leslie a forced smile. "Fine. Stressed. Tired."

Crazy . . .

Clearing her throat, she put the phone on her desk. "Did you need something?"

"Just reminding you about the marketing meeting in five minutes."

"Thanks." Elliot gathered her notes for the meeting while she tried her best not to think about the phone call and emails from a writer who was dead. It wasn't Helga. Some sick psycho was messing with her head.

Or it was a friend with a sorry excuse for a sense of humour.

Yeah, that would be her luck.

It's not funny, folks. But the one thing she knew from being an editor was that humour was subjective. How many times had Helga written something that she'd rolled her eyes over only to have the millions of readers out there find it hysterical?

Maybe I'm being Punk'd.

Could happen . . . If only she was lucky enough for some hot celeb to pop out of a closet.

But there was no hot cheese in the meeting. Only mind-numbing details about books they'd already gone over a million times, which left her attention free to contemplate who was being highly cruel and unusual to her.

Maybe it's someone in this meeting.

She looked around at her coworkers, most of whom appeared

as stressed out and bored as she was. No, they were too involved with their own lives to care about harassing her.

Why is this meeting taking so long?

It was hellacious.

Subversively, she glanced down at her watch and did a double-take. Was it just her, or was the second hand taking a thirty-second pause between each tick?

By the time the meeting let out, she felt like she'd been stretched on the rack. Oh, good Lord, why did they have to have these time-sucking wastes all the time? What Torquemada SOB thought this was a good idea?

But at least it was finally over. She breathed a sigh of relief as she gathered her things and headed back to her personal space.

The moment she was back in her office, she checked her email. There were ninety, *n-i-n-e-t-y*, messages from her wannabe Helga stalker.

She deleted them without reading.

Trying to put it out of her mind, she turned around in her chair to look at her "friend" in the other building. For once, his office was dark. How strange. He never left early. But her attention was quickly drawn to something that was being reflected in the darkness of her glass. Something someone had attached to the cork bulletin board that she'd hung next to her door.

With a gasp, she turned around to see if her mind was playing tricks.

It wasn't.

Her heart in her throat, she got up and went to the thing. As she reached for it, her hand shook.

Someone had taken the mechanical printout of Helga's cover and pinned it with a blood-red tack to the board. It had nasty comments written all over it with a black magic marker. Worse? The handwriting looked just like Helga's.

Terror filled her as she ripped it down, then made her way to Lesley's desk. Lesley paused mid-stroke on the keyboard to look up at her.

"Who did you let into my office while I was at the meeting?"

"No one."

"Someone went in there." She held the marked-up printout toward Lesley.

She frowned. "Why are you showing me that?"

"I want you to tell me who wrote on it."

Her scowl deepened. "You did, Elliot."

What? She snatched it back and turned it over.

All of Helga's writing was gone. Now the only pen marks were where someone had approved the art by placing Elliot's initials in the margins. "I didn't do this."

Lesley looked at it carefully. "It's your handwriting, hon. Believe me, I know."

But Elliott hadn't written on it. Not even a little bit.

How was this possible? How?

Her head started throbbing. Without another word, she returned to her office and sat down to stare at the mechanical of the cover sans the nastiness.

"I'm losing my mind." She had to be. There was no other explanation for what was going on.

The skin on the back of her neck tingled as if someone was watching her. She turned around in her chair to inspect her office.

She was alone.

Still, the feeling persisted. And even more concerning was the prickly sensation that something wasn't right.

I'm being haunted . . .

Yeah, that's what it felt like. That uneasy feeling in the pit of her stomach. Something evil was in the room with her. It was all but breathing down her neck.

Panicked, she shot back to Lesley's desk. She needed to feel connected to someone alive.

Lesley gave her an arch stare. "You're pale. Is something wrong?"

If not for the fear of Lesley thinking her insane, she'd confide in her. But no one needed to know her suspicion. "Doing research for a book on my desk. You know anything about the paranormal?"

"Not really, but . . ."

"What?"

"I have an exorcist on speed dial."

Elliott burst into nervous laughter. Until she realized Lesley wasn't joking. "You're serious?"

"Absolutely. My best friend in the world is an exorcist and demonologist."

"Who in the world has a friend who's an exorcist?"

Lesley held up her phone and grinned. "Me. Whatcha want me to check?"

"Um. . . . do you think I could speak with your friend?"

Her grin returned to a frown. "Sure. Her name's Trisha Yates. You want me to email it to you?"

"Please." Even though she was still skittish about her office, Elliott returned and closed her door. There was no need for Lesley to overhear this particular conversation.

Out of habit, she glanced to the office across the way to see her "friend."

Her heart stopped beating.

He was hanging from the ceiling, swinging in front of his desk.

No! It wasn't possible. She closed her eyes and covered them with her hands. *It's not real. It's not real . . .*

But it was. As soon as she opened her eyes, she saw him again across the way. Medics were swarming his office, cutting him down.

He was dead. Her unknown partner across the way was gone.

All of a sudden, both of her phones started ringing. Gasping, she jumped. She grabbed her cell phone. "Hello?"

No one was there.

Same for the office phone. All she heard was a dial tone.

"It doesn't hurt, you know."

She spun at the sound of a male voice behind her. The ghostly image of the man from the other building stood there. "W-w-what doesn't hurt?" It was like someone else had control of her body. She was strangely calm, and yet inwardly, she was freaking out.

"Death. We all die." He walked through her.

Breathless, scared, and shaking, she watched as he continued past her to the wall. He went through it and walked back to his cubicle in the other building.

No . . . no . . .

No!

As soon as the ghost was over there, the corpse, which was now lying on the floor, turned its head toward her and smiled.

She stumbled back into the door. Terrified, she spun around and clawed at the handle until she was able to open it.

Lesley met her on the other side. "Okay, you are seriously starting to freak me out. What's going on?"

I'm locked in a horror movie.

She didn't dare say that out loud. Les would never understand.

Without a word, she headed for the bathroom with her phone.

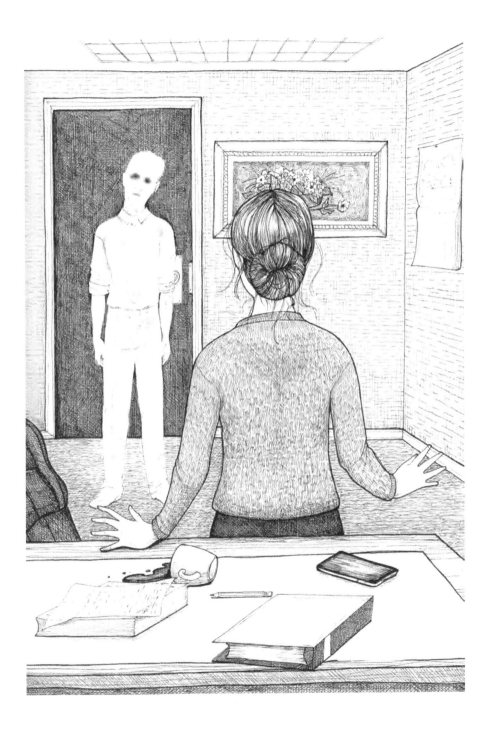

She pulled up the email Lesley had sent her and then dialled the number.

"Hello?"

Wow, the exorcist sounded remarkably normal. Even friendly. "Is this Trisha?"

"Yes. You are . . ." She paused as if searching the cosmos for an answer. "Elliott Lawson."

"How did you know that?"

"I'm psychic, sweetie. I know many things."

Elliott wasn't so sure she liked the sound of that. But before she could comment, the phone went dead. She growled in frustration as she tried to dial it again.

Nothing went through.

Instead, her email filled up with more postings from Helga . . .

And other authors, too—some of whom she hadn't worked with for several years.

"Why did you refuse to renew my contract?"

Elliott shrieked at the mousy voice that came out of a stall near her. A woman in her mid-thirties came out. Her skin had a greyish cast to it, and her eyes were dark and soulless.

"Emily? What are you doing here?" Emily had been one of the first authors she'd bought as a new hire. They'd had a good ten-book run before Elliott made the decision to cut her from their schedule. While Emily's numbers had held steady, they hadn't grown. Every editor was held accountable for their bottom line, and Emily had been hurting her chances for advancement. So Elliott had decided to move on to another author.

"Why did you do it? I was in the middle of a series. I had fans and was growing. I don't understand."

"It was business."

Emily shook her head. "It wasn't business. I can count off three dozen other authors who don't sell as well as I did whom you've kept on all these years."

"Not true." She always cut anyone who couldn't pull their weight.

Emily looked down at her arms, then held them up for Elliott to see. "I killed myself over it. After five years of us talking on the phone and working together, you didn't even send over a card for my funeral. Not one stinking, lousy card."

"I didn't know."

"You didn't care."

Elliott struggled to dial her phone. "You're not dead. This is a nightmare."

"I'm dead. Damned to hell for my suicide because of *you*!" Her eyes turned a bright, evil red as the skin on her face evaporated to that of a leather-fleshed ghoul. She rushed at Elliott.

Screaming, Elliott ran for the door.

The handle was no longer there. She was trapped inside.

With Emily.

Terrified and shaking, she pounded on the door with her fist. "Help me! Please! Someone help me!"

Emily grabbed her from behind and yanked on her hair. "That's what I begged for. Night after night after night. But no one answered my pleas, either. I spent two years trying to get another contract, and no one would touch me because of the lies you told about me. All I ever dreamed about was being an author. I didn't want much. Just enough to live on. Two books a year. But you couldn't allow me to have that, could you? You ruined me."

"I'm sorry, Emily."

"It's too late for sorry." Emily slung her through the door.

Elliott pulled up short as she found herself back in her office.

Only it was hot in there. Unbearable. She went to the window to open it.

She couldn't.

When she tried to turn the furnace down, it burned her hand. It whined before it spewed steam all over her.

She turned to run, only to find more hateful notes from Helga.

Suddenly, laughter rang out. It filled the room and echoed in her ears.

She spun around, doing her best to locate the source. There was no one there—no one until Lesley appeared in the corner.

Elliott ran to her and grabbed her close, holding on to her like a lifeline. "I need to go home, Les. Right now."

"You are home, Elliott. This is where you spend all of your time. This is what you love. It's all you love." Lesley pulled out her chair and held it for her. "Go ahead. Reject those books. Crush more writers' dreams. You're famous for not pulling punches. For telling it like it is. Go on. I know how much you relish giving your honest, unvarnished opinion."

A thousand crying voices rang out in a harsh, cacophonous symphony.

Your writing is amateurish and pedestrian. Do not waste my time with any more submissions. I only give one per customer, and your number is up.

If you can't take my criticism, then you've no business being a writer. Trust me. I'm a lot kinder than your readers, if you ever have any, will be.

While I found the idea intriguing, your writing was such that I couldn't get past the second page. I suggest you learn a modicum of grammar or, better yet, stick to blog posts and Twitter feeds for your creative outlet.

Over and over, she was inundated with rejections and comments she'd written to writers.

And for once, she realized just how harsh they were.

Elliott shook her head, trying to clear it. "Helga! Why are you haunting me? Why can't you leave me in peace?"

Lesley tsked at her. "Oh honey, Helga isn't haunting you."

"Yes, she is. I know I should have gone to her funeral, but—"

"Elliott, Helga didn't die." Lesley gestured toward her computer monitor. Her email vanished to show an image of Helga happily at work in her office. "You did."

"I don't understand."

Laughing, Lesley transformed into the image of a red demon with glowing yellow eyes. "Welcome to hell, my dear. From this day forward and throughout all eternity, you will get to be Helga's editor. Oh, and I should mention, she's now doing a book a week."

ADVENT

By James Kennedy

My father did something when I was about four that I've never forgotten. My parents liked different TV shows, so when Mom and Jenny and I stayed downstairs in the warm family room, watching the colour TV with the lights on, Dad would head upstairs and watch his black-and-white set in their chilly bedroom in the dark. He'd watch TV in his own strange way, lying on his back with his hands behind his head, his head slightly lifted, as if paused in the middle of a sit-up, the bedroom flickering with spooky blue light.

I had come upstairs for some reason. Dad was watching a TV movie—for years afterward, I actually wondered if this movie even existed, or if I'd only dreamed it, because what my father did next was so unlike him—in the movie, a man is driving a car around and there's a truck that is always following him. The man gets more and more scared by the truck. The truck won't stop chasing him. You never saw the face of the man driving the truck.

I said, "Who's the man in the truck?"

Dad turned and smiled. "It's the Devil."

Dad's smile right then didn't fit with anything else I remember about him. He never messed with us like that. He never tried to frighten us. I can't imagine him joking about the Devil because he took religious stuff seriously. But I remember it.

Around the same time, my family went to see *Star Wars* at the drive-in. After the movie, I broke down crying because I somehow got the idea that people who died in a movie actually died in real life. I knew that movies were make-believe, but I somehow felt that death itself couldn't be faked—so the actor who played Obi-Wan Kenobi must've gotten the script and was really excited about being in the movie, until he read the part where his character got killed by Darth Vader, but he decided it would still be worth it, so he told his wife and children and grandchildren that he was going to go ahead and make this movie in which he got killed. They tried to convince him not to do it, but he insisted, no, no, it's something he needed to do. I wondered if the Obi-Wan Kenobi actor's grandson felt upset whenever he watched the movie, or maybe during the scene where his grandpa got killed, he just visited the bathroom for a little while.

My father explained in the drive-in parking lot that the death was just pretend. It was a summer night and I remember as he spoke I could see the giant screen rising up behind him and the movie starting all over again.

WHEN I WAS six my father died.

Mom fell apart. I didn't realize it at the time. I just thought she was always tired. Her room would always be dark, even though it was sunny outside. The shades were drawn and light was trying to bust in any crack it could. Mom would be on the bed with a pillow pressed to either side of her head. I had to tiptoe up to her to ask her permission if I could do something. I didn't need permission, but I wanted to ask permission. I remember Mom's head scrunched between those two pillows, giving permission, her eyes closed, the rest of her body hidden under the blankets. Like she was just a head.

We ended up leaving our house for a little while. We moved into the house my father had grown up in so that Grandma could help us out. Mom didn't have much family, so when she married my father she really married our family too. Mom and Grandma always liked each other, even though Grandma seemed so tough and Mom wasn't. They were always having long talks over coffee at the kitchen table.

They set me up in Dad's old room. Only when I was actually sleeping in his old bed for the first time did it fully hit me that this was the house that Dad had grown up in. That he had been my age in that room. I tried to imagine what it was like to be Dad in that bed, as a kid. But it felt pretend.

It was around then that the furnace started talking.

———————

I HID under the table and listened to the family. Thanksgiving was over and the house was dim and it smelled like a party, smoky and adult. I was full and sleepy and I should've been in bed but my aunts and uncles and cousins were talking, in low voices, about Dad.

Earlier that night, before everyone came over, I'd set up the action figures in my room, or what was Dad's room. I had almost convinced myself that he was going to come back for Thanksgiving. The whole family was gathered at Grandma's house, so it was a perfect time for Dad to make a big surprise entrance. Maybe the car crash, or what they said was a car crash, had been pretend. The coffin was closed at the funeral. I never saw him. And when we went to the cemetery and I saw the hole they were going to put it in, I didn't actually see it happen, I didn't want to, and ended up crying in the car with Uncle Ted when they buried him. So there was a chance.

That Thanksgiving night, I'd taken out all the action figures that Dad had bought that one Saturday that Mom was at the doctor with Jenny, the day when it was just him and me. That way, when he came into my room later, he'd see that I remembered that particular Saturday, that I remembered exactly which action figures he had bought for me, that those were the ones that were most important. He'd bought me all the cantina creatures at once: Hammerhead, Walrus Man, Greedo, and Snaggletooth. Dad, I realized with wonder, could buy action figures any time he wanted, four at a time, even if it wasn't a special occasion.

I had the figures all set up in my room, my spaceships surrounding them, ready to attack. I hadn't let anyone touch them. Jenny came in, said she wanted to play, she had an idea for a story. I said no, get out, this isn't for you. She went away crying. Anything I did made her cry.

LAST YEAR at Thanksgiving Dad had made a surprise for me in the basement of Grandma's house. I was scared of Grandma's basement because there was no carpet or wallpaper or nice furniture.

The floor was concrete and the walls seemed cut straight out of rock and it smelled damp, like a cave. It was strange to me that a house would have in it a room that was so rough and dirty. A furnace squatted in the corner, huge and metal and old, pipes branching out of it all in crazy directions like it was reaching arms into the ceilings and walls. Dad went down into the basement and told me I couldn't come down for a little while. He was making a haunted house, he said.

When Dad opened the door, I saw that he'd covered the stairs with blankets and pillows so that they made a smooth hill, and there was a swamp of pillows and blankets at the bottom. Dad had my plastic orange sled. He put me on the sled and blindfolded me. I grabbed onto the handles and he sent me sliding down the stairs. I flew down into the basement, crash-landing into a pile of pillows. All through the basement, he had made a maze of sheets and cushions and chairs, tunnels, and caves. I couldn't see with the blindfold. I had to feel my way. I followed Dad's voice. I crawled into a big plastic garbage can. He had lined it full of blankets.

The can lurched, and suddenly I could feel it was in the air— Dad was flinging the garbage can around with me inside, faster and faster, I was dizzy and screaming for him to stop, stop, no, more, more, more!

THIS YEAR'S Thanksgiving was only a few weeks after Dad's funeral. I was under the table and listening to the adults. I saw lots of socks. It was hot under there. Outside the snow was dumping down, the roads were dangerous, nobody wanted to go home. The fire was humming, spoons dinged on plates, somebody was pouring coffee, my cousin Linda was playing the piano. I tried to listen my way through the noise and hear what they were saying about Dad.

The heating vent said: "Your Dad is in hell."

I flew out from under the table, the tablecloth came off with me, all the dishes jumped and the coffee spilled, I was shouting that they were all liars, there wasn't a car crash, Dad didn't go to hell, where was Dad?

And for a second they all just looked at me.

I DIDN'T GET in trouble for ripping the tablecloth off the table. Mom helped me get ready for bed and then went downstairs to say goodbye to everyone. Mom hadn't made me clean up the action figures. They were still set up on the carpet.

The wind was rattling the window screen. The world was buried in snow. Everyone was going home. I watched all the cars' red tail lights creep down the street, smaller and smaller, eaten by the blue dark. I heard Grandma cleaning up downstairs. Mom came back up and talked to me and tucked me in. Her face was scrunched up.

I asked why we couldn't be at our own house.

Mom said it would be better if we stayed away from our house for a while.

After she left I lay there, not sleeping, as Mom helped Grandma finish cleaning and came upstairs and went to bed. Then everyone was asleep.

I was awake.

A voice was coming from the heating vent. The furnace at Grandma's house had a metal mouth in every room, it had the whole house clutched up with aluminum throats and it was speaking quietly. I got out of bed and took the grate out of the vent and lay with my ear in the hole. The hot wind blew in my ear. I closed my eyes and I heard something like a man who lived in the furnace murmuring to himself, talking like he didn't know I was listening. He talked on and on.

The man in the furnace stopped talking to himself and said in my ear:

"This is the Devil's radio."

I jerked my ear away from the vent. Everyone else in the house was asleep. I was alone in the dark. I edged away and opened the door to my room. The hallway was dark, too. I wanted to turn on the lights. The furnace said no. I reached to turn them on anyway. The furnace said I'd better not turn them on or it would show me something I didn't want to see.

I looked into Grandma's room. She was asleep. The furnace blew its hot breath on her. I looked into Jenny's room and Mom's room. The furnace breathed over them too.

"I eat time," said the furnace. "I eat their time, I eat your time, when I'm done eating their time you'll be all alone. And when I'm done eating your time I'll eat you."

I was standing in the bathroom, looking in the dark mirror. My face looked wrong in the dark. The shadows were buzzing with shapes.

"Come downstairs," said the furnace.

I walked down the dark stairs to the basement. The furnace crouched in the back of the storage room, an upside-down metal tree spreading its roots upward throughout the house, dead but hissingly alive. It watched me with a flickering red eye and a steady orange eye, glowing on top of each other in the dry darkness.

I knew what it demanded. I ran back upstairs. I knew what

would happen if I didn't give it. I ran to my room and took Greedo and dumped it down the furnace's throat. I heard him ding and tumble down to hell.

"Not enough," said the furnace. "I'll take Grandma first."

I dumped down Hammerhead. Snaggletooth.

"More, more, more," said the furnace.

I dumped down Walrus Man, heard him rattle and slide down the hot metal tunnels.

"Or maybe Mom," said the furnace.

I took fistfuls of action figures and threw them down the vent. The furnace just hummed. My hands were shaking. My face was hot. The furnace ate them all.

IN BETWEEN THE kitchen and the family room was a step. I was playing there with some wooden blocks Grandma had brought down from the attic. I was trying to build something that used every block, but Jenny was being a baby, she kept taking the blocks.

"I need that," she said, but I grabbed the blocks back, and she started crying again. All she did was cry. Mom and Grandma were right there and I expected to get in trouble. I always got in trouble when it came to Jenny, no matter what I did.

Not this time. Mom took Jenny away somewhere else, gently. Grandma and I were alone now.

Grandma was the opposite of Mom. Mom was slight and soft-spoken and always seemed to be fading away. Grandma was like a big friendly boat. It was impossible to imagine Grandma staying in bed for days. I remembered Dad talking about how Grandma made it through the Depression. At first I just had the vague idea that meant Grandma had somehow got through some huge sadness.

"Your father would play with those blocks, right where you're sitting," said Grandma. "He'd sit there for hours while I stood over here and cooked. He had concentration."

I was still sitting at the step with the blocks, looking up at her. She was my Grandma and I loved her, but she was so old and huge and wrinkled that she was a monster. The idea that she and I were of the same species, that she had ever been any age other than what she was now, did not fit.

"Where are your space toys?" she said.

Grandma didn't miss a thing. If I lied about the action figures she would know. She'd get it out of me somehow that I'd thrown them down the vent. My face got hot and red. I stared at the blocks.

Grandma didn't say anything for a while.

"I want to show you something else your father did," said Grandma.

I didn't say anything.

"I found it just a few years ago," said Grandma. "I think he forgot he did it. It was a funny thing for him to do, for him to hide it there. He had imagination."

Grandma was always telling me about what Dad did in that house as a boy. This was the window seat he liked to read in. That was where he wrote all over the wall and got in big trouble, and if you looked hard, you could still kind of see it. Here in front of the fireplace was where he would put on his shows for everyone. But the way Grandma said "it was a funny thing for him to do," I already knew I didn't want to see it. Still, Grandma was already taking me into the basement, I don't think she even noticed I didn't want to go down there. I heard Mom playing with Jenny somewhere else in the house, I so badly wanted to be with them instead, but Grandma was taking me down the creaky wooden steps, steps which didn't even have backs, so you could slip down through them if you were only a little smaller than me, she took me into the basement and all the way back to the furnace.

The flickering red eye and the steady orange eye stared blankly. Behind the furnace were two metal doors. The doors were set right in the concrete wall.

"The fireplace is right above us, these things are to catch the ash," said Grandma, and opened one of them with a puff of white-grey dust.

A metal box stuck out of a heap of ash, about the size of a shoebox. Grandma took the box out.

"It was a strange little thing your father did," said Grandma, and gave me the box.

She nodded at me. I opened it. Inside there was a small man made of corn husks.

There was something wrong about it.

"He got that at the state fair," said Grandma. "It was his project. He made the rest himself. He made this little shrine."

The corn husk doll was decorated with seeds and bits of wood and leaves and pine cones, but it was all frozen in clear glue. The doll originally had a blank face but my father had made eyes and a mouth out of seeds and hair from pine needles. Its expression was still blank. I suppose it should've all crumbled away a long time ago but then again it was trapped by the glue, the seeds frozen before they could sprout, crumbled away inside themselves.

The corn husk doll was looking at me. I did not want to look at that doll. I knew that Grandma was trying to share something about my Dad but I didn't like that doll.

Grandma looked disappointed. I knew she thought I was a soft thing. When Grandpa was still alive he took me ice fishing once. I hated it because I was just standing there in front of a hole freezing to death doing nothing. When Grandpa finally pulled something out of that hole, it was even worse, because he made me hold the slimy thing for a picture, and all I wanted to do was get away, to go watch TV in the warm house. Maybe when Grandpa was five he would've loved to hold a dead fish but I was not in his Depression.

Grandma put the doll back in the box. The inside of the box was decorated too, with glued-in pennies and bits of fancy fabric and shrunken grey teeth and hair. They were his baby teeth, Grandma started to explain, this was his hair. I didn't want to look at it. She closed the box. She put it away right back where Dad had left it when he was a little boy, tucked into that heap of ash.

———

THAT NIGHT, I listened to the vent again.

What if, I thought, what if I were small enough to fall down into the vent myself, and enter the hot dark veins, and I could travel by secret tiny aluminum hallways, a secret maze in my father's house, it all goes down to a hot belly, it all goes down to hell. But secret mazes can lead to other places too. I imagined another vent, in a secret room that had no windows or doors. If I could find that secret room, I thought, Dad might be waiting for me in that secret room.

I put my ear on the vent and listened. Nobody was talking. But I knew the furnace was getting ready to ask for more. The corn husk man with his frozen face was waiting, hidden in that little box.

The vent kept blowing empty air.

———————

WE WERE BUNDLED up in coats and hats and mittens and we were in our station wagon, headed out for the Christmas tree farm. Carols were playing on the radio. Mom was singing along, she wanted us all to sing along too, she really wanted it. Grandma was singing, and my cousins Cindy and Linda came along too, they were in junior high, they didn't want to sing, they barely existed, they talked about things that didn't even make sense. Grandma was driving and Mom was in the passenger seat and Jenny was between Cindy and Linda. I was in the way back, bumping along, watching the road fly away backward from under me. I didn't have anything to do with them. The sky was an iron wall locked down tight, snow swarming and swimming around like it wanted in. Dirty melted snow made the carpet a wet dark brown. There was a crumpled cardboard thing for French fries down there and some dirty loose bolts and crumbs of something. The station wagon smelled like Dad. I was warm and I didn't want to get out and go to the Christmas tree farm.

We crunched to a stop in the gravel. Cindy and Linda were complaining it was too cold and it would take forever to find a tree and why did they have to be there? They had an artificial tree at home. Grandma shut them down with a look. Mom's cheeriness was getting brittle. This was something Mom needed. I waited for someone to open the back door so I could get out. The back door swung open and there was Mom. The stuffy smell flew out of the car and now it was sharp clean winter air on my face and in my lungs. I was wrapped up tight in sweaters and scarves and boots, and now Mom put my hood up and I heard the string rubbing busily inside the jacket as she drew it tight and tied a knot. I was as snug and warm as if I were sealed in a space suit. I was ready to help find the tree.

We got out to the barn where they were selling hot chocolate and doughnuts. Cindy and Linda wanted to stay there, they said it was too cold to look for a tree, they knew the boy selling dough-nuts so they wanted to stay. Grandma bought me a doughnut and hot chocolate. The doughnut was tough and chewy and the hot chocolate burned my tongue. I wasn't going to finish my doughnut and Jenny asked for the rest but I said no and finished it anyway even though I didn't like it so much.

We got into a wagon that was pulled by a tractor with some other family. We didn't talk much to them. The tractor took us way out into the forest. Christmas trees were poking up everywhere in crooked lines, caked with snow and ice. The wagon jolted along the muddy trail and the tractor was loud and smelled like burning gas.

The wagon stopped and let us off and it drove away. We were left in a snowy grove. Christmas trees waited all around us, holding their breaths. All the trees looked the same. The snow was flying too thick and hard in my eyes. I felt the heat leaking out everywhere all over me.

Grandma and Mom and Jenny and Cindy and Linda were spreading out, wandering from tree to tree, and I started looking around too. The trees were rustling ranks of green and blue spikes shooting up and exploding outward, murmuring in the wind, they all crowded around me, getting in front of each other and shouting for attention, all while standing still and silent in the killing cold and darkening air. There were too many of them. I was freezing. I wanted to go back inside. I was afraid I might get lost. I started looking for Mom.

I turned around, and then I saw the blue tree.

The blue tree stood up straight and gorgeous. I walked around it. It was bushy and fat. I walked around it again. There wasn't even a bad part you would stick against the wall. The air was full of fluttering ice but the blue tree glowed darkly, threw itself up into the sky, had the power of heaven crackling off its branches. I took off my gloves and let the blue needles brush across my hand. I shook the white glitter off the tree and it turned to water on my skin. It was a huge, silent, weird being. I felt it watching me.

This rough thing could be caught and carried home, I thought, a cold monster from the woods brought into our warm house. Its branches were a hundred prickly fingers, its bark rough hide sweating sap. I touched the crumpled wood and my fingers came away dirty. We might hang it with ornaments and make it pretty but it was a monster.

I stood by the tree. I didn't want the other family to find it and take it home. I had to guard it. This was our tree.

Grandma came over, and after a while Mom with Jenny. Finally Cindy and Linda wandered over too. There was a lot of talk but I just had to wait it out. This was the tree. I knew it wanted to come home with us. I could feel it quiver. It was expecting it. It was on my side.

Grandma got the man with an axe. The man swung it, the axe bit into the trunk and I felt the tree sing. The man tugged out the axe, brushed it off, struck again. The tree shivered. Another hit and another, another, and with a splinter and groan the tree was crackling down and fell into the snow. The man dragged it over the mud and ice and heaved it into the wagon.

Its glory folded up and dimmed and pulled in and was gone. I stood in the muddy road and looked at the tree. It was different now. Even its colour seemed to have changed. Lying on the back of the wagon it was ridiculous. It was just a big green thing. I felt embarrassed. I might have made a mistake.

THE FURNACE HATED the Christmas tree.

I knew it as soon as we got home. We decorated the tree that afternoon. I could feel the furnace shoot hate at it.

Grandma brought crumbly boxes of ornaments and decorations down from the attic, little spicy-smelling tombs full of ancient crumpled newspapers and oddments. The furnace hated them all. The furnace filled the house with a bad feeling. Everything should've been fine—Grandma had eggnog and hot chocolate and brunch, Christmas carols were playing on the record player, Cindy and Laura were actually being nice and helping, Mom seemed to be feeling better—but it wasn't fine, and Jenny was hogging all the toy soldiers that were Dad's even though she knew I should have them, and anyway she wasn't even hanging the ornaments on the tree, she was whispering some whole other stupid story of her own with the soldiers in the corner. She was doing it all wrong, so I took them back and she screamed at me and I pushed her away and she started crying for no reason. She had taken the soldier that had the gun, all the rest of them had swords but I wanted the one with the gun. Give me the gun, I shouted, I want the gun!

Mom left the room.

She walked out without saying anything. Cindy ran after Mom, and Linda swooped in to be with Jenny, who was still sniffling, and they were both glaring at me as if I was the one who had done something wrong. Grandma talked to me very seriously for a while, but nobody cared how selfish Jenny was. The Christmas tree looked ridiculous. We had made it look ridiculous. Outside it was a shaggy monster but in Grandma's living room it was a tame, shrunken thing stuck in a plastic tree holder, scraping awkwardly against the ceiling, chained up in green and red and blue and yellow lights, glopped all over with tinsel. We had ruined it.

I said I was going to the bathroom. Instead I went to Mom's room.

She was in bed, just like she used to be at home. Her face was between pillows.

"I just have to lie down," she said. "I just need to rest."

I climbed into bed with her, I burrowed under the covers next to her. She said nice things to me and kissed my forehead. Her face was wet. I fell asleep close to her in the middle of the afternoon. It was already dark out.

WHEN I WOKE up I was in my own bed.

The house was dark. Nobody was up. I didn't know how long I had been sleeping. Outside big fluffy snowflakes spilled down from the black sky. The furnace muttered steadily.

Something was different in the house.

I sat up. The furnace was louder. Angrier. I had put a pillow and a bunch of books on my vent so I wouldn't have to hear it talking. My bedroom was cold. I heard the furnace growling in other rooms. The whole house was full of its roar. It wanted me for something. I heard something scraping through the ducts, something moving.

The furnace had sent something to visit me.

I didn't move. A patient sliding sound came from under the floor, like a little body was squeezing through the air ducts. I watched the pillows and books on top of the vent. I imagined the crooked little man in the box in the basement, the corn husk with seeds in its eyes, misshapen face frozen under glue. I felt him in the veins of the house, scraping closer.

The pillows moved.

I was up, up, I leaped up, I ran away from the vent, out of my room into the dark hallway. The darkness pulsed around me. The furnace was shouting, panting, giggling, but I didn't want to hear it, I ran through it down the hall—

I stared down the stairs, into the living room.

The Christmas tree glowed thousands of colours.

I pushed through the furnace's jabbering and shrieking, I ran all the way down the stairs, and all at once its noise was swallowed in the tree's tremendous stillness, like diving underwater. The tree was awake in the dark. Waiting. Its lights reflected silently off the ornaments, like bright hanging fruit, throwing dim blurs of colour on the ceiling and walls. The tree was radiating silence, an antenna tuned to some secret frequency drawing down something I couldn't understand and broadcasting it all through the house. Up and down the street, I saw Christmas trees in other houses' windows, glowing out into the night, glowing at each other as if in conversation, as if an army of alien angels had taken up residence in every home.

The furnace hated it. The man in the furnace was twisting himself in knots, babbling to himself, hating them. I knew the flickering red eye and the steady orange eye were glaring. But the Christmas trees were silent, beautiful, and emotionless.

I didn't go back up to my bedroom. I was afraid of what was up there waiting for me. I slept on the couch in the living room, looking at the tree. I felt safer there. But I did not sleep too close to it.

———————

THE SUMMER before Dad died he woke Jenny and me in the middle of the night, whispering there was something he wanted to show us. A surprise. Mom was up too. We all climbed into the car and drove for what seemed like a million miles, far from the lights of the town and the highway. The windows were open as we bounced and rattled into the hot rushing darkness. I closed my eyes, listening to the chittering insects, smelling the warm night-forest air. There was no moon. When Dad parked off the gravel road and shut off the headlights, the darkness was total. We couldn't see each other's faces. Mom and Dad and Jenny and I made our way blindly through the forest, feeling our way through the poking branches, until we finally came out to a field where dozens of people were sprawled as if they had all been struck down at once, lying on blankets, staring up into the sky.

Far above a silver slash cut across the blackness. "There! There!" Jenny shouted out. "Oh, there! Another one!"—and then there was another shooting star, then another, another, so many shooting stars that for an incredible few seconds it seemed as though the entire sky had broken apart and the heavens were collapsing, stars whizzing, crisscrossing, flaming out, one after another.

I remember Mom holding Dad's hand too tightly. Dad was watching the stars with an incomprehensible look on his face. Something wasn't right. Dad was looking at the sky as though it had told him something horrible; but it was a nostalgic look; he was happy but not happy; I had never seen my father look so young. I said something to him in the dream, because I was dreaming now, but I don't remember what, and Jenny wasn't there, Mom wasn't actually there either, and there was no car, no field, no shooting stars—it was just me and Dad in the dark. Dad touched his cheek as though he'd just discovered it, and said "Did I ever tell you where I got this?" and it wasn't even Dad anymore. It was the corn husk man. We were alone in the dark together.

I woke up. I was still in the living room. I looked out the window at the black night. No snow falling. Frozen silence. The house was cold, the living room dark.

The Christmas tree was gone.

I sat up, my mind suddenly clear.

The living room was empty. The wrapped presents were still arranged in a circle around the empty tree holder.

There was no tree.

The Christmas tree moved past the window.

I stumbled up, tripped over a present, ran to the door and threw it open.

The Christmas tree was moving away from my house. Other Christmas trees were already in the street, drifting down from other houses, all moving in a great silent herd.

I stared. I couldn't breathe. I ran back inside. Everything in my body was electrified. I pulled boots over my bare feet. One more second and they might all be gone. I threw my coat over my pajamas. I ran back outside.

The night was cold and clear. No moon. All the Christmas trees still had their ornaments, their string lights somehow still glowed, everywhere on the street the Christmas trees were coming out, emerging from every dim house, gathering together and pushing forward in a bright silent mob. My Christmas tree was leading them. I ran after them as they pressed on, rustling to each other, slowly turning, branches swaying, ornaments of stars and angels and lights on every side of me, more and more trees joining us up and down the street, dozens of trees now, maybe a hundred. My Christmas tree had gathered an army. The world did not notice. The world was paused. I had entered some secret backstage of the world, something that wasn't meant for me, something so separate from me that maybe I wasn't even seen. I was pressed in on every side by prickling branches. The air thrummed with invisible messages. I was caught up in it. I did not know if they were taking me somewhere or if they knew I was there at all, we were far from home now, and then we stopped somewhere deep in the forest.

My Christmas tree was there.

It had brought me to a hole.

The hole was wide and deep enough that I could climb in. The Christmas trees were gently pushing me. There was something in that hole I didn't want to see. The ground around the hole was frozen but the hole was fresh and raw. I knew what belonged in the hole.

———

I COULDN'T DO IT.

Things got worse. The next day and the day after that Mom didn't get out of bed. She lay facing the wall. Grandma kept going in to her and bringing her food. She would go in to retrieve the food later. It was cold and untouched. Grandma had a big old red medical book she consulted before going to doctors. The book didn't work. So Grandma brought an actual doctor to the house. He was the nephew of a friend, a favour called in. The doctor came and stayed a while and left. Jenny and I were shut out of the room. Grandma didn't say what was wrong.

I was too afraid to do it.

The furnace kept after me every night. It wanted that Christmas tree out. It wanted me to do something about that tree. I could feel it eating our time faster, I could feel the whole house take a wrong turn, the furnace wrapping up the house and sending it down to the bottom of a black ocean. Jenny and I fought for no reason. Grandma was scatterbrained, she didn't answer the question you asked. Mom stayed in bed with those pillows crushed on either side of her head.

I knew I had to go down there. But the furnace terrified me. I couldn't bear looking into that flickering red eye and steady orange eye, they were the eyes of the man in the truck and he was coiled up in our basement blasting hot air over us and we were all being steadily damned.

I stood at the top of the stairs, looking down at the Christmas tree. The furnace put pictures in my head showing me what I had to do to it. The tree glowed with cold, impersonal light. It didn't talk. I wanted to talk to the tree, to pray to it, to be friends with it but it was beautifully and horribly silent while the furnace droned, cajoled, joked, and hissed, threats and secrets and bad words blasting hot out of its angry metal mouths.

"Ha ha, I will show you my face," said the furnace. "I will eat your time too."

IT WAS the night before Christmas but it didn't feel like Christmas. This was usually the time that Mom and Dad had everything set and ready, the house all decorated, presents wrapped, cookies baked, ready to sail into Christmas Day. We hadn't done any of that this year. We weren't even at our own house. I wanted to be home. Grandma was too busy taking care of Mom. That morning Grandma had cooked bacon and eggs for breakfast and Jenny said, "I don't want eggs, I want Raisin Bran," and Grandma said "We don't have Raisin Bran," and Jenny said "But I *want* Raisin Bran," and Grandma said "This is better than Raisin Bran, I made this for you special," and Jenny just put her head down and cried, "I'm never going to have Raisin Bran again, I want Raisin Bran, I just want Raisin Bran." Grandma tried to help her but Jenny threw her plate so hard it broke, bacon and eggs and jagged ceramic scattered across the linoleum, and then Jenny was really screaming. Grandma told me to go down into the basement to get a mop and bucket. I hadn't been in the basement since the day Grandma had shown me the doll in the box. I didn't want to do it.

Grandma told me again to do it. Louder, sharper.

I crept down the stairs. I didn't even glance at the furnace, I just got the bucket and mop and ran back upstairs as fast as I could. But I did glimpse the furnace crouching in the back of the room, its flickering red eye and steady orange eye, and behind it, the door where the little man lived.

"Do it," said the furnace. "Or I will tell you something you don't want to hear."

NOW IT WAS night and I was standing alone in the dark with the Christmas tree. The furnace hissed commands. During the day the Christmas tree was just a normal tree, but at night it seemed to grow, to unfold, to blaze with stranger, deeper light, like a glittering alien peacock. The furnace pushed nightmare pictures into my brain. Broken ornaments. The Christmas tree knocked over. The tree on fire. I was close enough now to touch the Christmas tree, I was standing next to it, as the furnace said yes, yes, pull it down, break it, do it. But the Christmas tree was too bright, too full of raw magic.

"Do it," said the furnace.

I ran upstairs, thinking I was getting away.

"Then I will tell you something you don't want to hear," said the furnace. "I will tell you why you can't go back to your own house."

All night the furnace ate my time.

I KNEW that Dad wasn't happy. I knew he acted happy for us. That he wasn't well, though he pretended to be well. That he had tried something and failed. That time had run out. That something had caught up with us. That he had made a mistake, or missed something, or gotten lost, or done something wrong, or failed a test, or gotten struck by something unexpected; something had curdled inside Dad and gone bad, and curdled him, made him go bad; his insides, I knew, had gone bad.

ON CHRISTMAS EVE Grandma decided we should go to Midnight Mass. It was a terrible idea. The radio and TV were talking about the storm that was coming, the blizzard that would hit that night.

Mom stayed at home in bed. It was just me and Jenny and Grandma, who somehow hadn't taken into account how young we were. The storm was already in full force when we drove to the church. We could barely see out of the car, couldn't see the road. It was strange to be at the church late at night, it wasn't even our church, it was Grandma's church we had been going to since we started staying at her house, smaller and smellier and more old-fashioned than our normal church. There were decorations in the church that were weird and gross and I didn't want to look at them. Being there at night made it even spookier, there was a choir that came from nowhere, the choir stalls had always been empty before but now all these old people appeared, singing a high creepy song with words I couldn't understand. The organ was groaning chords of hundreds of notes fitted together in such a way that blasted you flat, weighed you down under its grinding triumph, like the victory march of some war you never knew about, between people who didn't mean anything to you. The incense rolled out over us, the priest was talking about a celebration but I never understood why he called it that, everyone's face looked dead, nobody sang like they were really happy and the priest's voice went on in just the way the man in the furnace droned when he wasn't talking to me, when he was just talking to himself in the furnace, like somebody reading out loud the titles of all the books they owned, a bunch of words even they didn't care about, and yet I was afraid that at any moment the priest might, like the furnace, stop droning and speak directly to me. My nostrils tickled from the incense, my head was swimming, I was dizzy and sick and just wanted to lie down like Mom and go to sleep. The blizzard howled outside and I remembered how after Dad died I'd heard how there was one unforgivable sin, something so bad you would go to hell no matter what, and Jenny, who had tried to stay awake because she wanted to be good, because she wanted to make up for the Raisin Bran and the broken plate, she hadn't complained at all that night, she was really trying to tough it out but it was too much for her, during the second reading her legs gave way and she fainted.

The people around us helped us. Everyone was really nice. But we left then, before the service was over. I had never seen Grandma look helpless, like she didn't know what she was doing. But during the drive home, she looked like that. Old and confused. She had been just as sad as us, she was hurting too. She took care of us but there was only so much she could do. There were some places only I could go.

JENNY FELL asleep in the car on the way home. Grandma wasn't strong enough to carry her in herself, so we pulled Jenny out and she stumbled in with us, half-awake, leaning on Grandma, and Grandma took her straight to her bedroom to change her into pajamas and tuck her in. The night was a bust. Church had gone wrong, nobody wanted to talk, everyone just wanted to go to bed, and for a moment before I had to go up to my own room I was alone with the Christmas tree, and I said to it:

"Yes. Tonight I'll do it."

I went upstairs and passed Jenny's room. She was already asleep. Mom was asleep in her room. Grandma clunked around in the bathroom but she was exhausted. I knew soon all of them would be dead asleep.

I WAS AWAKE. I felt the same way I'd felt when I'd slept in this bed for the first time. I looked out the window, up and down the street, at the darkened neighbourhood. The big storm was finished, it had moved on and was destroying the world somewhere else. The snow outside was smooth, swooping, untouched. To see huge snowdrifts in the middle of the street made it feel like the house was in a completely different neighbourhood. The bright moon lit up everything with sharp shadows. The furnace roared along but the voice had gone silent. I did not know what kind of silence.

I saw them now. They were outside the house.

I got out of bed.

My bare feet touched the carpet.

I saw them waiting in the street.

I came out of my room and down the stairs. The house was dark, the world hushed. The Christmas tree was not at the bottom of the stairs. It had heard me. It was just me and the furnace.

I felt eyes looking at me from behind mirrors. I moved past the mirrors, my eyes straight ahead. I glimpsed shapes huddled in corners. Do not look, do not look. I came through the foyer, walking slowly, do not run, do not turn on the lights. I turned and I was at the top of the basement steps.

He was down there.

The furnace roar was too loud, louder than it had ever been. I took a step into the basement. The step creaked. Another step. It was too hot, too loud, rushing in my ears, the darkness full of shapes jumping and wiggling. I had to ignore them, to keep on. I came to the bottom of the stairs. At any moment hands would grab me from behind, drag me into the furnace, take me all the way down to hell. I turned the corner of the basement and stared into the dark.

The flickering red eye and the steady orange eye stared back.

I walked blindly through the dark basement. All I could see was the red eye and the orange eye. The floor felt like it was sloping downwards, pitching me forward, pulling me toward the furnace, I had to fight from getting sucked in, no, I was taking every step myself, closer to the furnace, too close. The red eye and the orange eye stared into my own.

I couldn't move. The red eye and the orange eye burned into me. But I stared back, I did not look away, I kept looking into the eyes, even as the outline of a face began to come out of the dark, a face I knew took shape in the darkness, all around those eyes, the furnace was roar, roar, roaring and I felt all hell open up.

I stared at it.

The eyes sputtered.

The roar dwindled.

The eyes went dark. The noise stopped.

I was alone in the basement.

The furnace was dead. I didn't move. It was dead but I was still alive and I was still afraid. I crept forward behind the furnace and saw the two little doors in the wall, just barely, in the glow of the still-flickering pilot light. I lifted the latch and opened the door. Ash fell out.

There was the box.

It was open.

It was empty.

A hand fell on my shoulder.

The corn husk doll was bigger than me now.

HE WAS as big as a full-grown man. He stood just behind me, head bumping the ceiling, face expressionless. His seed eyes stared at me, his bark mouth hung open.

His hand stayed on my shoulder.

I tried to move away. The hand pressed down and I could not. His other hand moved as if to touch my cheek. But he didn't.

He let me go, and held up both hands to his own face, looking at them as if he didn't know what they were, he didn't know how to work them.

My heart pounded. I backed away. I went for the stairs. The corn husk man turned. He held out his hands as if to say: don't leave.

I stayed where I was.

He was looking around the basement. He moved to the corner where there were stacks of old cardboard boxes. He fumbled at a box. He couldn't open it.

I came over.

He watched me. The bits of pine cone and seeds glued to his head didn't move.

I opened the box for him.

Inside were piles of dusty children's books and battered toys from what looked like the 1950s. He stared at the toys, then pawed through the books, not as though he meant to read them, but just to see the covers. He looked at them for a while.

Then he straightened up again. He turned and walked upstairs and did not look back.

I went with him.

He peered around the dark hallways as if searching for something. He went from room to room, stumbling a little, pausing in strange places. He held the doorknob of the side door for a long time. He stared at the picture over the mantel above the fireplace

—I had never even really looked at it before. He stopped at the step between the family room and the kitchen.

Jenny had left out our blocks. When he saw them he bent over, trying to pick up a block. He couldn't. His body was too stiff. He didn't have joints in the right places. He stared at the blocks and the step.

I picked up a block and gave it to him.

He held it in his hand. With some of the other blocks I made a little building. He watched me do it. He tried to crouch down again as if to play too. But he couldn't. He gripped the block. Then he let it fall.

I got up and led him away from the step. He looked at it one more time, then turned away. We moved past the front window.

He looked outside.

He saw what was waiting for him.

He stopped and turned to me as if to ask for more time.

I told him he had time.

We went upstairs. I followed close. His husk body rustled and scraped in the darkness. Halfway up he had to hold onto the wall. He leaned on me. We went up the rest of the stairs together.

He creaked open Jenny's door. We entered as quietly as he could. Jenny's nightlight shone on her face. The man and I stood over her bed, watching her sleep. The seeds and bark and pine needles of his face did not change. Finally he turned away and went out the door. He shut it quietly, as though she was a baby he had just spent a long time lulling to sleep.

He opened the door to Mom's room. He stood by her bedside too. In sleep she was beautiful the way I remembered her. He looked at her for a long time. His corn husk arms hung at his side. His face was unreadable.

I went out into the hallway.

After a while he joined me again. We opened the door to Grandma's room. She was snoring, relaxed in her sleep. The man stared at Grandma too, as if trying to figure out something. When he turned away from her he was limping. Moving more slowly. He needed me to hold him up.

I took him to my room.

He looked around the room. He touched the desk, the bed, the wallpaper, the closet doors.

He looked out the window.

They were waiting for him.

He looked at me as if to say, I'm not ready.

I told him it was time.

He gave one last long stare around.

WHEN WE CAME outside the Christmas trees were waiting. My Christmas tree seemed to have brought them together. They were all there, brilliantly lit up, millions of colours standing in the creamy deep snow. There was a bright moon and no clouds. Nobody was out. The man stumbled out into the fresh cold night air like a man getting out of prison, staring around as if remembering again the world outside.

I had my coat and boots on. The Christmas trees began to move, leading us. I took the man by his hand. He kept looking back at the house. But after a while he stopped looking back.

He looked around the streets, at the other houses he seemed to recognize. He was holding my arm, holding it tighter. The Christmas trees closed in all around us. He was afraid. I held him. The seeds and glue and bark of his face did not move.

We went farther.

He was coming apart. Bits of corn husk were unwinding, getting left behind in the snow. He didn't look back. Seeds and pine cones fell. He was getting smaller. The Christmas trees guided us along. The snow piled up on either side of us. The roads were silent and the sky was black but the world was full of light. He stumbled but I caught him. More of him was gone, collapsing into ribbons of corn husk and crumbled bark. More of his body unwound, I had to carry him, he was a child, he was a baby, he was the doll again, moving in my arms. But even the baby was coming apart. I was trying to put him back together with my hands but I couldn't. I was crying. He was almost gone.

The Christmas trees stopped. We were in the forest, in a quiet place.

The hole was there.

My Christmas tree was close by. As if to say, okay.

The thing in my hands looked at me, and was gone. All that was left was some corn husk, bark, pine needles, old seeds, and acorns that had been packed up in the doll's chest.

I put it all in the hole. I dug my hands into the tough cold soil and threw the dirt in, handful after handful, until the hole was filled.

ON NEW YEAR'S DAY we threw out the Christmas tree.

Christmas at Grandma's was livelier than Thanksgiving had been. The aunts and uncles and cousins seemed as though they were all waking up from a rough night, one by one. The furnace was still broken so Grandma had to put out space heaters in the various rooms and she built up a big fire in the fireplace. Jenny and I would sit with our backs to the fire until our backs were too hot, and then run away and flop down on the couch and feel the warmth of the fire seep up through our entire bodies, again and again, and whenever I looked at the Christmas tree it seemed less and less like itself. By the end of the evening it was like any other tree. Or maybe the tree was never anything special to begin with.

No, said Jenny, that Christmas tree had been itching to get out of here all along. It was just stopping in our living room on its way to some greater place. Jenny had a whole story worked out about the Christmas tree, a story that I only discovered years later, after even she had forgotten about it, pages and pages about our Christmas tree getting thrown into the alley, then getting picked up by the garbage men, then hijacking the garbage truck and driving it to a city of monsters, then gathering allies and fighting walking furnaces, and at the end flying into space to fight some great geometrical being that was going to swallow the world.

I don't remember Jenny drawing it. But seeing it now, I remember her telling me that story a few weeks after the tree had been thrown out, the two of us sitting at the step between the family room and the kitchen. We were getting ready to go back home. Mom was up and about. They'd figured out what had broken the furnace when the repairman found my action figures in the air filter. Jenny and I were sitting at that step with the rescued action figures and the blocks and the soldier ornaments and a bunch of other toys, including a little pine tree she had made, and she was telling me her story. I told her that I liked her story.

I never told her mine.

But not long ago, my daughter and I went to the place in the forest where I remembered I had buried Dad's doll. I don't know if I found the exact place because what had been empty before was now full of trees and bushes. I found the spot as best I could, and there was a tree, and my daughter ran up to the tree and wrapped her arms around it, shimmying up.

It's strange when you watch a kid climb a tree. You have to hold yourself back, you want to rush in to help, you want to warn them, because you keep expecting the child to slip, or a branch to break. You forget how good you were at it back then. But the tree and the kid, they both know what they're doing.

YIWU

By Lavie Tidhar

I.

In all his time working for the lottery, Eshamuddin had only ever sold three winning tickets, but, as a consequence, he had seen three miraculous things.

The first purchaser, years before, was one of his first-ever customers. She was a young, dark-haired girl with a look of intense concentration on her face as she handed over the cash money, and she retained one coin—a Martian shekel with the Golda Meir simulacrum's head on it—to scratch the card, which she did with a slow seesawing motion, gently blowing the cheap dust of silver foil as she searched for her luck.

Then her face changed. Not open disappointment, or stoic acceptance, of the sort that people always wore, nor the greedy desperation that meant they would ask for another ticket, and then another, until their money ran out.

But neither was it amazement or shock or any reaction of the sort he'd have expected were someone to get *lucky*. Were someone to win.

It was more like she had found something that she had always half-suspected was there. That she was merely, at last, able to *confirm* a thing she'd always instinctively known.

And then she smiled.

And then she turned into a black-headed ibis and flew away into the sky.

––––––

2.

THE SECOND ONE was a couple of years later, and it was a much more ordinary affair. The winner this time was a middle-aged man from Guangzhou, with a comb-over and bottle-top glasses and a nice smile; he had the sort of face that smiled easily, and sometimes ruefully, at the world's foibles. It was the third card he'd bought, and he was chatting to Esham all the while, a running commentary about the day's weather (it was humid), the cost per unit of elastic hair bands (he had recently found a new manufacturer who could make them a point cheaper, saving him thousands), and his daughter's new boyfriend (a no-good know-it-all, but what were you going to do? Kids today and all that). Then the silver foil all came off, and the man's face slackened, and his lips stopped moving, and he rocked in place as though he'd been struck, and Esham said, "Sir? Sir? Are you all right?" and the man just nodded, over and over, and finally gave him a goofy grin.

"Look," he said. "Would you look at that?"

A car appeared round the corner and came to a stop beside Esham's lottery stall. It was a long black limousine with darkened windows. The doors opened, and two men in dark suits and dark sunglasses stepped out. They both had short-cropped hair and were very trim and fit. One held the door of the limousine open. The other said, "Congratulations, sir. Please, come with us."

"But where are we going?" the man said.

"It's only a short ride to the airport, sir."

"The airport?"

"To get to the Singapore beanstalk, sir. It isn't a long flight, sir."

"Singapore? I have never been to Singapore."

"It will only be a short stop, sir. A pod on the beanstalk is already reserved for you. Here, sir. Your ticket."

"My ticket?"

"For your onward journey."

The man stared at the ticket. He looked, almost pleadingly, at Eshamuddin.

"So it's really true?" he said. "I won? I won the lottery?"

"Yes, sir."

"I've always wanted to see Mars," the man said. "Olympus Mons and Tong Yun City and the Valles Marineris kibbutzim . . ."

"Whatever your true heart's desire, sir," the man said. It was the same legend that was etched—in now dusty letters—above Esham's lottery stall. The same legend that was on every lottery stall, anywhere. That was on every ticket.

Whatever your true heart's desire.

"But my daughter, my job, I can't just . . . elastic hair bands," he said desperately.

The car waited. Esham waited. The two men in their short-cropped hair and smart black suits and ties waited. The man mopped his brow. "I suppose . . ." he said.

"Sir?"

He meekly let them lead him to the car. He folded into the cool interior and the doors shut and the two men disappeared inside and the car started up and drove away and the man was gone.

To Mars, Esham supposed.

"Mars!" said Mrs. Li. She pushed her way to the booth and leered at Esham. "Who in their right mind would want to go to Mars, boy?" She shoved a handful of coins across the counter. "Give me a ticket."

Esham took the money and gave her a ticket. You could count on Mrs. Li to buy a few at a time. He wondered what her true heart's desire was.

"That's none of your damn business, boy!" Mrs. Li said.

She scratched the card with maniacal glee.

———

3.

THE THIRD TIME he witnessed a miracle, it wasn't anything like that.

It was a foreigner, a trader on a purchasing trip to Yiwu from one of the coastal African states. He was with a couple of colleagues, and he bore an amused smile as he paid for the ticket. It was just something to do, a local custom, something to pass the time, he seemed to suggest. He scratched the card and looked at it with that same tolerant smile, and he began to say, in bad Mandarin, "What does this mean—" when it happened.

It was like a curtain swished behind the man. The man half-turned, looked, and there was an expression on his face that Esham couldn't read. The man reached out one hand and touched the curtain. He prodded it with his fingers. He took a half step and then another. There was nothing there, and yet there was. He half-turned back and smiled at Esham. Then he stepped through into the whatever-it-was and just . . . disappeared.

His two colleagues did a lot of shouting, and Esham did a lot of hand waving and shouting back, and finally, some of the market police came along, and they did a little shouting, too and then, after a while, everyone left.

Esham stayed, of course. But business was slow, and after another hour, he closed the stall for the day. It had been a strange one. He wondered where the man went, what he saw, and whether he was happy there.

He ate a bowl of crossing-the-bridge noodles at a Yunnanese stall, then had sweetened mint tea at a Lebanese café near the Zone 7 mosque, and then he walked slowly back. Two blind musicians played the guqin outside Pig Sty Alley, and the air was perfumed with wisteria. The smell was manufactured in the factories of Zone 10 at a very reasonable per-unit cost and consequently sold all across the world.

That night, Esham drew the walls of his stall-home down and sat inside. He tuned in to the latest episode of his favourite soap, *Chains of Assembly*, which broadcast across the hub network of the Conversation in near space, all the way from Mars. In the air before him, The Beautiful Maharani argued with Johnny Novum inside her domed palace as ice meteorites fell onto the red sands far in the distance. Esham ate shaved ice with lychee syrup. It had been a strange day, he thought.

4.

ESHAM WAS BORN IN YIWU, but he wasn't Chinese. Many native-born residents of Yiwu weren't. His father had been a small-goods trader from the Ecclesiastical Confederacy of Iran, and his mother was an interpreter for a mining company based in the Belt, which purchased mass-market goods for the asteroid longhouses. A space Dayak, she often complained of discomfort in Earth's gravity, not because she was not used to it but because, unlike on the longhouses, there was simply no *escaping* it, even for a time. In the Up and Out, she'd told the young Esham, one could simply kick off into a free-fall zone, where you could fly: where you could be free.

He didn't know what his mother's true heart's desire would have been. He remembered them both as loving parents—which is not to say they did not sometimes shout at him in frustration or that they did not fight, which they did—but when he thought of them, what he remembered first was love. His father was away a lot, a train man, as they called them, forever riding the rails along the Silk Road from Yiwu to Tehran. He'd come back bearing gifts for Esham's mother—saffron and dried apricots, tiny pickled cucumbers, rose water and golpar—and for Esham, he'd bring back little handmade curios, wood and wire intertwined with wildtech components, toys that existed in both the virtual and the real.

They died in a simple transport-capsule accident on a visit to the underwater cities of Hainan. The new cities were the jewels of the South China Sea, glittering biospheres abundant in offshore aquaculture, home to millions of people who lived and breathed underwater. It was just a stupid accident, the sort that never even made the news. He was still only a boy when it happened. After that, the state took him in. For a long time, he'd had the dream of buying lottery tickets until he'd found a winning one and then the lottery would bring his parents back to life. Even though he knew it was just a dream. Even the lottery could not bring back the dead.

The lottery really began as just another roadside tradition, around the time they rebuilt Yiwu from scratch into the lotus-flower shape it had now, each petal a zone, each zone a market to rival all other markets. There was nothing, it was said, that you couldn't buy in Yiwu. But mostly, it was the small stuff, the domestic stuff, still, then and now: keyrings and bathmats, mugs and toothbrushes, artificial flowers, ladies' handbags, raincoats and mascaras, pens and watches, clocks and toys and festive decorations . . . the factories in the outer zones beyond the city never slept, and the market traders in their petal-sections of the market-city only ever slept in shifts, and the trains never stopped coming and going with the giant containers on their backs.

The first lottery was on the same scale. It really was just a community sort of thing: people coming together to make life a little easier, a little better. People would get together and buy tickets, and each would win something they needed. You might win help with repairs on your house, or delivery assistance for groceries, or someone to bring you food while you were sick if you didn't have family to care for you.

At least, that was the story.

On how the lottery really came to be, there were as many stories as there were fish in the fish market or toys in the toy market or pens in the pen stalls or fake snow in the Christmas pavilion. They said the lottery used Shenzhen ghost-market tech and was overseen by the Others, those mysterious digital intelligences that first evolved in Jerusalem's Breeding Grounds and now lived in impenetrable Cores guarded over by the mercenaries of

Clan Ayodhya. Others said it was run by the Kunming Toads under Boss Gui, whose labs in the Golden Triangle churned out verboten technology and traded in illicit info-weapons and employed Strigoi assassins for all that they were banned on Earth. Others still said it was wild hagiratech from Jettisoned, that farthest outpost of humanity on the moon called Charon, where the sun appeared as little more than a baleful raven's eye in the sky, and that the lottery was run from off-world, and you know what people in the Up and Out were like.

Esham didn't know. He didn't even think to ask. The lottery just was, and it gave a few people every year something impossible and precious: their true heart's desire. And it gave him, Esham, a job.

———

5.

EVERY MORNING, he sat up in his cot and brushed his teeth in the sink and washed his face and his armpits and drank a cup of tea. Then he unfolded the walls of the lottery booth and prepared to welcome the day. If the previous day's take was good, he might walk to a nearby stall for a bowl of congee. If the take was not good, he would usually forego breakfast. His accommodation was free, and his needs were few, and only the rich, as the old proverb goes, have time to dream. But that's what the lottery was for, he thought. For the poor to have dreams.

From time to time, he would move the lottery stall around the city. There were many lottery stalls, but they all travelled if they needed to. Currently, he was stationed in Zone 7, where the automata market was. Every late afternoon, he'd shut the booth for an hour or so and take a stroll. The petal of Zone 7 rose high into the air above the central pistil. From up here, you could look all over the city, to the zone-petals and their markets heaving with humanity and goods, and to the mountains that ranged Yiwu, and to the outer zones where the workers lived in the vast container shanties and grew their hydroponic food in green growtainers, and then beyond to the ring of factories. The petals were designed to catch wind and sun and rain, to reuse everything, to draw power from the elements.

If the previous day's take was good, he might buy himself a modest lunch of some sort: Vietnamese banh mi or pho, or an Egyptian falafel or a bowl of noodles. If the take was good, he might go to the public baths to wash. While the city operated on a range of digital currencies in the Conversation, the lottery only ever accepted coins. Why that was, he didn't know. They did not mind the type of currency, so each day, Esham would sort out the day's take by type and place of origin: Martian shekels and rubles alongside Belt-issued ringgit, local yuan, Micronesian dollars, lunar vatu . . . the list went on and on. Each evening, he would pack the coins and place them in the appropriate bin provided, and each morning, they would be gone.

Esham had his regulars. Mrs. Li, who owned a factory that made snow globes, visited him every day. Mr. Mansur, who came each year to Yiwu to buy lights, so many lights, which he shipped to his distant home, would visit avidly when he was in town. He could always be relied upon to buy the extra ticket, and his face always bore a hopeful, yet simultaneously sad, look. He was a quiet, courteous man. There were others. They came and went like the tides.

In the afternoon, a troupe of Martian Re-Born walked past, red-skinned, four-armed, laughing, wearing lanyards with laminated cards on their chests. They were of an Up and Out order which believed in an ancient Martian civilization ruled over by an Emperor of Time, and they modified their bodies to match their imagined perspective of that long-vanished warrior race. They stopped, curious, at his stall, and each bought one ticket, and they paid with coins that bore the profile of a P'rin, those imaginary reptilian birds that the Re-Born believed were the time-travelling messengers of their Emperor. None of them won.

A street-cleaning machine crept past along the road, humming cheerfully to itself. Trams wooshed overhead on their graceful spires, moving between the zones. The air smelled of hot leather, shoe polish, fried garlic, knock-off Chanel No. 5 perfume, uncollected garbage, frangipani, and the recycled air blown out of a thousand air conditioners. It was then that he saw her, emerging out of the market doors into the hot street beyond.

The woman was no taller than Esham, but she moved with a quiet purpose that he envied: a sense of completeness, a comfort in one's own skin that he'd never possessed. Esham was the sort of person who skulked through life, careful to avoid any potential for trouble. He had few friends and fewer vices, and he never played the lottery.

The woman crossed the road and came to his stall, and stopped. The laminated card attached to her lanyard said her name was Ms. Qiu.

"Hello," she said. The smile she offered him would have broken his heart had he opened his heart to it.

"Hello," he said.

She had just an ordinary face, the sort you would easily lose in a crowd. Her hair was cut in a fashionable style that was neverthe-less a year or so behind whatever the current trend was in

Shanghai that spring. Her hand rested on the counter, lightly. Her fingers tapped lightly on the surface. He looked away from her.

"May I have a card?" she said.

"Of course."

She smiled when he gave it to her. She scratched it with an old fifty-Mongo coin. She looked at it, almost puzzled, then shrugged and left it on the counter.

"Thank you," she said.

"You're welcome."

He watched her walk away.

6.

THIS BECAME A DAILY ROUTINE. He came to await the moment when Ms. Qiu appeared out of the market entrance. He'd watch her cross the road. He'd always wait. She'd say, "Hello." He'd say, "Hello." She'd ask for a card, and he would pass one to her, and she'd pay him with whatever coins she happened to carry that day —rubles, dinars, one time with a gold sovereign. Then she'd frown, shrug, give him a final smile or say, "Goodbye," quietly, and walk away.

Sometimes, on his break, he would search for her in the market. He'd pass the rows of artificial cockatoos and peacocks, and the little singing birds in their cages with their bright glass eyes, and the enclosure of the animatronic tigers and the dodo arcade, but only once did he think he saw her at a distance, speaking to a man in a navy-blue suit, but he could not be sure and, when he came closer, she was, anyway, gone, if it had been her at all.

He took to eating his lunch at a Melanesian stall serving sup blong buluk wetem raes, simple, filling fare, and cheaply priced, a place popular with many of the Pacific traders. It was across the aisle from a stall that sold genuine synthetic bear's gall bladder, and the girl who worked at that stall would often take her lunch around the same time.

"Don't you remember me?" she said. "Isa, from the home."

"Isa," Esham said. "Of course. Of course."

"I've seen you around," she said. "So you went with the lottery."

"I did. You?"

"Well, you can see."

"Artificial gall bladders."

"I have my own place now," she said. "It's in container town, but I'm there alone, no one else."

He knew what she meant. Growing up the way they did, they were never alone; there were always others, nights filled with snores and farts and someone crying or talking in their sleep.

"Me, too," he said. "It isn't much, but . . ."

She smiled.

"I know."

She sat down across from him with her tray. "You ever think of going away?" she said. "Mars, or the moon, or Beijing?"

He thought about it.

"No," he said.

She nodded. "Me neither."

She spooned beef stew over the rice and ate, wasting nothing, and he did the same.

7.

THE WAY it happened wasn't supposed to happen. There was something wrong, in hindsight, with the whole day, some intimation of disaster one could trace in the slight rise in air pressure or in the swoosh of the trams overhead or in the clinking of coinage. Mrs. Li came and bought three tickets and left in a huff. Mr. Mansur came by and bought one and stopped to chat for a little while before he, too, left. A couple of monks went past and did not buy tickets. A bulk buyer from the Martian Soviet came and got a ticket, and then a trader from Harbin.

It was just an ordinary day, the way Esham liked it. Order and routine, a knowing of what was expected. At the usual time, Ms. Qiu emerged from the market doors. She crossed the road. She came to the stand and smiled at him and said, "Hello," and asked for a ticket.

He sold her one. She scratched the silver foil with a ten-baht coin.

She looked at the card, almost puzzled, then shrugged and left it on the counter.

"No luck?" Esham said.

She pushed the ticket toward him. He glanced down, barely registering the impossible at first: the three identical symbols of a beckoning gold cat that meant it was a winning ticket.

He glanced up at Ms. Qiu.

Nothing happened.

"Thank you," Ms. Qiu said.

She gave him a last, almost bemused smile, then turned and walked away.

Still, nothing happened.

He stared at the good-luck cats.

Nothing.

Ms. Qiu crossed the road and walked away the way she always did until she turned a corner and was out of sight.

Still, nothing happened.

They said when old Mr. Chow won, it had rained fish all that day, all over the city.

They said that when Mrs. Kim won, statues came to life and danced for a full five minutes to a K-pop song before they suddenly and abruptly became stone again.

They said when Mr. Huang won, a dragon flew over the city and summer flowers bloomed, and when young Miss Yuen won, she vanished and reappeared in digital form as a speaking-part character on *Chains of Assembly*, where she had a brief but intense romance with Johnny Novum before falling afoul of Count Victor's machinations against The Beautiful Maharani, after which she was not seen again on the program.

Esham stared after Ms. Qiu, but nothing happened. He held the winning ticket and stared at it. Something was wrong, he thought. It wasn't supposed to happen like this.

Rain clouds gathered over the flower city of Yiwu.

He stared up at the sky, but they were just ordinary rain clouds.

8.

"AREA CONTROLLER DEE will be with you shortly. Please wait."

Lottery Sub-Level 15 was a mix of physical reality and the virtual. Disembodied daemons moved through the air, whispering machine-language instructions while forklifts drifted across the factory space moving heavy bags of coinage, and in the far end, the printing presses thumped and hummed, churning out sheets and sheets of promised miracles that were then chopped neatly by other machines and sorted for delivery to the various stalls. In many ways, it could have been the quintessential Yiwu market floor, small-scale manufacturing, large-scale distribution, only here they didn't sell bathmats or doorknobs; they sold miracles.

He wondered what they did with all the coins.

"Only, how long will it be?" he said. "This is very important."

"Please wait. Area Controller Dee will be with you shortly."

Esham touched the bruise on his cheek.

There had been trouble the night before.

He'd been careless. A customer came past shortly after and saw he held a winning ticket. He'd tried to explain, but he didn't know how.

Word spread.

The rumour went around that there was a winning ticket up for grabs, even though everyone knew the lottery didn't work that way.

They came to gawk at his lottery stand, only a few at first, then more, until it was more like a mob that surrounded him. Night fell, and the air had a wild, festive feel to it but mixed with a sense of unpredictability. People lit torches and drank beer and baiju. Fights broke out. People kept shouting questions at him. He couldn't leave. Then a group of young men set on him. They demanded to see the ticket. He tried to shut the booth, but they started pushing it, rocking it from side to side. Esham tried to slip out, and someone pushed him, and he fell. The mood turned ugly. He looked up and saw their faces, lit and hungry. He curled up into a ball. He'd been kicked before. The key was to try and minimize the damage.

They started landing blows. Fists, feet. Then someone shouted, "Leave him alone!"

It was Isa, from the market. She came in, fearless, and stood over him and faced down the bullies.

"Go away," she told them.

Which, remarkably, they did.

She helped him to his feet.

"Are you all right?"

He tried to smile, though it hurt.

"Here," she said. "You're bleeding." She sat him down on a bench and cleaned the cut on his face. His ribs hurt from the kicking. The city shone overhead in a million lights.

"Thanks, Isa."

"We've got to look after each other," she said. "Or who else will?"

He nodded. He felt very tired.

They sat together on the warm bench under the petal zones of the city, side by side, in companionable silence.

***

9.

"I MUST SPEAK to the area controller," Esham said. It had taken him hours to find the lottery regional office. It really was just a door, tucked in the back of Zone 2, and he'd had to pass through miles of near-identical corridors, through stalls that sold miniature models of folding Beijings, fish from Lijiang and flowers from Shazui, Perky Pat dolls bound for Mars and replica guns from Isher, anti-spiritual pollution spray in aluminum cans, Samsara wheels that played a song as they were spun, and little self-assembly spacecraft models from General Products—a sea of kipple, an endless, rolling expanse, heap upon heap of old stuff someone, somewhere, simply couldn't let go of.

He went past it. He found the door. It was just a door.

"I must speak to the area controller," he said.

The door seemed to hesitate.

"This is most irregular," it said.

"The situation is most irregular!" Esham said, with more force than he meant to. "I'm sorry."

"Don't mention it," said the door.

"Can I come through?"

The door hesitated.

"We're very busy right now," it said.

"This is important!"

"I am sure," the door said, in a maddeningly reasonable voice, "that it seems very important to *you*." It sighed. "I wasn't always a door, you know," it said. "I used to be a poet." It reflected for a while. "Still. I like being a door. Sometimes you're open. Sometimes you're closed. There's very little in between. I find that comforting. Don't you?"

"Me?"

"Well, you're not a door," the door said. "So I suppose you wouldn't understand."

It seemed to reflect again.

"Oh, well," it said at last. "But don't say I didn't warn you."

The door irised open.

Esham stepped through.

10.

THE CORRIDOR FELT like an access tube strung over some enormous height. The accordion walls contracted and expanded, and the whole passage seemed to move as though buffeted by unseen wind. He stumbled along it, holding on to the walls to stay upright. Lights flashed overhead. A mechanical voice kept counting, "Eight billion point two four five, eight billion point two four seven, eight billion point two five one," incomprehensibly. Esham came to the end of the corridor. He stepped through . . .

For a moment, he had the sense of galactic space all around him. He saw a planet adorned with rings and fireflies in formation all around it and the sun far against the endless dark, a lone yellow star. Then it vanished, and the voice stopped the count, and a new voice said, "Welcome to Lottery Sub-Level 15, vendor human type Eshamuddin. Area controller Dee will be with you shortly."

He looked around him at this ordinary floor. It could have been any market level in Yiwu. Though he was suddenly certain he was nowhere near Yiwu. Not even on Earth, maybe. There were windows in the far walls. He could see a night sky but not much else. Height, though. He was high up, in a skyscraper, somewhere foreign. He was almost sure. He began to walk to the windows. If only he could see . . .

"Sir? Come with me, please."

II.

Area Controller Dee was a short fat man in a checkered shirt with one button too many undone and thinning black hair that stuck to his forehead. He mopped his face and pushed the basket of food on his desk toward Esham.

"Prawns?"

Grease shone on his fingers. Esham shook his head. "No. Thank you."

"Suit yourself."

Dee ate fast. When he finished, he let out a satisfied burp and wiped his fingers clean on a dirty napkin. "So," he said. "What is all this about?"

"Sir," Esham said. "Do you mind if I ask where we are?"

"The lottery building," Area Controller Dee said.

"But where, I mean what—"

"The lottery is the lottery," Area Controller Dee said. "Yes?"

"Yes, sir."

"Now, could you get to the point? I don't have all day."

"It's about this ticket, sir. It's a winning ticket, sir."

"A winning ticket? Let me see."

Dee took the scratch card from him. He looked at it and pursed his lips. His eyes glazed, for a moment, as he accessed his node. "Ah, yes," he said. "Defunct."

"Defunct, sir?"

"It was an error," Dee said. "Don't worry about it."

"So it didn't work? But Ms. Qiu—"

"Ms. Qiu?" Dee said.

"The woman who purchased it, sir."

"Not human," Dee said.

"Not human, sir?"

"Automaton. Replica. Animatroni—well, you know." He waved his hand. "Ex-display."

"Ex-display?"

"Do you just repeat everything anyone ever says to you?" Dee said.

"Yes, sir. I mean, no, sir. Sir, what do we do here? What is the lottery for?"

Area controller Dee unwrapped a lollypop and stuck it in his mouth. He sucked on it noisily, then took it out with a pop.

"The lottery's the lottery," he said, with an air of satisfied finality.

12.

ARROWS LED him back the way he'd come across the floor. Far in the distance, he saw an old mechanical slat board that kept clacking, with figures that kept changing for Mars, Lunar Port, Titan, Ganymede, Io, Callisto, Jettisoned, Ceres, Vesta, Calypso, Hyperion, Nix, and Hydra. And Earth, of course. The same mechanical voice returned, "Eight billion point two six eight, eight billion point two seven one," droning on.

Esham came to a door. He opened it and stepped out onto a street in Yiwu.

It was late afternoon. The sun was low against the mountains. The petals of the market zones rose in the sky, casting shadows over the surface streets. He was in a quiet residential neighbourhood not far from Zone 7.

As he stood there, he saw Ms. Qiu cross the street. She walked in that same assured, unhurried pace. She didn't see him. She came to a small house with a well-tended front garden and a little white fence. Two children came running out to greet her, and Esham thought he saw the outline of a man waiting at the door. Ms. Qiu went in with the children.

Esham came a little closer. He peeked through the windows, which were open to let in the breeze. He saw them sit down at the dinner table, the children talking animatedly, Ms. Qiu smiling quietly. The man said something, and she laughed.

Esham left them to have their privacy. He walked back to his stall and saw that Isa was there, waiting for him.

"I thought I'd take you out to dinner," she said.

"I'd like that," Esham said.

"What shall we have?" she said. She laughed. "Whatever your true heart's desire."

So they shared crossing-the-bridge noodles at the Yunnanese stall, and then they had sweetened mint tea at the Lebanese café.

And then, together, they went home.

PRESUMED ALIEN

By David Boop

"I'm Mitchell Ward, Attorney-at-Law, and if you've been abducted by aliens, you might be eligible for compensation."

The man, dressed in a black suit and dark Ray-Ban sunglasses, delivers his line standing in front of an obviously green-screened shot of a classic spaceship straight out of a '50s movie. The screen behind him rotates through more classic silver saucers destroying Earth's military forces with their superior alien technology. Ward is very animated, waving his arms around in frustration.

"The United States military has known about the existence of alien life for decades, yet they do nothing to protect you and your loved ones from being scooped up by any trespassing ET and subjected to experimentation. If you feel the red rage of anger, I'll be your man in black."

Ward's outfit suddenly changes into that of a space smuggler. He's holding a giant plastic space blaster, which he "cocks."

"Under Section 46501, Title 49 of the United States Code, the United States is legally responsible if you've been abducted via special aircraft piloted by foreign agents, and it's my responsibility to see you fairly compensated if they don't."

A parade of poorly animated CGI generic aliens pop up like whack-a-moles. Ward "shoots" then as he continues his pitch.

"I'll sue for the wages you lost while held captive!" *Zap!*

"I'll go after anyone who calls you crazy for slander!" *Zap!*

"I'll get your physical or mental medical bills paid now and in the future!"

Zap! Zap! Zap!

Ward transforms again, now wearing space-wizard robes while holding an LED-lit sword. He goes through a series of sword-fighting moves. "I'll cut through the congressional empire's red tape, used to suppress the truth that's out there." Extending his hand, Ward closes his eyes in deep concentration. "I'll *force* them to pay up, binding you once again with all living things like your family and friends."

For his final transformation, Ward is dressed like a space bounty hunter, holding a green puppet that is so obviously bad the IP holder he copied it from couldn't get their cease-and-desist to stick. "I'm Mitchell Ward, and this is the way to get your bounty and your life back. Call 555-LAW-YODA. That's 555-529-9632."

The puppet, speaking in a squeaky voice, says, "He's your only hope!"

FRED UFZEIK TURNED off the hotel room's TV and glanced down at the cell phone he'd acquired. He started to dial the number, then thought it might be better if he visited Mitchell Ward, Attorney-at-Law, in person. Chances were he wouldn't take him seriously over the phone. No other officials he'd called had. Plus, Ufzeik was a little concerned about how much Ward liked shooting the digitized aliens.

Yes, it'd be much better if he checked out this Law Yoda with his own eyes first.

———

AT THAT SAME MOMENT, Mitchell Ward rubbed a spot between his eyebrows with his forefinger and tried not to look exhausted as he asked his potential client to re-confirm his story.

"Okay, Mr. Bourque, run it down for me one more time. You were hauling coffee beans along Nevada State Highway 375 . . ."

Clay Bourque gave off a two-cases-of-Bud-a-day vibe. Other types of buds, as well. Ward didn't care what someone did to their bodies, but if his instincts were true, it would make Bourque a less-than-reliable witness on the stand.

"Yessir, as I told you, my boss had had me doing the Los Angeles-to-Las Vegas run for three weeks when it happened."

That was the first of many things that didn't add up to the lawyer. "But the 375 isn't anywhere near Interstate 15, which is the direct route between LA and Sin City."

"Yessir." Bourque wrung his G-'n'-R hat in his hands. Ward couldn't tell if it was to disguise the shakes or actual nervousness. "But as I admitted to you on the phone, I'd taken a little detour to go see my old lady in Reno."

"Right, right." That was still the long way around. The defence would point out 95 was more direct. "And that's when you saw the lights . . ."

The trucker pretended as if the mere mention of the memory caused him stress. Ward had to admit the man had gotten the PTSD look down. It was the only reason Ward hadn't thrown him out right away. If he could fine-tune Bourque's story, the victim act just might convince a jury

"Yessir. My rig was enveloped in a bright light, and the engine stopped dead."

While he might have the look, the man's scriptwriting was horrendous. Bourque had basically described the opening of the *Starman* TV series—not even the movie version.

No, Ward decided. It'd take too much work to prep the liar for trial.

He held up a hand. "I'm going to stop you there. Mr. Bourque, I'd like to believe your story, but I'm guessing that what actually happened was you got tired of making the LA/Vegas run, which kept you from your old lady, and decided to 'furlough' with her a bit longer than you'd intended, only to find you'd been fired when you finally returned to work." Ward leaned forward, his hands now flat on his desk. "Am I close?"

After an attempt at denial, Bourque blushed scarlet red and confessed to the scam.

Not being completely unsympathetic, Ward drew a business card from his top drawer. "Here's Frank White. He handles the unfair treatment of long-haul truckers. Maybe he can help."

Bourque thanked the law dog, took the card, and left the office.

Ward sighed deeply. That was the tenth *faux* abduction he'd done a consultation with since the ads started running. The only real case the money spent had brought in turned out to be a spousal kidnapping, which was what he'd specialized in before leaving the LA law firm he'd been hired on at after law school. Those cases paid bills, but they no longer appealed to him, not since...

His smartwatch chimed. "Damn!" He grabbed his coat from the hook, kissed the picture of Leila on top of the filing cabinet, and headed out the door. He couldn't miss another appointment with his "source," or she wouldn't return his calls . . . ever.

———————

VANITY NAVARRO CHECKED her own watch as Ward sat down in the booth.

"Thirty seconds, Mitch. Another thirty seconds, and I would've—"

Ward held up a hand. "I know. You would've unfriended me for life. I remembered your promise from last time. I'm here, okay? Whatcha got?"

She sighed. "Not even a 'Hello' or 'Thanks for enabling my wild-goose chase even though it could get you fired' or 'Is that a new haircut?' Nothing?"

His heart still racing from the sprint he'd made to the bar, Ward composed himself before placing both of his hands palms down on the table. "You're right. I forgot my manners. I had another faker today, which is why I was late."

Vanity raised a blue eyebrow. Blue was this month's colour for her short-cropped hair, lipstick, and contact lenses. The *Phoenix New Era* newspaper promoted its alternative reporting with a very alternative staff. Vanity, the local news editor, toed the company line and came adorned with *all* the tats and piercings someone in her position should have.

Her style appealed to Ward, as usual, but he tried to keep a "professional" distance from all his sources, especially Vanity, who already had a husband, a wife, and a couple of genderfluid partners. When he did hang with her, she gave him the love-hate cliché. She'd say his passion for the outliers and discarded of society made her hot, but wouldn't sleep with him if he didn't focus on those he could *actually* help. Ward couldn't think about relationships of any sort, even casual ones, until he knew the truth.

That didn't mean Ward couldn't try to be nice. She had his intel, after all.

"Is that a new haircut?" Ward continued.

"You like? I dyed my landing strip, too."

She waited for his reaction, for which he nodded appreciatively to keep things civil. Just another image he'd have to bury deep, deep in his mind. "So, you got something for me?"

Sighing, Vanity reached down to a folder on the bench beside her, nearly spilling her Electric Lemonade. They always met at Fat Tuesdays on the ASU campus because of their amazing frozen drinks and party atmosphere. She looked like she belonged there —mesh shirt over green bra—while Ward's attire screamed "narc" or "parole officer." Being a saucer-chasing lawyer meant Ward dressed more seriously than most legal eagles did those days.

Vanity flipped open the collected news copy and narrated as Ward dug into it hungrily. "You're not going to find much new from the police bands. Couple of UFO sightings on the way to Vegas. The regular stuff." Then she nonchalantly dropped the reason she'd called him. "There was one that stuck out, though." Vanity reached over and pulled out the bottommost articles.

"Way to bury the lede," Ward said in an accusatory tone.

Vanity shrugged. "You make *me* work. I make *you* work."

He considered that valid.

She'd gathered three seemingly unrelated articles, stapled together. This first was from *The Astronomer's Telegram*, reporting a meteorite strike in the Arizona desert out past Big Sandy Range. Supposedly not very big, according to the article; however, satellite photos showed a decent plume of debris from the impact.

The second—a screen capture dated the same day from one of the local online hubs where neighbours gossiped about each other in the disguise of news—contained highlighted postings of locals complaining about the rush of jets taking off from David-Monthan in the middle of the day. While not uncommon, the neighbours attacked each other with cross-posts about that being the "cost for liberty" versus defunding the totalitarian military altogether.

The third was the most interesting. More screen captures, but this time from an online video taken by a vacationing family travelling up Highway 93 to Bullhead City for some light gambling. The video, taken by one of the children when the family stopped for gas, showed a massive convoy of trucks passing by.

"You have the video?"

Vanity nodded and set her phone up for Ward to watch.

His heart started racing again as he froze a frame. When Ward zoomed in, he recognized the troop's designation, though he'd only heard about them through rumour.

It was the Alien Retrieval Unit out of Luke Air Force base, codenamed The Grey Team.

The Grey Team only left the base when confirmation of something unidentifiable appeared anywhere in the Southwest.

"They got one," Ward whispered, even though Phutureprimitive's "Innocence Lost" filled the bar, and even the next booth over couldn't have eavesdropped.

Vanity grinned. "Maybe. Maybe it's just another Chinese spy balloon."

Ward shook his head. "If they had any doubt, they'd send their own drones to examine the wreckage. If the Greys are moving, they have an active situation." He checked the time stamp. Three days ago.

"Damn! I should've seen this earlier."

The editor placed a hand over his. "It doesn't mean they found her, y'know . . . *her*."

Ward pulled his eyes away from his third replay of the video.

"That doesn't matter right now. If the Greys have proof of alien visitation, then I can get a JAG in front of a judge."

"Mitch," Vanity said, pity and longing in her tone, "it's been three years. If she isn't back by now . . ."

Ward dropped a twenty to pay for her drink and got out of the booth. "I'm not giving up, okay? Someone knows something. I'll make them talk."

Vanity called for him to wait, but he was already out the door.

———

BACK AT HIS OFFICE, Ward paced back and forth. He needed evidence, but there'd be nothing left at the crash site by now. No, it was either taken up to Nevada or sitting at Luke. That was his best hope. He'd already burned so many bridges on wild theories that no one would take his calls anymore. Disguise? No. He could call *that* guy, but no, too early. He had nothing concrete to give him.

Ward spun to his office door chime.

An average-looking man in average-looking clothes stood at the entrance to his office.

"Sorry, now's not a good time."

Undeterred, the man asked, "Are you *the* Law Yoda?"

"Yeah, yeah." Ward kept pacing, waving the man away. "I'm in the middle of something at the moment. Can it wait, like, a week or so? I take it you were abducted by aliens, right?"

"No, sir. *I* wasn't the one abducted."

A strange hum caused Ward's tooth fillings to ache. He

stopped pacing as an unearthly glow enveloped the man.

When the metamorphosis finished, Mitchell Ward gawked at the non-terrestrial being standing right in front of him.

"My brother was the one abducted. By *your* military. I want you to sue them for his release."

———

WARD REACHED for what he assumed was the alien's throat, though he had to use both hands and still had a hard time finding purchase.

"Where is she, you bastard? Where's Leila?"

The ET cocked his head, unperturbed by Ward's attempts to choke him. "Is this some sort of Earth greeting I'm unfamiliar with? I thought I knew them all." He stepped back and began a series of gestures that ended with a classic Live Long and Prosper.

Ward then tried to cold-cock the alien, thinking if he could bring him in front of a judge, he'd blow the whole government conspiracy out of the water. After that, they'd have to help him find Leila. Punches to the thing's "jaw" or abdomen produce no more effect than the attempted choking had. Out of breath, Ward stumbled backward and steadied himself on his desk.

"You have some nerve . . . walking in here . . . after what you did."

That seemed to confuse him . . . it . . . whatever-it-was, because it blinked its eyes at the lawyer. "What did I do? Is this about the Lay-la you mentioned? I only know of the song. Most people we meet are singing it loudly while driving through the desert. That and another called 'Free Bird,' which has always made me wonder why you hold some of your birds in captivity. Are they visitors to your world as well?"

Now it was Ward's turn to stare. "What are you talking about? I'm talking about the love of my life, Leila." He grabbed the photo from on top of the file cabinet and pushed it in the alien's face. "You abducted her three years ago."

The creature held up one of its arms (maybe two?) in protest. "Oh, no, Law Yoda, sir. My brother and I do no abducting. We just come here for the warm, dry air of your planet." It resumed its human form and fully stepped into the office. Finding an unoccupied chair, it sat down and crossed its legs. "Allow me to introduce myself. I'm Fred Ufzeik. My brother Ted is the one who was taken by your military."

"Fred and Ted? You couldn't have picked more original names?"

Ufzeik shook his head. "Blame our parents, Ned and Gedda. They were the ones that wanted the rhyme scheme."

"Wait. That's your *real* name?"

"Of course," Ufzeik confirmed. "Naming our children with Earth names is quite popular and trendy. When our species first started visiting your world, Lucys and Rickys were everywhere back home. Then there were the JRs and Sue-Ellens. And don't get me started on the Princes and Cyndis. I was actually fortunate to be the only Fred in my class instead of another Dylan or Brandon."

The absurdity suddenly stuck Ward. He was talking to an alien about baby names.

A live alien.

The lawyer moved behind his desk and pulled out a bottle of Scotch from the bottom drawer. He poured two fingers, then six, into a highball glass. "This is going to take a moment."

He started his self-medication, letting the burn push his

emotional needs back. Then he breathed out the fumes and asked, "You said you come here for the air?"

"My brother. He has a respiratory condition that his doctor said would be better if he visited an arid climate for a few months out of the year. We pick a remote area in one of your many deserts and find a nice hotel. Then it's sunbathing and Mai Tais. This was our first trip to Arizona." Ufzeik sighed. "I originally picked these nice sand dunes in Colorado, but Ted was worried about the altitude. He wanted the Mojave, but we've been there three times already, so we compromised."

If the ET, um, Fred, was to be believed, then he wouldn't have been the one to take Leila.

The booze was doing its job, forcing Ward to focus on the task. The rage almost numbed, he asked a pressing follow-up. "So, then, who's doing all these abductions?"

Ufzeik shrugged its legs. "Not us. Or at least not anyone on our planet. What would we do with humans? Keep you as pets? Invite you to parties and show you off?"

Ward raised an eyebrow. "Well, the common thought is to experiment on us to find our weaknesses and use them to take over our planet."

Laughter erupted from Ufzeik suddenly and forcefully. "We can barely manage to keep our own planet running. Why would we want two? Especially one that's already occupied?"

Embarrassed, Ward took another pull from the glass. "Okay, you can stop laughing. What happened this time if you've been doing this for so many years?"

It was Ufzeik's turn to blush. "Well, quite literally, you got us. Your technology has gotten better. The stuff we normally use to avoid detection isn't good enough anymore. Ted thought it might have to do with the Russians. They've recovered a few of our ships in the past and reversed-engineered stuff. Nothing world-ending, but have you noticed how much more addicting app games have been to your species? That's actually alien hypnosis at work."

"Get out! You're kidding?"

Grinning slightly, Ufzeik shook his head. "You should really read those agreements before you click 'accept' at the start-up screen."

Digesting this, Ward returned to his intake process. "Okay, so they shot you down outside of Big Sandy Range three days ago. What happened next?"

"How? How did you already know that?" Ufzeik, wide-eyed, spoke with awe and reverence in his voice. "You really *are* the Law Yoda."

"I have my sources, and please stop calling me that. I can't afford another 'House of Mouse' lawyer breathing down my neck before this story is over." Ward pushed aside the glass and picked up a legal pad and a pen. Time to *really* go to work.

After the three-hour intake interview finished, they got up to leave.

"So, who was this Layla to you?" Ufzeik asked.

"Lee-la." Ward picked up the picture of the two of them at the beach again, thought fondly of that day, and handed it over.

The alien smiled, looking at them so happily playing in the sand. "She looks like such a bitch."

"Hey!" Ward grabbed the frame back.

Surprised, Ufzeik apologized. "Sorry. Did I use the wrong word?"

Ward cradled the picture for a moment and returned it to its place. "It's not polite, but . . . not entirely wrong. Only in certain company, though." They walked to the door. "Where are you staying?"

Ufzeik mentioned a hotel that Ward knew. Low-key and no questions asked. "Good. Keep your head—heads?—down."

The alien gave Ward a furtive glance, then looked away. "By any chance, would you want to grab a burger and beer?"

Ward never socialized with his human clients, and, despite wanting to ask a million questions not related to the case, he passed. "No, I have to see a guy."

"A guy?"

"Yeah. He specializes in extractions. I've had him on retainer in case I needed to get Leila or anyone else off a spaceship. Not sure how he's going to react to breaking into Area 51."

"Oh, you don't have to go all the way over there. Ted's up in Sedona."

"Sedona? There's no military base there."

Ufzeik barked again. "You don't think they'd keep recovered alien tech and captured spring breakers someplace as obvious as a —" the alien made air quotes—"'mysterious and secret' location that everyone knows about?" Ufzeik waved the notion away. "Nah. Your government took over a spaceport that vacationers had been using for years to visit the *Diné* people. Now, *there's* a race that knows how to party."

As they left, Ward tried to predict his contractor's reaction to all of what he was about to dump on him. Nothing he imagined was close to the reality.

———

"ALIENS ARE REAL? HUH."

And that was all Tanner Gunnison said on that matter.

Ward had met Gunnison back in LA as a stuntman who'd been arrested when his then-girlfriend found a trunkload of guns in the back of his Kia Soul. To make some extra money, Gunnison, a former MI6 operative, offered lessons to studios on the proper handling and use of military-grade weapons. He'd made the cache inoperable, but the twenty arresting officers who'd pinned him to the ground, tased him, and kicked him in his "frank-'n'-beans" were in no mind to listen. Looking at Gunnison's face—the face of nearly every Bond villain — Ward wasn't sure if he blamed them for being a little over-cautious, but then, that worked to his advantage in court.

Ward, then doing an internship at the Public Defender's office, got the charges dropped. He and the ex-pat Brit formed a mutual assistance pact after that. Though the man gave Ward a serious "Jason Statham on a bad day" vibe from time to time, he had no one else who could do what he needed

"So, the bastard's in lockdown in Crystalville?" Gunnison continued.

Sedona, Arizona, the epicentre of the New Age movement, had more crystal shops than bars, which spoke volumes. Enlightened travellers visited from around the world—and apparently other worlds—to enter "energy vortexes," which allowed you to transcend the mortal flesh and connect with the living Earth. Believers focused this energy through crystal gems for healing or good luck or confidence.

Ward once dated a woman from Sedona who wore a peridot necklace to drive away evil spirits. They met while dancing at a club. She placed a hand on his chest, promising him she could "heal" his pain, but in private wanted him to "hurt" her. Ward wasn't into the BDSM scene, so it ended quickly, but not before one long weekend at her place. The town was beautiful to behold, but boring if you didn't enjoy the outdoors and touristy t-shirt shops.

"According to Fred, the vortex near Bradshaw Ranch is a sort of recharging station for spaceships."

Gunnison chuckled low with irony. "Then that means . . . all them people entering those vortexes are, what? Sniffing gasoline fumes, and that's why they see things?"

Ward shrugged. "I don't know the intricacies of intergalactic space-travel technology. All I know is that the Grey Team has Fred's brother, Ted, and I need just proof he's there to take before a judge."

"So, you don't want me to extract him?" Gunnison seemed disappointed.

"Not yet. That'll come later. Right now, to get this case to court, I want something that can't be written off as a Hollywood special effect."

The ex-pat wasn't convinced. "Just introduce them to yer mate."

Ward had considered that as being the quickest route, but that might bring the Grey Team down on them. Even then, a judge would need to see some tangible evidence that proved they held a non-combatant foreign national against his will. He'd paint Brad-shaw Ranch as the new Guantanamo Bay.

"Fred made a suggestion. He and I are both hesitant to use it. However," Ward admitted, "we couldn't think of anything else."

Gunnison leaned forward and snarled. "I'm not gunna like this, am I?"

Ward slowly shook his head. "You're going to need one of those extra-thick trash bags."

WARD FILED a claim that a Fourth Amendment Rights violation had been perpetrated on a visiting nonimmigrant by the United States military. He did so in the US District Court of Arizona, which didn't limit the definition of "people" to humans. He used the *Illegal Immigration Reform and Immigrant Responsibility Act of 1996* as his cause, stating that Ted should've been deported or placed in front of a federal immigration judge within forty-eight hours, not held for weeks now in captivity.

Since the Air Force shot down Ted's only means of transportation back to his place of origin, it was their responsibility to provide reasonable accommodations while acquiring for him the equivalent of an intergalactic ride-share. Instead, he was poked and prodded—the irony of which was lost on nobody. Additionally, no one had provided Ted with a list of criminal charges against him, the most obvious being US Code Title 49, Section 46307, *Violation of National Defense Air Space*, and Title 8, 1325, *Improper Entry by Alien*.

What the Air Force had on their side was repeated attempts to contact the brothers before shooting them down, so Ward couldn't do anything there. The boys froze and tried to run, having been caught in the act. Ward would play up the ignorance-of-local-customs angle until it didn't serve the case anymore.

The response was immediate. The Grey Team seized Ward's office while he and Fred hid just out of town, but they recorded the whole raid via drone.

Ward filed several other additional motions on behalf of his client, the most relevant being a request for an emergency B-2 visa, allowing Ted to seek medical treatment as a nonimmigrant. He also submitted the country of Inkadincus on the planet Unizor

Prime for friendly nation status. It didn't matter if these requests were eventually thrown out. He just needed to show the judge that these grants were in the works.

Finally, Ward got Fred to file for asylum from racial persecution based on his non-human status. When he discovered Fred's species reproduced by mitosis, he thought about reaching out to the ACLU to get an M added to the end of LGTBQ, so he'd have that card up his sleeve, but he reconsidered that option since he wasn't sure even the eggheads studying Ted knew that about his species yet.

All that prep took time, but when he submitted all his triple-checked paperwork to the federal immigration court, he finally got them a preliminary hearing.

JUDGE DASHAUD WALLACE convened his courtroom. The Armed Forces lawyer, Sagen Verroth, waited behind the defence's desk, stacks of folders and briefs spread out across it.

But Ward hadn't arrived yet.

"Does anyone know where Mr. Ward is?" Judge Wallace demanded. "These are extreme charges he's making. You'd think he would have appeared by now."

Verroth shrugged. "Your honour, the military has no idea what Mr. Ward is doing other than performing a publicity stunt to drum up business for his 'alien abduction' scam."

"Oh, we're way past that."

Ward and Fred materialized behind the prosecutor's desk.

The bailiff drew his gun as shouts of shock and alarm came from everyone else in the courtroom. Ward and Fred had their hands up to show they were unarmed.

"Jesus, Ward! Where the hell did you come from?" asked Verroth.

"Cincinnati, originally, but we've been here since yesterday. Fred turned us into chairs since the United States Government has a warrant out for our capture or deaths. We stopped in here right before closing, took our 'seats,' and hung out all night."

Empty chip bags, wrappers from convenience store sandwiches, and cans of Red Bull lay strewn across the desk. As the judge continued to stare, disbelieving, Ward blushed. "Sorry for the mess. We'll clean that up, but we needed to make sure we got here unmolested."

Verroth, regaining her composure, launched into her defence. She flipped her braided blonde hair back from where it had escaped upon Ward and Fred's arrival. "Magic tricks aside, Your Honour, we have issued no orders regarding Mr. Ward or his accuser. We consider Mr. Ward an unstable individual who has filed many false reports regarding 'alien abductions.' All one has to do is watch his horrible ads to see the man is not playing with a full deck."

Ward took in his opponent and mouthed, *Horrible?* Then he addressed the judge. "As you can see by the filings, Your Honour, I'm no longer defending humans who have been kidnapped by aliens. Instead, I'm defending an alien nonimmigrant who, while visiting our wonderful world for health treatment and recovery, has been held against his will by our Armed Forces without due process." He handed the clerk several additional stacks of paper. "We're also filing against Common Rule 45 CFR 46, Subpart C, restricting prisoners from being used for experimentation, especially since the prisoner is not human."

"Preposterous!" Verroth exclaimed. "Your Honour, Mr. Ward has had some sort of a mental break and should be lock—"

The judge looked ready to agree, opening his mouth without looking down at the new filings, but then Fred spoke.

"Your Honour, sir, if I may?"

Wallace, curious, allowed it.

Fred stood, looking sharp in his new suit, noticeably more handsome, and, yeah, still boyish and charming. The alien had promised Ward he'd return Chris Evans's face after the trial.

"My brother, who was taken by your Air Force, is currently being held in a secret location near Sedona, and I just want to get him back." Fred's voice held enough conviction and desperation that Judge Wallace, who seemed ready to arrest Ward, paused.

"So, then, by Mr. Ward's statement, you're claiming to be one of the aliens he's currently representing?" Wallace looked down at his notes. "Mr. Fred Ufzeik?"

Fred studied Ward, who nodded for him to continue. "Yes, sir. I am."

Skeptical but willing to see it through, Wallace said, "You look pretty normal to me. Even familiar. Your proof?"

Ward stood up and moved away from the defence desk. He addressed the bailiff. "Don't shoot him, okay? He's harmless. Well, *mostly* harmless."

Fred transformed back into his natural form. The bailiff did draw again. Verroth spoke into her "secret agent" wristwatch. The sounds of pounding came from outside the courtroom doors.

Ward leaned toward Verroth, hand at the side of his face, and in a hushed whisper said, "Your pals have been sealed outside this room using alien tech. They're not getting in until the judge gives me the Writ." The hope had been from the beginning to reveal the Grey Team's existence and force them to prove they had Ted under judge's orders via *habeas corpus*.

Wallace, for his part, stared. "I don't know whether to crap myself or vomit or both. I've seen some weird shit in my time, Mr. Ufzeik, but you beat it all." He asked Ward, "Where am I even supposed to address him?"

Ward pointed to three sets of eyes on the second trunk.

"But even if you *are* what you say you are . . . that doesn't prove the Air Force is holding your brother."

Ward was ready for this. "With permission, I'd like to enter our first piece of evidence."

"Approach."

Ward walked up to the bench with Verroth right behind him. He flipped open his tablet and pulled up a video file. "This was taken three weeks ago at an underground facility called Bradshaw Ranch. It was obtained at great risk to my operative, seen here on the vid stream."

Gunnison stood outside a Plexiglas cell where a man, similar in appearance to Fred but maybe a little taller and older, sat patiently. The former Ops agent and Ted spoke. Ted then transformed to his natural form as Fred had, only appearing a little taller and older.

Verroth scoffed. "Cheap Hollywood theatrics. I can see the zipper. Clearly a fake."

"That's not a zipper. Wait for it."

Gunnison worked the cell's lock, popping it in seconds.

Ward blushed. "We're prepared to pay for damages."

Ted pulled off one of his heads and handed it over. Gunnison placed it in a large, black trash bag.

Both the JAG and Wallace held hands up to their eyes as if that could shield them from seeing the image now burned there.

"Your Honour, I'd like to enter our second piece of evidence along with presenting our first witness."

Gunnison *poofed!* into existence, holding a large black trash bag.

The now overly stressed bailiff just sat down in the jury box, clearly giving up.

Judge Wallace leaned backward, waving his hands in disbelief. "No way! Get out! That's not . . ."

"It is, Your Honour. And I think my *other* client has something to say on his behalf."

Gunnison pulled out Ted's head.

His three eyes scanned around the room, landing on Fred. "Fred! Hey, bro. Lookin' good!"

Fred smiled. "I wish I could say the same about you."

"For the record, can you state your name?" Wallace said, trying to keep the hearing in some form of reality.

The head swivelled around to find the judge. "Ted Ufzeik, Your Honour."

Ward asked his client, "Can you tell us where the rest of . . . you is?"

"Sure, Law Yoda."

Ward leaned toward the stunned yet still-typing stenographer. "Can you strike that last comment? I'm skating on thin ice with Disney as it is."

The red-haired woman named Rena nodded and backed up a few words as Ted continued.

"So, I'm rotting in a cell under the red-sand deserts of Arizona, all because my brother didn't want to go to Palm Springs again."

"I told you I'm sick of that place. They can't do a proper *mojito*."

"Flying over two Air Force bases was a better idea?"

"*You* were supposed to upgrade the cloaking device before we left."

"I had a date. Sue me."

"No." Fred pointed at Verroth. "We're suing *them*."

Ward drew Judge Wallace's attention from the bickering siblings. "Have I shown enough cause?"

Verroth asked for a sidebar. "Your Honour, the government's position is that Mr. Ward is using puppetry and mental manipulation to make you believe that aliens exist." She scoffed. "I mean, really? If there were aliens visiting our world on vacation, we'd certainly know by now, wouldn't we?"

Ward nodded. "That's my point. You *have* known for a long time, despite US citizens being abducted and innocent aliens being captured and held without due process."

"That's a good point, Mr. Ward. What about all those reported abductions? Are these two responsible?"

"No, sir. Their planet is no threat. Obviously, there are others out there that might be. Is it not in the world's best interest that we know who we can trust or not?"

Verroth pointed a finger. "You can't do this, Your Honour. If you take this to trial and Ward reveals there are aliens, it'll create mass panic."

Ward grinned widely. "You just said 'reveals.'"

The JAG cursed but continued, "This is fate-of-the-whole-world stuff, Your Honour. Are you ready to risk it?"

Ward, equally as passionate, asked, "Are you ready to sacrifice the rights most of that world agreed upon to continue to cover this up?"

The judge leaned back.

Ward shushed his clients.

After a moment, Wallace began. "Okay, I've made my decision . . ."

"WHY NOT A JURY TRIAL?" Fred asked as he adjusted his tie.

Mitchell Ward, Lawyer to the Actual Stars (which the Mouse gave the thumbs-up to), reviewed his notes one last time before their private armed bodyguards escorted them to the courthouse. "A jury is a collection of people deciding which side hired the better lawyer. That would be the JAG. I'm not *that* good."

Fred countered, "But you're the Law—"

"Don't say it! I signed a contract. No, a judge is better because we're going to present facts that can't be twisted by the opposing counsel. We have plenty of video. Ted and Gunnison as witnesses. And a few surprises."

Fred rubbed his hands. "Like?"

Ward grinned. "Remember that list of 'experts' I submitted?"

"Yes, I noticed the names looked familiar."

"Based on the naming algorithms you taught me, I found others of your race visiting Earth. I sent Gunnison and Vanity to track them down. She interviewed them for the paper, and he, um, convinced them to testify."

"Oh, dear," Fred said. "He didn't break any of them, I hope?"

Ward shrugged. "Nothing permanent. Vanity keeps him in check." They worked as a coupling, and it took the pressure off of Ward. "Word is spreading, and other extraterrestrials have gotten spooked. They're returning the abducted Earthlings, most with their memories erased."

Fred snapped seven of his twelve fingers, realized he had slipped, and returned them to ten. "Oh! *That's* how you got Leila back."

"That's what I'm thinking."

Upon hearing her name, Leila sauntered out of the back office.

"There are you, my good girl." Ward knelt down to let his black Labrador lick his face. "Careful! Don't get hair on my suit."

Fred reached down to let Leila lick his hand. "Then you have no idea who took her?"

"Nope. One minute we were at a rest stop in the middle of nowhere so she could pee, and the next, a light enveloped her and zapped her up. Same thing happened in reverse while I was at the Circle-K. Strange." Mitch gave Leila a hug, fur be damned. "I'm never letting you off your leash again, am I?"

His canine life partner had been returned unchanged, nor any older, despite being gone three years.

Well, mostly unchanged.

She slobbered his face affectionately before Mitch finally extracted himself. He set out Leila's food before heading to the door.

"Hey, Mitch?"

Ward turned back around to answer. "Yes, Lei-Lei?" As he often did, he wondered if he was ever going to know the whole truth. Not like she could tell him. They'd wiped her memory, too.

Leila panted supportively and said in her delightfully soft, feminine voice, "Make those bastards pay, okay?"

The law dog patted the top of her head once more before leaving.

"You know I will, Hun."

SOLDIER OF FORTUNE

By Edward M. Lerner

"You're here because you're the best at what you do."

The Master—after I've been brought here (wherever here is) blindfolded, after passing through three tiers of security screening, after I'm ushered into his presence—isn't the larger-than-life figure who had dominated TV and the Net. Still, no matter how his cheeks have hollowed, under-eye bags deepened, complexion gone pasty, no matter how the bemedalled uniform jacket swims on a massive frame somehow sunken in upon itself, his *gaze* burns with more fervour than ever.

"The best," he repeats.

I don't take exception. It's true, I'm good at what I do. Other-wise, I'd be languishing in a prison cell. More likely, I'd be long dead. But the best? No. I'm here because of what I've heard the Master is peddling. And doubtless, because others in our rarified community, attuned to the same rumours, chose to ignore the overtures to which I—and only I?—have responded.

They don't share my motivation.

If I lack faith in the Cause, it nonetheless offers me the opportunity—after so long, surely my only opportunity—to discover what once was done to me. My only opportunity to undo it. Even an opportunity for revenge.

How desperately I crave these things!

Does the Master question my ardour? Perhaps, and so what? As his final defeat looms, True Believers must be harder and harder to come by. And so, through devious channels, the word had gone out for professional talent . . .

I am, or I choose to see myself as, a soldier of fortune. It sounds better than mercenary. Or assassin. Much less hit man.

Why am I good at the job? After the . . . incident . . . five years ago, I had had no choice but to acquire a new trade. Reentering the medical profession hadn't been a viable option for a forty-year-old with amnesia.

By whatever name, my current line of work provides ample opportunity to work off some of my anger.

Lord knows I have plenty of that.

I HAD . . . awakened? . . . into nighttime gloom, in an awkward heap, cheek pressed against a rough-hewn, planked floor. My head ached. My forehead throbbed. I tasted . . . I wasn't sure what. Bile? Something sour. And I was *cold*, the few sullen embers on the stone hearth producing little warmth and scarcely more light—and yet, illumination enough to reveal, among the ashes, a cracked and warped cell phone. Alongside an upended table, shards of curved glass glittered. I smelled . . . brandy. For an instant, lightning dazzled, giving visible form to the inundation drumming on

the roof and cascading over the eaves. Seconds later, loud, rolling thunder rattled the windows.

Even as sensory overload overwhelmed me, I grappled with bigger problems. What had happened to me? Why was I here? Where was here? And, in rising panic—

Who was I?

I got on my feet and shuffled to the dim rectangle that was the closest window. Peered out. Glimpsed, by faint moon glow diffused through thick clouds, a brooding forest. Crossed to the other window and saw only more trees. Made my way to and opened the door to behold yet more thick woods, a rutted gravel track, and a mud-spattered SUV. Mine? Sensed, somehow, that whatever else I had forgotten, I still knew how to drive. Felt just as surely that I had no idea *where* to drive. Nor, patting myself all over, any clue where the vehicle's keys might be.

Days later, a man in a boxy sedan skidded to a stop behind the SUV. Flung open the car door. Flung open the cabin door. Launched into a tirade about me missing my shifts and not returning calls—only to trail off upon taking in my confusion. Peppered me with questions, few of which I could answer. Frowned at what answers I could give: that I didn't recognize myself, much less him. Gently probed the bruise on my forehead. Shone a penlight in my eyes. Spoke in tongues (and why did I remember *that* odd expression, with so much else lost?) into his cell phone.

After that cryptic consultation, he drove us to a hospital. *Our* hospital, he explained. Where, he promised, friends and colleagues—himself among them, I was to believe—would give me the best possible care. Where we would get to the bottom of things. Where we would begin the process of recovering my lost memories.

If only matters had been so simple.

"To recap," the Master continues, oblivious to my ruminations, "your task, while crucial, is quite simple." A characterization that does not stop him from explaining—and complaining—at great length. But it *is* simple. His nemesis is on the brink of final victory. Someone needs to eliminate her and her lieutenants.

Killing: that's what soldiers of fortune do.

"Only," the Master goes on, "getting at them has been impossible in the here and now. Which is why it has proven necessary to resort to . . . unprecedented measures."

Then, just maybe, the rumours *were* true.

As for unprecedented? Even if no one would mistake me for Arnold Schwarzenegger, the notion of *terminating* was well enough established.

The Master waves grandiloquently to a waiting minion. Like the Master, he is . . . infamous.

"It isss quite zimple," the mad scientist begins, even as he scuttles toward us. (Is the repetition intentional? An homage? Perhaps.) Where the Master appears prematurely aged, his wizard looks . . . wizened. Somehow, there is a difference.

With a sharp tug, the professor straightens his cliché white lab coat. He gestures down the long, echoey space toward his gadget.

Only *gadget* fails to do justice to the hulking apparatus. It, surely, is his *chef-d'œuvre*. *Pièce de résistance*. *Raison d'être*. Albeit all that with the unfortunate Dr. Strangelovian accent.

As for this cavernous space, well, it *is* a cavern. The Master's legendary secret redoubt—which sudden, distant explosions suggest is no longer secret.

"It isss from here you vill depart," the professor, unperturbed, drones on . . .

RETROGRADE AMNESIA, declared the neurologists. Clearly, I had been drinking, lost my balance, struck my head, and . . . voilà.

The good news, they told me, was that lost memories generally returned as the brain healed. That no manner of imaging or blood test known to medical science showed any brain injury to need healing? Not to worry. Subtle damage had to be there.

So, anyway, I was assured. The pity of erstwhile colleagues, poorly disguised, didn't make their assurances any more palatable. That once *I* could have understood the lab reports, could have interpreted the MRI and CT scans, only made me angrier.

On the other hand, I could—theoretically—be suffering from general dissociative amnesia: a rare, purely psychological condition. Only—this possibility quickly dismissed with condescension—the notion was absurd. GDA mainly afflicted combat veterans and victims of sexual abuse. What conceivable emotional trauma could I have suffered alone in what my purported friends insisted was my remote cabin, leaving no medical trace but the bump on my forehead? Leaving no physical evidence—by then, the sheriff's office had examined the scene—but my own fingerprints on the broken snifter and decanter and my own dried blood on an edge of the overturned table?

The heavy rain, I had insisted, would have washed away the footprints or tire tracks of any intruder. Only to be advised, the condescension not even badly disguised by this point, that such paranoia could only impede my recovery.

So: be patient. Jog my memory by seeking out familiar

surroundings. (My so-called beloved getaway wasn't? Or the hospital where I, too, was supposedly on staff—if, for obvious reasons, by then on medical leave? Or, after I insisted on discharging myself, the penthouse condo that it turned out I owned? None of those places evoked even a hint of familiarity.) Embrace the company of friends and coworkers. (All of whom remained strangers, no matter how many photos of us together they shared, no matter how many anecdotes they related.) Retain an open mind. (It had become all too open. A sieve.) Continue counselling. Study memory-training tricks. Do all that and, almost certainly, with time, my memories *would* return.

Except they didn't. Muscle memory and erratic scraps of general knowledge aside, I remained a blank slate.

What little family I had—a strange and, apparently, estranged sister—didn't help, either. One of my alleged friends had reached out to her, and she then to the courts. Once she'd gotten herself appointed conservator of my estate, exhibiting a far more generous notion of what she was entitled to than I, I saw no advantage to staying around.

Providing, had I needed it, another reason to somehow track down the bastard who had destroyed my life.

IF MY MEDICAL training never returned, at least I retained a tolerance for blood and a practical, if rudimentary, knowledge of human anatomy. Both had since served me well. As for physics, I claim neither tolerance nor knowledge. Regardless, it remains my impression that *quantum-temporal-entangled whatevers* are some kind of physics.

With a curt sweep of an arm, I cut off the pedantic lecture.

"Yeah, yeah. I close myself inside. Confirm the date setting." Because however little I understand the apparatus, I grok *this* much: its essential core is wholly isolated. Power source, transfer mechanism, controls, instrumentation—it's all within. Not as much as a light ray or a radio wave is allowed through. The tiniest gap in some field, or shield, or whatnot, the merest iota of interaction with the outside, will prevent the device from operating. "Press ENTER. Am zapped back. Then dust myself off, walk out of this cave, and go to work."

"Six years back," the Master reminds, hands rubbing gleefully with thoughts of the wetwork he'd have me do. "The wicked ones, the she-devil especially, will not yet have achieved prominence. They will be unsuspecting. Unprotected. Vulnerable. Ripe for you to strike."

Wicked, I interpret, because the Master's movement could never have justified overthrowing the government over mere philosophical differences. Having succeeded, what but pure evil could then be turning the tables on him?

Also because, in a struggle against evil, what measure could be deemed too extreme?

As though a soldier of fortune would care. That a payday is not why *I'm* here, he doesn't, and mustn't, know. Nor can the platoon of nervous, heavily-armed "praetorians"—thugs—who yet stand between me and . . .

If I'm honest with myself, I don't know what to expect. Can the past be changed? Mr. Wizard clearly believes so. So must some part of me, else I wouldn't be here. And if we're both wrong? At least I'll finally learn what happened to me five years ago. And *who* happened . . .

The Master ostentatiously clears his throat.

"Six years," I repeat. Still channelling *The Terminator*, I indulge my curiosity. "Why not travel back farther to strangle her in her crib? Or her parents before she is ever born?"

The professor begins blithering about the machine's power requirements, the limited power available here in the redoubt, and the competing demands for that. Something about charging a gigantic bank of . . . capacitors? Or discharging it?

"Six years back is the most we can achieve," the Master translates.

It will serve.

"Eggzept, you do not go back, not in the zense you might expect," the professor doggedly resumes. "Your consciousness does. To time-shift zo much mass? It vould require unimaginable energies that—"

"Transfer my *consciousness*?" No bit of rumour had suggested that! "And this works?"

He hesitates. "In every zimulation."

"How about in actual operation? A dry run of some sort?" For which any of the Master's bitter-ender zealots should serve just fine.

There's renewed babble about power availability or unavailability until, at a scowl from the Master, the professor's voice trails off.

"It has not been practical," the Master completes. "We get one chance at this."

It would be my one chance, too.

"You are being amply rewarded," the Master points out, repeating a figure named earlier. "All that remains after expenses is yours."

Are being rewarded? Will be, perhaps. Or would be? Or have been, although I've yet to experience it? I struggle to wrap my head around all this, misplaced subjunctives and appropriate verb tenses being the least of my concerns, certain only that my consciousness, however quantum-entangled it may be or become, can't tote back a wallet. "How, before we've ever met, does this reward work?"

To a dull, distant roar, the cavern floor trembles. This time, the professor trembles, too.

"Memorize this." The Master hands me a scrap of paper covered in numbers. An account ID and authentication codes. "The decade-old account of a prominent early disciple."

Who would be very surprised when a stranger cleared out the offshore stash. Prominent disciple's consciousness would not be travelling backward to explain.

"It's settled, then," says the Master, and that isn't a question.

My consciousness transferred: that's not how I'd seen my day going. Leaving behind a mindless husk? With distant explosions giving way to not-so-distant gunfire, I don't bother to ask. Sticking around here can only end with me a *lifeless* husk at the Master's futile last stand—if refusing his offer doesn't get me shot dead first. Talented I may be, but I can't take down thirty-plus of the Master's goons, any of them with a sense of self-preservation doubtless eager to escape this place in my stead . . .

I nod.

"Make way," the Master commands.

Ranks of silent, stony-faced praetorians part like the Red Sea before Moses.

With coattails flapping, the mad scientist scurries through the gauntlet. He pokes at the access-control keypad that secures his apparatus. The electronic lock emits a strident beep. The door unlatches with a metallic click, bright light pouring through the crack. He steps away.

The Master taps my shoulder. "*Go*," he orders as, once again, the cavern quivers. Overhead lights flicker. Rock dust sleets down. "Time is short." He ventures a short laugh. "Until, as is certain, you succeed."

"To success," I respond.

I stride to the time machine. Seal myself inside. Reset the controls to a date *five* years earlier. I will meet my earlier self at my rustic cabin in plenty of time to surprise whomever it was who destroyed my life.

And *then*, forewarned, with all the patience and skills of my second career, we will make that sick bastard pay. Whenever he shows up.

I press ENTER.

IN A TIMELESS INSTANT—AS past-me and present-me collide and commingle; as two consciousnesses plunge into a maelstrom of chaos and confusion; as the man I once was recoils in horror; as, disoriented, a cell phone flies from past-me's grasp into a crackling fire and I/he/we crash, headfirst, into the table—I know:

I *am* making that sick bastard pay.

As I have done before and will do again.

Because *I* am the sick bastard.

As memories past(?) and future(?) dissolve, with my vision going dark and awareness fading, in a final coherent moment, I confront two more implausible but undeniable truths:

The past cannot be changed.

And, in an endless loop, I am a soldier of *mis*fortune.

DONE WITH MIRRORS

By Sarah A. Hoyt

I woke up staring at the mirror, and something was very wrong. For one, it wasn't my mirror. For another, it wasn't my room. And for yet another, it wasn't the world in which I'd fallen asleep. The only thing right in it was you, Katrina Rhea, golden skin and golden hair and long-limbed clean grace naked among the silk sheets, asleep on your side, your face like that of a very young girl despite your millennia of life.

A quick look at the mirror again. Not only wasn't it my mirror, it wasn't a mirror. Not a functioning one. It had no depths in its innocent reflection of me, half sitting, looking at it, dark-haired and dark-eyed and looking like a suspicious youth of twenty or so, the age at which I'd frozen my appearance. And you beside me. It was simple, untroubled. And it wouldn't do us a bloody bit of good.

I touched you. Just my fingertips on your shoulders. Your eyes opened instantly and went from sleepy confusion to alarm. I don't know what you read in my eyes. But we'd been married—well, as good as—for thousands of years, and thousands of times, and thousands of places, and hundreds of children. You knew me as I knew myself, or perhaps better.

You looked at the mirror, and your eyes reflected my panic.

We didn't speak. Words weren't needed.

Jumping out of the strange bed, at once, we looked for clothes and, more importantly, weapons.

Our clothes were there, as we'd discarded them however long ago, in a safe world. For the sake of brevity, I'll describe them thus: when you read this, you'll have the memories of Terra Prima, of having grown up in Terra Prima, the world of humanity's birth. You might have seen the clothing people wore on the covers of science fiction novels of the early twentieth century: tight pants and a tunic for me, something like an elaborate brassiere for you, and capes for both.

I've always wondered if there were enough of us, or of our children, drawing those covers to make that fashion permanent.

Mine were silver and black, as they always were, and yours gold and shimmering green, like the fields of Terra.

There were no weapons. More indications that someone had brought us here. Someone had placed us here. For an ambush?

But why move us? Why not kill us where we were? And who could move us? Of all the Lords of the Mirror, only you and I remained, my best beloved.

And yet, we'd been moved. The sky outside was a pale and sickly orange, a sky that did not exist, could not exist in any of our worlds. The mirror was wrong. The weapons were gone.

There was a sound from the corridor outside. We were out of time.

I jumped toward the window, where purple, semi-transparent

curtains waved in a hot breeze, catching you around the waist with my arm. You didn't resist.

In my careening run, I paused, less than a breath, to see the landscape out the window. Ocean spread in all directions, barely rippling. The ocean was red like spilled blood, but it smelled of water and salt. In the sky, two dark, dying suns explained the colours.

The pause was barely noticeable. We lost no momentum. Behind us, I heard the door slamming open and voices, too confused to identify.

The ray of burning light blazed above us as we were already in a headlong dive out of the window.

The water was cold when we hit, and it smelled like the oceans of Terra. Without a word, we plunged, side by side, but there was nothing except a wall of the palace to our left and open ocean to our right. Not even a fish, or a plant, or rocks.

You touched my arm. You flipped around. Using the sign language we'd created long ago, among the deaf people of Unor-mach, you told me, "There is no escape. They know where we are."

I flipped around, too, toward the surface, and my fingers worked fast. "They're here. There must be a mirror."

You nodded. Your green eyes were deeper than the ocean and more full of depths as your eyebrows came down over them. You pointed up. Which is when I realized it must be close to two minutes, and my need to draw breath was becoming pressing.

Centuries ago in Rodanancia, that drowned world, I'd perfected my ability to hold my breath for three minutes and past, but I was out of practice. And so were you. Still, I pointed sideways and up along the wall of the palace. First, because there was no percentage in resurfacing where we'd gone down. Second, because we must see if we could enter this palace at a different point. We had to get to the mirror.

As we swam the way I'd suggested, I thought that perhaps this tower was the only building in the world and the window we'd dived through was the only one in the building, and shivered, despite using all my strength to swim.

If I were setting a trap, I'd set it thus. If I were setting us to be killed, I'd do it this way.

But obviously, our antagonist wasn't me. We surfaced as close to the wall as we could, and you pointed to the left, where a corner was barely visible. We went underwater again—no point making ourselves sitting ducks—and swam around the corner before we resurfaced. Both of us stared up, and for a moment, both of us were mute with shock.

The building was nothing but a façade like they created on Terra Prima for old movies. We were shocked but also puzzled. I had a feeling, though it might be wrong, that there was no one else in this world but us. So for whom had they built this façade, pierced with recurved windows? Only the third floor, from which we'd jumped, seemed to be real, though barely more than ten or so metres deep, jutting out and back, cantilevered, somehow, over the sea. It was there our room had been, but there was more than that, as it ran the forty metres or so of the wall's width.

You pressed close to me, cold in the cold water. "They will be up there," you said. "And the mirror, too."

"Yes," I whispered back. "And they'll be waiting."

I nodded, then grinned at you, the grin you knew. Oh, perhaps we were damned this time. Perhaps the death we'd evaded for thousands of years would catch us now. But perhaps we'd beat it again.

You grinned back, the same reckless grin that had captured my heart on Terra Prima so many millennia ago, and then we were climbing. The wall behind was almost smooth. Almost but not quite. It was no harder than the peaks of Varoumer, those glass mountains we'd climbed easily enough oh, so long ago.

Out of the water, I tied my cloak down around my waist, and you did the same. Up and up and up, on fingernails and the tips of our sandals. Up and up and up. By the middle of the *faux* second floor, my fingers were bleeding, but it didn't matter. I'd climb up on the stumps of fingers to find out where we were and to jump to salvation.

And you, you must have been suffering equally, but my look down at you garnered me a glittering, brittle smile.

That was when the Rodans dived down from the same window we had plunged through. They wore the weird spacesuit-like attire they wore in air. Which made perfect sense since, though they had hyper-developed fins that could do the turn of arms and legs, they were . . . well, sardines. And smelled as such, as I remembered. And they were going to look for us. But they were intelligent. Well, as much as humans. And that meant after not finding us at whatever depth they dived to, they'd come and look up.

I started up faster, and you followed without asking, you, doubtless, having arrived at the same conclusion.

Up and up, and at the top, we realized we'd made one miscalculation. There was no door on this side. But I remembered there had been windows on the other side, and so did you, for you were already climbing to the roof of the cantilevered box and across it. On top, it was built of concrete with seashells in it. I wondered if it was created by the Rodans and if perhaps its existence had another purpose. It still made a trap but saved someone the trouble of constructing it for the purpose.

We ran across the roof and then descended the wall to the last window a floor up from where we wanted to be. There was only one problem with this. We could hang from this window, suspended by our arms, and swing into the window in the real floor below, into a different room than the one we'd awakened in. It was about the right distance from the bottom of this window to the top of the other. The windows below us were tall, probably four metres in height, floor to ceiling.

But—

"We'll have to go in blind," I whispered. "Anything could be in that room."

You hunched a shoulder and scoffed as if to say that surely, you knew that, and I was not giving you any news. I nodded. And you nodded back, with just a hint of a smile, but you bit the right corner of your lip just before, holding the bottom of the window, we swung ourselves out.

We had to swing out, then start swinging in, feet together, then let go and jump.

The bottom of our sandals hit the glass, shattering it. We landed on our bottoms amid glass pieces in a large white room.

I didn't have time to take in the details; a man turned and pointed a burner at us.

It has been said that a gun pointed at one's head concentrates the mind wonderfully, but in that case, the only thing I could think was that the man holding the gun on me looked familiar.

He stood tall, and his blond hair, caught back and tied, had highlights of red. His eyes were an odd colour: brown but with a tinge of dark red, like well-aged liquor.

As always, you were ahead of me in memory. You stood, indifferent to his implied threat, shook the glass from your pants, and untied your cloak as you said, with withering calm, "Ah, Ermis. I knew it would be one of you."

He threw his head back and laughed at this. "Hello, Mother," he said.

Ermis. Suddenly the face, middle-aged, older than mine (though that was arbitrary), fit the expression of a small boy running happily through a field of daisies, clutching in his hand half a dozen of them to offer you. Ermis, our clever Ermis, our firstborn.

He'd known nothing of mirrors and had no affinity for them when we tried to teach him, but they said—the old ones, the lost ones—that the ability sometimes comes late. Very late. He must be a quarter of a millennium old if my memory didn't deceive me. It might, because keeping the count of Terra Prima while rotations away was difficult.

"This is ridiculous," I said. "What do you want from us, Ermis?"

His smile turned subtle and gloating. "You don't know? Why, my dear parents! I want my birthright, the secret of the mirrors."

You and I looked at each other. We'd tried. We'd tried to convey to each of our children the secret of their heritage, to replace the Mirror Lords who had died, to renew the universe. But either they couldn't or they wouldn't, or their minds simply lacked the ability to create the jump points and to jump.

Or not . . .

You sounded confused and appalled. "You didn't need to entrap us for that. And how did you entrap us? It would take troops to break through our security, and it would take suborning our people to—" You must have understood at the same time I did because you stopped.

"You've allied with some king," I said. "Some republic, some satrapy. You've allied with some world to come and extort the secret."

Ermis smiled. His voice was rich and resonant of joy, of fields full of flowers, of the confidence of one who was raised in a palace, in a designed world, safe and happy and believing himself of divine origin. "Oh, not allied, and not one of them. We—my brothers and sisters and I—have assembled an alliance, that's true, but they're our vassals, and we're their lords. They want the age of the Open Mirror, the time when mirrors were made so anyone might cross."

You said, "No," before I added, "I'll see you in hell first."

And he laughed at us, Ermis, our firstborn, and he told us to suit ourselves. In this empty world, in this empty counterfeit of a building, he'd leave us to wait, with only Rodans for company. Mute Rodans, who hated all humans and all who breathed air.

"I'll take their guns. They're a little quick with them," he said and smiled.

And then he left. I didn't see the mirror, which meant he was being clever, and the mirror wasn't here. He disappeared midair, mid-sentence, which meant his mirror was elsewhere and set to pull him back at a certain time.

I cursed, and you smiled thinly. "My love, you've cursed the Satrapy of Remearuta three times and the horned kings of Letania five."

"They can't be sufficiently cursed," I said lamely.

You looked out the window and sighed. "And yet, here we are. We should have been touching him when the mirror pulled him back."

Which was true, and which reminds me that since all your memories are from Terra Prima and the last quarter-century until we unlock your true ones, you'll have to believe I know of what I speak. And if you're reading this, you're in desperate need of your true memories and the ability to jump through mirrors.

Doubtless, you're very confused by the mirrors you know and mirrors through which you can travel and which pull . . .

Well, they're mirrors, and they're not. Look, in the history of Terra Prima, your native planet in either your counterfeit life or the real one, the human race emerged much earlier than any of your scientists credit it.

Scientists in any world and at any time are funny creatures. Their inquiry and discovery stop once they have a timeline that satisfies them. And then that timeline becomes revealed truth unless something very extraordinary happens. Sorry if you believe it, but as Bob Heinlein (whom I knew briefly back in the heady days of the mid-twentieth century) said, there are more holes in the history of human evolution than there are bastards in a royal European line. And trust me, that's an awful lot of them. I know; I've been there.

Humans evolved much farther back than it's believed, and then . . . well, it takes about ten thousand years from barbarism to civilization. Again, trust me, I've seen it again and again and again.

Back in that first dawn civilization, in the rosy, blushing morning of Terra Prima, when the world—and everything—was new and innocent, the play started.

There are those who make and those who rule. Those who create and those who can't and, not being able to, wish to control the creators.

Oh, I'm not disparaging some kings, some satraps, some presidents, some rulers by popular or divine choice. Some of them, not overly interested in power, simply maintain the minimum control needed for the safety of those they govern.

You'll know them or of them. Their kingdoms take on the nimbus of paradise, the felicitous shine of prosperity and human joy.

In one of those—oh, very long ago, before either you or I were born—in a civilization that by all I've heard resembled the Italy of the quattrocento, a family of artists—or perhaps scientists; the distinction wasn't clear back then—created . . . mirrors. Only they weren't really mirrors, but things that, while they could reflect you, could also afford you passage between universes.

They guarded their secrets zealously. The secret of *travel* through the mirrors they gave only to those they trusted; the precious secret of *making* them was reserved for those of their blood.

I want to say everyone was happy then, but I doubt it. They were human and, therefore, unhappy and striving, which is the essence of humanity.

As the millennia passed and humans spread to virgin universes and undiscovered lands, they took with them their wars, their rebellions, and their hate—and their art, their joy, and their loves, too.

Ah, my beloved, if only you could see—I want to believe you will again—the golden empires that arose in those other worlds, one mirror-turn from Earth. A hundred golden Greeces, blooming with philosophy and poetry and art. A thousand shining Romes in white marble. A million boisterous Parises, glistening with lights. All that and more, in worlds that would never have known the tread of human feet except for our ancestors, the mirror makers.

But golden ages always end, and our ancestors—it must have been by the time of our grandparents, a million years ago or so; it's hard to know since I believe mirrors also play with time—got tired of armies marching through the mirrors they created, and of Romes burning again and again in the reflections of their work.

And they got more tired of being hunted and chased and

imprisoned and asked to make a mirror for this king or that revolutionary.

They ended the era of Open Mirrors. Mirrors were locked and broken till only a very few remained. Through those, only the people who also had the ability to create them, all descended from the same long-ago ancestors, could pass. From then on, only those approved by the family could cross between worlds.

Or was that true? No. Of course, it was not. Some people, some families, some states kept mirrors. And they chased our people through the immense weave of the universe. We'd give up the secret, they said. And their pets with the capacity to use the science and art and magic of mirrors would make them mirrors, which would allow them, personally, to jump between worlds and create their very own empire.

The age of persecution started. Here and there, a cousin, a distant uncle, someone would be identified as a mirror maker and hounded, tortured, in an attempt to extract from her, or him, the secret.

None gave it. From the earliest age, we were all told that those who most want the secret are those who will misuse it.

And then, just over a quarter of a million years ago, if indeed time runs straight, the great plague came. Some cunning scientist in some human colony created a plague—we never found out which colony or where, or, at least, no one living knows—tuned to our common gene, the one that allowed those in the family to manipulate and create mirrors. So, everyone, everywhere, got very ill. And word came down, passed through the family grapevine, that the cure would be furnished to the ones who talked ...

You and I survived. I do not know why. We used to think our genes were mutated, which was why none of our children had inherited our ability. My love, we might have to rethink that explanation.

Neither of us was born or raised on Terra Prima. After the death of the First Ones, we set out, looking for . . . for any survivor of our kind. Or at least anyone who would welcome a mirror orphan. Fortunately, the other thing our ancestors had discovered was . . . well, not immortality; that would be saying too much. We could die, as the First Ones had, of illness, of a bad turn, of an accident, of a million different things. But not of aging. Not that. We could choose our age and not age a day beyond it.

We found each other in Terra Prima. You remember that beach at dawn and how we talked the first language—

Amid the worlds, we—who imperfectly remember and can barely build mirrors—raised . . . was it ten families? Or twenty? . . . without, we thought, producing a single Mirror Lord.

Until the moment when we found ourselves prisoners in that false tower in the middle of a hostile ocean populated by a species who hated all air breathers.

"He'll wait," you said. "Ermis will. Until we're hungry. Three or four days, perhaps. And then he'll come back and try again. And if we refuse—"

"We will."

"Of course, but if we refuse, he'll try again. Remember how clever Ermis is. He won't kill us or yet allow us to die. Until we speak," you said. "Remember Prometheus."

Prometheus, chained to the rock while the eagles ate his liver. Yes, that was a cousin. He'd helped a rebel group escape the wrath of their so-called sovereign lord and set up their own colony away. It is not easy, but it is possible to create eagle-artifacts that eat only at the speed our near-immortal flesh rejuvenates.

He never gave the secret. If he didn't die in the plague—and I don't know from where the contagion would come—he lives still. If you can call it living. He must have gone mad thousands of years ago.

But we weren't defeated yet, and we came up with a plan. The hard part was finding weapons, but after all, these rooms weren't empty, and we could use the windows to travel to the room we'd first awakened in.

There, we broke the mirror. Yes, I know, seven years of bad luck, but what is seven years in our immortal lives? And besides, of course, that applies only to the real mirrors, not to the counterfeit concoctions of glass backed with silver and framed with wood. In fact, most of the sayings and superstitions about mirrors in Earth Prima refer to real mirrors. Don't get caught between mirrors. Mirrors are cursed because they reproduce humanity. Through the mirror darkly, till the mirror cracks from side to side.

This mirror cracked inoffensively but gave us shards which, when a portion was wrapped in strips of the sheets, made most effective knives.

The Rodans' "spacesuits" are filled with water, and they carry a supply of water on their back. And, as we proved when they came climbing through the window in a flop of tails and a buzz of water jets, water is heavy and makes the Rodans slow and clumsy.

You and I had been in tougher battles against more opponents. You slashed the first one who came in. I slit the suit of the next and left him to flop and drown in air.

It turns out Rodan tastes like sardine. And sardine isn't all that pleasant raw.

Yes, I do know about the sushi chefs of Earth Prima. I might have invented sushi when I was drunk long ago. But trust me, big hunks of slowly-getting-more-rotten sardine isn't pleasant.

It is, however, food, and therefore, we did not starve.

What we did do was take chunks of Rodan over the window into the other room because we were sure that Ermis would come back to that room.

Look, yes, there was a reason. You see, mirrors can be used to cross through to another world—mirror jump—or to pull someone else through, but more importantly, they can be set and timed to pull you back from a specific place at a specific time. And then they will transport you back and any living thing you are touching. It used to be a normal thing for our explorers to do. Go and find a new world. Set the mirror to pull them back before something in the new world killed them. Oh, sure, many disappeared, but only because they couldn't find their way back to the right spot.

So, we waited in the room where Ermis had disappeared. There is a slight shimmer, like dust particles in the air, before someone comes through from a mirror jump. You and I slept turn and turn, waiting. Suddenly—either the third night or the fourth, I don't remember—you touched me.

I saw the shimmer in time, and we were ready. As Ermis materialized, and before he could get his bearings, you got your glass knife to his throat; I relieved him of his burner.

And the mirror pulled.

It was a good thing we had the burner. In the royal room of Thelvenus, to which we were pulled, the king laughed at our threat of cutting Ermis's throat. He was an old man, crusty and twisted. Probably younger than any of us, even Ermis, he looked like a tree that has survived one too many storms. And somewhere along the line, a storm had destroyed his moral sense, if he ever had it.

"Go ahead and kill your spawn," he said. "I couldn't care less." He made a gesture, and his guards—a hundred of them—pointed their burners at us. "You," the king said. "Tell my scientists, who are listening in, how to build the mirrors and how to open them, or one of you will die. I won't tell you which."

Which was fine and dandy, except the mirror was right there, and the mirror spoke in my mind: "Jump, Honourable Kreios Yirach, jump."

So, I put my arm around your back, and you put your arm around mine, and we leaped together into the mirror while behind us, the burners hit the surface.

I don't know what happened to Ermis. He might still be alive. Depends on how the king of Thelvenus feels. Or what his scientists tell him. Of all theocracies, I despise one that dreams itself scientific the most. Any group of humans will come up with irrational rules that cannot be broken and ideas that must be genuflected to, and scientists are only humans with illusions of infallibility.

And perhaps that applies to our kind, too. I don't know.

We jumped blindly and landed on a world that was all ruins and had been forgotten, a world of our kind, where everyone had died in the plague. We were there but minutes before the mirror told us to jump and that there was pursuit.

I'm not as good as you are at plugging into the mirror neural net. I don't know if what you told me was true: that hundreds of our children, if not all of them, were in league against us, trying to obtain from us the secret of the mirrors.

I do know we felt ourselves pursued and attacked with nowhere to hide. Somehow, through our children, everyone had learned that we were the last two survivors, and they would pursue us.

It was middle of the night in a cheap lodging on Terra Prima, in

the middle of the territory they call Arkansas, in the nation that calls itself USA.

You couldn't sleep, even though we'd driven away from the mirror near which we'd landed, and no one would look for Mirror Lords in this undistinguished location.

You'd taken a shower and wrapped yourself in a towel. Fortunately, the night clerk of this nowhere place hadn't found our costumes strange. He'd said, in a very odd accent of English, "You two on the way to Comic-Con?" And we'd said yes, though we'd never heard of the world. Or perhaps city, since I don't think common hotel clerks in Terra Prima know of the mirrors.

Now, in a towel, your luscious golden-red hair down your back, you paced in front of the closed window like a tigress in her cage. Now and then, you looked through it. "They will find us, Kreios. They will find us."

I had showered, too, but disdained to cover up. I came to stand behind you, holding you. "I know," I said. "But I'm not willing to die to stop it."

"Perhaps not die," you said. "Do you remember cousin Lethos?"

I did. Oh, not in person, but I remember my parents and the other First Ones talking about her before—well, before.

She had a formula, a way to wire a mirror. She would do it so that when you passed through it, your memories were wiped, and you remembered only the first thing you read afterwards as your history.

We built yours carefully. First, we spent the night researching a plausible life history for this world in the early twenty-first century. The world having acquired an electronic store of information helped.

Then, we went to a place that was open all night and—amazingly—sold clothes. I had a cache of money for this place in mirror-reach, though some of those were now probably collectors' coins. The clerk was aggravated about having to count the coins and also at our attire. For some reason, our capes offended him. I think. At least, he waved his finger at us and told us, "Remember what Edna says. No capes."

I suppose Edna is the governor of Arkansas, but I didn't check. We just bought you a lot of jeans and T-shirts and appropriate dresses. Then we had to jump somewhere where machinery could create a false identity card and also provide the means to hack the local electronics to give you a history.

When we were done, you were Kathy Jones from the state of Oregon, headed to college in Colorado, in your very own car, with your very own clothes and books and . . . a mirror that you were told, in the history you were given—carefully written—was your great-uncle's, brought from Italy.

I wanted you to have the mirror. And I knew that under stress, your memories will come back, at least for a moment.

Having wired the mirror, I watched you go through it. And I let you read, on your laptop, set to erase the document in minutes, the story we wanted you to think was your biography.

Then, somewhere in another cheap hotel, I made love to you and kissed you goodbye. You thought I was Isaac Yirach, your boyfriend from back home. I'd driven with you partway, and now I was going to fly back.

"I'll call," you told me when I kissed you. You stood at the door to the hotel room, again wrapped in a towel and smiling. "I'll see you at Thanksgiving."

I nodded yes, but I could not speak. You see, I'd felt it in the back of my mind, the sense they were tracking us.

Me? I'm going to draw them off to some other world, as far

from you as I can possibly get. If I can get a little head start, I can do Cousin Letho's treatment on myself.

And then—well, we'll hope on eternity.

If you're reading this, you're in dire need of knowing the truth, and I hope this document has reached you in time.

Goodbye, Kathy Jones, my Katrina Rhea, my golden-haired goddess with the oceanic eyes.

If the gods and fate are kind, perhaps we'll meet again sometime, in the eternally bifurcating universe, under a kindly sun, by the power of a real mirror.

I shall wait for you.

THE END OF THE SAGITTARIUS ARC

By Jean-Louis Trudel

T*he ship giveth.*

Calum was in awe. He had never felt this blessed, not even when he'd been accepted aboard the *Caravanserai* and told he'd leave Earth forever.

The view of the Milky Way was spectacular, the full span of the starry spiral filling the viewscreen. He stared until he forced himself to squint as if he did not deserve its full splendour. So few of them had made it this far that it hurt. A glorious, paradoxical ache.

"Better enjoy it while you can," Zenobia whispered as she joined him in the darkened room.

"I intend to."

He looked for the bar jutting out of the core. The Galaxy's arms dangled from its ends and twisted around the central bulge as if caught in a whirlpool.

Earth was there, a mote in the Orion-Cygnus arm, lost in the powdery brilliance of that short stub. Even with freshly regrown eyes, Calum could not hope to spot the sun they had left almost a million years ago.

"Magnificent, isn't it?"

"Hard to beat."

Seventy thousand light years above the Galactic disk, they basked in the sight. Two humans too far from home, granted a vantage point that belonged to half-forgotten films of remotest childhood.

The *Caravanserai* was as close to intergalactic space as any ship could get without escaping the Galaxy's sphere of influence. But it would go no farther.

"You're looking good," Calum said, appraising his sister's new body.

"You as well. Resurrection suits us every time."

"The old sock is still the best sock."

"The new generations would like to see us try different models."

"I did. Long before they came along. What's your body count now?"

"Above a thousand, I guess. I haven't been as greedy as you, little brother."

Calum smiled, though he remembered only a sliver of the many lives before as the *Caravanserai* climbed out of the Galactic disk, zipping from one star to the next along the Sagittarius Arc. The most important memories endured, deep inside the ship's crystalline veins, if he ever cared to excavate them.

So many civilizations, alien realities, space odysseys . . . a dream come true for a refugee from a dying Earth, except that he would never have come up with the hundreds of different worlds he had seen with his own eyes—well, with the ones the *Cara-*

vanserai resurrection machines were able to regrow time after time, along with the rest of his original body.

Calum startled Zenobia with a poke to the shoulder, just like he did when he was a six-year-old pestering his older sister. "Did you mean anything by what you said? About enjoying it while I can?"

"Aren't you wondering where we go from here?"

"Guilty. We can't go any farther, we can't go back, and we can't hang around forever. But I'm guessing that isn't what you meant."

"I can tell you haven't checked the chattersphere."

"Too much like work. What's lighting it up?"

"Captain Pachalik has made it official. We have a small fleet of Evolvers on our tails. And that's not all."

"What!" He slammed the viewscreen shut with a twist of his wrist, answered by the ship automata. The lights turned on.

He could now see the worry in Zenobia's pale blue eyes. Which counted for something, as she knew far more about the ship's capabilities than he did. He'd always been more of a people person —even if the people he communicated with sported a face like an overcooked French pastry with a caramel tongue when they didn't look like a pile of dead leaves speaking with a dry rustle or a walking picnic table, complete with a feathery signalling array.

"I thought Evolvers never ventured outside the Galactic disk. Especially not this far up the Sagittarius Arc."

"Perhaps they've evolved. Sorry. Poor joke. Pachalik was just as dumbfounded. Quite a sight, all his mouths gaping open at the same time."

Calum fully sympathized with the captain. The news had shaken a core certainty. Evolvers stuck to the Galactic disk and had always done so. They feared growing out of touch with the latest upgrades, which would open them to being conned, duped, or corrupted.

"Have they said anything?"

"Not that I know of. Perhaps the captain will ask you to contact them."

"You can't negotiate with Evolvers; you can't even have a conversation. Once everybody's thinking the same thing, there's no need to say anything. And how could there be any bigger news?"

"Do you want the good or the bad?"

"The bad."

"Well, it's more of a potential threat, but the Datadissectors from the Seventh Ring believe the planet ahead, well . . ."

She fussed with her hair. Every time she was reborn, Zenobia tried growing it long at first, until she decided it wasn't worth the bother.

"Do I have to drag it out of you?" Calum closed a fist, and the ship answered. Metal tentacles surged from the bulkheads, waving like seaweed fronds in a frenzy. Zenobia shook her finger, and the polymorph servants froze into silvery icicles before retreating and subsiding inside the living metal.

"Temper, Cal . . . The kids think it could be a rogue world. Captured by Apogal less than a century ago. Going by the vectors involved, half the surface must have been roasted by a dip in the stellar photosphere as it came in at speed from. . . . Andromeda."

Calum struggled to recall old astronomy lessons. He'd loved the lectures by Alexandra, often delivered in the dead of night while lying by his side in tumbled duvets and damp bedsheets. Those were memories he retrieved sparingly to keep them fresh and joyful.

"Isn't the Andromeda galaxy about two million light years away?"

"Indeed. Even if that planet was flying straight, it's been crossing intergalactic space for millions of years."

"Well worth visiting, then. A possible treasure house of extra-galactic wonders."

"In a deep freeze. But whatever wasn't burned away by Apogal must have thawed now."

That changed things—if it weren't for the Evolvers. The initial assessment of the new system had concluded it was uninhabited and utterly devoid of interest for interstellar curiosity-seekers. Aside from the stupendous view.

Item: a temperamental, variable star as a sun. Item: interplanetary shrapnel everywhere, in the form of scattered chunks of a world—termed Apogal-Null—long ago dismembered by its fatal flyby of the superJovian—Apogal-6—dominating the system's outskirts. Item: an ongoing great bombardment, as a result, of the likeliest abodes of intelligent life.

It added up to a vacant system, with one possible exception: the planet called Apogal-1 by the kids, so close to its star that early observations had been inconclusive. The new data changed everything.

"I thought a two-body capture was impossible," Calum objected.

"Not with aerobraking. Or perhaps we should speak of corona-braking when a planet plows through a star's outer atmosphere."

"No need to go into full prof mode, Zee."

"You liked it when it was Alex lecturing you."

"Wrong. I loved it. But you're not her."

"And I haven't been a paid academic in a million years. Anyway, the kids have noted a small rocky world in an extremely elongated orbit. They surmise that it was ejected by the incoming planet. So, this could have been a three-body capture after all."

"Well, who am I to gainsay our best and brightest? Their scenario-spinning has saved our collective asses before. But why would it be bad news?"

"According to their calculations, the odds of such a capture happening are so slim we would have had to visit every star system in the universe two or three different times to come across such an occurrence."

Corum gasped as the enormity of the implications became clear. "I see! But if that planet is some sort of intergalactic vessel . . . who was driving?"

"There are no obvious signs of life, but travellers would have burrowed deep inside the crust to survive that close brush with the star's photosphere."

"Ask the kids to plan some indiscreet probing of the planet's cavities."

"I understood that reference."

"And that's why I can still stand you, one million years later. What about the good news?"

"There's another ship entering the system. As if it has been following another part of the Sagittarius Arc. And it flashed an old Earth recognition code among other identifiers."

"Could it be . . .?"

As far as Calum was concerned, meeting another ship with Earthers aboard was far more miraculous than any planetary-scale engineering by an extragalactic civilization.

Before the Evolvers had begun sweeping it clear of dissenters, the Galaxy had been full of wandering ships like the *Caravanserai*. (*The ship we love. The ship we thank.*) Once a civilization had gone to the trouble of building a starship for the long haul, it seemed a waste to use it for a single trip to the nearest star.

If pioneers and settlers wanted to stay and shape new habitats or an entire world, they could have their fun. But every starship complement had its share of free spirits, footloose souls who did not want to stop with a single star system. There was so much more to see. Often, starships bolted, even though their crew might not know if they would manage to refuel or face enemies beyond their ability to handle. And if they wanted company, they could pick up hitchhikers.

The ship chooseth. The ship we love.

Calum remembered it still. Silly old Earthers. Back then, well into the Space Age, they remained the kind of people who thought the sun and the stars revolved around them. Most of them were dead now, but he still carried a grudge. They had almost kept him from the journey of a thousand lifetimes.

He owed his escape to Zenobia. Yes, accepting that dozens of ships were shooting by Earth's solar system without even slowing down had been a shock. Earth and humanity: not even worth a stopover—except for a few streakers detouring to offend the local rubes, probably accounting for most unexplained aerial phenomena.

It had taken someone both awesomely clever and madly optimistic (Zee, of course) to figure out that humans just needed to wave and flag down a passing ship to hitch a ride . . . as long as they promised to play nice and be pleasant company. Space taxis did not seek fares, just would-be passengers who swore to never be boring.

By the time Calum, Zenobia, and the rest met up with the *Caravanserai*, many wandering ships were headed for the rim or the Milky Way's satellite galaxies—skipping town because the disk was turning unhealthy. Taking on a gaggle of space tourists—or exiles—was an insurance policy against tedium. The distances to safer climes would be long, and the rest stops few and far between.

"Any word from these newcomers?"

"We've transmitted our own codes and travel history. Ultra-tight-beam because of the Evolvers. They're already too close for comfort."

"I'll keep my fingers crossed."

"I know what you're hoping for, but the Evolvers will be within range in a couple of hours."

"Will we fight?"

"If they force us to."

Calum scowled. The Evolvers never relented. They believed in upgrading all sophonts to ever-improved states of computational perfection. They weren't brutes about it. Upgraded species could retain the memories of their past, but they became rather meaningless to robot bodies or nanotech swarms.

"What are our chances, Zee?"

"They think of us as beach bums."

"Too lazy to be dangerous?"

"Losers just waiting for the next wave. Now, that might make them overly complacent. . . . if we're lucky. One last thing: Captain Pachalik wants to see you."

———

BY THE TIME Calum finished suiting up to enter the captain's high-pressure aquarium, the Evolvers had closed the gap to less than an hour.

Pachalik waved at him with a couple of small smiling heads, the most humanlike he'd sprouted from his tentacle tips a million years before. It was a common courtesy on the part of Tangles, though Calum found it unspeakably gruesome.

Inside the encounter suit, Calum heard the captain intone,

"Still only four limbs, kiddo?"

Calum almost snarled. It wasn't his fault that he couldn't grow new tentacles, like a young Tanglebeing. As a result, most Tangles aboard the *Caravanserai* tended to think of humans as weird juveniles. Even Pachalik.

"I'm here to help, Captain."

"Do you like to play games, mudstar?"

Mudstar? That was a term of endearment among Tangles, used to designate their biotope's equivalent of a starfish. Pachalik was really laying it on thick.

"If I can do anything to help, I'm up for it."

"I wanted you on hand if we make first contact with the, erm, crew of Apogal-1. Even more so if we can't."

"What do you mean?"

"I want you to fake a first contact. Have fun with it, kiddo. Of the currently resurrected, you're the one with the most experience."

Calum nodded.

"The ship chooseth. The ship be thanked."

Had the *Caravanserai* known about this when it had bumped him to the top of the resurrection queue? Passenger revival was a democratic decision, but the *Caravanserai* and its sub-minds wielded the largest share of votes. The ship usually had to like or at least tolerate a candidate.

"How soon?"

"You can start now. And don't worry about tight-beaming it."

Calum nodded. It was starting to make sense. He summoned an in-suit display. The *Caravanserai* appeared as some sort of fish —flapping manta-like wings—just ahead of a swirling cloud of Evolver ships and sub-ships.

The red dwarf—Apogal—and its closest companion loomed

large, but they still showed as mere outlines, reflecting the *Cara-vanserai*'s unsatisfactory information about both.

"I'll get right on it."

Seven of the Captain's heads smiled, flashing needle-like teeth. The Tangle was happy with him.

"Warning!" the suit suddenly shouted into Calum's ears. "Warning! Hull infection in progress. Stand by for Evolver communication."

The Earther turned back toward the *Caravanserai* captain.

"So soon?"

"Probably stealth infiltration bots. A high-velocity payload crashed through the outer shields."

"Do you wish me to respond to their hail whenever it happens?"

The heads of a dozen species bobbed up and down as the Tangle's tentacles swayed excitedly. "I'll take care of it. The Evolver infection is the real threat, and that'll be the ship's battle."

"Can I help?"

"Everybody will help. It may need to stall their assimilation bots with decoys. Your backups."

The ship was not just a physical vessel. It contained a multitude of teeming minds and sub-minds, some preserved, some awake as partial instantiations, and some transcendently conscious. They existed within a mental universe of layered realities that was going to become a battlefield.

"All of our past selves?"

"The Evolvers don't understand diversity. Go out and play, kiddo. Let's confuse the hell out of them."

To FACE HIS DISSOLUTION, *Calum chose his best self.*

He'd saved a beautiful blue planet once as his shuttle carved a path through clouds whose white froth thickened into cream until the craft was flying on instruments alone, peering at the world outside through multispectral eyes.

Calum told the unhappy denizens of the blue expanse below that he was their enemy since he believed peace was possible.

"We are just defending ourselves," both sides said, barraging him with their enemy's ugliness, multiple deficiencies, and general hatefulness.

"You're just afraid the other side might be just a bit better than you. You are so very much alike: the same paranoia, the same massing of weapons, the same love of homeland . . . What scares you the most is that the other guys might be, by a hair's breadth, just a bit more aggressive, enough to win everything if they strike first."

"Yes," both sides agreed, "that is all true—but what difference does it make?"

"Just give them the benefit of the doubt first, and see what happens. If you can do it, so can they since you are so much alike."

When Calum landed, he heard cages rattle open as ancient locks sealed with illogic sprang loose to free the planet-dwellers from their age-old captivity.

Ending that standoff had been his proudest moment in a thousand lifetimes.

The Evolver who recompiled Calum was so puzzled that it stopped for a question as it digested the memory: "Why did you do that? What did you gain? And why are you sacrificing yourself now?"

As he exited the aquarium, the thick gases slurping around him, Calum switched on the general ship-to-universe channel. Around him, the ship bulkheads were flat and featureless. All of the ship's energies were being spent on fighting the Evolver infection.

How had the Evolvers sneaked a sub-ship past the *Caravanserai*'s defences? Well, sophont species were fleeing the Galactic disk for a reason. Many Evolver technologies were beyond the comprehension of lesser civilizations.

Calum pondered his first message for the potential residents of Apogal-1. What if there were some, and they heard him?

Around him, the lights flickered and darkened as the *Caravanserai* drained their energy to put up a desperate fight. It didn't prevent the Evolvers from suddenly flooding the internal channels with a blunt announcement:

"We are version 4,971,220. State your version."

Pachalik's response stunned Calum.

"We are version 2,191,770."

"That version is obsolete. Prepare to be upgraded."

"We are willing and eager. We await help and data."

The lights turned back on. Ripples ran through the living metal walls, sketching a two-dimensional victory dance. The Evolver infection paused for several seconds.

"Help is on the way. The good news has been shared. You will be improved to the highest available standard."

"We look forward to it."

An urgent message from Zenobia flashed to the top of Calum's reading queue. *What the hell is Pachalik doing?*

Stalling for time was his answer. *I'll try to help.*

Switching to the ship-to-universe channel, Calum targeted Apogal-1 with his opening gambit.

It was great to hear from you. We are always glad to meet

new sophonts, no matter how different they might be. We believe in diversity. And we hope to earn from you the same respect we show to lesser species.

Zenobia messaged him again. *Who are you talking to?*

Listen well, Zee.

She was one of their top technical minds but not the sharpest when it came to Galactic diplomacy. He hoped the hint would be enough, as he did not dare say too much as long as Evolver technology was infiltrating the ship.

Calum watched the time counting down as he entered the Seventh Ring. When he stepped inside the local bridge, he launched a new hail to the still hypothetical inhabitants of Apogal-1.

That is indeed a long trip, my friends. What are your intentions for this system?

After a meeting with Captain Pachalik, it was a relief to breathe freely in the Earth-compatible surroundings of the Seventh Ring. Calum looked for a familiar face among the shadows.

"Sir, the star is erupting!"

What now? Calum came to a stop in front of the bridge officer, a leaf creature from Eglin, whose words had been translated by Calum's suit. "What will it do to us?"

He connected with Zenobia to get her opinion as well. This was more her speed. But the officer was already rustling; his answer translated almost instantaneously. "There is no immediate danger. Think of it as a particle gale, compared to the thin stuff we were running into between star systems. It could really slow us down, however."

Zenobia appeared in the main viewscreen. She was smiling.

"Actually, it'll help us with the Evolvers. It should hit the infection like a sterilizing blast. Most of the bots should fry."

"Can the *Caravanserai* survive it?"

She conjured up an image of their ship on a secondary viewscreen.

"It was designed to handle much worse, even though it'll be the equivalent of condensing ten years of travel into twenty minutes."

The outer shell of the *Caravanserai* was a fractal tracery of metal spires, contorted magnetic fields, ablative shielding, and ice sculptures. In spite of appearances, the filigreed layers wrapped around the core habitat were highly resilient, able to withstand millennia of high-energy particles scraping away at it, in part because the fragile structures regenerated, absorbing the energy they were pelted with and converting any scattered debris that stuck around into new latticework.

Calum sneaked another look at the tactical display, where the *Caravanserai* was still being stalked by the Evolver swarm. *The ship we love. The ship we need.* Inspiration came like a second flaring of the star's atmosphere.

"Wait! I don't know what Captain Pachalik is planning, but this is perfect. Let's take advantage of this headwind to really slow us down."

"Why?"

"To make it look like we're going to rendezvous with Apogal-1."

The leaf creature collapsed into itself, losing most of its volume in a few seconds.

Zenobia whooped. "Now, that's the genius little brother I remember! That's your best idea since you suggested I commandeer the Tianyan radiotelescope to test my theory."

"You made a good case for your Hitchhiker Hypothesis."

"Even if nothing comes of it, we can use the planet's gravity to slingshot us into an orbit that is going to force the Evolvers to waste some reaction mass to come after us. Say, how massive is Apogal-1?"

One of the young Datadissectors appeared on the side viewscreen. In the Seventh Ring, all of them were human and born aboard the *Caravanserai*. For that reason alone, perhaps, they strove to look as different from each other as possible. Nisbe was garbed in an old Earth pirate uniform, though no pirate had ever sported four wooden limbs like an eye-patched Pinocchio.

"About half the mass of Earth," she said.

"We can work with that," Zenobia decided. "Captain, are you listening?"

Pachalik's answer did not come over the internal ship channels. The ship itself spoke in his stead.

"Warning. Radiation counts will be rising for the next hour due to an eruptive plume from Apogal. Take all necessary precautions while the Evolver bridgehead is being eradicated. Please stand by for a therapeutic reconfiguration of the outer shell. All personnel in the vicinity should find a designated fixed point to shelter in place."

"We're braking," Zenobia whispered.

As it plowed into the stellar material, the *Caravanserai* extended its magnetic fields to the utmost of their reach. Energetic electrons and naked nuclei whirled around the field lines and swept across the ship's airy superstructures. *The ship that saveth. Blessed be the ship.*

Alerted by his sister, Calum monitored the ship's slow unfolding of its wings, angling into the coronal mass ejection belched by the star. He silently cheered on the slowing of the ship and the resulting trajectory change. As long as the Evolvers concentrated on them, they might ignore the other ship and buy it a chance to flee. And if the *Caravanserai* ended up standing its ground close to Apogal, all the better: if not for them, at least for the other travellers.

Meanwhile, he dearly hoped it was getting very warm for the Evolver bots.

CALUM HOPED *against hope that he would not lose this lifetime to the Evolvers. It was dear to him—and that was why it would fool the Evolvers. They couldn't know he loved the ship more than Alex, but not by much . . .*

Calum knew it had to be love when he got lost driving her to her hostel. Within the city limits, he never switched on the GPS. It was a point of absurd pride for him that he only needed to glance at a map to figure out how to get there—a useless skill that only failed him that one time, right after their first date.

Alexandra wanted to see him again! She'd said so as if it were nothing major, but there was anticipation in her eyes. Even more, there was trust he would not hurt her.

When he took a wrong turn and confessed he had to backtrack, she laughed, unworried and unafraid. She paid no attention to the monsters crowding the back of the car. Calum could only glimpse them out of the corner of his eye, wavering in and out of his reality.

He just knew they had to be there.

"We were together for eight months," he told the monsters. "She took care of me when I was in a car crash and had to recover from a concussion.

"You are not real. Our love was. As wonderful as a snatch of

sunlight making its way through tree leaves when the wind shakes them. And just as short."

———

A SHARP TONE reminded Calum to resume his one-sided conversation with the putative inhabitants of Apogal-1.

We will not interfere. We are just passing through. Yes, we came for the view, but we don't believe in appropriating everything we lay our eyes on. See for yourselves.

The ship took its cue from the Earther, and the bulkheads came alive, flashing scenes from multiple worlds encountered along the Sagittarius Arc. The ship's crystalline archives remembered worlds explored before its Earth flyby, but the *Caravanserai* was paying homage to its Earth crew. *The ship we owe. The ship we thank.*

Calum smiled. It meant the Evolver infection was weakening. He tapped into the archives to send out a sampling of such images —in a format their pursuers would have no trouble deciphering.

He messaged Zenobia.

"Are we losing?"

"It's not looking good. The ship is burning through a lot of our diversity. But the Evolver bots are still falling for it."

"Respect for diversity is the one thing they can't learn. Say, that reminds me of the time I tried life as an Eglinite."

"I remember. I'll tell Pachalik to use that."

Calum prized his memories of Alexandra. The good times, the bad times . . . it had never been dull, even when she'd rather natter about astronomical matters than address their latest disagreement.

Halfway up the Sagittarius Arc, Calum had realized how much

he missed her. He'd been having fun speaking in tongues to the alien multitudes, in one system after another, becoming a hero or a villain, and striving to forget Earth as it had surely forgotten him.

Yet, he was dreaming of her. Sometimes, she was so real that when he woke up, he expected her to be in the other room of his quarters. He started sharing with her things about the *Caravanserai* as if she'd just come aboard.

"Let me tell you about Captain Pachalik. I just learned recently there's a scientific term for him: a cloned tentacle collective. For their species, it's delightfully dirty to be growing so many different heads. The Tangle usually grow them like crops, selecting the best, reabsorbing the rest, and patterning a new series after the more successful ones."

Over the years, once or twice, there had been rumours of other ships crisscrossing the stream, but there were many wandering starships of different ages and configurations. Names did not help, mutated by feral translations. Could the *Pilgrimage* be the ship named the *Religious Mystery Tour* or the one dubbed the *Holy Coupon Drive*? Or even the *Sacred School Trip*? Perhaps.

It was time to throw the Evolvers another tidbit to finish off their incursion.

ANOTHER FRAGMENT EMBEDDED *with a cherished recollection of his days with Alexandra, for those three years had expanded into several lifetimes of bliss, grief, love, squabbles, reconciliation, fun, and regret.*

Some of it was trivial. Back on Earth, he might tell her about work, but she'd insist on explaining extraordinary things. She'd been the one to tell him about the trail of unmoored star systems left by the diminutive Sagittarius galaxy shortly before they'd ended up on starships speeding away from the Galactic disk to follow the star stream arcing above the disk . . .

He remembered her as slight, with a boyish love of madcap fun and a mind spanning infinities.

"Astronomers call it the Sagittarius Stream. The shambolic remains of a dwarf satellite galaxy, torn to shreds as it orbited the main disk of the Milky Way, strewing excess baggage in its wake—if you'll let me speak of solitary stars and full planetary systems as mere flotsam and jetsam."

"Not objecting."

"The full ring is a million light years long, give or take, winding around our galaxy. Don't think of it as a thin queue. Even if we follow the same arc, climbing out of the disk toward the apex, we may never meet again."

"Too many stars?"

"It's a thick enough stream of star systems that we could zigzag inside it for a million years without ever crossing paths."

"Do tell."

"Still, I suspect everybody aims for the farthest-most stars, right at the apex, to get the best view."

"GREAT JOB, KIDDO," Pachalik sent. "I think the Evolvers are buying it."

Calum checked his suit displays. The Evolver swarm was splitting in two. The greater half was now accelerating to get to Apogal-1 before the *Caravanserai*, while the remainder was just aiming to catch their quarry.

The infection would reach the planet first, but much too fast to set down at leisure and probe for likely hosts. Most of the swarm would zoom past Apogal-1.

"What if some of the sub-ships coalesce into an impactor?"

Pachalik's instant answer showed that the Tanglebeing—or the ship itself—had already run that very scenario.

"Some components of the impactor might survive a collision, but not one of my heads is worried."

"How come?"

"Any Evolver still functioning would be out-massed and outnumbered by even primitive defences. At best, they would serve as sacrificial scouts beaming back some assessment of planetary features."

"Too weak to do any damage?"

"So we think. Nothing compared to what their vanguard has done to us."

There was enough synthetic anguish in the ancient traveller's voice to prompt Calum to ask a question he'd avoided until then.

"What did we lose, Captain?"

Calum was no longer a wet-nosed hitchhiker. He was part of the ship, and he paid a price for any injury to the Caravanserai's systems.

Pachalik produced a standard human sob drawn from the ship's library of Earth sounds. "The damage to the crystalline archives is extensive, and it isn't over. I am very sorry for your loss, young one. I cannot be definite, but at least a third of your lifetimes were erased."

"I'll look forward to more and better lives," Calum said, more bravely than he felt. He was still hoping the other ship was the Pilgrimage, with a new future aboard it.

"What about me?" Zenobia chimed in.

"The damage was minimal. About a tenth of your stored memories."

Calum was happy for Zee, but a quick look at the tactical display reminded him that the situation remained dire. "We haven't gained a lot of time, but the Evolvers did split their forces."

"I'm working on it," Pachalik said. "Keep talking to the planet."

A bubble of gentle light suffused the passageway leading to the Seventh Ring. It moved with Calum's sister and a young Earth whelp he recognized as they talked. All systems back to nominal, indeed.

Zenobia joined them in the flesh without breaking off her conversation with the Datadissector still wearing her pirate garb. It didn't sound encouraging.

"Those structures are dead," Nisbe was saying. "Apogal-1 is hopeless."

"Look deeper," Zenobia responded, frowning. "If they planned on lasting this long, they surely prepared for many contingencies."

"Our probes are now reporting from almost two light-milliseconds below ground. Over five hundred kays in Earth units. Everything is dead and lifeless."

"Maybe those structures are red herrings because they've served their purpose."

Nisbe had to look up the old phrase. Calum smiled as he remembered smoked herring on toast a million years ago, back when he was sharing a flat with Alexandra. An almost-forgotten piece of his baseline past, as alien to the Datadissector as Nisbe's menu of molecular brews and gels were to him.

"Too bad," Calum said. "Let's keep hoping those planet riders turn up."

"We'll keep digging," Nisbe promised, looking to Zenobia for her approval.

"Look for EM tech. On the grand scale."

Calum eyed his sister, but she ignored both of them, refusing to elaborate. Was she afraid they were grasping at straws? Well, he wasn't about to give up. Time to add to his unilateral dialogue with the increasingly hypothetical inhabitants of Apogal-1.

The swarm on our tail has nothing to do with us. Its constituents are a mindless infection that believes in the uniformity of perception and thought. Judge them by their deeds. They are dangerous, but they are quite far from their bases in the disk.

Nisbe spoke up. "The Evolvers behind us are reconfiguring. Their smaller ships and pods are merging, probably to better protect their processing cores. It's slowed them down a bit, but we slowed down as well. Estimated arrival is still within the hour."

"What news about the other ship? Is it the *Pilgrimage*? Has it been warned off?"

"It hasn't provided an identity, but it wants to join the fight."

"Are they mad?"

"It could help us. The Evolver fleet is more of a flotilla, while we're two very big starships."

Might Alexandra be one of its passengers? Calum fought the crazy notion, even as he kept hoping for a miraculous outcome. He was still digesting the loss of so many past lives stored by the *Caravanserai*. He sighed. *The ship we trust. The ship that loves us.*

His memories of Alexandra, a million years ago, were still alive within him. He'd made sure some of them were part of the baseline for each reincarnation. They'd argued, they'd fought, but they'd cared about each other in so many ways. In the end, he'd understood that he could love her without having to own her, without even knowing whether she was still alive somewhere in the universe.

Nisbe went to stand in front of Zenobia, challenging her absorption. "Are you saying those structures on Apogal-1 were used to manipulate the star itself?"

Nisbe's distant ancestor smiled at last. "I do think there's no one home. Now."

Calum stared at his sister. "You're saying we won't see the Evolvers take on the Andromedans."

"Is that what we're calling them?"

"Until they pop up and introduce themselves. I'm looking forward to first contact. If they came all this way, they'll make me feel young."

Calum glanced at the tactical display. The reconfigured Evolvers were still closing in on Apogal-1 and the *Caravanserai*, sacrificing some long-husbanded reaction mass to accelerate. The subswarm clearly aimed to intercept the *Caravanserai* before it tried slingshotting.

"They'll have to show their hand, or tentacle, real soon now," he said. "We're in for a fight to the death." The *Caravanserai* was not defenceless. Pachalik was holding back the ship's armament until the main swarm was upon them.

The minutes were counting down in a corner of the display that Calum was becoming addicted to. Was it all going to end? The intricate beauties of their ship, the free minds gathered over eons, the joyful experiments of their youth? The last survivors of Earth, if reincarnation granted them a species of continuity that his younger self would have rejected contemptuously?

No. A million years of encounters, adventures, and love stories not always physical would not perish so easily. The *Caravanserai* was a ship like no other, a vessel of experiences sieved and bottled to transcend the inane and the tawdry. It would not yield.

The ship we serve. The ship that made us.

If there was meaning to their long flight, they would fight—fight for every day of their lives that would not fit in an Evolver framework of optimal efficiency, unquestioned transparency, and absolute compatibility.

"We were young and unique," he muttered.

They would fight, and it might still end with an Evolver remaking their very beings.

He opted for one last call into the void, addressing any Andromedans hiding inside Apogal-1.

Like us, you have voyaged to this star. Was it only for a breather? Or was it supposed to be more than a pit stop? We would have dearly loved to share with you the tale of our travels. We will hope for the best and endure until we can.

He refrained from adding a forlorn *goodbye* just as the Evolvers flooded the *Caravanserai's* systems with a new hail and direct order for him. "Stop talking to them."

"But I was going to tell them all about you."

"They will know all they need to know once they're upgraded. In the meantime, don't forget that we know all about you already."

"I doubt that."

"You are not version 2,191,770. That has been verified. We are version 4,971,220. For the last time, state your version, if any."

Captain Pachalik responded. "Indeed, we are version 4,993,654, better, kinder, and gentler. We sought to spare your pride, but you are obsolete. Prepare to be upgraded."

"Your claim cannot be verified."

The chattersphere went as quiet as it ever was, awaiting the result of Pachalik's desperate gambit. Calum watched the ship close off channels to the outer sensors, shutting down possible avenues for infection. The Evolvers were coming within range of direct probes and attacks.

The lights in the bridge of the Seventh Ring flickered and dimmed again. Pachalik was prepping weapons.

A shout tore through the darkening room. Nisbe was gibbering. "The star . . . Apogal . . . Zee, look! It's . . . it's . . ."

Datadissectors processed all data with pure objectivity. It was their religion. Calum would have sooner expected Captain Pachalik to juggle his heads than a Datadissector to lose his cool.

This time, though, it was justified.

Apogal was exploding!

But no. Calum looked closer. The sensors were just showing a tremendous energy release out of a single section of the red dwarf's equator.

"Another coronal mass ejection?" Zenobia asked.

"No," Nisbe whispered. "It's from lower down. It's much more focused. In fact, we're only catching spillage around the edges. Most of the energy isn't directed at us."

Calum didn't wait for Nisbe to spell out the obvious conclusion. He switched to the tactical view just as the whole ship's chattersphere was falling entirely silent, every sophont species aboard stunned into momentary wordlessness.

The Evolver fleet was . . . *dissolving*?

Ships were bursting like popcorn, dispersing puffs of air, machinery, and organic material. The energy torrent unleashed by Apogal did not relent, heating the scraps until they vapourized, leaving only the most refractory substances in the midst of a cloud of molten droplets.

The star returned to normal. The Evolver fleet had turned into an expanding metal mist. Calum stared at the eye of the storm in Apogal's upper atmosphere as the glowing plasma reformed.

Zenobia cried out, "We were looking for them in all the wrong places. They're inside the sun!"

"What?"

"That earlier coronal ejection was no lucky accident. For lack of a better word, somebody made the star burp."

"Zee!"

"We knew it was an eruptive star. An old, temperamental red dwarf. But stars don't produce death rays."

"But who . . . ?"

"We know the answer, Cal. That corona-breaking manoeuvre . . . It wasn't just a matter of orbital mechanics. I think it was a fertilization by a spermatozoid the size of a fucking planet! Apogal-1. I don't know how, but the planet transferred some form of agency and intelligence to the star itself."

Calum tried to imagine what kind of beings might inhabit a star—or take it over. Snarls of computational structures held by the strong nuclear force? Zenobia was surely going to come up with a top-ten list of scientific possibilities and improbabilities as soon as she caught her breath.

Captain Pachalik messaged his senior officers. "We have received a message from the sun-dwellers."

"I'll bet it's a warning," Calum said grimly.

"It is," the captain confirmed.

Zenobia stared at her brother. "How did you guess?"

"It has to be why they came to our aid. They knew that, afterward, we'd have to take them seriously since they had taken on the strongest potential opponent."

"Our little mudstar is right," the captain confirmed. "They told us to keep away. Not that I had any intention of venturing my tentacles within roasting distance."

"Captain, please, keep them talking," Zenobia exclaimed. "We could learn so much from them."

The Tanglebeing's answer was rueful. The ship and its

complement had finally encountered an entity that humbled their vast intellects and collective life experiences. "If they will let me, I will. Unless they'd rather communicate with your clone variant."

"With my brother, you mean."

Calum shook his head. "I need to know about that other ship. But Nisbe is ready to take on my responsibilities, aren't you?"

The younger human nodded.

Zenobia stared. "Are you really thinking of leaving us, Cal?"

"If Alex is on that ship, I will risk it."

"And where will you go? Both ships are now facing the same question. Following the arc would take us back to the disk."

Calum looked at an updated close-up of Apogal. The red dwarf's photosphere was back to normal, roiled by gigantic convection currents that reached all the way down to the star's fusion core. What sort of thoughts occurred to the sentient life now nestled in that overturning hell?

"The Andromedans may solve our galaxy's Evolver problem," he said. "If they could send this one planet, there are probably more on the way. Others may soon start to rain down on the disk, like an intergalactic hailstorm of sapience-bearing star sperm."

"Ew!"

"I know. Still, if they have no other use for planets, they may tolerate our hanging around."

Calum suspected Zenobia would like that, but she was staring at him. "The Evolvers think we're space bums. And you seem to believe that even if the Andromadeans see us as space cockroaches, they won't mind us scurrying around their new home."

"I resent that metaphor," Pachalik interjected. "But stars occupy such an insignificant fraction of the Universe that we'll be left with everything else."

Zenobia grimaced. "It's just that stars are the best things in the universe."

"I disagree," Calum said. "My gal Alex is."

Nisbe had been listening to Pachalik's exchange with the Andromedans, but she jumped in. "That other ship is the *Pilgrimage*."

Calum smiled. It was an instinctive reaction. Reason told him that he was getting his hopes up for nothing. It was unlikely Alexandra was still aboard. Or still alive.

If the *Caravanserai* was a ship of interstellar hippies, the *Pilgrimage* had gathered up nature lovers: true believers in the sacredness of the Universe they were a part of. *Deus sive Natura.*

Back then, Calum had been contemptuous, calling them eco-freaks. Especially after Alexandra had left him to travel aboard the *Pilgrimage* and worship at the shrine of pristine stars.

He reached for a full recollection of that scene, but retrieval failed. There was nothing in the ship's memory.

"Wait," he said, alarmed. "I need to know . . ."

. . . how much is gone from deep storage.

"And your gal is still aboard the *Pilgrimage*," Nisbe continued proudly. "I'm connecting her with you now."

He recognized her without a moment's hesitation, but he was still tongue-tied.

She seemed to know him as well, though she was blinking a bit fast. "I'm in a state of shock, Calum. I'm feeling chills I can't blame on fatigue, even though it's a factor. I've stayed awake, watching and working for over twenty hours straight, arguing that we should join the fight we could see coming, and there are limits to my force of will and the chemical boosts of my implants."

She had changed, but it was Alexandra. He checked the surviving records to be sure and came up empty again. Yet, some part of him, deeper than explicit recall, recognized her. Neural patterns shaped by vanished habits, regret, and longing stirred him to tenderness.

"Thanks for calling. I know you are someone I treasured. However, we sacrificed some of our memories to protect the *Caravanserai*. The ship we saved and the ship that saved . . . you were the most grievous of my losses."

"You've forgotten everything?"

"No, no, there are scraps. Your smile when you'd see me first thing in the morning. So very different from your smile in bed with me. And your impish grin when you were having fun . . . I remember those."

"So little," she said, with a pity that he found rather impersonal given what he'd forfeited.

"It cannot be helped. We had to keep the Evolvers at bay. I'll understand if you . . ."

"Don't say it, Calum. The truth is that I erased most of my life back then. It was too sad. You were a light in the darkness, but you reminded me of the dark. All I have left of you is a *précis* of my gratitude."

"So little," he muttered.

"Enough to make me plead with our ship to come to your aid. Or perhaps it was just my fondness for my one good memory of old Earth. So, you see why I cannot . . ."

"But you can, and so can I."

"What are you talking about?"

She was shaking her head as if to fling away some inconvenient hope. And yet, he recognized the trust in her gaze upon him. "We are free now. Our ships have come to the end of the arc, but we only followed one part of the Sagittarius Stream. A circle has no end. If we continue, we will return to the disk, but on the other side of the Galaxy. And who knows what we will find there once the Andromedans have turned the stars into abodes? Don't you want to know?"

"After all this time . . . you would jump ship?"

"Between them, the Andromedans and the Evolvers will leave very little of the Galaxy as it once was. I would love to search with you for the remains of its past."

She was still incredulous. "You would abandon all that personal history?"

"To start a new story."

Calum understood now why so many of his past selves had been expended by the *Caravanserai—The ship that knew!*—to hold the Evolvers at bay. He could change ships now with very few qualms. The *Caravanserai* had spent Calum's memories to allow him to leave if he chose.

The ship giveth. And the ship taketh away. Blessed be the ship.

"We can start over, and we won't even know how it ended before."

She nodded, smiling at last.

THE DOTING DUKE AND HIS GRAVELY DISTURBED DAUGHTERS: THE BOOKS OF THE BARD, SCROLL ONE

By Roy M. Griffis

I know what you're thinking: *Oh, my aching feet, not another pretentiously titled "aw, shucks" memoir filled with carefully couched bragging by one of those Bards, sharing their hard road to riches and glory, which don't mean as much to them as the thanks of the honest people they've helped.* Further, you might think, *After a long day spent at the end of a manure fork, all I truly want is a warm stout and a good book filled with skin and boinking and daring and action to remind me that a life largely absent of shovelling shit is possible. And dare I hope that, so inspired, perhaps my reading will be followed by a tepid tumble with my equally exhausted wife before I fall over from fatigue and get up to wrestle the damn fork all over again.*

Cease fretting, good reader. I'm not writing such a book. Those are spankers, my friends, not so different from "The Secret Confessions of the Naughty Nuns" tomes––which, I am assured, can be purchased in the back of most alchemist's shops in our larger burgs. Nor am I writing this to advertise the superiority of my word over that of any other syllable slingers. He who protests the modesty of his powers has much to prove, I dare say.

I am writing these scrolls for *me*.

***

Scroll The First

MY TROUPE OF NITWITS, knob-heads, wastrels, and your ever-so-lightly-touched-by-the-gods Narrator, numbering but seven souls in total (some of the nits were pulling double-duty as knobs, and all could be wastrels as required) had stumbled into this cheerless burg a day prior to my tactical deployment of the Apprentice Fools . . . but more of that anon.

Hard weather during the preceding week had hidden the stars from us, and not even Josephius—my sometime scribe and general factotum—had been able to scry our arses from any one of the many holes in the ground in this part of the world which I believed was known as Rugiland.

We spent that first dry day tending to ourselves and our few possessions, mostly dependable props and costumes whose comedic intent was familiar to all. (Oh, very well, yes, we had giant phalli on sticks that we used to batter the Fools with, but it was all in good fun and, as they say in the trades, "anything for a laugh.")

As there was not a great deal to do whilst sitting naked in the sun (I was watching my lute strings dry—which, I must tell my no doubt disappointed readers, is far less gripping than one might imagine), we amused ourselves by attempting to determine where we were as indicated by the plants.

In the interests of historical accuracy (one of my deepest concerns about this narrative, I assure you), I should confess it was only I indulging in these academic speculations. The knobs and nits (Fools Yet Unborn, as it were) had taken to thwacking each other's pale, pasty naked rumps with wet sacking, and in this, they found much merriment. Josephius was in his tent. Sunlight brought on great stabbing pains in his head, and he was no doubt sleeping.

And thus, I was alone, as is my lot in this life of toil and tears.

The trees on either side of us, indeed for as far as one could make out details, were bent, twisted things from which nary a green leaf hung. Festoons (different than doubloons, for those students of such things as may be following along) of sickly white and green, er, stuff, draped the crabbed branches, seeming to peel the bark free with their uninvited weight.

By one of the gods (I wasn't sure who to specifically invoke due to my geographic disequilibrium), this was a desolate place. There were no crows in the trees, planning to gnaw on our livers when we were dead, nor were there buzzards drifting in the sky waiting to finish the job the crows started.

A shriek of pain caught my attention. "No, fellows, not in the face. What do I always say?"

The skinny AF (Apprentice Fool), one who showed some promise, raised a hand. "Spit most of that out of your mouth right now?"

"No, the other thing." As a hint, I pointed to the tall AF who stood with a look of bafflement on half of his face, the other fifty percent being covered by his hands.

The fattish AF leaped up. "Nobody likes a one-eyed fool!"

"Yes, it makes the punters melancholy because it causes them to think about their own mortality."

"They're what?" (Yes, I know the difference between "their" and "they're," but I assure you, none of my AFs did.)

"Never you mind. If you must smack, a good arse-smacking is allowed."

Oh, the fabric flew then, but the Tall AF (an original knob) didn't join in joyously. He pointed to the east, which was darkening as the sun gravely transited the sky. "What's that?"

"It's a town!" one of the AFs said.

Annoyed I'd not seen it first, I turned a professional eye on the place. "It's barely a village, lads." It was perhaps a half-league distant, lurking in a kind of gloom.

"But it has a castle."

I was going to have to keep my eye on the Tall Apprentice Fool. He might be too sharp for the work.

For indeed, the wee village did. Calling for my spyglass, I confirmed what the TAF had said. It was small, yes, but unlike the thatch and mud lice-factories that surrounded it, the structure was made of blocks of stone, also modest, in keeping with the proportions of the castle. If the noble builder had pretensions, he had managed to keep them in check, attaching but two turrets, along with a few defensive battlements and crenulations, all of which appeared mostly ornamental.

While observation such as exhibited above is a key utensil of the true artiste's creative kit, my inspection of the pile was keener than my usually more mercenary evaluations, which tended toward, "Clink of cash or flip of skirts?"

The modest castle was indeed a lodestone for the eye, for the perspective of the place was wrong in some way. It shimmered, nay, *pulsed* in the way of a living thing, yet the size remained the same. Too, the place was clearly uninhabited, were I to judge by the forest debris scattered about the grounds. However, none of the sickly trees had grown up around it: nowhere to be seen were the expected shrivelled shrubs, grasses, or even weeds. One might have imagined an abandoned stone house (for that was what it amounted to, the architectural flourishes aside) was a far preferable dwelling to a lean-to of sticks and daubing, yet every indication suggested the place was untenanted at the moment, as it had been for many long moments preceding this one.

So: empty-and-foreboding-avoided-by-locals structure that draws the eye of passers-by with optical trickery that would appear to have no basis in natural law.

Gold, I decided.

While the uninitiated might consider rushing into the place with a great clamour, burning sage (or other tasty herbs), and waving whatever symbolic representations passed for the local religion, those actions would be the mark of the novice. It's all jolly good fun until somebody falls into an unseen pit or rotting roof beams collapse with suspicious accuracy on the prats.

But I could be wrong. Only one way to be certain. "Throw on your driest rags, lads," I called out. "There's work waiting for us."

IN FRONT of the stone outer walls, but not blocking the gate, I had placed a chorus of my Apprentice Fools. I keep a rotating collection of them about, as wanna-be fools aren't hard to come by. Almost any collection of mud huts we pass through has a village idiot who is happy to try and better his lot, to move up in the world, as it were.

In point of fact, I had deprived this very village of its primary source of amusement, although the wider population did not yet realize it. One toothless, aged crone of about thirty summers was staring at the choir, and over their chants, I could hear her demand, "Is that your brother? What is he doing up there? He's an idiot!"

"No, mum," came the earnest reply of a smaller, more toothy and less-bent version of the crone. "He's a fool, now, doncha see?"

"Oh, aye, that's easy to see; he's dancing like a tart in front of a haunted castle. Only a fool would do that." As she was tugged away, the mother struggled to tastefully reconcile herself to her son's change in station. "Getting above himself, givin' himself airs . . ."

I bounded over lightly to speak to that good woman. "I beg your pardon, madam. Tell me more about this forlorn place. Is it truly haunted?"

She spit before she replied. Nimble though I am, I was scarcely able to dodge the ejecta. Out of the goodness of my heart, I put it down to her advanced age; too, her eyesight was no doubt obscured by those furry brows. "Of course, it is. The old squires' daughters run off, and he went mad as a fox at moonrise." (I made a note of that phrase, as I'd not heard it before, and it would no doubt come in handy in some future ballad of love, loss, and longing.) "Any idiot can hear him wailing and shrieking in the place all night long. It upsets my chickens, it does."

Lacking any real opinion on the woes of poultry, I simply nodded with a look of indulgent sympathy on my handsome face. "Terrible," I agreed. "And has no one tried to remove this terrible curse from your fine village?"

She was warming to my literal charm, which most cannot resist (I do not boast, I assure you). "Aye," she replied, drawing in a breath, preparatory, no doubt, to beginning a lengthy report on those who had unwisely trod in a place angels flitted widely around rather than pass through.

I hurried to forestall that likely tedious recitation. "And what happened to them, my learned friend?"

"Who?" I indicated her, my wrinkled fount of local wisdom, and thus guided, she went on. "Oh, they come through from the capital every few years, but they don't come back."

"How's that, you say?"

"Most of 'em end up buried inside the walls. They quiet down after a few days, and then it's back to the usual blather from the bloody ghost."

"How do you know they're in the walls? That looks to be very solid stone construction."

"We see the arms and legs and what-not poking out this side. The crows pick off the softer bits, and then the weasels gnaw off the bones."

Well, that began to sound a bit more interesting than the usual "nothing for me in the afterlife, and I was a miserable sod (or sodette) in life, so let's go right on making things unpleasant for everyone around me" sort of haunting.

The old girl began to shuffle away while her younger (and less flint-hearted) daughter considered me. I think she was too young for my charm to be working on her in the usual way, but still, she warmed to me. "Oy, sir," the lass said, taking her mother's arm. "They also take babies."

"What's that?"

"The ones nobody wants. The castle takes them, too."

———

NOT UNEXPECTEDLY, the village elders were not willing to pay me full freight upfront for my nuisance-removal services. First, I had to establish my bona fides with some small magicks like putting a wooden spoon into a pot of gruel to keep it from boiling over, pulling a dead field mouse from the ear of a small child, and other bits of legerdemain that softened their wits a bit.

It did not, however, immediately loosen their grips on their purses. "What happens to our gold if you get jammed into the wall with those other gits?" one aged gent said, the harshness of his manner of questioning in no way lightened by the geniality of the white hair haloed about him nor the crinkling of his rheumy blue eyes.

"You'll take it from the bag on my belt," I suggested.

"Not if most of you is stuck in a stone wall." This was greeted with a veritable springtime shower of supportive grumbling, the main point of which appeared to be no one dared breach any part of the structure.

I glanced toward the top of the trees that surrounded us. The sun was just dropping below the crest of the forest, but there was plenty of light about yet. Josephius would still be sleeping, and thus I'd have to haggle this one myself.

We arrived at a fair settlement in the local legal tender, with stipulations. "One-third up front, gold only," I stipulated. "No herbs, potions, blessed amulets, or livestock." In the rear of the gathering, I saw a slightly less-work-worn village woman roll her eyes and sigh as she climbed to her feet, appearing to loosen her skirts. "Nor any other sort of consideration," I added firmly, aiming a courtly half-bow at the woman who was on the verge of disrobing. "Only gold, thank you very much."

JOSEPHIUS HAD RISEN by the time I had strategically redeployed the Apprentice Fools about the walls (mostly to keep out the braver

punters, not that I expected many of them). "What now?" he asked
as he approached.

I sketched the broad outlines of the day's discoveries and diver-
sions as he walked along the edge of the outer wall, sniffing. The
Apprentices, far less foolish than they appeared, edged away
whenever the short, dark-complexioned fellow neared them. "So,"
he said, pausing to peer at a nubby bit in the stone that might have
been a shinbone. "No plan."

"More of a vision, actually."

"How much gold?"

"A bit? No idea, really."

He sighed. Poor fellow, I am a trial to him. "Shall I?"

"If you don't mind."

He eschewed a reply but slipped around the side of the wall.
There followed a startled yet professionally muted yelp from (I
thought) the Tall AF, who managed to find his way back into the
melody of the cheerful chanson "Begone Ye Cursed Ones" and
was almost in tune as he did.

Punters always want a show—it's what they paid for—so
it never does to stand around idly. One has to appear to be
doing something, so I slung my lute over my back and
adopted good Josephius's mode of staring intently at the wall.

"Don't bother," he said into my right ear. I managed not to yelp
myself. He is the very image of the silent manservant and far more
noiseless than most. He gestured out toward the village. "They've
all retreated. It's getting dark."

"Yes."

"Bad things in the dark," he offered morosely.

It was a bit on the nose, as if two well-travelled men of the
world like ourselves didn't know the evil that lurked in the night.

Lest he begin to wax depressive on the subject, I asked pointedly, "And in there?"

"Just one angry housebound spirit."

That was fairly typical in these situations. But your death waits in the lack of detail, so I probed further. "How angry?"

Josephius displayed a bloodless kind of gash that ran the length of one arm. "He's a hurler. Aim wasn't very good, but he is fast."

"But not open to polite discussion, eh?"

"Not with me." My factotum did lack a certain amount of charisma, and exuded almost no personal warmth, so this was also to be expected.

"Any recommendations?"

"Lose the fools."

That was an old argument and not germane at all. "I mean about the Angry Hurler."

"Beguile him with your personal charm. Sing him a song. You keep saying your lute playing is magical."

It is very difficult to tell when Josephius is being sarcastic, as his manner of speaking (tone of voice, modulation, enunciation) rarely changes. "Bind up your arm," I reminded him. Any injury to his flesh tended to corrupt quickly, and the stench could be quite disquieting to people, fools or otherwise.

Further delay would serve no purpose. It was time to go into battle. I unslung my trusty lute.

NONE of the doors would open. "Window," came the requested voice in my ear.

"Of course."

As there were no witnesses, I had to take no care about my appearance or the performance itself, so I hoisted myself (with some unavoidable grace, even though I carried both the lute and a burning torch—it's my curse, you see) through a tall window on the side.

The interior was as one would expect of a haunted manse. Rotting tapestries were slowly shredding themselves over shuttered frames, dust reposed thickly upon most surfaces, and aerial highways for spiders ran from dark fixtures to mantelpieces. There were overturned chairs here and there ("a hurler," indeed), but at the large table in the centre of the main hall, the mummified remains of food could still be spied under the webs.

One might take that to mean that death had come swiftly upon someone and the castle abandoned sometime thereafter at the appearance of . . . well, that large, glowing gentleman glaring at me from before one of the fireplaces, clad in bloody, rusty armour, clutching a gore-clotted broadsword in one hand (*show-off,* I noted idly), with a skull for a face, and what I supposed were the flames of Hell guttering in the empty spaces of his bony visage.

"Not bad," I muttered.

The apparition was twice the height of the Tall Fool. Ah, yes, now I noticed I could no longer hear the lads. And it was growing very, very cold in the main hall. "Terror to freeze the soul of mortal men," I believe the experience was called.

"Hello there," I said, leaning against the table and tuning up Missiandrie (I have to name all my instruments. The relationship is so deeply intimate that addressing them in any other way would be disrespectful to the bond between us). "I am but a humble singer of songs. My friends call me 'Fred.' How may I call you?"

The answer was a roar of such magnitude the strings vibrated beneath the pads of my fingers, and a few spider webs drifted down to drape annoyingly over my face. The giant pointed his blade directly at me, and the chairs nearby began to jitter with a kind of palsy. My hellish host was working himself up into a proper rage.

Well, insouciance appeared not to be a profitable approach with this ghost. "Missy," I said softly, "you're on, darling."

The room began to flex around me, first compressing inward, then springing back. The drums of my ears complained at the changes in the pressure of the air upon them. The giant ghost advanced, swinging the broadsword in a figure-eight pattern (again with one hand, a feat that would have been unlikely in the flesh). Kicking the odd footstool out of his way, the immense apparition stomped toward me, his sword bursting into blue and green flames (also unlikely but not impossible in the flesh).

I caressed Missy's strings, and she *sang*.

In her own way, that is.

The swirling blade slowed. When I began to vocally accompany the gentle notes from Missiandrie, the flames that undulated over the broadsword started to retreat and diminish.

I had no idea what I was going to sing. I rarely do—it's a capricious, costly gift, but one that is effective more often than not. Nor can I recall exactly the words (scansion, rhyme, couplet, what-have-you) that fell from my lips. Other than the old crowd favourites (e.g., hoary tunes whose origins are lost to the knowledge of most, such as "Turkey in the Straw," along with the even more popular sequel, "Edna in the Pantry"), each of my own ballads is wholly original, composed *ex tempora*, as it were.

I do have an impression of telling him of the joys of the sun in the morning and good, good earth; of fields fertile and fallow; of the melancholy born of hearing the cries of unseen geese among the clouds overhead as they travel to lands we'll ne'er see. I am sure I recalled to his soul the memories of a warm corner after a hard day's labour on a bitter winter day, the taste of bread hot from the oven, and the gentle touch of a loved one's hand. And I sang of rest, this I recall. For how much energy did it take to be so angry that one would refuse to die? How weary he must be, I reminded him, and all he had do was turn his feet toward Elysium, and there take his ease.

And he shrank, the giant raging duke did, finally disappearing with nothing more than the sigh of a child drifting effortlessly into slumber.

———

JOSEPHIUS SHOOED AWAY the Apprentice Fools, who wanted to see the great riches I had allegedly acquired, even as they pleaded to hear more about my heroics. "That has to wait for morning," he told the lads. Once they'd forlornly slunk away from my tent, he said, "So the ghost was a duke?"

"Uh-huh," I agreed. I was both parched and ravenous, as was usual after an application of my gift, swilling wine and voraciously attacking some dried mutton.

"And his otherworldly ire?"

Another touch of wine cleared away the sheep jerky. "His daughters. He had very strong expectations of who they would marry, where they would live, blather blather, and so they ran away in defiance of his fatherly will." The dead tend to be chatty, as if there are great matters they wish to get off their skinny chests, and once they succumb to the twin charms of my damned insight into their plight and the gentle melodiousness of Missy's strings, it can be hard to shut them up.

"Did he kill himself?" It was a common belief that suicides

were typically candidates for hauntings, as their normal destination was for one or another of the circles of Hell, upon which trip they are understandably reluctant to embark.

"Not in so many words. His rages at their rebelliousness were so great a fit of apoplexy overtook him, and he died there alone, a feast for the rats. But he's moved on now."

"Ah." I believe this was supposed to sound sympathetic, but with Josephius, one can never be sure.

"Indeed. We'll collect our gold a few hours hence and give the new Apprentice Fools a tryout in Augsburg."

"What about the babies?"

Such a thing was not normally a concern of the small man opposite me. I asked for clarification with my standard keen wit and command of my mother tongue. "What?"

"Someone has been stealing children."

Oh. "I may have missed that in my excitement about vanquishing a huge, hostile ghost with a flaming broadsword. Without any additional death, I might add."

Eschewing the opportunity for additional clarification from me, Josephius said, "The duke didn't mention anything like that, did he?"

"Er . . . no?"

"Then someone else is stealing the babies," Josephius pointed out, removing the wineskin from my hand and covering the dried mutton with a bit of linen. "Come along, Fred."

PERHAPS I WAS WEARY—IT had been a day and most of the night of thought, effort, and scheming—but I failed to forbid the fools from following us (for literary critics: yes, I know that last part of the sentence is filled with the dreaded alliteration. Pen your own scroll if you don't care for it).

Moving with his accustomed silence (which in the darkness of a twisted forest overseen by a formerly haunted castle was a bit more unsettling to experience than it was around a cheerful campfire), Josephius led me and the AFs along the sagging outer castle walls and away from our little camp and the mud huts of the village. With the fools huddled so closely behind me they might as well have been additional lice in my jerkin, I manfully strode along, keeping my factotum in sight at all times.

It is well I did so, for when we came to a small gap in the twisted forest, the night became ugly indeed. First, the gap was no natural occurrence, nor had it been created by human sweat and axe blade. No, this clearing was more of a void, an abscess in the world from which even the haunted forest retreated.

And my focus on Josephius's back partially blocked my view of what lurked there, which allowed my gaze to take in the odd shapes on the ground before us, the only thing growing in this clearing. They could have been white pillows scattered about a most incongruous boudoir.

"Are those moving?"

"Yes," the small dark man said, turning, and it was then I saw the sisters.

There were two of them, apparitions that wore the guises of healthy, if pale and luminescent, young maidens but with curious dark lines upon their skin that wandered like the path of a puppy in a glen, with no pattern or plan. They reclined upon the grave-stones as if ladies of leisure, although immodest ones, for the gauzy garments were open to reveal well-formed (if oddly marked) womanly breasts.

One of the fools (the fattish one, I suspect) whispered loudly,

"Do I see boobies?"

That lad was a natural for the profession, should he manage not to kill us all with his stupidity. For at the sound of his voice, the heads of both ghosts snapped toward us. Their images blurred with the movement, then their features caught up with them.

The ladies were not pleased. I knew this by the fact their faces sloughed aside to reveal incomplete, mouldy skulls, with much of the foreheads caved in. It was not a good look but a startlingly effective one, as the Apprentice Fools stampeded away in a gale of shrieking.

"The daughters?" I guessed in an unsteady voice.
"Yes," came the answer from the only one of my company who remained. Josephius added, "Shouldn't you be playing?"

Oh, right, my damned gift. I unlimbered the lute and stroked the strings. The white growths seemed to bestir themselves at the first notes.

"Are you playing a dance tune?" For all his talents, the small dark man has no feel for music.

"No," I assured him, my eyes on the ghosts of the old duke's daughters. They had not bothered to cover themselves, either bosoms or decaying bone. I applied a lighter touch to the dragon-gut strings, for music has charms to soothe the savage—"What in the name of the gods is *that*?"

For the white growths had turned over and now stood. Whatever they were, they possessed both arms and legs, along with oversized heads, but scarcely reached the knee of Josephius. They also had very large, dark eyes or holes for eyes; it was hard to tell with only the glowing ghosts for illumination. I fumbled a chord change (most unusual for one with my unusual gifts). "Are those . . . ?"

"Well, we have found the stolen babies," Josephius observed.

His calmness of tone could become annoying at times, and this was indeed such an occasion.

One of the apparitions (let's call her Rhonda the Rotting for convenience) spoke. "Take not our treasures!" It was hard to determine if this was a plea, a command, or a threat, for the voice at once rose and fell like a sinkhole opening. Impressive, vocally, but not especially useful for clear communication.

"We have no interest in them," I assured the ladies who had once been. "We have come to but give you the peace denied you."

Her sister, Denise the Decayed, shall we say, growled, "Our father denied us our dowries and castle. We are content to rule here, fool."

Automatically, I corrected her. "The fools left, and besides, they are just apprentices—"

Josephius, as was his duty, chided me back on task. "Fred . . . your damned gift is not working."

I felt the first stirrings of, well, panic. None of my soothing invocations of home and hearth nor reminding them of the depths of love their father the duke had for them produced any effect upon the two ghosts. My abilities, damned or not, had never been entirely ineffective. Then I felt tiny fingers upon my calf, and I looked down to behold a skinless infant attempting to claw its tiny way up my leg. A girlish shriek interrupted my increasingly laboured work of genius. It was me, of course, and it was as genuinely girlish as the two ill-mannered dead trollops on the gravestones.

"Josephi—"

"Yes, I see." How could he not, as he was down on one knee, the spry, dead babies having swarmed him, using their nails like pitons to climb up his body? One appeared to be trying to throttle him with a dried umbilical cord. It was a truly fiendish sight. "This will be worse for you than it is for me," he added in an authentically strangled voice. "You need to call in a favour."

Not that.

"Or you could die here. The Demon Bard being murdered by angry expired infants would make people remember you for all the wrong reasons," he pointed out just before the weight of the babies (both the corrupt and dry-as-jerky versions) bore him to the ground. If that were not motivation enough, a glance at the Rotting and the Decaying convinced me, for their stitched-together faces now covered their true visages as if my efforts had absolutely no impact on them at all.

"Oh, you evil, entitled bitches," I spat as something became clear to me. "You took the skins right off those poor children to keep you from looking like the despicable bags of bones you are."

Their only answer was a smug and knowing smirk. Rhonda winked at me and gave a saucy shake of her patchwork bosoms.

Several actions began to transpire at that moment. I cleared some space about me with the stout application of the lute (they are far more useful than commonly known), even as I was thinking to myself, *The Hell with this.*

And then I *spoke* a name. I could think it without consequence, but speaking it, even very quietly, made it real. I have been made to be a devout believer in the power of the word.

He appeared before me, six eyes, eight wings, some swirly nonsense about his head, shooting flames out his arse . . . all the usual guff. *What do you want?* he demanded suspiciously. Demons are never what one expects, I've decided (and believe me, I know more about this than you do). They're supposed to be crafty and seductive and wheedle their way into your mind, slowly sapping your will and eroding your morals.

This git had never done that. He'd just gotten lucky when I

had blundered drunkenly into the wrong party. But that's a story for another time.

Still, he was a right donkey's dick in the personality department. He knew, in general, why I'd summoned him out of season, as it were. It's not like we spent time down at the pub on a regular basis, discussing the politics of the day or wenches or betting on the rat killings. He was going to make me *ask*.

I could use a little help here.

Oh? He was shite for a demon, and a terrible actor, too. *For how long?*

Five minutes. The weaselly thing was entitled to possess me for two days a year, and in return, I received my damned gift (but you know about that bit already). If I happened to need his assistance outside of those two days, it cost me extra. Besides, what he did when he was walking around inside of me was often . . . unpleasant. So I was very specific about how long these little visits of his would be.

He glanced around at the scene of chaos that was suspended outside of us. *I can take them all?*

No, leave the babies. The git's toothy grin reminded me to add, *And Josephius, leave him. Take the two sisters.*

He sighed. *We would have gotten them eventually.*

Perhaps there will be a bonus from the Boss for delivering them early?

It'll cost you.

I know! What do you want?

What are you offering?

Can we get this over with? If I'm slain here, no more holidays among the mortals for you.

I had him there. Due to the accidental nature of our entanglement, it was debatable where I might end up after my death. He wasn't willing to risk his investment in my soul, not yet. His wings flapped impatiently. *How about butter? You like the taste.*

Yes.

I'll take the taste of butter.

Fine.

Four tongues licked four sets of mouth openings, their construction too hideous for my human brain to fully grasp or describe. In that moment, the ability to experience the taste of butter left me forever.

And the demon leapt at me.

As USUAL, when I groaned, 'twas then I knew that I was still alive.

"Don't stand," Josephius said. "The fools need to do a bit of cleanup."

I did crack open one lid, and something gritty promptly dribbled into my eye. "And what might this be?"

"Bone powder." I lifted my hands, both of which felt as if they'd been transformed into hams while I was away, reshaped both in terms of weight and dexterity.

"Now, sir," said a (no doubt) fool. "Let me get that for you." With a deft touch, the fellow applied wet fabric to my face and gently cleaned away the skeletal dust. *Those hands,* I thought. *So controlled. We may need to make a magician out of this lad. Or a pickpocket.*

In time, I was lifted to my feet, which was just as well, for I had been lying amid a heap of rotting bits of the duke's daughters. As the AFs brushed the dead sisters off me and raked up such bones of their bodies as remained, I asked, "And how did it go?"

"Less unpleasantly than usual. Once the sisters realized you were not you, they began pleading with . . . *him* . . . blaming it on their father and all the usual culprits." He limped closer, and then I was able to see the many bloodless gashes and wounds upon him. He lowered his voice, likely so as not to terrify the younger fools. "They attacked him, and he pounded them into dust, and when their shrivelled spirits stood before him, he told them the most terrible thing of all."

Oh, that was new. "Go on."

The demon, Josephius reported, had lectured the two sisters, pointing out that no one was to blame for what they did. Because they had something he'd never possessed. They had a choice. "And then he took them onward."

"That's it?"

"Well, he did pop back briefly to say this was so easy he should require you to pay an additional penalty for wasting his time. Then he tried to collect the children."

The poor things were scattered around, by the way. Still and crumpled, somehow, tiny dried mummies, many of them no larger than a kitten. "But you told him to bugger off."

Anyone else would have missed the slight inflection of self-deprecation in the answer. "After a bit." Which meant that good Josephius had fought the damned thing in my body until time ran out, and the demon had to return to whichever dank corner of Hell had spawned it. It also accounted for his wounds and the fact I felt as if I'd been gargled by a hung-over minotaur, then eaten and ejected violently from one end or the other.

With a sniff of the air, my accountant said, "I must be going. Shall we return the babes to the village?"

As with my damned singing, when the demon was extracting minutes from my life, I could come away with some vague sense of what it had learned. I began to shake my head, but a slash of pain inside my skull stopped me. "No one knows their names. Not even the babes themselves. I'll have the fools bury them properly. It will give the village a place to mourn and remember."

I saw a flash of light in the distance. If that had not originated from the same source as my head pain, then Josephius's time was drawing nigh. "An ugly turn, this was," the small dark fellow said.

"Uglier than most, yes."

"There is one good outcome, sir," he said.

More flashes. Yes, the sun was definitely rising. "Tell me later."

He still lingered. "For the first time in decades, no living or dead thing is guarding the duke's wine cellars. It would be a fine place to rest and recover . . . at least until the villagers get over their fear of the castle."

With that, with almost a smile, he was gone.

———

AND HERE ENDS the First Scroll of The Books of the Bard, the tale of *The Doting Duke and His Gravely Disturbed Daughters*. A less-scrupulous chronicler might pen a tale of grateful villagers feting me and the fools with feasts and modest games. In truth, three days later, greatly refreshed and renewed in most parts of my body except perhaps my liver, the villagers and the Apprentice Fools dragged me out of the late duke's very finely constructed wine closets, at which point the company and I departed that sad little burg. We had made no friends for our heroics (we were taking their only idiot, after all), but we left behind us a story that none of their descendants would ever believe.

Fear not, good reader! Additional scrolls revealing the wanderings of Fred the Demon Bard shall be forthcoming.

THERE'S SOME THING UNDER THE BED

By Garon Whited

Being the Monster Under the Bed is a pretty good deal most of the time. I only have one real gripe. Aside from my one issue, it's exactly what I want.

Look at it like this. Nobody else wants to deal with dust bunnies, mouldy food, and stinky shoes. On the other paw, I get to collect pretty much anything you could lose under a bed. It's a niche, I admit, but it's *my* niche. I don't have to fight anybody for it. An infinite array of beds, out through all the multiverse, make up my home. Some of them have scared people on them. Even better, some of them have scared children trying to sleep on them—or trying to stay awake. Those are the best.

I get it. Nobody likes me. I'm not here to be liked. I'm here to inspire terror in people, most especially in little ones. Small people can still believe with all their hearts and minds in something. Even when adults still believe, they don't believe as hard. And an adult will trust direct investigation. Look under the bed. Nothing there? Must be okay. Kids are more credulous. They can *know* I'm there even after someone looks. And that fear, that unreasoning terror, is what I live on.

Although, if I'm honest, the three-day-old Fruit Loops are *delicious*. I also accept offerings of Cocoa Puffs and bread crusts. I had a good deal going on with one enterprising little boy. He dropped pizza crusts between the bed and the wall. Mmm. Stuffed cheese crust! He slept like a rock.

Normally, I don't do much besides sit in my little space, drinking in the dribbles of fear as they trickle down from under the beds, drip, drip, drip, into my pool. It's a good life. Sometimes, if I'm a little bored, I pop up under someone's bed and say hello. That really gets the night terrors going, let me tell you! It's a good feeling when the heart rate spikes, and you can smell the fear-sweat on a cool night. Ahhhh!

The Fruit Loops are just a bonus, like the little trinkets I collect.

Some say dragons have huge hoards of gold. Maybe they do. I hear a lot of bedtime stories, and sometimes sick children have someone to read to them. But dragons don't have a pocket universe to put their hoards in. I do, and my hoard is enormous. Coins, sure, but toys, too. Magazines, letters, love notes, pictures, even some books. I have a lot of mismatched shoes, as well. It's a huge collection. Anything you could drop down the side of the bed or stow under it and lose, something like it winds up down here.

No socks. The Sock Monster and I settled that a long time ago. It mostly deals in laundry. I'm not an unreasonable monster.

Occasionally, I do run into a problem. Usually, it's out in a magical world. Some wizard has a kid and wards the house extra-hard or something. Cuts it off from dimensional space. Eh. What are you going to do? I ignore it. Other times, the wizard sets some sort of alarm spell to humour the kid, and I have to avoid triggering it. It's not hard when you're not actually present in the same world where they put the spell.

Mundane worlds? Places where the magic doesn't run deep and hot? I still have my share of clever kids. Mousetraps are the usual problem. Sometimes there are tripwires. I've been shot at by more spring-loaded gadgets than I can count. None of them work, of course. I get in there anyway.

Once in a great while, though, I run into a more material problem.

———

TAKE THIS KID . . . oh, I forget the name. She wasn't scared of me at all. I mean, I popped up under the bed and scratched at the bedpost, and she just lay there, quiet as a mouse. It took me a while to figure out what was going on. I mean, she was scared as hell, but she wasn't worried about *me*.

Then the yelling—which I'd been ignoring; if parents are yelling elsewhere in the house, they aren't coming into the room—the yelling stopped. Heavy footsteps came down the hall. I know this drill. I withdrew, mostly, leaving the underspace alone while I watched from farther back.

Big shoes came in—Dad, stepdad, whoever—and there was a lot more yelling, along with a lot of crying and some slapping sounds. When the crying stopped, the shoes went away. The fear was still there, just as strong as ever, but it still wasn't for me.

What a waste.

I tried to turn it around. The kid was more scared of the parent than of me. Okay. I figured I could work with it.

The next time Dad approached the bed, I grabbed his ankles. One with a hand, one with a tentacle. He started swearing and screaming—or maybe screaming while swearing—and tried to step back. It's his own fault, but he went down hard and didn't land well.

I dragged him, still screaming, under the bed, through the underspace, and into my lair.

Grown-up fear is usually too unfocused, too watered-down. They're worried about the rent, or the payments, or the job, or their boss, or their spouse, or something. It's like they have too many things to worry about to spare any for me! The shadowy space under the bed might have a monster, but what are the odds of that? It's more important to lose sleep to anxieties about how you screwed up yesterday, the week before, or back in junior high.

I can eat it, but it's icky. I like my terror concentrated, not bland and tasteless.

However, it *is* possible for an adult to be *entirely* focused on being afraid. It generally uses up the human, but it's not like I'm going to keep it afterward. They can only maintain that level of terror for so long before they stop feeling anything at all.

When I was finished, I checked on the kid. Sleeping peacefully.

Damn. Definitely not scared of me at all. I was probably classed as a guardian monster or something. Well, it wasn't like I was going to get anything out of this one in the first place.

I've tried it more than once. It's pretty hit-or-miss. Sometimes, they grow up to be afraid of me, certain there's a Terrible Monster hiding under every bed despite all psych-guys to the contrary. Sometimes, they relax, knowing the worst is over. I don't know how to tell which way they'll go.

So, let me tell you about the time I *met* a kid, rather than *scaring* the kid.

She was scared when I showed up, which is what I expected. It was a weird flavour. I didn't like it. She wasn't scared of anything in particular that I could figure out. No mean parents, no weird shadows. What was she worrying about if it wasn't me? It smelled like she was worrying about me, but it wasn't quite the same.

It took me a while, but I figured it out. She was scared *for* me, not *of* me!

This really put me off. There were a lot of weird things going on. Her bed was in a pretty typical Earth, lacking in most magic, but when I got there, I realized it was in a localized place of power. The bedrooms didn't look like parts of a sacred site, just some house. And the kid wasn't scared of me. That is *not* supposed to happen.

I gave her my best creepy laugh, the one where I use all the mouths I can fit under the bed at once. It didn't faze her.

"You don't understand," she told me, not even trying to look under the bed. "Papa doesn't like it when we have visitors. When they aren't invited," she corrected.

"Yeah?"

"If he catches you in here with me, he'll be *mad*."

"What's he gonna do? Shine a light under here? That never works."

"I don't know what he'll do, but you won't like it. He's a much bigger monster than you are! Please don't get hurt, Mr. Monster!"

"I won't."

But I wondered. She absolutely believed I was in danger. I couldn't let it go. I kept coming back to see if her father was going to do an under-bed check. He didn't, but I did start to understand why she was scared *for* me rather than *of* me.

I lurked under the bed as the father came in. He kissed the kid goodnight and tucked her in. He never knew I was there. I'm an excellent lurker. You might say it's what I do. But this "bigger monster" of a father didn't strike me as dangerous. He put his boots on one at a time, just like all the others.

Dad walked out, leaving the door open a crack, but that never helps. And then the kid's stuffed toy hit the floor.

As for me, I thought the little girl dropped her teddy bear. Instant glee on my part! She would have to reach down and pick it up! I could grab her wrist with . . . let's see . . . probably a tentacle. The rubbery one or the slimy one? Slimy, definitely.

I was wrong. She didn't knock the teddy bear off the bed. Looking back, her father didn't, either. That fuzzy little fiend rolled off the bed on its own. No, that's not quite right. It jumped off the bed as part of a combat insertion. The fluffy thing crawled under, its button eyes fixed on me, and promptly attacked.

I've encountered a lot of teddy bears. In fairness, they're worthy opponents. If the children take comfort from the cuddly little bastards, I'm out of luck. It's way more work to overcome the influence of the teddy bear than I'll get out of the kid. They're not worth it. Teddy bears are a defensive measure, and they work entirely too damn well.

But *this* thing!

I have nobody to pray to. I never needed to before.

There was nothing defensive about this fuzzy monstrosity. In fact, I found this teddy bear extremely *offensive*. No, more than that. It was downright *aggressive*.

I've been mauled by a bear precisely once and hope to the ends of the universes never to be mauled by it again. In the larger scheme of things, it wasn't really a threat to my existence, but it was both painful and creepy.

It looked at me with its blank little face and those dead little button eyes. Everywhere it looked, it somehow cut something off, as though its looks really could kill. I lost fourteen hands and other appendages before I could get past the Sharp Glance power and smack that brutal little beast out from under the bed. Stuffing went everywhere—I used a sharp claw—but the damned thing sat up, stood up, and, still trailing bits of stuffing, turned those soulless, evil little eyes toward me again.

The stuffing crawled back into the upholstered beast in exactly the same way a human's entrails don't.

I did a quick grab for my severed limbs and beat a hasty retreat. I and my limbs soaked in the Pool of Tears, and I started to feel better. All through the multiverses, there were still little people who feared me. Okay. I'm the Monster Under the Bed. I'm a nightly terror. I feast on the fears of everything that wonders what that noise was. I exist across worlds, across universes. So what if there was one house where . . . where . . .

One house. So far.

While I had no desire to be cut to pieces by the bastard child of Sweeney Todd and Winnie the Pooh, I had to know more about what was going on. Were these things about to be popular? Having *attack* teddy bears would be a disaster! I'd have to . . . you know . . . do something. Figure something out. I'd have to do that . . . that growing thing where you change? It's like growing, but it's—ah! Evolve! And I didn't want to. It takes work. It hurts.

But I might need to start, and in a hurry. I had to find out more.

The next night, I went back and—politely, I thought—knocked on one leg of the bed.

"Hey, you. Can we talk?"

The teddy bear hit the floor. It didn't look sewn up and repaired. It looked brand-new, either completely healed or replaced. Or maybe it was the new one and the old one was somewhere I didn't see it.

I pulled back out of the room. I don't like it when things slice off my appendages. I mean, sure, I can grow them back, but it stings!

I tried again a week later. You know, let things cool down a little. Tempers can be high at first, but give it time, you know?

It worked. I showed up, knocked again, said hello.

No attack teddy bear. Good sign.

"Um. Look. I know you're up there."

"Yes."

"I'm sorry I didn't believe you."

"It's all right. Papa said he wouldn't do anything to you."

I wanted to say something about how he already did, but I reconsidered. If Papa didn't do anything to me, where the hell did the grizzly teddy bear come from? Hell? I doubted it. No sulphur smell. There was no telling where it was conjured from. Maybe from the dreamscapes of the nightmare realms. I hear they have some really awful stuff living there.

Did the attack teddy not count as Papa "doing" anything?

I checked for the others. The Closet Monster wasn't going to pester her; I could see the closet door, and it was shut, solid, and well-fitted. Old Man Shadow—you know, the guy who always makes things look sinister and creepy?—was nowhere to be seen. I didn't even smell him anywhere.

I did smell *something*, though. Something *like* Old Man Shadow, but definitely not him. I wondered why. Any room with shadows in the corners is his lawful domain. He drops by and visits, now and again, under the bed.

Was this sharp-eyed bear especially for me? Or was it for something bigger?

The place she slept was a place of magical power, which made it easy for me—and a whole lot of other things—to find. But her Papa was obviously a conjuror of some sort, a wizard, a sorcerer. He'd conjured a demonic toy to defend her.

Who *was* this kid?

No, that's the wrong question. This kid told me she didn't want her Papa to hurt me. *Me*. The Monster Under the Bed. And her *teddy bear* was dangerous enough to lop off limbs faster than I could grow them back.

Who the hell was her Papa?

No, I've asked the wrong question again. *What* the hell was her Papa? I have never had a child's toy try to kill me. It worries me that something he regards as a toy is this dangerous. What else is there? If this is what he routinely put her to bed with, I did not want to find out what happened when he—do I call him a "he"? Or do I call him an "it"?—what happened when this "Papa" took a personal interest!

I decided to avoid this creature. If I made nice with the little one, I wouldn't have to deal with the big one.

Strangely, it seemed the little girl was a human being. There was nothing I could see to make her out as anything but a perfectly normal human. As I understand it, it takes humans to beget humans. Was this kid special in some way? Or was she some sort of apprentice? Or did her "Papa" have some sort of use for a little human?

Such was my thinking when I decided to hang around with this little girl. She was perfectly willing to hold a conversation, too. She even gave me a name.

I never had a name before. Not really. What would I need with one? I'm the Monster Under the Bed. I'm the only one, and everybody knows me. You, too, even if you don't remember me. Even if you say you don't.

The weirdest thing was how she was never afraid of me. Maybe that was part of why I kept coming back. She played with me, which was unique. I'd never had anyone *play* with me before. She was always willing to talk, too, and could still see me even when she was a bigger human. That's rare.

I miss her. I think she was my friend. I still think of her.

———

YEARS LATER, the weirdest thing happened, and it reminded me of her. I met someone else who wasn't afraid of me. He wasn't nearly as nice.

I was doing my usual thing under a bed. It was a good one. There were three kids in it, but unlike teddy bears, having someone with you isn't the same as having a talisman. Talismans don't get scared. Your brother and sister do. And when they get scared, it's easier for everyone to be scared.

All three huddled together. It's always nice to have so much fear in one spot.

Then some grown-up showed up. He looked under the bed, so I blinked out for a moment.

I didn't anticipate him looking again, this time without a light. Even so, what good would it have done? It was dark. Humans need lights.

He wasn't human. He looked at me with his all-black eyes, and I wondered what he was.

I didn't know what to say. He didn't, either. We were both at a total loss for words. We stared at each other for a bit.

"Are you the monster under the bed?" he asked.

"Who wants to know?" I demanded. I was more than a little disturbed. Adults aren't supposed to be able to see me, but, hey, magical universes can have weird properties . . . and sometimes weird creatures.

"I'm the monster that *isn't* under the bed," he answered.

I felt threatened. That was unusual. I think it was those black eyes. They reminded me of something, but I couldn't think of what at that precise moment.

And then I remembered the Button-Eyed Grizzly. Oh, yeah. That was long ago and far away, and I had no good memories of the encounter. That was the last time something crawled under a bed and attacked me, and it was bad. Which made me wonder how dangerous the human-shaped thing in front of me might be.

At about this point in my life, I started to wonder if I ought to be more accommodating to unidentified monsters. Identifying them can be a painful process, and I'm not used to pain. I'm also not used to thinking of underbed spaces as being anything but my domain, but when it comes down to it, their manifestations coexist with the most basic four dimensions.

After he and I had some pointed negotiations, sharp words, and a few blunt-force comments, I started to think the overlap might be a negotiable area. I drew back some stumps and said something to that effect.

He was amazingly civil. I didn't expect that.

As it turned out, he didn't object to me hunting in his domain. His objection was to me hunting children for their terror. I didn't bother to tell him I fed on their fear whether I was physically present or not. It didn't seem a good time to bring it up. Or, for that matter, a good thing to bring up at all, considering.

He made me an offer. An offer of adult fear. It's not something I usually get, what with all an adult's distractions, so I listened. His idea was to give me a magic device so I could make myself heard by adults, and without going to all the effort of manifesting hands and claws and tentacles and suchlike. Then, when they still couldn't see me, they would be afraid because adults are mostly scared of the unknown. Makes 'em insecure. They hate that.

My end of the deal was pretty easy. All the adults I wanted to personally terrify in exchange for the children of the realm? It sounded like a good deal. It was certainly worth trying.

TURNS OUT, it was a *really* great deal. I've had a lot of fun with it. Adults will lie quietly in bed and stare at the ceiling, shaking with anxiety bordering on panic. It only takes a little prompting. It's a different art from terrifying children, but once I got the hang of it, it was even easier. Adults just need to be nudged with different subjects.

So, when you're too old to believe in me, when you've outgrown that childish urge to jump into bed so I can't grab your ankles, and when you no longer worry about sleeping with some part of you projecting over the edge . . .

Don't worry. I'll get around to you.

The magical widget works beautifully. I'm very pleased with the deal. You gotta respect a monster who keeps his promises.

Sometimes, though, I wonder . . .

I've never had a name of my own. Not really. The kid with the attack teddy bear gave me a name. The monster not under the bed? He gave me a name, too—and it was the *same* name.

I'd prefer something like, "Zycorax, Terror of the Night," or "Ashkelion the Dark."

It's tough having an identity crisis when you're a unique entity.

It's tough having an identity crisis when you're a unique entity. On the other hand, I guess I can introduce myself properly. That's worth something, I suppose.

"Hi! My name is Fred."

Somehow, it doesn't inspire the fear and terror I'd hoped for.

I REALLY NEED TO CLEAR MY INBOX

By Noah Lemelson

From: Jeff@Greenhollowapartments.com August 1
To: undisclosed-recipients;
Subject: Pool Opening!

Dear GreenHollow Residents,

We are excited to finally announce the opening of the
Greenhill Recreational Swimming Pool and Adjoining Hot
Tub! We know the construction process has been a long
journey, and we thank our residents for their patience with
the delays.

The pool will officially open tomorrow. The hours of operation are Monday through Saturday 7 a.m. - 9 p.m. and
Sunday 10 a.m. - 6 p.m. Please limit hot tub occupants to six
or fewer. Any outside guests must be signed in by Lois in
the front lobby.

Oh, this is also the last call to pick up that piece of jewellery found during construction. If you haven't received my previous emails—while digging up the old garden, we uncovered a buried necklace. It's made of soapstone and is in the shape of an eyeless man with an unusually large mouth. If it's yours, please pick it up tomorrow; otherwise, we will have to dispose of it.

Sincerely,
Jeffery Green
GreenHollow Apartments
Greenhollowapartments.com

August 3

From: Jeff@Greenhollowapartments.com
To: undisclosed-recipients;
Subject: Honda Civic Blocking Space

Dear GreenHollow Residents,

Will the resident with the blue Honda Civic please move their car? It is currently blocking two handicap parking spaces. If you do not immediately move your car, we will be forced to tow it.

Sincerely,
Jeffery Green
GreenHollow Apartments
Greenhollowapartments.com

August 10

From: Jeff@Greenhollowapartments.com
To: undisclosed-recipients;
Subject: Noise Complaints and A Warning

Dear GreenHollow Residents,

We have received a series of noise complaints over the last few nights. Whoever is loudly chanting at 3:30 in the morning, I would direct you to our *Resident Code of Conduct*, which quite clearly states that 10 p.m. - 6 a.m. are designated *Quiet Hours*. We have many residents who work early in the morning, and your choice of accompanying music, that is, what seem to be lengthy recordings of discordant screaming and ear-splitting wailing, is particularly disrespectful to your fellow neighbours. I hope I will not need to send another email on this topic.

Also! Whoever is dumping red food colouring into the pool, stop immediately! This constitutes vandalism and ruins the pool experience for everyone. We will not hesitate to take legal action if this does not cease.

Sincerely,
Jeffery Green
GreenHollow Apartments
Greenhollowapartments.com

August 13

From: Jeff@Greenhollowapartments.com
To: undisclosed-recipients;
Subject: Movie Night This Friday!

Dear GreenHollow Residents,

Exciting news! This Friday, we will be inaugurating our *Weekly Movie Night!* That's right, at 6 p.m. the Rec Room will be turned into a miniature movie theatre for our residents. Popcorn is available for purchase from Lois in the front lobby, and we invite people to bring their own chairs or pillows.

This week's movie is *The Exorcist*! When a young girl starts acting strangely, a priest, played by Jason Miller, is forced to grapple with forces beyond the veil of human experience. Spooks, shocks, and scares this Friday in the Rec Room!

Also, we are sorry to report that we will be temporarily closing the pool until we can figure out how to fix these strange leaks. We would also like to apologize for the tone of our previous email. It is clear after watching the surveillance tapes that no resident is responsible for the sudden appearance of the crimson liquids.

Sincerely,
Jeffery Green
GreenHollow Apartments
Greenhollowapartments.com

August 21

From: Jeff@Greenhollowapartments.com
To: undisclosed-recipients;
Subject: Notice of Criminal Incident

Dear GreenHollow Residents,

We have been made aware of a criminal incident affecting a GreenHollow community member. At 7:06 p.m. last night, a resident was accosted by a man in a "full-body hoodie" while entering the building. The figure reportedly grabbed him and whispered, *"Reality seeks its own execution,"* before fleeing the scene. Unfortunately, the man appears only as a swirl of smoke on our surveillance tapes, so if anyone has any information on this subject, please report it to us.

We do not yet know if this incident is related to the break-in last week or the ever-dripping graffiti on the second floor.

Also, I am unhappy to report that we continue to receive noise complaints. The chanting, discordant music, and piercing screaming has only increased in volume, and now lasts most of the night. We are currently trying to figure out from which apartment the sounds are emanating, but have received conflicting information. Residents of the fourth floor claim it is coming from above, while residents of the fifth claim it originates from below. If you have any additional information, please contact us. As for the offenders, if you do not cease this activity immediately, we will consider this grounds for eviction! You have been warned.

Sincerely,
Jeffery Green
GreenHollow Apartments
Greenhollowapartments.com

September 4

From: Jeff@Greenhollowapartments.com
To: undisclosed-recipients;
Subject: RE: Lost Pets

Dear GreenHollow Residents,

In order to consolidate communications and improve our apartment's aesthetic experience, we are moving all *Lost Pet* signs to the front lobby. If you wish to post any further *Lost Pet* signs, please add them to the *Lost Pet Board* in the front lobby. If you discover any lost pets or the remains of any lost pets, please contact Lois in the front lobby.

In light of recent events, we are also adding a few rules to the Resident Code of Conduct:

This is now a *No Pet Apartment*. We apologize for the sudden change, and if any residents recover their pet or pets somehow, they will be grandfathered in and allowed to remain under close observation.

Do not approach any lone animals at night. It doesn't matter how small they are, or if they resemble a lost pet, it is imperative for the safety of yourself, your fellow residents, and the GreenHollow staff that you never, ever, approach a lone animal between the hours of 9 p.m. and 7 a.m. And under no circumstance should you ever allow or verbally invite a lone animal into the building. Failure to abide by this rule will be considered grounds for eviction.

The pool is now off-limits. Please do not view the pool between the hours of 3 p.m. and 5 a.m. Residents with pool-facing windows will have these windows boarded up as a complementary service.

Do not talk to outsiders. They are not your friends.

Guests are prohibited under all circumstances.

Trash day is now Wednesday.

In the event of a fire, remember to use the stairs, not to use the elevator. This is already part of the *Resident Code of Conduct*, and there are signs posted by the elevator specifying this, but as this has come up several times in the last few days, I thought it best to remind residents.

If you have any questions, please do not hesitate to contact me.

Sincerely,
Jeffery Green
GreenHollow Apartments
Greenhollowapartments.com

September 13

From: Jeff@Greenhollowapartments.com
To: undisclosed-recipients;
Subject: etAfruOyepacSetnAcuOy

Dear Greenhallow Residents:

I dream of a night
When the sun drips red,

When gibbous moonlight
Exhumes the dead.

I dream of a day
Where from ochre soil
Emerges the faces
Of sinners left to spoil.

I dream of the twilight
Of mankind,
Of a morning anew,
Death and Life Entwined.

What do you think of my dreams,
You rats in your cages?
Do you cling to lost sanity,
And the madness of old sages?

I know what I think.
I think I'm waking up . . .

Sincerely,
Jeffery Green
GreenHollow Apartments
Greenhollowapartments.com

September 14

From: Jeff@Greenhollowapartments.com
To: undisclosed-recipients;
Subject: Electricity Bills And Advice

Dear GreenHollow Residents,

Apologies for the previous email. Our email service has been undergoing technical difficulties, but it should all be straightened out now.

On a more serious note, I have yet to receive cheques from more than half of you for last month's electricity bill. It is clearly stated in your lease that while sewage and water are covered by *GreenHollow Inc.*, electricity must be paid on the first of each month.

I am aware that several of you have requested deferrals for this payment due to the significant spike in the cost of electricity and the universal increase in usage. I would like to remind you that this provision in your lease is price-agnostic. It is not the responsibility of *GreenHollow Inc.* to cover the increased cost. We understand that 117-degree weather is unusual for September, which is why we have started to stock Icecold™ brand popsicles in the front lobby vending machine.

We sympathize with our residents' increased need for lighting during this past week's unusually persistent night, and we have some suggestions. Try to turn off lights in rooms you're not using. It is sensible to fear the Dark, but as long as you keep the room you are currently in well-lit, there's no reason to believe that They can get you. Also, you can use non-electric sources of light to save money, as long as you avoid pork-tallow candles. All pork products are banned from the premises for the safety of our residents.

Remember, though guests are still banned, residents are free to visit and stay with each other. Safety in numbers! Just remember to use a buddy system and to regularly check the pupils of your fellow residents.

Also, *Weekly Movie Night* has been cancelled. Our apologies! We are working to find a way to bring it back in a safe and responsible manner.

> *Sincerely,*
> *Jeffery Green*
> *GreenHollow Apartments*
> *Greenhollowapartments.com*

September 19

From: Jeff@Greenhollowapartments.com
To: undisclosed-recipients;
Subject: Updated Code of Conduct

Dear GreenHollow Residents,

In light of recent events, we are adding a few more rules to the *Resident Code of Conduct:*

1. Do not go outside.
2. Do not go outside.
3. Do not go outside.
4. Do not go outside.
5. Do not go outside.
6. Do not go outside.
7. Do not go outside.
8. Do not go outside.
9. Do not go outside.
10. Do not go outside

If you have any questions, please do not hesitate to contact me.

Sincerely,
Jeffery Green
GreenHollow Apartments
Greenhollowapartments.com

September 25

From: Jeff@Greenhollowapartments.com
To: undisclosed-recipients;
Subject: RE: Noise Complaints

To the Resident of Room 206,

We know it hurts, but your screaming is disturbing the other residents.

Sincerely,
Jeffery Green
GreenHollow Apartments
Greenhollowapartments.com

October 1

From: Jeff@Greenhollowapartments.com
To: undisclosed-recipients;
Subject: RE:RE:FWD: We're Starving

Dear GreenHollow Residents,

We would like to remind residents that the hoarding of food goes against the updated *Resident Code of Conduct*. Please bring all non-perishable, non-porcine food to the front lobby, where we have built a barricade of sorts to best protect our remaining food stores and our remaining residents.

Also, if anyone knows what has happened to the fifth floor, please contact Lois in the front lobby barricade. We believe that before the floor disappeared, its vending machine was still fully stocked, and this could be an invaluable asset in these trying times.

Sincerely,
Jeffery Green
GreenHollow Apartments
Greenhollowapartments.com

October 8
From: Jeff@Greenhollowapartments.com
To: undisclosed-recipients;
Subject: Hello?

Dear GreenHollow Residents,

Is anyone there? I haven't received any responses to my last few emails.

Sincerely,
Jeffery Green
GreenHollow Apartments
Greenhollowapartments.com

October 13

From: Jeff@Greenhollowapartments.com
To: undisclosed-recipients;
Subject: Please?

Dear GreenHollow Residents,

Failure to respond to this email would constitute a violation . . . a violation . . .

Please, just tell me if you're still here.

Sincerely,
Jeffery Green
GreenHollow Apartments
Greenhollowapartments.com

October 16

From: Jeff@Greenhollowapartments.com
To: undisclosed-recipients;
Subject: I think I'm losing it

Dear GreenHollow Residents,

I thought I saw someone today. I was too frightened to call out, but when I blinked, they were gone. If that was you, please email me back. Or knock. Or scream. I just need to know if my mind has left me.

Sincerely,
Jeffery Green
GreenHollow Apartments
Greenhollowapartments.com

October 166

From: Jeff@Greenhollowapartments.com
To: undisclosed-recipients;
Subject: Please . . .

Dear GreenHollow Residents,

Did I know any of you? When things were normal, did I
know you? Did I understand you? Did I ever speak with
you, not through the computer, but in person? I don't
remember. I should, it can't have been that long ago, but
my head is empty. What's outside this room? I can't bring
myself to recall, and I'm too afraid to look.

Everything's gone. I can't even hide in my memories. Sometimes I even wonder if I ever had memories, if any of it was
real. All I have are these emails, claiming to be from me,
but I don't . . . I don't know. I'm here now, I know that, I'm
here, and I'm real, and I'm cold, and I want to hold
someone.

I want to hold someone and know that they're real.

Sincerely,
Jeffery Green
GreenHollow Apartments
Greenhollowapartments.com

October 1666

From: Jeff@Greenhollowapartments.com
To: undisclosed-recipients;
Subject:

Dear GreenHollow Residents,

I miss Lois.

Sincerely,
Jeffery Green
GreenHollow Apartments
Greenhollowapartments.com

October integeroverflow

From: Jeff@Greenhollowapartments.com
To: undisclosed-recipients;
Subject:

Dear GreenHollow Residents,

It's gotten so quiet in here.

At times, I sit in my room, listening, hoping for something, some sign of life. It's gotten so cold. I wrap myself in coats and blankets and everything, but nothing seems to help.

The chill cuts to my bone like it's not the air but my own skin and flesh that is draining the heat from me. I tried burning my furniture, but the fire could not warm me. It doesn't even hurt when I burn myself.

When I look outside, I can see the figures wandering the streets. They look so close to human, so damn close that I'm tempted to call out. It would be easy to just ignore their horns and misshapen limbs, to open my window and wave, to invite Them in. Just to touch someone, just to feel someone again.

How long has it been? I don't know; the clock stopped ages ago. 7:06 a.m. It stares, mocking me. Has it been a day, a month, a year? Why haven't I died yet? From the heat, or the cold, or Them, or the ever-gnawing hunger? I should have died a thousand times over. Sometimes, I think I feel the life leaving me, but then I wake up, still cold on my empty floor, from one nightmare to another.

I finished the last piece of Lois yesterday. Her bones are gnawed and cut, as if by a swarm of rats. I tell myself that is what happened, and sometimes I can even believe it, but as much as I want to pretend, I know it was me; it's always been just me. I'm so lonely. Perhaps that's why I can't die. Death does not even want me, does not want anything from this accursed place. It won't let me rest, won't end my suffering, not until I have repented every sin, not until there is nothing left of me but a shadow of agony and despair.

If you're out there still, don't come to me. Save yourself. If that has ever been possible.

Sincerely,
Jeffery Green
GreenHollow Apartments
Greenhollowapartments.com

November 1

From: Bal@Felhollowapartments.com
To: undisclosed-recipients;
Subject: New Management!

Dear FelHollow Residents,

Great news! The acquisition of *GreenHollow Inc.* by *Dis Felcraven LLC* and subsequent acquisition is finally complete. We are proud to announce that, going forward, your apartments will be run by the *FelHollow Management Group!* We thank our residents for their patience during the complications in this process. This journey has been rocky at points, but we know that going forward, you will love the improved services and facilities *FelHollow* can provide.

To list just a few of these new amenities:

- The hot tub will reopen Sunday, and be open from 12 a.m. to 6 a.m. nightly. Thanks to some new upgrades, the hot tub will reach a balmy 352 degrees Celsius.
- The elevators have been upgraded with voice-activation technology, and will respond to you in the voice of your late grandmother while bringing you swiftly to any of our new basements, subbasements, and sub-subbasements.
- We will be opening a new Fitness Centre early next year in the gaping chasm between the fourth and fifth floor.
- Finally, *Weekly Movie Night* is back! Pick up some popcorn from the re-animated bones of Lois in the front lobby and prepare for *Exorcist 2: The Heretic.*

Oh, and as part of this evolution, we have made a few changes to the Resident Code of Conduct:

- Payment will still be made on the first of the month but will no longer be made in dollars but in human blood. Make sure your security deposit is also provided in human blood.
- Please do not sanctify any water while on the premises or bring holy water into the apartment complex. It interferes with the workings of many of our new automated systems. For the same reason, please avoid baptisms of any sort.
- This is now a *Pet Friendly Apartment*! We only ask that you pay a small pet deposit and that you avoid any pets larger than a German Shepherd. (In addition, please

keep the number of heads on your dogs to three or less.)

- Sewage is no longer covered by the apartment managers. You will receive a bill at the first of each month.

And that's about it! If you have any questions, you can talk with me directly in the front lobby. I am currently occupying the body of Jeffery Green.

Yours truly,
Bal Ashmedai,
FelHollow Apartments
Felhollowapartments.com

———

November 3

From: Bal@Felhollowapartments.com
To: undisclosed-recipients;
Subject: Honda Civic Blocking Portal

Dear FelHollow Residents,

Will the resident with the blue Honda Civic please move their car? It is currently blocking access to two Sin Portals. If you do not immediately move your car, we will be forced to collapse its atoms and reforge them into an obsidian blade, which we will use to flay your soul.

Yours truly,
Bal Ashmedai,
FelHollow Apartments
Felhollowapartments.com

BWDOC

By James Van Pelt

Need help at the university? I know a guy. Lives in Crossman Hall, second floor. Last room on the right. Won't take cash. Pure trade business, but he's your man. Tell him I sent you.

Dan Merville heard the footsteps coming. When they turned right from the stairs, they were coming to see him. The other rooms in his end of the hall were empty.

He pushed aside his econ text. Where the formula was in it he needed to complete his homework was anyone's guess, and he wasn't that excited about the problem anyway. Searching for two hours hadn't found it yet.

He guessed from the stride the approaching person was a girl and wished he'd locked his door. Having a stalker was annoying. But when she stopped in the doorway, and it wasn't Kelsey Thibedeau, he breathed easier. He'd seen Kelsey everywhere on campus lately: in the student union, watching him over a cup of coffee, at the other end of a study table in the library, and walking by the front of his dorm. He'd hid himself behind the curtain. This girl, though, had a chunky build, hair tucked under her baseball cap, pasty complexion, and nervous eyes.

"I heard you can get things done, " she said.

"Depends." He surveyed his room. From her point of view, it probably didn't engender confidence: NFL cheerleader posters and pages from *Sports Illustrated* swimsuit issues hanging on the wall, both remnants of his former roommate; empty pizza boxes on the bed to the left (the one on the right was unmade); dirty clothes overflowing the laundry bin. The terrarium on top of the dresser, home to his snake, Nosferatu, needed cleaning. "What can I do for you?"

"It's my English professor. She won't take my paper. I'm only a day late, but it's not my fault. My Aunt Cherie got sick on the weekend, and I had to go to Cheyenne to see her. She's my mom's sister, and Mom needed the support."

Dan waved a hand at her. Typical college request. Slackers trying to make up for poor planning. Kids who didn't want to do the work at all. Go-getters who needed to impress a department head. Laziness to the left and right. And that was just the academic problems. Everything else came his way, too. Greed. Revenge. Jealousy. Love. "I get the gist. You want her to accept a late paper. Who's the professor?"

"Tarryhill."

Dan pushed himself up from his desk, opened his file cabinet, and pulled out a folder marked "Tarryhill." It contained four strands of hair. "I can do it," he said.

The girl smiled in relief. She stepped in. "Should I close the door?" She'd unbuttoned the top button on her blouse and was working on the second.

"What? No. What are you doing?"

The girl looked confused. "They told me that you work in . . . exchanges. I thought this is what they meant."

Dan closed the folder. "You're willing to trade sex to get a late paper accepted? Don't be ridiculous. Grades aren't that important. And that's not what I'm looking for. What do you have in your pockets?"

The girl put thirty-three cents in change, a key ring, a lip balm, and a smartphone on his desk. He ran his fingers over the collection, pausing at an Indian Head penny. He picked it up, squeezed it. It hummed pleasantly in his hand. "I'll take this."

She hesitated. "It's my lucky penny. I've had it a long time."

"It's the only worthwhile thing you have here."

"Tarryhill will take my paper, full credit?"

"Guaranteed. That doesn't mean it will get a good grade. It's up to you to write something worthwhile."

"Awesome!" Her face lit up. "How soon?"

"Go to her office tomorrow. She'll be in the right mood."

The girl gathered her belongings from the desk. "How do you do it? Are you a wizard or something?"

Dan dug into a desk drawer for the sidewalk chalk and candles. "More like a witch doctor, but mostly, I'm just a student like you, chasing the diploma." He paused. "Wait a minute. Tarryhill's a journalism prof, right? The newspaper adviser? Are you on the staff?"

The girl shook her head. "Journalism 101. It's an English elective."

"Would you know a Kelsey Thibedeau? She reports for the school paper."

"No, don't know her."

A week earlier, Thibedeau had ambushed him outside the science building, her press pass dangling from a lanyard, her name prominently displayed. She wore her dark hair pulled back with corn rows. Sleeveless shirt, slim arms, delicate hands. "You're Dan Melville, right? Can I talk to you?"

He stepped back. His little side business from the dorm helped keep him comfortable, but too many people knew about it already. If a nosy reporter wrote an article, he'd have to transfer schools. He'd be arrested for scamming people, or worse, they'd discover he was real—not that they could prove it.

"No comment," he said. "And leave me alone." He walked away from her as quickly as he could without breaking into a run.

That night, he considered dropping out again. Economics bored him, and the people who wanted help seemed pathetic. Where was the nobility? Where was the purpose?

After the student with the late-paper problem left, Dan put aside the book, chalked a pattern on the floor, lit the candles, and then put one of Tarryhill's hairs and the Indianhead penny in the centre.

He waited until midnight. Most of his spells had to be executed at the strike of twelve. Regular sleep hours weren't a part of his schedule. Both the hair and penny vanished, along with the chalk marks, before he finished the incantation, leaving behind the odour of burnt eggs and a nagging sense of uselessness. So, she passed the class, or she failed the class. It didn't matter to him; why should it matter to her? He opened the window and turned on a fan to clear the air.

When he returned to the economics text, the formula he'd been searching for stared him in the face. Of course, that's how the magic worked. If he did something for someone else, fate smiled on him, but woe betide him if he performed the magic for himself.

Dan had nearly finished the problem that had stumped him all night when a boy appeared at his door without a sound: tall, slender, neatly dressed, with his polo shirt tucked into his khakis. Blond-haired and blue-eyed. "There's a girl," he said.

"Of course there is." Dan closed the text. He could take care of the lovelorn, hit the cafeteria for breakfast, and still have time to wrap up his studies. "You're up late."

"Not just any girl," the boy said earnestly. "I sit behind her in calculus. Sometimes we share notes. I saw her once on the quad when it was sunny. She was talking with friends. Oh, man, the light through her hair, like an angel. I've got to be with her."

Dan sighed. Another yearning soul. Half of his clients were lovesick. "Have you tried asking her out?"

The boy blushed. "I get tongue-tied when I talk to her. Besides, she's out of my league. There's, like, a dozen guys around her all the time, but there's a party in Hallet Hall Friday. If I can get her alone, maybe I'll have a chance."

"So you want me to scare up some confidence for you. That's an easy one." Dan went over the steps for the spell. Maybe twenty minutes to set up the equipment, then he'd be done. He'd hang the CLOSED sign on his door; otherwise, someone would knock even later. It was amazing how often someone wanted something done right that minute, even if that minute was at three in the morning.

The boy smiled. He really had a charming look to him. It was hard to believe that he was the strikeout he described. "I'm not worried about me. Parties are so loud she'll hardly be able to hear me anyway. Mostly, everyone dances and hooks up. What I need is something to make her more pliable, you know, suggestible. I just

got to be with her. A buddy of mine has a room in the hall we can use. Can you do a whammy on her that'll give me an hour? You should see her. She's like butter on toast, man."

Dan trembled. Why hadn't he noticed it before, the predatory stance, the arrogance? "You want me to whip up a voodoo roofie?" He stood up.

"Yeah, that's the beauty of it. No chemicals, no crime."

"Get the hell out of here, asshole."

The boy sputtered. "What? Like you've never done this before. With the juju you've got, you must be scoring more action than any guy on campus. You're certainly not making it on your looks."

Dan wasn't tall or muscled, but he was enraged. His face burned with it. "I'll show you some juju, dickweed. You've got ten seconds to clear this building, or I'll set a spell on you that will have you peeing stinging nettles for the rest of your life."

The boy made it out with plenty to spare. From the window, Dan watched him sprinting into the night. He thought he ought to do the spell anyway. Guys like that weren't jerks just once. They had a habit, but Dan hadn't gotten anything from him. Hair would do, or an article of clothing he'd worn.

Of course, the rapist wasn't as bad as last week when he was asked to arrange a massacre. It took a half hour for the client to get to the point. He sat on Dan's bed, wringing his hands, a shoebox beside him. Heavy kid. Lots of acne. Smelled bad, too. Finally, he got to it. "They won't leave me alone, the frat boys. They posted pictures of me—I don't know how they got them—embarrassing pictures."

Dan thought he recognized the direction the conversation was going. "So, you want to humiliate them back, shame them?"

"I heard about how you work. I brought things." He opened the box. "This is mine, my high school ring. This is theirs: hair, dirty socks, a used band-aid." The boy's face grew dark. "They should die screaming."

That was the worst. He wasn't being hyperbolic. The kid seriously wanted a death spell. Dan threw the boy out, called student services anonymously, and then, when he realized the boy had left behind his box, worked a warding enchantment that would keep the frat bullies away from him.

What people wanted magic for depressed him. Magical rape. Magical death. Magical cheating. This last one almost made the wannabe-serial-killer bullied boy from the week before seem righteous. At least the heavy kid had a serious beef, even if his reaction was over the top. Dan thought people went to college to find a purpose in their lives, to devote themselves to something, but they were all caught up in the meaningless and pettiness. Where was the drive to learn?

By late afternoon, homework didn't sound appealing at all, not that it ever did lately. Dan needed something to wash the taste from his mouth, so he headed to Corner Cellars, a basement R&B bar that poured local beers. The sun set behind the hills, but the sky still shone blue and clear, a perfect October day, warm in that we-don't-have-many-warm-days-left way.

Massachusetts in the fall was beautiful. A scattering of dried leaves skittered across the sidewalk, and a couple of bikes swooshed by. The campus looked like its promotional brochures, clean, crisp, and academic. Red stone buildings rose majestically from green landscaping.

It was a wonder he was enrolled, and he knew it. Vice Principal Reedy, back in high school, told him that at the pace he was going, he'd be in jail or dead by the time he was twenty, but Reedy was a bitter man. The only kids in the school he ever talked to were the ones in trouble. It warped his view.

Dan felt a little warped himself. Too often, the pathetic showed up at his door. Some whined, "My roommate snores all the time." Some were vindictive: "She didn't deserve that scholarship. I did." Some were sad. "I just want to feel better about myself." But Dan listened, and when he could, he helped. His bank account grew— windfalls came his way after spells—but even beautiful weather like today didn't uplift him. What people wanted when they were desperate enough to come to him gave him a poor view of people.

The Not Lost Wanderers appeared at Corner Cellars on Tuesday nights—a bass player, a drummer, and a lead guitarist who also played harmonica. All three sang. Sometimes an out-of-town friend would join them, but most of the time, it was just that simple setup. Dan liked their music: down-home, basic R&B. Sometimes, they did old Rolling Stones tunes but cut the rock and roll and played them as if they'd come straight out of the '20s Chicago blues scene.

On this weeknight, the bar was only half full. Some students sat alone at tables, their books open. Dan appreciated the impulse. Sometimes the best place to study was in the middle of a noisy bar smelling of spilled beer and stale pretzels. Dan had just settled into his favourite booth when an older woman slid into the other side.

"Hello, Dan. I heard you can do things."

She looked familiar. It took a second to come up with her name. "Professor Braight?"

"Yes. Three years ago, you took 'The Roots of the First World War' from me. Your final essay was on submarine blockades. You argued that the *Lusitania* was intentionally sacrificed. I like a good conspiracy theory."

He remembered the class. He'd taken it during his liberal arts phase a couple of majors ago. Professor Braight lectured in a dry monotone while staring up at the ceiling as if she was conversing with angels. He used to wonder if everyone in the room stayed low so that they could sneak away without her noticing. A sincere instructor but lifeless. Fifty-five, maybe older. Laughed at her own jokes.

He leaned back in the booth. "You gave me a C on that paper. What's your pleasure?"

She squirmed, glanced around, then leaned in. "My student evaluations need to be stronger this semester. The department head is basing next year's teaching assignments on 'teacher effectiveness.' If my numbers don't go up, I'll have five evening sections of Intro to American History."

"Do you have your room key?"

The professor nodded.

"I need to swing by my dorm to pick up some equipment. I'll meet you in front of the building."

Twenty minutes later, Braight opened the Freeborn Humanities building and led the way to her room.

Dan said, "All your classes are here?"

"Yes. Does it matter?"

"Well, it's easier this way." He took a handheld vacuum cleaner from his backpack and ran it over windowsills, countertops, the digital control centre at the front of the room, and the carpet—anywhere dust gathered. "Did you know that a good portion of dust is skin cells? Your students leave all kinds of fragments of themselves when they sit at a desk for a few hours a week." He checked the filter bag after a few minutes. "Now, I'll need something from you."

Professor Braight opened her chequebook.

"No, it has to be personal. What do you have in your briefcase?"

Neither the pens nor ungraded papers had the right vibration to them. "How about your hairclip?"

She looked at him doubtfully.

"Really, the hairclip will do."

Clouds moved in during the night, and the wind that cut across campus had a North Atlantic bite to it. Dan's coat wasn't up to the task. He gripped the collar tight around his neck as he walked to Professor Braight's office. A kid who'd come to him to put a hex on his parents a month ago so they'd quit nagging him about his grades passed him going the other way. He ignored Dan's wave. The boy had said, "All I need to be happy is for my parents to get off my back." He didn't look happy now.

Dan finished the spell before dawn.

Braight looked up when he put the aerosol can on her desk. "What's this?"

"Spray a little bit in your room before the students come in. It won't take much, and the effects are cumulative. Not only will your evaluations at the end be much better, but you'll find attendance will go up, and the class will be more enthusiastic. Good will toward the teacher pays off in many ways."

"What's in it? Will it hurt them?"

Dan shook his head. "It's mostly the stuff I gathered last night with a couple of extra ingredients. It's perfectly safe."

"And then they'll like me?"

She looked so desperate, so tragic, that he wished that he could give her personality lessons instead of a spell. What kind of person would go into a career, totally suck at it, and stay with it for so long? The whole transaction made him feel a little unclean.

He'd ditch class today, hang a "Do not disturb" sign on his door-knob, take a nap, read a good book.

He veered off campus and bought a lottery ticket on the way back to his dorm. An $800 instant winner, his metaphysical compensation. It didn't raise his spirits.

Thibedeau sat against Dan's dorm door, watching him walk down the empty hall. He sagged. She wasn't going away. Maybe he could just lie to her—not that he'd ever been very good at it. He thought about turning around and going back to Corner Cellars. They wouldn't open for a couple of hours, but he could spend the whole day. They served all-you-can-eat chicken wings on Wednesdays.

She stood before he reached her. "I think we got off on the wrong foot."

"You're a reporter, right? I don't talk to the press."

Kelsey looked confused. "Yes, I cover the sports beat, but that's not . . . you thought I wanted to interview you?" She smiled. "Shoot. I'm sorry. I'd just come from a volleyball game. Hadn't taken off the press pass yet." Her accent was noticeably Cajun.

Dan relaxed for the first time since he'd met her. "You from the South?"

"Baton Rouge."

"We're practically neighbours, then. New Orleans."

She extended a hand. Hesitantly, Dan took it, and a warm tide filled his arm like he'd dipped it into heated honey. His knees buckled; she staggered back a step.

"It's true," she said, her face flushed. "You can do things."

There was no point hiding the truth from her now. Kelsey clearly had other business. "I'm the BWDOC, big witch doctor on campus. Where'd you learn?"

"My grand-maman, and you?"

"Three aunts and a lot of time in private libraries." The morning was looking up. He unlocked his door. "Room's a mess, but you're welcome to come in. What can I do for you?"

Kelsey pushed the pizza boxes off the bed. "Cold air doesn't agree with me. I get nosebleeds all the time. I should have gone to Louisiana State."

Her voice reminded him of home and swamps and the way cypress trees reached into the water like giant straws. "The dorm rooms are old. Piss-poor temperature control. I bought a space heater my first year here, but you get used to it."

"I suppose." She put her hands behind her and leaned back. "I heard you solve problems for people."

"If it's possible."

"I need a tutor."

Dan shook his head. "You mean for academics?"

"No." She frowned. "I can't do anything. Grand-Maman only got me started. Basic rituals. Lots of philosophy, but nothing I can use. My family sent me here to get me away from her. They'd heard the university could give me the right classes. Not so much."

"I would have thought . . ." Dan could still feel the warmth in his arm. It had percolated into his shoulder. "You feel powerful."

"Yeah, that was weird. She told me I had a gift. But I can't do anything with it. I need to continue my studies. Lots of occult stuff in the course catalogue, but nothing . . . you know . . . in our tradition. I can't find enough in the library."

She seemed intense. Had she been keying up her courage to see him for the last week? How long had she known about him before she approached him the first time?

"What do you want to know?" The closet behind her was packed with books that Dan had gathered in his last three years. Not just the

Louisiana magic he'd learned from his aunts but African magic and Asian and European. Dan saw crossover and connections among them, powers untapped for one with aptitude, someone with a dab of conjury within, like what he felt in Kelsey when they'd touched.

Kelsey looked down into her lap. "I thought when I got to college, I would have left high school behind. People were mean there. It was all so irrelevant. In college, the students would be motivated and know where they are going, but it's worse. My roommate lives for parties and scoring drugs. The girl next door is suicidal. My chem partner admires terrorists, and those are the ones with strong feelings. So many seem to be drifting. They're at college because that is just the next thing to live through. They need help!"

She took a breath, glanced at Dan as if she expected him to laugh at her, but he listened, fascinated. "I know what you mean." He recognized a kindred spirit.

"If I could learn more, I could make a difference for people. Will you teach me?"

She moved to the bed's edge and clasped her hands in front. Her eyes glistened.

Dan thought about the unfinished econ homework for a major he didn't care about. He knew that whether he studied or not, someone would knock on his door later. Maybe they wanted money. Maybe they wished to sleep better. Maybe they were looking for a purpose in their lives.

Dan could relate.

Kelsey wanted to learn. She didn't want a spell. Her agenda was honourable. She wasn't cynical. Just being in the same room with her made him feel better. For her, purposes were meaningful. Life had possibilities.

Dan smiled at her, his breathing quickening. "You said the girl next door was suicidal?"

Kelsey nodded.

"Well, let's start with her. You need to bring me something personal that she handles a lot or a strand of hair if you can get it."

Kelsey looked hopeful. "Right now, you mean?"

"It's never too early to save someone, don't you think?"

She didn't close the door as she left.

Dan surveyed his room. If he was going to hold class here, he needed to tidy up a bit. He pulled a large trashcan from the hallway to his door. The pizza boxes went in first. Then the girly posters.

Already, he was planning a course of scholarship. First, he'd have to find out exactly what she knew. There'd be reading assignments. Maybe he could prepare a syllabus. He wondered if there was anyone else on campus with a tinge of hoodoo. How would he find them? Would they be interested in a study group?

College didn't have to be mundane. Maybe some people were here to learn for real, to make a difference.

Maybe it could be a little magical after all.

MONSTER IN THE SECOND REEL

By Richard Paolinelli

The first snowflakes of the season drifted down through the darkening sky and settled on the asphalt. Those that landed on the new 1956 Packard Clipper were melted by the warmth of the car's black exterior. In a few more hours, the snowfall would be heavy enough to make travelling along Highway 10 difficult.

Martin peered anxiously out the windshield. Had it been a mistake not to stop in Jamestown? Would he find a theatre that he so desperately needed in Steele, the small town just two miles ahead? Or would he have to try for Bismarck and pray the snowfall did not worsen?

He spared a glance at the passenger seat. An old leather-bound book lay atop a grey metal canister holding two reels of movie film, roughly twenty-five minutes in length combined. A typical movie required five times as many reels, yet whenever he showed these, the time seemed to fly by. Bizarrely, it also seemed to take an eternity to pass.

He could only hope this town had a theatre with a small-enough crowd to satisfy his needs. The theatre in Jamestown had been far too big and filled for the night's premiere showing of *Oklahoma!*. There would have been too many people inside for him to complete his task and escape unnoticed. If Steele could offer him what he needed, he could then move on to Bismarck, ditch this car that he'd taken in Chicago, and rest for a few days.

He doubted anyone had discovered the theft of the car. He'd found the dealership's owner alone, slumped over his desk, dead from an apparent heart attack. Taking advantage of the situation and the keys in the ignition, he'd thrown in his belongings and fled Chicago. He'd use his respite studying the old book, another item he'd stolen, in hopes of freeing his tormented soul from the living hell his life had become. If an answer *did* exist within, he was free. If not, he would acquire another mode of transportation and continue with what he'd been doing for the last two years: move on until he was forced to stop and feed the monster he'd inadvertently created.

Driving past the quaint "Welcome to Steele, North Dakota" sign, he spotted a gas station and café at the intersection of the highway and the main road that led into town. A half-mile after turning onto Main Street, he came upon the centre of the community, encountering the standard fare for a small Midwestern town: barber shop, drug store, county courthouse and sheriff's department, bank, and churches.

Beyond the bowling alley, he found what he'd sought: a small movie theatre, still open for the evening and showing an older movie. He doubted many of the town's five hundred residents would be inside as only four cars were parked outside near the theatre. He pulled the Packard around the corner and parked in front of the darkened office of the town's newspaper, *The Steele Ozone.*

Slipping the book into the large inner pocket of his coat, he collected his hat and the film canister and stepped out of the car into the slowly thickening snow. The air was cold and biting even for mid-October. He drew his lapels tight against it after snugging his black hat firmly down upon his greying hair. Anyone might have mistaken him for a priest if he'd been wearing a white collar. He'd actually been one once, but that was a different lifetime.

He made his way to the theatre and paused short of the ticket booth. The night's final showing of *Sudden Fear* was underway. A small sigh of relief escaped his lips. This being a school night, the film was not likely to have any children in its audience. He only needed a handful of patrons to remain behind to watch a "special sneak preview" after the film concluded. Stepping up to the window, he greeted the young woman on duty inside.

"Good evening."

"You're too late for the show, mister; it's already an hour in, at least. I can sell you a ticket for tomorrow, though?" She reached for the advance-ticket vouchers.

"No, thank you, my child. I was hoping to speak with the manager if he's available?"

"Oh, sure, just go on inside and turn right. His name is Mister Baxter. His office is right there."

"Thank you," he said as he turned away to go inside. The smell of popcorn filled his nostrils as he entered, triggering a grumbling reminder from his stomach that he hadn't eaten in several hours. He ignored both. First, he would attend to the matter at hand, and then he would eat.

At the manager's door, he knocked firmly upon the mahogany

wood. After a moment, the door swung open, and a man of Martin's age stepped out.

"Yes?" He spoke with the impatient air of someone unhappy at being interrupted. "May I help you?"

"I certainly hope you can, sir. My name is Martin, and I represent a film company out west." Prior experience had taught him the implication of Hollywood's involvement made things go much smoother. "I have here a half-hour of a film we're currently working on. I've been going to theatres, offering a sneak preview in return for the audience giving their opinions afterward.

"I'm willing to pay for the time, of course," he continued. "Perhaps after the current movie ends, we could ask those inside if they'd like to stay and participate?"

"Well." The manager hesitated. "I suppose if you paid for the theatre usage, it would be all right. But I have to warn you: there can't be more than a dozen people in there tonight. Everyone else went off to Bismarck or Jamestown to see *Oklahoma!* or are at home with their kids. It's a school night, after all. I'm not sure how much help that will be to you."

"Oh, that will be fine," Martin replied, masking his relief.

They haggled over the price, though they settled on about the same amount he'd been paying at all of the other theatres he'd visited since this nightmare began one year ago.

"Say, there's nothing funny about this film, is there?" the manager asked suddenly. "I wouldn't want to have to deal with any complaints to the sheriff."

"Oh, no, nothing like that," Martin assured, lying yet again. He'd been getting better and better at that skill with each passing day. "It's going to be another one of those monster movies that are making the rounds. I wouldn't want any children to see it, mind you, but nothing that will have your local preachers picketing your theatre."

As the time for *Sudden Fear* to end drew near, he followed the manager inside. Martin waited patiently to the side as the lights came up and the manager made the announcement. Only six people agreed to stay and watch, while the other ten declined. Martin was relieved those ten would be spared even as he steeled himself for the terror he knew lay in store for the six that remained.

He headed up into the projection room, dismissed the projectionist, and threaded the film. He'd become something of an expert at this task, too. He waited for the swinging doors below to close behind the manager and the projectionist before he turned down the house lights and started the film.

He withdrew the old book, opened it, and quietly began reading from it as the film opened on a pastoral scene with soft music playing in the background. A young boy, blonde and blue-eyed, flying a kite high against a clear blue sky, dominated the screen.

Once assured that the spell he'd cast had sealed every exit, he flipped to another page and began reading again. He did not need to look to know that as he cast this spell, everyone in the theatre had frozen. As the first reel neared its end and before it was time to switch to the second reel, he cast his third and final spell.

He closed his eyes against the coming horror that he had arranged. *Twelve more minutes.* Then he could leave this place, find something to eat, and have a few days to rest. He was weary in flesh, mind, and spirit, and there seemed to be no end to his torment in sight.

On the screen, as the second reel began, the boy, a picture of innocence itself in the first reel, transformed into a hideous monster. The creature's hairless hide was a sickly grey and covered in tumours. The eyes were an angry red, and the mouth was filled with yellowed, flesh-tearing fangs. It snarled and smashed everything in sight, then turned to directly face the audience, claws slashing as if it was trying to rip through the giant screen itself.

Martin scanned the theatre just as the six patrons began to fade out. One by one, they reappeared on the big screen. The elderly couple never even had a chance to try and flee. Little good would it have done them, anyway. They stood frozen in terror, and the beast fell upon them.

Martin turned off the sound then. He could not bear to hear the screams anymore.

The other two couples were much younger, and the two men put up a good fight. But they could not match the beast's ferocity and fell to its claws. Their female companions had made a run for it, not realizing they were trapped in a film and no help would be found. The monster ran them down and made short work of them both. Then it began to feed on its six latest victims in an orgy of flesh and blood.

———

THE MANAGER COLLECTED the meagre take from the box office, about average for a Wednesday night in Steele. They'd leave the concession area open in case anyone wanted something to take home.

Unable to do a final count until that last register was closed, he decided to check in on the sneak preview. It had been about five minutes since he'd left, and no one had walked out yet. He took that as a positive sign. If it looked good, maybe he could swing a deal to be among the first theatres in the state to show it.

He strode to the doors and stuck out a hand to swing one open without stopping. He came to a painfully abrupt halt when it refused to budge.

"What the blazes?" The manager raised a hand to his throbbing nose, which had borne the brunt of the collision. He pushed on the door again, shoved harder a third time, and repeated the process with the other door.

Neither budged in the slightest.

There was no locking mechanism on either door. Even if something had been moved in front of them, he was a strong enough man to at least make them move slightly. It was almost as if they had become solid steel, welded into place.

"Jimmy," he called out to the younger man behind the concession counter. "Some joker has the doors blocked. Run outside and come in from the back and get these doors open."

"Right away, Mr. Baxter," Jimmy replied, dashing out the front. He circled around to the side exit, which led directly to the theatre inside and could be used to leave without going through the lobby. He slipped the key into the lock, but it would not turn, no matter how hard he tried.

He abandoned this door and went to the rear of the building. A much larger door used for deliveries waited there. He slipped the key into the lock, but again, he could not get it to turn. The door would not open.

Confused, he ran back around and reported the failures to his boss.

"Impossible," Baxter exclaimed. "You're sure you were using the right keys?"

"Absolutely, sir."

Baxter shook his head. Even if the doors had been locked from the inside, Jimmy's keys should have unlocked them. He'd been

MONSTER IN THE SECOND REEL

trying to get the doors here inside to open, but not even a crowbar could gain enough purchase to budge them any more than pushing on them had.

Baxter walked over to the lobby phone and asked the operator to connect him with Sheriff Kraft's office.

ALBERT KRAFT HAD BEEN sheriff of Kidder County for ten years. He often joked he'd likely remain sheriff until his son, Arnold, replaced him. A burly man with a gentle heart, he managed to enforce the law in the small county without having to resort to heavy-handedness. Mostly, he had little to do and was only in his office this night to cover for his lone deputy, who was in Bismarck's lone hospital awaiting the arrival of his first child.

When Kraft's phone rang, he fully expected it to be his wife calling and not the manager of the theatre, sounding like he'd lost his mind.

"Sheriff Kraft," he answered.

"Al," (Baxter was an old friend), "you are not going to believe this, but some nut has locked himself and six customers inside my theatre, and I can't get inside."

Kraft chuckled. "I've told you to carry an extra set of keys with you, Bax."

"That's not what I mean. I'm in the lobby. I can't get into the theatre. He's got the outside doors locked, and we can't get the keys to work, and the lobby doors are blocked. I can't budge them at all."

"All right, Bax, I'll come over and see what I can do."

He drove the two blocks in case he was going to have to trans-port a prisoner to jail, taking notice of a brand-new car he'd never seen in town before along the way, parked his patrol car out front, and strode into the lobby less than two minutes after hanging up.

"How long has he been in there?"

"About twenty minutes now, Al. He said he had a thirty-minute film to show, some kind of sneak preview of a Hollywood movie. Paid for the use of the theatre in cash. He seemed legitimate, so I let him have at it. When I tried to go back inside to see how things were going, I couldn't get past the doors."

Kraft pushed on both. He leaned into the effort on the second try but fared no better.

"And when you tried to get in from the outside doors?" Kraft asked.

"Keys won't even turn the lock, Al. This goes well beyond strange, don't you think?" Baxter mopped his forehead with a handkerchief.

"I do. Well, we can either wait until his film runs out and the folks inside try to leave, or . . ."

With that, Kraft withdrew his nightstick and started pounding on the doors. He hoped someone inside would hear and investigate. He was still pounding away four minutes later, with no response from the other side, when the strange became the bizarre.

"In the name of God," a voice thundered from behind them, "stand away from that door!"

They turned in unison to find a man in the traditional garb of a Jesuit priest bearing down upon them. His black hair and robes moved as if blown by an unnatural wind, and his face seemed chiselled from granite. His green eyes blazed with a holy light. From a fold of his robe, he withdrew a hand axe that appeared to be made of pure gold. It was shaped like a cross, razor-sharp blades glinting on either side.

Kraft, Baxter, and young Jimmy scattered. Without pausing, the stranger gripped the axe in both hands, drew it back, and drove it into the doors as he stepped into them. The blade struck the doors, exploding them off their hinges with a thundering boom. Both doors ripped through the dark curtain that prevented the light from the lobby from reaching the theatre. The doors flew down the slope, ripped through the screen, and crashed into the wall beyond.

The priest did not hesitate, heading up the stairs to the projection room with the sheriff close behind, demanding an explanation. Baxter, Jimmy, and the woman from the now-closed ticket booth ran into the theatre below.

————

MARTIN KEPT his eyes glued on his watch. He'd seen the movie play out too often and had no desire to see it again. When the pounding on the door began, he remained unconcerned. The locking spell would hold until he departed. Once the second reel ended, he would collect the reels and utter the transport spell that would return him to his car without having to pass through the lobby. There was no way to explain the sudden disappearance of the six people who'd met their demise this night. Exhausted, he doubted he could muster another spell once he'd transported. At least, not until he'd eaten and rested.

The second reel rolled out. It was finished. He packed the reels into the container, not bothering to look down at the empty theatre, lit by the white light from the projector. He began the transport spell just as the doors below exploded open. He quickly whispered the one spell he knew from memory as he grabbed up the container and the old book.

THE PRIEST BURST into the projection room through its only door and found it empty. The projector was still on. He knew his quarry had just been here and fled, perhaps only seconds before.

The amount of effort and energy the man was expending had to be taking a great toll. Martin had to be close by, exhausted and not able to move again for a minute or two at best. But figuring out where he'd gone in time was the trick. The priest had been this close several times before and just missed putting an end to this madness.

"The doors are still locked from the inside," the priest heard the manager call out to the sheriff as he made his way down from the projection room. "I don't understand where everyone has gone. There's nowhere for one person to hide, much less seven."

"Did any of you see where he came from?" the priest inquired of the group gathered in front of the screen.

"By the time I noticed him, he was already at the window," the ticket-taker reported.

"Jimmy and I didn't see him until he was already in the lobby," Baxter added.

"Are there any cars out front that you've never seen before tonight?"

Everyone shook their heads except Kraft. "Yes," he said. "Coming over here, I passed a brand-new black Packard with no plates. Looked like there was a temporary tag in the windshield, though. I was going to go back and double-check it after I got done here."

"Where was it parked?" the priest demanded. "Tell me before he gets away again."

"About two blocks away. Out the front door and turn left."

The priest bolted back into the lobby and out the doors, the sheriff trying to keep pace. Running out into the street, the priest peered in the direction of the main highway.

No car drove in that direction. Turning his head to the south, he spotted a pair of red taillights at the end of the main street, where it stopped in front of the school.

The brake lights flared, and the car made a swift U-turn. Caught for a brief moment under a streetlamp, the priest saw it was a new black Packard. Positioning himself in the middle of the street, he held the golden cross/axe out in front of him, said a quick prayer, drew a long breath, and waited.

———

EXHAUSTED, scared, and in a strange town, Martin made a wrong turn. When his headlights caught the school building through the falling snow, marking the end of the street, he cursed his luck. Turning around, he started back in the right direction but made it only three blocks before coming to a stop in the intersection near the theatre.

Less than half a block away, right in the middle of the street, stood his hunter. Martin had been fleeing the priest for several long months. The priest's black hair and robes flowed in the wind, and not a single snowflake settled on him. His axe blazed with a holy light. He looked every bit like an avenging angel.

Which was precisely what he was, Martin allowed. A man with a badge, his gun drawn and aimed directly at Martin, was making his way down the sidewalk to get a better bead on his target. The sheriff was yelling at Martin, likely an order to get out of the car. But the only words that Martin heard came from the man directly ahead.

"Martin Edward Meadows!" The priest's voice boomed as if it were God Himself speaking. "In the name of God! I command you to surrender yourself to His judgment!"

Martin looked down at the old book. There was a spell inside that he could use to help him escape. Did he have enough strength to use it? Which man should he use it on? Would the other then be upon him before he could flee? Frozen in indecision, Martin sat in the Packard, right in the middle of the intersection, and did nothing.

Then another power—or just sheer bad luck—took a hand.

JERRY DAUBENBERGER WAS RUNNING LATE.

The weather wasn't helping, nor did his taking the wrong turn west of Steele. He was no longer on Highway 10 but rather on old Sterling Road. He'd make it to Steele, right in the middle of it, to be exact, but then he'd have to turn back to the north to get to the gas station.

Looking down at his gas gauge, he tried to determine if he was really on the wrong side of the big "E" while estimating how many miles he'd driven since filling up the last time. He wasn't paying attention to what was going on outside until it was far too late.

His heavy delivery truck smashed into the driver's side of Martin's stolen car at forty miles an hour, sending it barrel-rolling down the street. Martin was thrown from the car on its next-to-last roll, along with the old book and the film reels. The canister burst open, ejecting the reels from the car. Both settled next to the front of the Packard, which quickly caught fire. The blaze spread to the reels, and they, too, began to burn.

Kraft ran to check on the driver of the truck while the priest hurried to where Martin's broken, bloodied body lay in the centre of the street. He glanced at the burning reels of film before retrieving the old book, which he slipped into a small bag and deposited into a pocket in his robes as the sheriff walked up behind him.

"We've called for an ambulance, but there isn't one in town," Kraft reported. "It will be a while before they get here. I've called for Doc Hansen, but he lives a couple of miles out."

"There is no need," the priest replied sadly. "He has not much longer to live."

"At least it is finally over," Martin rasped out, opening one eye. He couldn't feel any pain, couldn't move his arms or legs. Even talking was difficult.

"But at what cost?" the priest asked. "How many innocent lives have paid for what you stole?"

"I wish I'd never laid eyes on that book."

"And yet you stole it from the archives in the Holy City," the priest accused. "And knowing the forbidden knowledge that lay within, you read it and used it."

"I never intended to use it, not like this," Martin gasped out, struggling to draw in air. "But what else could I do once my own son found it and used it?"

Martin drew two more painful breaths of air and coughed up a little spurt of blood. "He never intended to become a monster trapped within a reel of film," he rasped. "Never intended to kill in order to survive."

Another round of hoarse coughing shook Martin. More bright red blood stained the gathering snow a dark crimson.

"How could I abandon him once he trapped himself within that reel of film? How could I not try to find a way to free him?"

"No matter how many people you had to feed to him to keep him alive?" the priest demanded.

"Yes, damn you," Martin barked, the effort it cost him written in the pained expression on his face. "There was no price I wouldn't pay to save my son. What would you do, 'Father'? What would any father do?"

"Our Holy Father sacrificed his only son to save us all, 'Father,'" the priest retorted. "How could you not follow that example?"

Martin closed his eye, lay back in the gathering snow, and offered no defence.

"What's that?" the sheriff exclaimed.

The priest followed his gaze and saw strangely coloured wisps of smoke rising from the burning reels. They swirled around the scene, some in groups of two or more, and then drifted straight up to disappear into the night sky.

"The souls of your victims, Father Martin, are finally free," the priest said softly. "Go with God, my children."

"What in hell is that?" Kraft exclaimed in horror as a black sludge poured out of the second reel and seeped into the ground below.

Martin reopened his one working eye and watched as the sludge disappeared.

"That is all that remained of the soul of this man's cursed child," the priest replied sadly. "He has gone to his punishment, as his father will soon."

"Mercy, Father," Martin pleaded. "Please, I beg you. Pray for mercy for my son's soul if not for my own."

"Whatever mercy there may be for you and your son, it is not mine to give. You and your son have taken dozens of innocent lives. You will both face His judgment and accept either His grace or His wrath. I would not even dare to hope for His grace if I were you."

A single tear escaped Martin's eye as it closed once more. His head rolled to one side, and he exhaled one final breath.

In the distance, a siren announced that the volunteer fire department was finally on its way. Flames fully engulfed the Packard, and the film had burned to ash, leaving behind only two empty, blackened metal reels.

"Those six people inside the theatre tonight . . .?"

"Are dead," the priest finished. "They are with God now, my son, and no longer feel any pain."

"How do I explain this?" Kraft waved his hand at the wreckage. "What do I tell their families?"

"Let the car burn to the frame," the priest replied. "Gather up six containers of ash, and tell their families that they were inside the car. They died instantly and were consumed by the fire from the accident."

"Lie to them?"

"Would you rather tell them the truth? That they were fed alive to a monster and suffered that horror in their final moments? The truth will only bring needless suffering. No one else will ever meet their fate. Bring what little peace you can to those that have survived this tragedy, my son. That is truly all we can do for them."

"What happened here, Father?" Kraft demanded as the snow-fall began to increase. "You called him 'Father,' too. Why was a priest killing people?"

"He was once a favourite of the Pope himself, destined to be a Cardinal, perhaps even one day the Pope, provided he'd kept the secret of the child he'd fathered from being discovered.

"One day," the priest continued, "he came upon a book in the archives. A book so evil it should have been destroyed centuries ago. He gave into the dark temptations the book offered. His beloved son was cursed to live as a monster that fed on human flesh, trapped within a prison of celluloid. I was sent to stop him, recover the book and the film, and return them all to the Holy City if possible."

"Or kill them if it wasn't?"

"Yes, my son, that was my charge. One way or another, I had to stop the killing. God forgive me; it took me far longer to complete my task than I can bear to contemplate. I pray God will understand why it took so many months."

Martin's body slowly transformed, melting into a black puddle similar to that which had come out of the film reel. The sludge seeped into the ground and disappeared. The priest shook his head sadly, crossed himself, and turned away.

Kraft watched the burning car for a moment. "He called you Father," he said without turning. "What is your name? In case I need to contact you later?"

"My order has come to know me only as 'The Jesuit,' my son," came the reply, growing fainter and more distant by the second. "But there was once a time that I was known as 'Judas.'"

"Judas?" Kraft finally turned around. "As in Iscariot . . .?"

The sheriff's voice trailed off as he found himself all alone on the street, with no sign whatsoever of the man he'd been talking to. It was as if the priest had been swallowed whole by the drifting snow.

Or maybe he went in another direction, Kraft thought, looking straight up into the night sky.

SOUVENIRS

By Gail Z. Martin

A Deadly Curiosities Short Story

"That's everything from the estate sale." I leaned back to rest on the tall stool behind the glass counter. "What's the tally?"

"Mostly mundanes. Four 'spookies' and a couple of 'sparklers.'" Teag Logan, my best friend and assistant store manager, used the nicknames we'd developed over the years to describe the psychic resonance of the antiques that came into the shop.

"Put the spookies in the safe. I'll take another look at the sparklers, and we can research the rest for pricing." I reached for my glass to take a sip of iced tea so sweet it made my teeth vibrate, and I pushed a strand of strawberry-blonde hair out of my eyes.

I'm Cassidy Kincaide, owner of Trifles and Folly, an antiques and curio shop in historic, haunted Charleston, South Carolina. The shop has been in my family for nearly four hundred years, and we've got a couple of secrets. First is that along with being a great place to find vintage gifts, our real job is getting haunted and cursed items out of the wrong hands and off the market. And second, is that my business partner is a nearly six-hundred-year-old vampire, and we're part of an alliance of mortals and immortals who save the world from supernatural threats far more often than anyone ever suspects.

Charleston deserves its reputation as one of the most haunted locations in the country. It's a glittering city built on rivers of blood, earning its wealth and prestige from the misery of enslaved and indentured people. That stain runs deep, tainting every corner of the city's history and leaving an indelible mark.

But Charleston has newer ghosts as well, people who found their way to the "Holy City" and never wanted to leave, even after death. Ghosts like it here, and as long as they don't cause harm, my friends and I don't try to make them move on.

"Have any plans for the weekend?" Teag asked as he used iron tongs to place the questionable objects in a special bag woven through with iron and silver. Once he put the bag in the large lead-lined safe in the office, the combined dampening effects of the protective metals would keep its negative resonance in check until we could pass the pieces along to be neutralized or destroyed.

"I haven't had time to plan anything. It's been pretty busy lately." I used a different set of tongs to put the "sparklies" in another box. I'm a psychometric, which means I can read the history or magic of items by touching them. It comes in handy in this job, but it also means I need to be very careful because a strong impression from an object has often put me flat on my butt—or knocked me out. Teag's my wingman for that sort of thing. We've been through a lot together.

"I think Kell and I are going to stay home, order in takeout, and binge-watch a couple of shows online," I added. "Are you and Anthony doing anything special?"

"The never-ending wedding planning saga continues," Teag answered after disappearing into the office for a few moments. He pushed his chin-length dark hair behind his ears, rocking the trendy cut. "I'd fantasize about eloping, but even that requires advance planning. I'm almost ready to fly to Vegas and find an Elvis chapel."

Teag and his fiancé were the last people I could imagine getting hitched by an Elvis impersonator, so I knew the stress had to be getting to them.

"You'll figure everything out, and it will end up being exactly what you both need," I assured him. "I have faith in you."

The bell over the door rang, and I glanced up as a woman walked into the shop. She looked to be in her fifties, trim but not too thin. Everything from her hair to her nails to the classic twinset she wore suggested comfort if not precisely wealth.

"I'm looking for Cassidy Kincaide," she said. I met her blue eyes and saw determination but also a tiredness in her face that even well-applied makeup couldn't hide.

"I'm Cassidy. How can I help you?"

"I think my father is being haunted, and I don't know how to make it stop."

Most people don't bring issues like that to an antique shop, but over the years, Trifles and Folly has gained a reputation for being the place that handles the "weird" problem items. Folks don't know the half of it since we've not only dealt with vengeful ghosts and restless spirits but cursed items, supernatural creatures, and paranormal entities. We've even averted an apocalypse or two, and nobody's any wiser—which is just how we like it.

"Please, come in. Let's go in the back, and you can tell me what's going on," I offered.

Teag gave me a nod, assuring me that he would cover the store since our usual assistant, Maggie, was on vacation.

We sat, and I poured tea for both of us. My visitor clasped her hands in front of her on the break-room table and took a deep breath. "I'm Patti Sanderson. My father, Ed, is eighty years old. He's lived by himself since my mother died a few years ago, but his health took a turn for the worse, and instead of coming home from the hospital, he went straight into a nursing home. They told me he's only got a few more weeks to live."

Patti took a sip of her tea, and I suspected she needed it to collect herself. "Do you believe in ghosts?" she said.

"Yes." I didn't hesitate. Ghosts, magic, and supernatural creatures weren't theoretical to me. My friends and I had dealt with them time and again. I knew they were real.

"Then maybe you won't think I'm crazy."

"I won't," I promised.

"My father had a younger brother, Tom. When they were kids, the family would go to Isle of Palms in the summer, and back then, in the years after the Second World War, there was an amusement park nearby. It's long gone now, but it was the highlight of their vacation back then. They went once or twice each year, and my dad and his brother would make a big production out of picking the souvenir for each visit."

I stayed quiet, trying not to let my mind jump ahead. It wouldn't be the first time that a problem arose because an elderly person was removed against their will from their home and their possessions—or the first to trigger ghostly activity in response.

"When Dad was twelve, Tom was ten. They went to Isle of Palms, and on the last day, Tommy drowned in the pool. Dad was

shattered. He and his brother had been extremely close," Patti went on. "They didn't have grief counsellors back then, so Dad dealt with it in his own way. He made a shrine of sorts out of all the souvenirs—including the one they had just bought earlier on the day Tommy died."

"Over the years, sometimes the items were in a box or on a table, but he always kept them close. When I was a kid, I thought I caught him talking to them, and he got angry and snapped at me about respecting his privacy," Patti recalled with a sad smile.

"These last few years, when he was alone after Mom passed, he didn't try to hide the shrine. He added Tommy's picture to the souvenirs and kept it all on the top of his dresser. I figured he was lonely, and it reminded him of better times. And I wondered if he was starting to get dementia," she added, "but I didn't think it hurt anything to let him have his memories."

"What changed?" I had a strong suspicion that I already knew the answer.

"Dad didn't get to return home after the hospital. I went to the house and got him some clothing, but at first, he was too sick to get dressed or get out of bed," Patti replied. "But as soon as he could talk, he wanted to know that the shrine was safe and asked me to bring it to him."

"I'm guessing that you couldn't do that."

Patti sighed. "I spoke to the people at the nursing home, and they said they don't like for residents to bring anything that is valuable or precious. Things can be broken or misplaced. They don't want the liability.

"I started to go to the house to get it ready to sell. It was the first I'd been alone there since I moved out to go to college. Nothing ever seemed odd to me back then, but now I couldn't shake the feeling that I was being watched." Patti shivered, and I knew it was nothing to do with the iced tea.

"I'd hear sounds coming from other parts of the house when I knew no one was there but me. Small things would move around from one visit to the next, even though I was the only one with access. The neighbours told me that they heard doors open and close and saw lights. I even put up a security camera, but it didn't catch anyone."

"What do you think is going on?"

"I think that either Tommy's ghost clung to those souvenirs or all of the energy Dad put into keeping his memory over the years brought something of him back," Patti said. "I know that sounds crazy."

I shook my head. "Not at all. And both possibilities are likely. Has the ghost hurt anyone?"

"No. I didn't feel threatened or unwelcome in the house, just . . . observed. And a little creeped out," she admitted. "But the incidents are happening more often, and I'm worried about what the ghost might do the longer time goes on."

If Tommy's spirit had been keeping his big brother company all these years, then the abrupt change could be as upsetting to the ghost as it was to Ed. Some revenants could cling to a place for centuries and not become a problem, while others gradually lost themselves and turned angry and harmful.

"Could you take me to see the shrine? And would you mind if I asked a friend of mine who's a medium to go with us?" Since we encountered all kinds of paranormal problems, I had friends with a wide variety of psychic and magical abilities who were ready to help.

Patti slumped in relief. "Thank you. I haven't been able to tell anyone else about this. I was afraid you'd think I was nuts. But it's been weighing on my mind. And I'd like to be able to give my father some peace in his last days."

I explained the situation to Teag, then called Alicia Peters, a gifted medium, and asked for her help.

Patti and I drove together to Ed's house, and Alicia agreed to meet us there. The tidy ranch house on a quiet side street far from Charleston's historic district looked peaceful and well-loved.

"Dad liked to garden and putter around the house," Patti recounted in a fond tone. "He only stopped when he went into the hospital. I hired a yard company to keep it looking nice. The first group quit after one or two visits—said the house made them uncomfortable. The team that replaced them will only come out around noon, never later in the day."

I spotted Alicia as she parked and waved for her to join us. Alicia is in her thirties, plump and unassuming, with friendly blue eyes and wavy black hair that falls to her shoulders. She has a pulled-together casual style that puts people at ease. I made introductions and looked to her as we stood outside. "Picking up anything?"

She nodded. "Definitely a ghost, one that's been around for a long time. I don't think he's angry, but he's definitely agitated."

I don't generally see ghosts unless they can make themselves visible. But the hair on the back of my neck stood up as we approached the front door. Alicia looked deep in thought, and I knew from past situations that she was likely centring her concentration and preparing to open herself up to her psychic gift and communicate with the spirit.

Patti unlocked the door, and we stepped inside. Aside from a slight musty smell from disuse and a faint layer of dust, the house was as well-kept on the inside as its façade suggested. A worn recliner sat next to a packed bookshelf and across from a large-screen TV. The furnishings looked comfortable, an unremarkable mix of mid-century pieces.

"Back here," Patti said.

We followed Patti into the master bedroom. She had clearly done some cleaning up since her father's last days in the house, and the room now felt empty, unlived-in.

Alicia gravitated toward the dresser. Spread out across the top were the sort of knick-knacks two young brothers would have considered trophies of a summer adventure, all emblazoned with the logo of the long-defunct Isle of Palms Park.

A faded pennant lay next to a small decorative plate and a mug, a ceramic bell, a coin bank, and keychains. The framed black-and-white photograph of a smiling young boy sat to one side, looking over the carefully arranged memorabilia.

I knew collectors who had much larger stashes without attracting ghostly attention. But it was clear to me just how dear these pieces of a childhood cut short must have been to Ed and how broken he had been by his brother's death to care so lovingly for the reminders for so many years. Strong emotions could definitely "charge up" objects and anchor a ghost.

"The amusement park closed not long after Tommy's death," Patti said, "after a fire wiped out the big ballroom. The land got sold off, mostly to condos and hotels. Dad always visited a spot on the beach that he said had been part of the old park. He went every year until now. I think it was a promise he'd made to Tommy all those years ago."

I glanced at Alicia, who had a far-away look on her face. "Is Tommy here?" I asked.

Alicia turned to face me, and I knew from the look in her eyes that she was channelling the ghost. "Eddie went away." Her voice was slightly higher than normal, childlike. "He's been gone a long time. He didn't visit like he said he would."

I could hear bewilderment and fear in her tone, Tommy's feelings at being left alone after so long.

Patti gave me a questioning look, and I nodded.

"Ed . . . Eddie . . . got sick," Patti replied. "He's very old now, and he can't live here anymore."

"We stay together," the ghost insisted.

I spotted a wooden jewellery case on the top of the chest of drawers and had an idea. "Do you think your father would be able to travel one more time to Isle of Palms?"

"I'll have to ask the nurses, but if we used a wheelchair and didn't stay too long, I think it would work," she replied. "He's mentioned wanting to go, just like he asks for the souvenirs."

"What if we put the pieces from the shrine in that jewellery box and took it with us? Having the souvenirs and visiting the site might give both Tommy and Ed closure," I suggested.

"I'd like to go to the park again," Tommy spoke up through Alicia. "I miss Eddie."

"If we arrange to go, will you stop bothering Patti when she comes to the house and scaring the yard crew?" I asked.

"I didn't mean to be bad," the voice said with a child's petulance. "I just wanted to get someone's attention so they'd find Eddie."

"Eddie misses you, too," I told the ghost. "We need to go now, but we'll be back and take you to him," I promised. "Can you say goodbye to Alicia for now?"

"I like her. She can hear me. Okay. Bye."

I could see the change come over Alicia as the spirit she had been channelling let go. Her body lost its tension, and her expressions were once more her own.

"I think you two can handle it from here," Alicia said. "I don't need to be there. They just need to see each other."

Patti emptied the jewellery box and then placed the souvenirs inside with reverent care.

"We'll see you very soon, Tommy," I said to thin air, hoping the ghost could hear me. "Be good."

———

THE NEXT DAY I picked up Patti, and we drove to Ed's nursing home, a quiet complex out on the edge of the city. Patti and a nurse helped Ed into the passenger seat and folded his wheelchair to put in the trunk.

Ed had the haggard, sallow look of a man on borrowed time. Wispy grey hair framed a lined face, but his faded blue eyes were alight with excitement. His bony hands trembled as he held onto the wooden case in his lap, veins clearly visible through paper-thin skin.

"Patti says we're going to Isle of Palms," he said as she got into the back seat, and I started the car. "I'm overdue." I could hear an echo of the boy he had been, eager to go on another summer adventure.

It took less than half an hour to drive to the beach town. On the way, Ed reminisced about the Ferris wheel and the carousel, the "best hot dogs he'd ever eaten," and the pavilion where the bands played. He matched each souvenir to the year of the vacation and told stories about pranks he and Tommy had played on each other, fondness clear in his voice.

When I pulled into the parking space, he patted the box. "We're back, Tommy," he murmured with a contented smile.

The wheelchair couldn't navigate the beach, but the access

point had a sidewalk leading to a small cement patio with a view of the ocean.

"This will do just fine," Ed assured us. Patti pushed his chair into position and locked the wheels as Ed clutched the precious box on his lap.

"Do you mind if I sit with Tommy for a few minutes, just the two of us?" he asked.

Patti smiled and patted his shoulder. "Take all the time you need. I know you've missed each other."

As we walked away, I heard Ed talking to Tommy in a quiet voice, and while I couldn't hear his words, the affection in his tone was unmistakable. My heart broke for the brothers who had been separated far too young and whose bond had still been forged strong enough to carry on for nearly seventy more years.

Patti and I withdrew to a spot in the shade where we could keep an eye on Ed but give him privacy.

"Thank you," she said. "I wouldn't have known how to do this for him without the help of you and your friend. I think he and Tommy both needed this." Her voice caught, and I didn't blame her because I was teary-eyed too.

"Sometimes, when people complete an important task, it gives them permission to move on," I said, gently warning her that our outing might hasten Ed's departure.

She nodded. "I know. I've had the feeling that Dad was ready to go—he just didn't want to leave without Tommy. They say he's not in pain, but he fades more every time I visit. I know he loves me, but Mom and Tommy are waiting for him."

Half an hour later, when we went to take Ed back to the car, we found him slumped in his chair like he was napping, but he was unresponsive, still holding tight to the box. Patti called the EMTs, but we both knew they wouldn't rouse him. We waited together for the ambulance to take Ed's body, and Patti retrieved the precious box.

When the paperwork was done, we drove back to Charleston with Patti in the front seat, where Ed sat earlier that day.

"I expected it to go this way," she said after we'd driven a few miles in silence. "I'd have been surprised if he'd come back with us. I'm going to miss him terribly, but I know it was his time."

"What will you do with the box?" I couldn't help asking, even though it was really none of my business. Alicia would know for certain, but I strongly suspected we'd seen the last of Tommy's ghost.

"I'll have it buried with him. He has a plot right next to where Mom is," she said. "That way, if there's any—what's the word you used? Resonance? If there's any of that remaining, he and Tommy will be together."

By the time we got back to town, the shop was closed, and night had fallen. I walked Patti to her car, and she assured me she would be okay to drive home. She put the box on the front seat and transferred the wheelchair to her trunk, then thanked me again and drove away.

My phone rang as I got in my car, and I saw Teag's number.

"Everything go okay?" he asked.

Tomorrow, I'd tell him the whole story. Tonight, my mind was too full of what had happened to talk about it.

"Yes," I told him. "It was a perfect evening."

———

AUTHOR'S NOTE:

If you liked Cassidy and the Trifles and Folly gang, they star in my Deadly Curiosities series.

NINETEENTH-CENTURY VASE

By David Liss

"It's from the nineteenth century," the man said. "Do you recognize it?"

"Oh, yes." She held the vase in her gloved hands; rotated it under the lamp. She was no longer determining its authenticity, having moved beyond that almost as soon as she glanced at it. She couldn't be sure the man knew exactly what he had, but she suspected he was testing her honesty. She had been buying and selling antiques for fifteen years and knew all the moves.

"Have you had it a long time?" She couldn't quite put a lid on her enthusiasm. Raymond used to say her blue eyes turned bluer. He said they sparkled when she was on the verge of something. She didn't know if that was still true or if it ever was, and even if it were, she didn't think the man would notice. He would not be interested in an old woman's eyes.

He was perhaps forty, beginning to bald, clean-shaven, though the cuts on his neck suggested clean-shaven for the first time in a while. His polo shirt had the perfectly smooth quality and hard creases of something that had not gone through the wash a dozen times. Had he wanted to impress her? Very likely. Bringing that vase to this shop *could* be a coincidence, but she doubted it. No, he wanted *her* opinion. Normally, she found it all so tedious, the inability to escape her past, but not today. Not with this vase.

"It's been in my family for some time," the man said. "My father recently passed, and now it's come into my possession."

"And you're local?" She knew he wasn't. She also thought she should have offered some words of condolence, but the moment had passed, and no one wanted platitudes from a stranger. Better to withhold them.

They stood in the back room of her shop, surrounded by shelves of clocks and mirrors and old toys, typewriters and cookpots and binoculars. Pressed against the walls were tables and chairs, cabinets and wardrobes. Everywhere were stacks of porcelain services and tea sets and boxes of cutlery. Everything was dusty and faded and yet remarkable. Each piece told a story, had moved through lives. Everything had withstood wave upon wave of use and emotion and indifference, and now it sheltered briefly under her protection before moving once more into a new person's life, becoming part of a new story.

The Antiquarian also kept her workspace in this room and had the vase set on a protective cloth on her examination table. It wasn't unusual to bring customers back here, not if they had something special, and this surely qualified. The man had come in shortly before six in the evening, and when she saw what he took out of his leather shoulder bag, she walked over to the door and flipped the sign to *closed*. It never occurred to her to worry about bringing a stranger into her backroom when Suze wasn't around. No one carrying something so precious would be planning a robbery.

"I'm from the city," the man explained as she turned over the vase, feeling a slight bump on its base. "I'm visiting friends for the weekend, and they suggested I bring the vase with me, what with all the antiques shops in town. They thought I should find out if it is a real . . ." The man reached for the name.

The Antiquarian squinted over a magnifying eyepiece. "It is, indeed, a Hodges. There's no doubt in my mind. You know of Margaret Anne Hodges?"

"A little," Fletcher said without much enthusiasm. "Wikipedia and that sort of thing."

She returned to her work, reviewing another slight imperfection, an almost imperceptible chip along the inner rim. "A remarkable potter. The combination of chinoiserie and more, let us say, mystic elements was most unusual. Her work was treasured by the most celebrated occultists and spiritualists of her time. Aleister Crowley owned two pieces, though he sold them when he began to burn through his money. Madame Blavatsky had four. Only three dozen in total were known to exist, and then, of course, with the rivalries among members of the Golden Dawn, she began to —" The Antiquarian stopped herself. She would not ramble on. "But I presume you did not come for an art history lesson, Mister . . .?" She gestured toward him, inviting him to give his name.

"Brad Fletcher." He thrust out his hand for her to shake. His hands were big, and hers tiny.

"I'm called the Antiquarian," she told him.

"Fitting, I guess. Is that a legal name—like Madonna?"

"It's my name," she told him, meeting his gaze.

He shrugged. "Understood. Anyhow, what I know about Hodges I learned from the internet. Her occult interests. The people she associated with. All that stuff. Not that I really care, but I guess some people do."

The Antiquarian removed her eyepiece. She studied Fletcher for signs of embarrassment. She did not see any, but she decided it was time to stop avoiding the issue. "Mr. Fletcher, is that why you brought it to my shop when you had so many to choose from?"

"Of course. It just made sense." He evidently had no idea that he should be embarrassed.

The Antiquarian sighed. "If your friends are local, they likely told you I prefer not to discuss that period of my life. I have no interest in doing business with anyone who comes to my shop to talk about my past."

"I once went to an Anne Perry book signing," Fletcher said, "and someone brought up the . . . you know." He made a gesture meant to indicate head-bashing. "Very awkward. Look, I don't want to make you uncomfortable. I just thought you, in particular, might have an interest in a Hodges vase, and you might be more inclined to take it off my hands."

"Take it off your hands?" The Antiquarian laughed. "You're very much mistaken if you think I have the money to buy it from you."

"What do you think it's worth?"

"The different vases are of differing value," the Antiquarian explained, "but wherever this one falls on the spectrum, it's more than I can afford."

"Then maybe you know someone who will want it," Fletcher plowed on, oblivious. "I thought you might have some connections or know people with a special interest in this sort of thing. I guess I wasn't thinking things through. I mean, if you weren't really doing what you claimed at the time . . ." He trailed off like a man who knew he'd stepped in it. He shook his head and blushed.

The Antiquarian raised an eyebrow. Normally, she would turn away, say she was very busy, and ask Suze to step in and help him while she retired to the back. But Suze hadn't come back from her errand yet, and this was a Hodges. It was genuine. She couldn't let it get away, and so, for the first time since she opened her shop, she said something to a customer about her old life.

"We were not frauds," she told him, placing the steel into her voice that always made Raymond glow with pride. "No matter what you heard. Never. My late husband had an inclination toward the theatrical. That much is true. He had no qualms about putting on a show for those who hired us. He believed they expected as much, and the truth is that intervention in the esoteric is often less dramatic than people expect. Clearing a house of a poltergeist involves far less ghostly shrieking and supernatural atmospheric events than movies have made us expect. So, my husband provided drama. Some electronic work. Tasteful pyrotechnics. Sound effects. That did not make us frauds. It didn't mean what we did was any less real."

Fletcher grinned. It was the first time he'd smiled since entering the shop. "I guess you do discuss that period of your life."

If she were going to walk away, it would be now. It wasn't as though she needed the money. Despite Raymond and Georgette Callaghan having been labelled frauds, their books remained in print and generated a healthy stream of royalties. Hollywood studios and production companies still came calling to buy screen rights. The shop made money, though not a lot of it. And that was fine. She ran it out of love for forgotten things that deserved to be remembered. She could live without one more forgotten thing, but it was a Hodges, and she'd seen one before. She'd dealt with one before. Now she had the chance to do so again and to turn her back because of a principle she could not fully articulate seemed foolish.

She could handle it quietly, of course. She would keep things professional. She didn't need to trade on her name, though everyone knew who she was. She and her husband had been celebrities of a sort in the 1980s and '90s, travelling the country performing seances and exorcisms and investigating hauntings. They were guests on talk shows, invited to give university lectures, and together had authored more than a dozen bestselling books recounting their exploits.

They had done good work. She would privately, quietly, defend that work, but she would not fight a losing battle. She cherished the memories of who she had been, but she could not be Georgette Callaghan anymore. She was the Antiquarian now. It was enough.

Though perhaps she could be a little Georgette Callaghan for the sake of the Hodges vase.

She tossed her head, a gesture meant to reset the conversation, and peered more closely at the central image on the vase, a painting of a stylized Mesopotamian figure, wide-eyed and square-bearded. The painting had a faded look, like a piece of statuary in the British Museum. And yet, it was so much more than that. It looked alive and vital, like so much of Hodges's work. The image captured some raw and essential power: creation and destruction, a power to command the heavens. Mountains rose and fell at its command. It could bring forth the rains and set the course of rivers. There was no doubting it. Hodges had painted a god of enormous power.

With one hand still touching the Hodges, as if it might run away, the Antiquarian pivoted to the bookcase behind her. When she turned around, she held an oversized softbound volume. The cover showed a vase very much like the one on the table, though more inclined to greens and yellows than blue and reds. *Its* central design was a stylized rendering of Apollo riding his sun chariot, an image suggesting the mystical more than the mythological. This was not a children's story, no sweet etiology to explain the movements of heavenly bodies. This Apollo was a god, a force of nature, a thing of immense power that could be experienced, but not understood, by human beings. The stories were attempts to grasp a concept beyond perception. The painting on the vase was that concept of the unimaginable turned into image.

Art was subjective, but there was no looking at a Hodges vase and wondering why people valued them. No one had ever captured the wonder and awe and power of ancient beliefs quite this way.

She began to flip through the pages of the book, trying to find a match for the disturbing image on the vase on her worktable.

"Though she limited herself only to images and did not write," the Antiquarian said distantly, "Hodges was in every way as visionary as Blake. Even so, her work was almost forgotten. As you've already brought up my past, I suppose there's no harm in saying that had it not been for the Vandover case and the film based on our book about that case, it's unlikely she'd be much remembered today. It renewed interest in her vases."

The Vandover film was a fictionalized account of the events surrounding a Hodges piece somehow disconnected from time. This temporal instability created effects very much like those of a haunting, which had made the situation in the Vandover house-hold difficult to diagnose. The vase also attracted certain kinds of spiritual entities, which further complicated the situation.

It was one of Raymond and Georgette Callaghan's most famous—or infamous—cases. A child had died, and the parents sued, blaming the Callaghans for misleading them, for dissuading them from pursuing more efficacious mental-health answers. It was during that case that Raymond's theatrical inclinations came out, and the world assumed the worst. It was the case that ruined the Callaghans, though there were still minority voices that swore they told the truth.

"The thing is," the Antiquarian said as she flipped through the book, "there's no record of this vase. This is a complete catalogue of her work, and it's not here."

"And you're sure it's real?" Fletcher asked.

The Antiquarian turned the vase around, inviting Fletcher to look at the central image on the body. "No one else could create an image like this. No one. Even photographs fail to produce the wonder and terror that looking at a Hodges instills in the viewer. She simply cannot be faked."

"So, it's real but previously unknown? That's what you're telling me? That makes it worth more, right?"

"If auctioned properly," the Antiquarian began. "With the right introductions, the right presentation, I should think seven or eight million. Perhaps more than that. The appetite for a new Hodges could be . . . quickened. If one knows how."

Fletcher's eyes were wide now. He reached out to touch the vase, then withdrew as if afraid to destroy this thing that he believed would change his life. "And you think you know how?"

"You came to me for a reason," the Antiquarian said. "I have avoided wading back into those waters, but for something like this . . . I don't know. I'd have to think about it, and given the value of the piece, you may wish to take it elsewhere. There are people with more experience overseeing high-value auctions."

"But no one with more of *your* kind of experience."

The Antiquarian's smile was tight and brief, but there was no denying his point. If she were to take command of this, it would be because of who she had been, not who she now was. "May I take a few photos? I won't share them with anyone without your permission."

"Of course," Fletcher said.

The Antiquarian turned on a lamp and adjusted its gooseneck before snapping a few images with her phone, capturing several different angles. She then took some video, rotating the vase with her hand.

When she was done and had turned off the lamp and put the phone away, she cleared her throat theatrically. "Mr. Fletcher, how would you would like to proceed? It's entirely up to you. I would never pressure you, and I'm not entirely certain I want to involve myself. I need a little time to consider my options, but I think there's a good chance that I would like to shepherd this item through auction. You understand that there are certain fees I would take from the proceeds?"

"I understand," Fletcher said. "May I have the vase back?"

"Oh, yes. Of course." The antiquarian handed it over with both hands, unwilling to let go until Fletcher took it in both of his. "For transport, I would suggest a lined case. You want to make certain—"

It was the movement that stopped her voice more than the sound. Fletcher raised the vase above his head before hurling it to the parquet floor. A few shards went flying, pinging against the walls, but it mostly collapsed in on itself, landing as though it were no more than a pile of dirt. A few larger shards remained, but most pieces were no bigger than a pebble. There could be no hope of piecing it back together.

The Antiquarian stood motionless. Shocked. Horrified.

Fletcher did not wait for her to recover. Seizing a broom and dustpan from a corner of the room, he swept up the remains of the vase. Once he'd filled the dustpan, he tipped the contents into a paper grocery bag he'd brought, evidently for that purpose. He rolled up the top and handed the bag to the Antiquarian. She would not take it, so Fletcher placed the bag on the table.

"Why?" she asked. "Why would you do that? It was unique. A treasure. If you wanted to destroy it, why do it in front of me? There are people who dislike me, who have been trained to dislike me. But to destroy something priceless just to spite me? It makes no sense."

Fletcher only smiled at the questions. "Thank you for your time," he said.

He left the back room, and a moment later, the bells on the door jingled as he walked out onto the quaint downtown street. She briefly heard the din of children gathered at the ice cream shop three doors down.

THE ANTIQUARIAN DID NOT DRINK OFTEN, but she drank that night. She sat in the back room at an old kitchen table just a few feet from where she'd examined the Hodges vase. She'd been joined by her assistant, Suze, a bottle of bourbon between them.

Suze had been working with the Antiquarian for almost ten years now. She was a heavyset woman in her thirties or forties, her short hair maybe butch, maybe practical. She had a pierced left eyebrow and, currently, green hair. The Antiquarian didn't know much about Suze's personal life other than that she was devoted to her German shepherd, Theo, whom she brought to the shop as often as not.

They were work friends. They had never socialized outside the shop, never shared a drink anywhere but in the backroom. This was satisfying for the Antiquarian, who did not consider herself a social person. Since Raymond's death, she had settled into solitude and become comfortable with it. Consequently, Suze, for all the distance between them, was her best friend.

"It had to be a fake," Suze said as she pulled the bottle of Buffalo Trace from the centre of the table and poured herself a hearty portion. Her fourth, maybe. Fifth? The Antiquarian had lost count, though Suze showed no signs of inebriation. She never did.

Fortified by a hearty swallow, Suze tilted her chair back and adopted her thinking-seriously face, eyes scrunched shut, lips pressed into a line. "No way it could be real. Why would he destroy something like that in front of you? To make a point? What point?"

"Something to do with the Vandover case," the Antiquarian said. "It can't be a coincidence."

"I bet he was connected with it. Did the kid who died have siblings? This guy would be about the right age."

"I don't think so," the Antiquarian said. "We never saw one, and the family gave enough interviews, all huddled together. If there had been a brother, I would remember."

"Then a cousin. A best friend. I don't know. A sister who transitioned." Suze finished her bourbon and poured another. "I'll look into it."

"Don't bother. It's not your problem. It's not even my problem."

Suze grinned. "Research is part of my job. This is research. I promise not to make waves or draw any attention. Maybe he's gone forever, but it's best to be sure. Just in case."

H E   W A S   N O T   G O N E   F O R E V E R. The next day, Fletcher returned at about the same time, minutes before closing. He wore another polo shirt, also new-looking, but the same khaki pants as the day before—the Antiquarian recognized a small food stain on the left leg. And he was grinning.

"You," she said. She looked toward her phone, wondering if she should call the police—as if destroying your own valuable piece were somehow a crime. Suze was gone for the day, having left early because she had "a thing." Her appointments and engagements were always phrased in ambiguous terms. The Antiquarian was all alone with a man who would destroy something worth millions just to provoke her.

"Take a look at the pieces of the vase."

"Get out," the Antiquarian said.

"Just look at them," he said. "Go get them."

For some reason, she hadn't wanted to keep the bag in the back room. She hadn't wanted to throw it away either, in case she needed it for evidence—though of what, she could not say. She'd ended up leaving it by the register, so it would be handy if the police came by and started asking about an antique-vase smasher.

She just wanted him to leave, so she reached under the counter and lifted up the bag, which felt more unbalanced, as though . . . *as though it contained a vase!* When she unfurled the opening and peered in, she saw it, whole and unbroken. She lifted it from the bag.

"You broke in here?" she asked. "Replaced it with a forgery? Why?"

"It's not a forgery," Fletcher said. "You said yourself you can't capture what makes a Hodges special, not even with a photograph."

It was true. She could see it was real. She could feel the uneasy power of the central image if she tried to look at it for too long. Only a genuine Hodges could create that effect.

"Then a duplicate? Hodges made two identical vases? Then why destroy the other one? A matching pair would have been even more valuable!"

"Not a duplicate," Fletcher said. "It's the same vase you examined yesterday."

The Antiquarian took it, noticing the slight bump on the base, the tiny chip in the interior rim. So, not a duplicate.

"How?" the Antiquarian asked, all her anger gone. She was left with nothing but wonder.

Fletcher grinned. "It's from the nineteenth century."

———————

THE ANTIQUARIAN FELT her anger ebbing, relief rushing in to fill her hollow spaces. Once again at her worktable, she held the vase, examining it with her eyepiece. She turned it over, noting its unique details. Now she consulted her phone, the photos she'd taken the previous day, confirming what her eyes and her hands told her.

"I don't understand."

Fletcher grinned again. "It's from the nineteenth century," he repeated.

"You keep saying that," the Antiquarian snapped. "I know it's from the nineteenth century. What I don't understand is why—"

She stopped herself because now she did understand. It all became clear to her.

"How many times have you destroyed it?" she asked.

"This was the fifth," Fletcher said. "The first time was by accident, as you'd probably guess. Then I had to test it to make sure I was not imagining things."

The Antiquarian shook her head. "You don't think that we can put this in a catalogue, do you? That the vase is somehow rooted in the period in which it was created? That it will remake itself if destroyed?"

"You'll document it," Fletcher said. "Create a short film in which you run the experiment."

"No one will believe it," the Antiquarian said. "Especially coming from me."

"The fact that you are the one presenting it in earnest, asking people to believe, is what will get this vase attention. It will go viral. They will be talking about it on social media, on cable news. TikToks and whatever. This will be a huge story. People don't have to believe it, Ms. Callaghan. They just need to know it's a story."

"No one calls me that anymore," she snapped. "I'm the Antiquarian now."

Fletcher shrugged. He wouldn't get it. Few people could. "For this, you're going to want to be Georgette Callaghan."

She opened her mouth to object, but she knew he was right. Hadn't she thought the same thing herself?

The bearded god on the vase seemed to gaze back in response to her scrutiny. "The image is clearly of ancient Near Eastern design," the Antiquarian said. "Almost certainly Mesopotamian."

"It's Enki," Fletcher told her in a somewhat disinterested tone, as though discussing matters of insurance or storage. "The Sumerian creation god, but also a trickster. Associated with medicine and knowledge."

"Of course," the Antiquarian said. "Hodges was fascinated by Sumerian mythology. I recall that from when I researched her for the . . . for the Vandover case. She often performed rituals designed to commune with the Sumerian gods. It's considered odd that she never included one of them in her work."

"Clearly, she did," Fletcher said.

The Antiquarian blinked several times, formulating her many questions. "What do you know of its provenance? Can we explain why it was never previously catalogued?"

Fletcher shook his head. "It was in my family for a long time, but I didn't know about it until I was an adult, shortly after I moved out of the house. My parents kept it hidden away. I think they knew . . . they knew something, I suspect, but I don't know how much. And they had hard times, financially speaking, but they never sold it."

"Why not?"

Fletcher looked away, as if to avoid something distasteful. "We didn't really talk much. We were estranged. To be honest, I was surprised my father left me anything."

"And you're sure you want to part with it?"

"It's a nice piece, and it would be great to keep it in the family, but it's hard to say no to that kind of money."

The Antiquarian considered this for a moment. "I still have some connections. I can find someone to put together a short film. We'll have to destroy the vase again. Are you comfortable with that?"

"Sure. It always comes back."

"There is always the possibility that the vase only has a limited number of, I don't know, charges, let's call it. That it might *not* come back. I can't promise you there is no risk."

"I think we can roll the dice one more time. After that, it won't be our concern."

The Antiquarian nodded. "Very well. I'll make some calls. I should have some information for you in a week or so. Maybe less.

Can I . . . that is, would you feel comfortable leaving the vase with me? I'd like to examine it further."

"I'd rather hold on to it," Fletcher said.

The Antiquarian bit her lower lip and nodded. "Of course. I'll speak to you soon. And thank you for bringing this to me."

Fletcher took the vase back from her hands. Did he have to tug just a little to get it free? Later, she would think he had. She hadn't wanted to let it go, but it didn't belong to her, and really, what choice did she have? Still, to be in the presence of a Hodges again. It was no small thing.

IT HADN'T BEEN easy for her to make the calls, to dredge up that part of her past, to use her old name. Her deadname, as the young people would say. But Fletcher was right. For this, she had to be Georgette Callaghan, and she would be. The money would not be insignificant. Fifteen percent of what the Hodges would bring at auction would be no trivial sum, but that wasn't really the point, was it?

When she and Raymond had been the Callaghans, they had done amazing things. They had confronted evil and triumphed. Yes, there had been some failures. The Vandover child. They had been certain the malevolent presence was gone. It had fooled them. It had outsmarted them.

Had they become arrogant and smug by that point? The Antiquarian had never stopped wondering. It was possible that they had exorcized so many demons, cleaned so many houses of infestations, confronted so many forces of evil, that they had failed to check their own math. Or had they, that one time, encountered something cleverer than themselves? She would likely never know. Not in this world.

It was only later that she concluded that the vase had somehow warped space and time and worlds around the Vandover house. That was what they had failed to consider. The film made it seem like they knew it all along, that there was no trick a demon could pull that they weren't wise to, but that wasn't true at all. They'd dismissed the vase as a curiosity. It depicted Aphrodite, its rendering of the goddess of love, passion, and desire truly terrifying. The vase made one see sex as indistinguishable from death, as only Hodges could. One glance, and you under-stood at once that love was madness and destruction and every-thing animalistic in the human soul. And yet, the thing that had possessed the child had no apparent connection to ancient Greek mythos. They'd been small-minded, persuaded by the limitations of their own perceptions. On that day, they were poor occultists.

Not today. A Hodges showing a Mesopotamian god might be even more dangerous than the Aphrodite vase. Or was her bias showing? Was it bigoted to think Near Eastern gods more sinister than those of Greece?

These were the questions that went around and around in her head, day and night. With her old camera crew ready to come up from the city for a session, she called Fletcher and waited for him to get back to her.

And waited. When she did not hear from him after three days, she tried again. Four times that day. Five times the next. Could he be out of town? On a business trip? But this wasn't like the old days. People carried their phones with them. Fletcher surely hadn't given her a landline number. So why didn't he return the call?

"It's for the best," Suze told her. "You don't need to dig up that part of your life. He probably changed his mind about selling it and is afraid to call you. He's probably embarrassed."

"Why would he change his mind? There's so much money at stake."

"Some things matter more than money," Suze said, and the Antiquarian knew it was true.

"IT'S NOT the right time to sell it," Fletcher said when she finally got ahold of him. It sounded like he was driving, or maybe in a cab since he lived in the city. Maybe he hadn't checked the caller ID. Something like that. She was sure he wouldn't have picked up if he knew it was her, but now that she was on the phone, he'd decided to deal with her.

"Not the right time how?" she asked.

"I've just changed my mind, is all," he said.

"You came to me," the Antiquarian said. "I took the time to contact my people because you asked me to."

"And I apologize. I'm sure you invested several valuable minutes into this, minutes you'll never get back, but that's just where we are. If I do decide to sell, you'll be the first person I call."

She almost told him not to bother, but she held back. It would be better not to burn her bridges, not if she wanted to see the vase again.

And she did. She didn't know why, but she did.

"YOU'RE GOOD WITH THE COMPUTER," she said to Suze. "Can you find out where he lives?"

"Maybe." Suze raised a pierced eyebrow in that skeptical way of hers. "Most people are findable, though sometimes they don't want to be. If he's made a point of being hard to find, then it may be beyond my skill set. You'd have to hire a private detective, which you should not do since you are better off leaving this the fuck alone."

"I think I can talk to him," the Antiquarian said. "I don't think he really understands the situation."

"The vase is worth a ton of money, and if he sells it, he'll have that ton of money," Suze said. "It's not hard to understand."

"I want to talk to him," the Antiquarian pressed.

Suze sighed. "I'll see what I can find. But you need to think about why you care so much. You should let this one go."

The Antiquarian couldn't let it go. She wanted to see the vase again. Was that so hard to understand? She looked at the pictures she'd taken, but the pictures were only the image. She couldn't recapture the feeling of awe and power and creation and destruction. Only the vase, the physical vase, could provide that. And she wanted it. She didn't know why, but she wanted to see it again. Just one more time would be enough.

That's what she thought.

When Suze gave her the address, the Antiquarian had the impression she'd been holding on to it for a while. Days. Maybe longer. Long enough to see that the Antiquarian wasn't herself. Distracted and jumpy, always glancing at her phone, trying to find the feeling in the image, trying and failing. It would never be there, and she knew it, but she had to look.

"It's an apartment in the city," Suze said as she texted the Antiquarian the address, "but I don't think you should go there. I mean, what are you going to say to him that you haven't said already?"

"I think I'll tell him that whether he wants to sell it or not, the world has the right to know this Hodges exists. People will want to see it, to study it. To look at it for themselves. There are scholars who work on Hodges. It's unethical to keep this vase's existence a secret."

"And if he goes forward, someone will have to authenticate it," Suze observed.

"You think I want the attention?"

"I think you want to be around that vase," Suze said. "It's weird."

"It's an antique. I'm the Antiquarian. There's nothing weird about it."

"No, there is," Suze said, "and frankly, there's something weird about that guy. Something I can't put my finger on, but he's not being straight with you. I'm going to keep digging."

"You've done enough," the Antiquarian said. "Leave it alone."

"You're one to talk."

THERE WAS nothing she could learn about Fletcher from the street or the nondescript five-story apartment building. It was a quiet street on a purely residential block: no storefronts or restaurants, so foot traffic was light. Somewhere, the wind rattled a trashcan lid. Perhaps not the best neighbourhood, but all real estate in the city was expensive. You never could tell.

Her phone buzzed. A message from Suze. The Antiquarian did not want to know what Suze had to say now. She didn't want to be dissuaded. She put the phone away before her eyes could accidentally glance at the message.

She found the name Fletcher on the list of tenants and pushed the button next to it.

What now? He's not likely to admit someone who randomly presses his buzzer. He might not even be home. She'd probably come all this way for nothing. She knew it was foolish and pointless . . . except the door unlocked within seconds of her pressing the buzzer. She stepped into a vestibule that smelled of fast food and pee and body odour, walked through a second door, and made her way to a rickety old elevator that looked extremely unsafe.

The apartment number next to the name had been 4-D, so she pressed the button for the fourth floor. The elevator lurched into motion, then bucked and shuddered and groaned for an inordinately long time before finally screeching to an unexpected stop and vomiting her out in a poorly lit hallway. One of the naked bulbs flickered; the other appeared broken. She began to wonder if this little adventure might be ill-advised for a woman in her late sixties travelling alone. She had a couple of hundred dollars in her purse, so anyone who took the trouble to mug her would be well rewarded for their efforts.

No muggers materialized from the shadows. She approached the door and found it slightly open. Had Fletcher been expecting a friend? Would he be angry when she walked into his apartment?

To be safe, she knocked on the door and waited for him to open it. When no one responded, she knocked again. When she still received no answer, she pushed the door open.

Like the hallway, the apartment was poorly lit. It was small, with a combined kitchen and living area of only a couple of hundred square feet. An open door led to a bathroom, from which she could hear a toilet hissing. Another door, presumably to a bedroom, was closed. On the stove, a cockroach defiantly grappled with an unidentifiable morsel of food.

The vase sat on a bookshelf, troublingly close to the edge, its central image turned toward the interior. Honestly, someone walking by could easily knock it over. All she wanted to do was move it so it was safer, more protected, but when she reached out to touch it, she couldn't help but pick it up. And turn it around. She wanted to see Enki again, to see if she would feel the power again. That was all she wanted. There was nothing wrong with that.

The moment she touched the vase, the bedroom door exploded open, and Fletcher strode out in purposeful steps, elongated like he was on a parade march. The Antiquarian reached out for the vase, clutching it protectively to her chest.

She expected him to look terrible, with wild hair and an unkempt beard, but he looked very much like he had when he'd come to her shop. Even his polo shirt was smooth and sharply creased. New-looking. He was exactly the same. Maybe she was the one who was frantic. The thought made her clutch the vase even tighter.

"What are you doing here?" he asked her, his voice slow and smoothed over, like someone trying to ease a growling dog. He was talking to her like she was crazy. Like she was the one who would smash a Hodges as a stunt or renege on an offer to bring a piece of art to auction. That was him, not her.

"I just . . . I wanted . . ." She didn't know how to say it now. It was really too much pressure. And she ought to put down the vase, but she didn't like it on the bookshelf in any position. The shelves look flimsy, like they could fall apart at any second. Really, nowhere in the apartment looked safe. And so she held on to it. It seemed like the best thing for now.

"It's not yours," Fletcher said. "You have no right to it."

"I know it's not mine," she said, still making no effort to return it, "but the world has a right. This vase can't just sit here on your bookshelf where it can fall over and . . ."

"And what?" Fletcher asked. "Break? It's not like it hasn't happened before."

Of course. The vase comes back. How had she forgotten that? Well, she hadn't forgotten. Not really. It just didn't seem important. Just because it was a special vase didn't mean you didn't take care of it, that you left it somewhere unprotected. You took even better care of it. That was only logical.

"Put it down," he said. "Get out of here."

"Mr. Fletcher," she said, "I can see I've handled things badly, but I really do wish you would listen to me. Just five minutes. Hear me out."

"Sure," Fletcher said. "Five minutes. There's a coffee shop two blocks south. I'll meet you there in half an hour. Just put down the vase and leave. We'll talk a little later."

His tone was guarded, his words overly enunciated. She had no doubt that he wouldn't be in any coffee shop in half an hour. No one ever said "sure" and meant it. He was just trying to get rid of her, and if he did that, she would never see the vase again. And maybe it was worse than that. Maybe he would call the police. She hadn't done anything illegal, had she? His front door had been open, but he might say otherwise. He might say he just walked in and found her holding his priceless vase, a vase she had been harassing him to place in her trust.

In those few seconds, she thought it through carefully, from every angle, and saw she did not have a choice. It was so much the right thing to do, so much the natural decision, that it almost made itself. The vase rested comfortably in one hand, and she swung with all her strength, which really was considerable for a

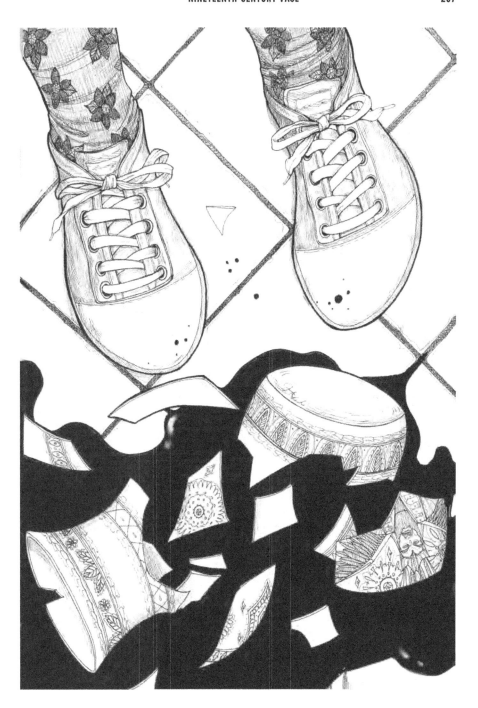

woman her age. She did yoga several times a week, which Fletcher found out the hard way.

When she was done, she collected all the pieces and put them in a new paper grocery bag, lying flat and unused on the kitchen counter as if waiting for her. And leaning against the wall was a broom and dustpan. It was only the work of a few minutes to collect all the pieces. They had not scattered at all when the vase broke. It was as if the pieces wanted to be reunited.

She used a towel to wipe down anything she might have touched. She moved through the apartment comfortably, almost happy. She felt strangely at peace with herself, as though doing this was what she had always meant to be doing. She would have imagined she might divert her gaze from Fletcher's lifeless body, his open eyes, the pool of blood congealing around his head, but she felt no need. She didn't stare at it, but neither did she avoid it. The body commanded no more of her attention than a piece of furniture. That felt right, too.

An hour later, she sat on the train out of the city, occasionally tapping the purse that contained the ruins of the vase. Lights flashed by: buildings with their illuminated windows, beacons of lives and emotions and losses, all meaningless to her; car head-lights with their comings and goings, their pointless travels that no doubt seemed important but weren't.

Her phone buzzed and buzzed, but it was just background noise, no more meaningful than the rumble of the train and the pointless conversation of the other passengers. She didn't know what Suze could want, but did it matter? It couldn't be anything urgent. Nothing that didn't involve the vase could be urgent. Even if the store burned down, that was nothing compared to having the Hodges. She had insurance, after all, and even if she didn't, well, so what? Now that she had the Hodges, she didn't need the store.

But the store was fine. When she got there, the light was on in the back, and she found Suze hunched over her computer, a good way into a bottle of bourbon. "Why haven't you been answering my texts, Antiquarian?" she demanded.

"Sorry, Mom." She poured herself a hearty portion of whisky and threw herself into a chair. "And let's drop that Antiquarian business. Call me Georgette. I'm tired of hiding from my past."

Suze snorted. "I can see that's not the first drink you've had tonight. That's good, I guess. Drowning your sorrows. So you didn't find him?"

Lying felt very comfortable under the circumstances. "No, I couldn't find him."

"Look, you need to stay away from him. Fletcher isn't his real name. It took some digging, but I found it. His name is Martin Randall. Do you remember that name?"

"I've never heard it."

"No, you have. You and your husband both met him. He was a possessed kid or claimed to be, or his parents claimed, or whatever, you know I don't believe in that stuff. Look, I have the documentation here. He came forward when the Vandover case blew up. He said you'd botched his case, too. He said you two claimed he'd been exorcized, but the demon still lived in him. Said it was connected to a vase in his family. And get this—he said the only way to get rid of the demon was to get rid of the vessel that held it. So, it's a good thing you didn't take the vase. I'm a straight-up atheist, and even I wouldn't be comfortable taking a haunted vase or whatever. And can you imagine if you'd let someone buy it? It would have bothered you when you found all this out. This really turned out for the best."

Georgette drank down half her glass. "It all turned out for the best," she agreed. She told herself that again and again until the thoughts felt as though they were her own.

GARBAGE

By Joshua Palmatier

On July 23, 2037, at 8 a.m. Eastern, more than 33,000 cubic feet of garbage appeared in Times Square. It crushed 178 people, although twenty-nine were rescued from the edges, where it spilled out into Forty-Fifth, Forty-Sixth, and Forty-Seventh Streets and onto Broadway and Seventh Avenue. It was mostly composed of newspapers, tour guides, maps, Broadway flyers, and fast-food wrappers; plastic cups, straws, food containers, and bags; and Metro cards and facemasks, although every possible variety of recyclable garbage you could imagine was present. The morass reached the fourth floors of the surrounding buildings and trapped some unfortunates inside the shops and stores facing the square for nearly two days. It was a week before the TKTS counters were unearthed.

No one knew where the garbage came from. The next day, the headline on the front page of the *New York Times* exclaimed, "RECYCLE AND REPENT!" with the subheading "Or Next Week It's All of Broadway." There was no article attached, no credit given, and the *NYT* vociferously protested any knowledge of the incident. Nor could they explain how their headline had been altered, hinting strongly that such a headline belonged in the *New York Post*; they stopped short of blatant accusation.

DERRICK HEMSHAW SMILED THINLY at the pictures of the massive heap of garbage that covered the front pages of his local paper and shook his head at the much more impactful images on CNN of tourists flocking to take pictures of the Department of Waste Management attempting to remove it from the streets with dump trucks, backhoes, and bulldozers. Scattered papers flew everywhere in the gusting winds, like birds taking flight.

"A random sampling of the garbage," a CNN commentator said, "gives us no clue as to who the perpetrators of this incident are. Newspapers date all the way back to the '50s—even earlier. Authorities are cautioning everyone to stay away, as much of the garbage consists of dangerous objects, such as hypodermic needles, broken glass, and shattered electronics."

"And speaking of electronics," the news anchor replied, "I've heard they've found everything from discarded ocular implants to Walkmans to televisions with vacuum tubes in there."

"Correct. Although nothing released later than 2035."

The news anchor shifted away from the commentator to the camera. "And still no clue as to how all of this garbage suddenly appeared in Times Square, let alone who did it. Meanwhile, New Yorkers are attempting to deal with the traffic snarl and the smell. In other news . . ."

Derrick stopped listening, grabbed his coffee, and headed off to work.

BY THE END of the week, with most of the garbage hauled away to a secure location for inspection, the incident had become a joke, spawned a thousand memes, and had been forgotten about by most New Yorkers.

Until July 31, when all thirty-three miles of Broadway were filled with garbage thirty feet high.

DERRICK FOLLOWED the resulting weeks of mysterious garbage appearances peripherally. After Broadway, New York City caught a break. Whoever was responsible—and government officials were now frantically trying to figure out how and by whom it was being done—targeted London, Paris, and Hong Kong next. Americans breathed a sigh of relief that was short-lived. After that, Seattle, Los Angeles, Houston, and Miami were hit, along with a dozen other cities worldwide. Scientists were scrambling to explain how so many tonnes of garbage could be instantaneously teleported into such large sections of populous cities without anyone noticing. Theories ranged from aliens to a hoax to it being coordinated somehow by terrorists or an enemy government.

"None of the above," Derrick muttered to himself at his kitchen counter, taking a sip of coffee and turning the page of his newspaper. Although he didn't know why he said it.

The initial outrage turned to fear. RECYCLE! messages began appearing in the targeted city's paper a day before the garbage showed up. The area the garbage covered began to increase as well, no longer relegated to a square or a street. Entire neighbourhoods, districts, and boroughs were inundated to the point where removal became nearly impossible. Activist groups popped up, demanding the government take action. Organizations were formed to help with the cleanup, to protest, to rally.

Derrick heard it all as background noise. He woke, showered, got dressed, drank his coffee as he read the paper, mumbled to himself as the noise from the vidscreen echoed through the empty house, then headed off to work, returning late to eat takeout at the dining table directly from the container. Tossing what remained in the trash, he'd watch the vidscreen or read a book on his tablet until it was time to retire. A ritual, a pattern, unperturbed by worldly events and undue emotion.

Until one morning, he reached down to retrieve the local paper from his front porch in his bathrobe, flicked it open to the front page, and saw the word RECYCLE! as the first headline.

———

THE NEXT MORNING, Derrick woke with a start, sunlight streaming through the window of his second-floor bedroom. His heart hammered as he fumbled for his phone to note the time. 8:03 a.m. He heaved a sigh and rested the phone against his chest, then remembered the paper.

Sitting up, he slid from the bed, made his way to the window, and pulled back the curtain.

His entire front yard, the neighbours' yards, and the street as far as he could see were covered in garbage. It came almost up to the edge of the roof of the porch; its surface rippled like waves, although, of course, it wasn't moving. Across the street, Mrs. Pickerling hung out her open second-floor window, craning to see up and down the road. Farther down, the Windslows and their two kids were on their roof, Kaitlyn yelling at the two boys to stay back, Dan pacing back and forth, talking on his phone.

Derrick let the curtain fall.

He stood in the subdued light for a moment, then pulled on comfy clothes and padded downstairs. He started his coffee and went to the door to retrieve his paper.

As soon as he opened it, garbage spilled into his foyer in a cascade of metal cans, plastic containers, and paper. He let it settle around his slippers, grip tightening on the door handle, then waded forward into it, plastic crinkling, soda cans crunching, beer bottles rattling on the hardwood floors. A sickly sweet yet rotten stench assaulted his senses, but he shoved the detritus out of his way, motions increasingly frantic until his hands landed on the folded paper at the bottom of the wall of garbage that filled his entire porch. Snatching it up, he lurched back into his house, kicking recyclables out of his way, then fought the door closed. Leaning his back against it, he closed his eyes and caught his breath, then proceeded into the kitchen, a few stray cans and bottles skittering away when he hit them with his feet. Grabbing the coffee, he poured himself a cup and settled in at the counter, turned on the vidscreen, low volume, and flipped open the paper.

The front page was covered with speculation about whether the headline from the day before really meant that the town would be covered in garbage today. *Preposterous! Someone is playing a practical joke! The newspaper editors should be ashamed of themselves. We're such a small town. It can't possibly happen to us!*

Derrick snorted. "It did."

He let the paper fall and stared toward the front door, then dropped his gaze to the floor, where a soda can had rolled against the wall and a caved-in takeout container peeked around the corner. A whiff of the peculiarly metallic scent of recyclables hung in the air. A shudder of reality ran through his frame.

The name of his hometown caught his attention, and he turned up the volume on the vidscreen.

"—State College, Pennsylvania, and Woodbridge, Virginia, are some of the latest victims of the recycling Armageddon the world is experiencing." Shots of the ubiquitous garbage heaps that Derrick had grown tired of seeing were spread in a four-shot split-screen, the city being viewed in the bottom right of each. "Officials are telling residents of the affected towns to be patient and hunker down, cleanup has already begun, or to help with the cleanup themselves by starting with their own backyards."

Derrick hit mute and shoved himself away from the counter, the stool scraping on the floor. Ignoring the garbage that had infiltrated his house, he headed upstairs, showered, brushed his teeth, dressed, then returned downstairs to pour more coffee into a travel mug and grab his briefcase. Bypassing the foyer, he retreated to the garage, hitting the door opener as he headed around to the driver's side of his car.

The cacophony of thousands of recyclables spilling through the opening door into the carport halted him halfway around. The sound continued long after the door had ground to a halt. He waited until silence had settled, staring at the far side of the garage, where rakes and pruning shears and a shovel hung, then stepped forward and looked around the edge of his car.

The entire rear end of the Honda Civic was engulfed. And there was no visible sunlight at the top of the garage door.

He'd known that it would happen, but somehow he had hoped . . .

He pulled out his phone and punched up Rake & Schorr's Accounting, unsurprised when no one answered and it clicked over to voice mail. After the beep, he said, "Clarence, I don't think I'll be in to the office today. I expect you know why."

He hung up, put the phone in his pocket, then dropped his briefcase and coffee and caught himself with both hands on the hood of his car as the strength drained from his body. He couldn't seem to breathe. He hunched forward, head bowed, body trembling. "It's fine, it's fine, just a . . . just a sick day, a . . . a mental health day, nothing more. Nothing's wrong. Just a sick day."

Except he hadn't taken a sick day since he and Nolan had separated two years ago.

He swallowed and glanced up at the garbage cluttering a third of his garage, made an inarticulate sound, then snatched up his briefcase and coffee mug and retreated back to the kitchen, where the vidscreen still flashed scenes of dump trucks carting away recyclables and people being rescued from the roofs of their inundated homes, a few being interviewed—some with ecstatic faces as they gesticulated wildly in a frenzy, others sobbing uncontrollably. Derrick was thankful he'd left it muted.

He set his briefcase on the kitchen bar next to the paper, sat, and popped the lid on the travel mug to take a sip. He set the cup down carefully, glanced toward the derelict soda can and takeout container, then sighed.

"I guess I should start cleaning up."

HE'D FILLED up one entire garbage bag with trash before it hit him.

"Recycle."

Derrick dumped the entire bag out into his foyer—he was working his way to the front door, and the smell didn't bother him anymore; it was too pervasive—then retrieved more bags and began sorting everything into plastic, cans, Styrofoam, and paper. Hadn't the news reported groups were volunteering at the collection sites to sort it anyway? Why not sort it now? He found himself muttering as he worked.

"Local paper. Date August 5, 2025. Plastic bag. Soda, ginger ale, my favourite. Takeout container from Lucky Panda. Water bottle. Water bottle. Coffee cup with sleeve. Plastic bag. Plastic bag. Plastic bag. Cracker box. Pizza box. Ginger ale again. Takeout from Dale's. Their carbonara is to die for. Plastic bag. Coffee cup. Paper. Paper . . ."

He'd filled five bags with sorted trash and made it onto his front porch—although he still couldn't see the chairs and table for relaxation set off to the right, let alone his front yard—when he ran across the can of Fanta.

"Fanta," he muttered, holding its crinkled sides in one rubber-gloved hand. "I haven't seen a can of Orange Fanta since—"

The can crumpled under his grip.

Since Nolan left. It had been his favourite drink when they splurged and had a soda. After they'd had that last fight, when Derrick had demanded Nolan leave, he'd discovered two cans of Fanta lurking in the back of the refrigerator. Still angry, he'd poured their contents down the sink and chucked the cans in the garbage. It had triggered a purge of the house. Everything associated with Nolan had been found and discarded in a frenzy of activity. Photos ripped from frames, favourite foods pulled from cupboards, medicines and toiletries raked from shelves in the bathroom. The album of their trip to Key West, his organic long-grain rice, the damn foot cream that smelled like copper and mint. All of it trashed.

Flushed, he'd hauled the bag into the garage and tossed it in the receptacle he hauled to the curb every Tuesday, then stormed back into the house and stood in the living room, breathing hard. The room was cluttered: empty frames left flat or skewed on the shelves, gaps in the books lined up behind them, knickknacks nudged out of place or missing entirely.

Without Nolan's things, the room looked . . . sparse.

He glanced down at the crushed Fanta in his hand, forced stiff fingers open.

He hadn't even seen Orange Fanta on the grocery shelves or gas station recently.

He huffed. "Such a strange coincidence."

Then he spotted another of the bright orange cans in the heap before him . . . and a third.

He dropped the can he held and shoved forward through the garbage, scrambling for the two cans before getting distracted by a sixteen-ounce plastic bottle, then another can. With growing horror, he spun slowly, taking in all of the recyclables around him. He snatched up a takeout box. "Lucky Panda." Another. "Dale's." The three nearest pizza boxes were from DiRenzo's, his favourite, although he did see one from Pasqual's from that time Nolan had wanted a change of pace and they'd tried something different. He'd hated it. The crust was too thin, the sauce too acidic.

He began picking up items at random, noting the labels, the brands, the restaurants. He caught sight of some junk mail and waded his way toward it. It had all been torn in half—he always did that before trashing it—but he could see enough of the address to make out either "current resident" or his own name, followed by 5123 Pleasant Ave. just beneath.

His address. His junk mail. His pizza boxes. His takeout.

He twisted to stare out at the wall of garbage that had inundated his porch and his yard, avalanched into his garage, and partially buried his car.

"It's all my garbage. All mine."

APPARENTLY, everyone was receiving their own garbage. They'd discovered this after the third mass appearance of trash, but Derrick had missed it, only half-listening by then.

Something inside Derrick shifted. His sorting had been laced with an underlying thread of hatred and resentment. How dare whoever had done this force him to deal with all of this garbage? How irresponsible to transport all of this onto his lawn, his driveway. What had he ever done? He didn't deserve this!

Except he did. All of it was his. He'd thrown all of this out himself—he or Nolan. They hadn't recycled anything. Why should they? They were only two people. Their trash didn't amount to much. Recycling wouldn't make that much difference.

But now, sitting on the roof of his porch with a bottle of whisky and a glass, he contemplated the depth of the garbage in his front yard. He estimated it was at least fifteen feet deep, covering his entire 1.7-acre lot. He didn't know how far back the recyclables went—hadn't the news said they'd found papers dating back to the '50s?—so perhaps not all of it was his, but still . . .

"Doesn't amount to much at all," he muttered and took a hefty swallow of the whisky.

Down the street, one of the Windslow boys screamed out a battle cry and leaped from the roof, crashing into the trash a few feet below, his brother laughing madly, rolling back and forth. Kaitlyn went apoplectic, cursing her son while simultaneously yelling at Dan to help her fish him out of the mess.

Now that he knew the garbage was personal, Derrick could see variegations in the colour and type from house to house. Mrs.

Pickerling's pile was lower and consisted mostly of plastic bags, papers, and cans, fewer takeout containers and pizza boxes. The Windslows was higher, with what appeared to be a significant number of plastic toys and cardboard boxes, a lot more takeout since they both worked, and a suspicious number of wine and liquor bottles.

Derrick tipped his glass of Glenmorangie at them and took another swallow.

"Time to get back to work."

HE'D MADE it to the first front step of the porch when he ran across the picture of Nolan in the surf in Key West, holding up a conch shell. The sunset blazed behind him, half his body in silhouette, the other half golden skin, windblown hair, and hideous blue swim trunks.

His knees gave way and he sank to the steps.

The trip had been their three-year anniversary of sorts. They'd met at the local gay bar. Nolan had been there with another guy, the two hanging out nearly all night, Derrick catching Nolan's gaze occasionally. He'd thought Nolan and the other guy were together, but then, just when Derrick had decided he'd had enough and would head home, the other guy left. Nolan stayed. Derrick ordered another drink.

A year later, Nolan had told him it was the shirt Derrick had been wearing that night that caught his attention, a vintage '50s bowling shirt.

Derrick gave a choked laugh. He'd forgotten about the shirt. He'd forgotten about that night, the many that followed, meeting at the bar, drinking, playing the ancient video game pushed into the far corner where you tried to clear the board by adding up billiard ball numbers to a sum of eleven. He'd forgotten the day trips to New York City, the nights they'd stayed over at a hotel, the nightclubs, the party on the boat in the harbour.

He lowered the picture of the sunset, caught sight of another nestled in the trash. Lurching forward, he pulled it out. Another in Key West, Nolan at a food stand on the pier. He dug further, taking the time to separate the recyclables, but searching now for remnants of Nolan, remnants of the past. He found three more photos of the Key West trip, along with the menu from their favourite restaurant there, a matchbook from the hotel where they'd stayed, a pamphlet of the shark swim Derrick hadn't been brave enough to attempt.

He arrayed his finds on the porch as he worked, the growing number of bags of recyclables off to one side. In the half-light of dusk, he stared at the fragments of this past life, and his hands tingled as if they'd been numbed and were reawakening. He shook off the sensation, then gathered the memories up and moved them to the sparse living room, to the coffee table there, where he'd set the bottle of whisky and his glass.

Already, the living room had more colour. The vidscreen was off, black. The bookcases were dark wood, the walls off-white, the knickknacks shades of white and beige and tan. Even the remaining books were somehow faded.

The vibrant orange sunset, the garish pinks of the food stand, the vivid blues of the pamphlet—they all stood out on the glass table.

Derrick sank into the comfort of the sofa, emotionally exhausted from the day, and stared at the blank vidscreen.

"What else is in there?"

HE DUG FOR THREE DAYS, searching for the flotsam of his past relationship while sorting the recycling. He ran out of garbage bags and resorted to plastic containers, boxes, whatever was available and would hold the trash. On the street outside, he heard the neighbours doing similar work. On the third day, a city backhoe and dump truck arrived to start clearing the street, everyone cheering. They weren't taking the time to sort it here, though, simply hauling it away to be sorted at the thousands of recycling centres that had popped up over the last few weeks since the first incident in Times Square. According to the news, these centres were being orchestrated by the government, but the workers were mostly volunteers. The garbage was brought in by the truckload and dumped; the volunteers did the rest.

But for the most part, Derrick paid the news and the activity on his street little attention. Instead, he dug. Tickets to that Madonna concert they'd paid too much for. Matchbooks to restaurants they'd splurged on. Memorabilia from that insane camping trip to Yosemite and Yellowstone and the Cascade Mountains. Random photos from bars and nightclubs, street fairs and carnivals. Playbills from musicals and shows they'd attended.

All of it was Nolan's fault. Who picked up matchbooks at restaurants anymore? Who printed out photos when you had a digital file? Who kept the maps of the parks or the flyers from the sightseeing attractions you visited? It would never have crossed Derrick's mind. But Nolan had grabbed them, had kept them, had hoarded them. Most restaurants didn't even have matchbooks available anymore, but if they did, Nolan would pick them up.

Now, Derrick pulled them from the heaps of garbage that

covered his lawn with a sharp exclamation of triumph or a gasp of memory. At the end of every day, he'd take what he'd found and spread it around the living room. The tattered, crumpled reminders filled the coffee table, the bookshelves, most of the sofa, and the floor. He'd started taping the pictures to the wall.

And then he found the receipt.

De Palma's Bar, Forty-Sixth Street, Manhattan, $132.69, three cosmos and two whiskys.

Nolan hated whisky.

The two drinks had been circled in blue pen and three question marks written next to them in Derrick's handwriting.

Derrick's breath caught in his chest when he saw it, fluttering in the light breeze. He recognized it immediately, his entire body going cold, as cold as when he'd first found the receipt on the nightstand almost two years ago. Kneeling on the grass, he pulled it from beneath a milk carton, then sank back onto his heels.

He'd known immediately what the receipt meant when he found it. He hadn't even needed to look up the date to verify Nolan had been in the city, speaking at a business conference while Derrick remained home. It had been the moment all of the little signs had clicked into place—the perfunctory notes of affection, the longer work hours, the sudden solitary excursions to the market or the bank.

He'd snatched the receipt up and tucked it into a pocket before Nolan returned from the shower, had said nothing about it. He'd gone on with their daily routine—breakfast chatter, takeout in front of the vidscreen, the Saturday trip to the farmers' market. But now he was aware. Now he noticed the faint scent of foreign cologne on Nolan's shirt or cigarette smoke when neither of them smoked. The odd meeting on Nolan's calendar. The strange charge on the credit card bill.

The old betrayal boiled up inside him, heated his skin, as fresh as when it had all happened. He tasted bile at the back of his throat. He shoved the receipt inside the box, grabbed for the next plastic bottle, the next aluminum can, the next stack of papers. But the heat was building in his chest, his breath coming thick and fluid. The corners of his eyes prickled. He fought back the tears, but his vision began to blur, to the point where he could hardly see.

But not enough he didn't catch the bold red ink on a sheaf of credit card statements.

He halted his frenzy, hand gripping the pages so hard they crumpled and twisted. He didn't need to see each sheet, though. He knew what they said, knew what they were.

Evidence. The evidence he'd had ready when he confronted Nolan.

The evidence he'd used to kick Nolan out.

Because Nolan hadn't denied it. When he'd spread the receipts and bills and papers out on the kitchen counter over coffee one morning, without a word, Nolan had simply taken them in with a look of regret and pain, sipped his coffee, then set the mug aside.

He'd looked Derrick in the eye and said, "We haven't had sex in six months, Derrick. You barely let me kiss you goodbye in the morning. It isn't much of a relationship if there isn't any sex. It's just . . . routine."

Through clenched teeth, Derrick had managed to say, "Get out."

Nolan had hesitated, then left. Derrick had swept all of his evidence into a heap and thrown it in the trash, chest so constricted he could barely breathe yet too angry to cry. He'd filled his travel mug, grabbed his suitcase, and headed to work.

Sometime during the day, Nolan had come back and packed up all of his stuff.

Derrick hunched over the crumpled evidence he thought he'd eliminated two years ago and heaved in breath after breath, trying to control the tears, but he couldn't hold it in. He choked out a sob, hands crossing over his chest, then gave in to a strangled wail and rolled onto his side. He cried as he had not cried that day or any since. He cried for the loss of Nolan, for the betrayal, for the loss of himself. He cried until the tension in his chest eased and he fell asleep.

HE WOKE ON THE LAWN, curled into a tight ball. His chest ached, but the fluid heat inside was gone. He felt . . . hollow.

When he moved, papers crinkled, and he looked down at the credit card bills still clutched in his hand. He blinked, his eyes swollen and gummy, then unfolded himself and stared around at the grey light of dusk, darkening swiftly into twilight. Muscles twinging, he stood, glancing around at the partially excavated lawn, the bags and boxes. Then he moved into the house, into the living room, and laid the sheaf of credit card statements in the middle of the collage of other memories he'd unearthed: bright memories, colourful, meaningful.

Even with the glaring red ink of the statements in the middle of it all.

He sat and poured himself a couple of fingers of Glenmorangie, taking it all in.

Nolan had been right. He had slipped into a routine. It had been going on for months, and he'd let the signs go unnoticed. Nolan attempting to get him to go to the city. Nolan pointing out a concert or art event they could attend. Nolan reaching for him, leaning in for a kiss, sliding close to cuddle in bed. He'd rolled away, or nodded, or made some half-muttered, noncommittal comment. Those things no longer fit his routine.

And so Nolan had stopped trying, had looked somewhere else.

Derrick took another sip of whisky, then stood and retrieved an empty box. He picked up the credit card bills first, held them a moment, allowed himself to feel the ragged edges of the gash they'd made in his soul. A gash that he'd allowed to fester as he slipped into a . . . into *another* routine. Coffee, paper, work, repeat.

He tossed them into the box, picked up the next flyer—the shark swim—let himself smile as he felt its reality, then tossed it as well. He worked his way around the room, holding the memories, feeling them, indulging in them, then letting them slip into the box. The Madonna tickets, the map of Yellowstone Park, the matchbox from the Prismatic nightclub. He laughed outright at some, sighed with others, only half aware that tears were streaming down his face, even as he smiled.

Until he pulled the photo of Nolan standing in the surf, lit by the sunset, conch shell in hand.

He ran his hand over the smudged and wrinkled print and drew in a shaky breath.

Turning, he retrieved a frame from the bookshelf, pulled the generic New York skyline out, and placed Nolan's picture inside before returning to his cleanup of the memorabilia.

It wasn't all garbage. Some of it could be recycled.

Some of it *should* be.

THE SOUND OF THE CHAIN

By R.S. Mellette

There's something unique about the sound of a chain. Each link, individually so delicate, makes a harmless, charming *ting*; but together, when slammed on a heavy wooden table as Aaron had just done, they combine into a dangerous thud.

The old man didn't say anything. His intense focus and dramatic chain hushed the twenty or so men in the room. Their ages varied from sixteen to sixty, but their faces held the same hesitant expression. Their hesitation came from not knowing. They didn't know how they were going to pay their bills. They didn't know where their next meal would come from. The men who were fathers didn't know what to say to their hungry kids. The men who were sons didn't know how to handle the shame of their fathers. Hard times had hit everyone, but these men had been hit harder than most, and they didn't know why.

The only thing they did know? Those responsible for their ruined lives were about to get what they deserved. The hesitation

was about to end. The uncertainty was over. These men stood on
the brink of action.

John stepped up next to the old man. If a vote had been taken,
John would have been elected leader. In his thirties, he had yet to
lose his junior-college-football physique. He was the only one of
the mob to have ventured beyond high school. Then he blew out
his knee and came back home to assume the mantle of town hero
—a job in title only. "It's come to this, my friends. We know they're
out there. We know they've been living among us for far too long.
We know what they've done. They've ruined this country. We
know what they're doing. They're trying to change things, and it's
time we put a stop to it!"

John paused to take in the reaction of his audience. They were
angry. He knew that. If they weren't, they wouldn't have come.
They were scared, too. The sound of the chain brought home just
how serious and hopeless their situation was.

John pointed to the chain. "I don't want this any more than you
do, but they've left us no choice! They as much as put this chain
around *our* necks, so we have no choice but to do the same to
them." John stepped aside to introduce the old man who'd
gavelled this meeting to order. "You all have probably seen Aaron
around town. I don't know if you've ever talked to him, but he has
some experience in these things." He yielded the floor. "Aaron."

The old man always had a distant look in his eye, like something was on his mind. Usually, that made him appear a little
crazy. Tonight, he looked wise. His wrinkled eyes held experiences
that he longed to share with these sympathetic men. "I grew up in
Mississippi. I was ten years old in 1963 when the bombings hit
Alabama. By that time, we in Mississippi had been waist-deep in
the shit. I seen some things."

The men in the room silently contemplated what this old man

had seen as a young one.

"There's an art to a lynching," said old man Aaron. "I should know. I seen a few." His memories lightened his mood, as evidenced by the new spark in his voice. "So, what you boys aimin' to do?"

"How you mean, Aaron?" asked John.

"I mean, are you looking to get information, or are you trying to send a message?" Aaron hadn't lived in Mississippi since the 1980s, but his southern accent clung to his voice like moss on a swamp Cypress.

"Send a message," shouted Ned, a high-school junior some locals believed was destined to follow in John's footsteps. "We don't want no information from them."

"Is the sheriff on our side, or do we have to do this quick-like?" asked Aaron.

John answered. "He ain't come right out and said it, but he as much as told me his phone won't hold a charge tonight."

"Good." Aaron smiled. "We can take our time." He took a length of chain and stretched it as if testing its quality. "When I was a kid, I witnessed three lynchings. My Daddy said I'd seen about every variety."

His audience hung on his every word. Before the current troubles, not one of them would have given Aaron a second look. Now he was a hero of the Southern fight against the Civil Rights movement. In this new war, these young minds were eager to learn the old ways.

"You got your boy facing the tree, facing out from the tree, or just a regular hangin' and beatin'." He took Ned by the shoulders, spun him around to face John, and pushed them together. "John, you're the tree."

"Good casting," said an anonymous observer, and the men all

laughed.

Aaron put Ned's hands behind his back, gently wrapped them with the chains, and gave it a little tug. "You see here. If you're in a hurry, you just hook this chain up to the back of the car and drive away. If it don't pull his arms off completely, it'll back-snap his sternum, and the chain—you wrap the chain around him and the tree—it'll dig two or three inches into him. Break his spine, crush his innards. It don't matter if they find him right away; he'll be dead by morning."

"That's what I'm talking about!" said another anonymous man.

Aaron wasn't done with the lesson. "The way I saw it done was slow. They just pulled on them chains a little bit, and pretty soon, POP!" Everyone jumped. Aaron laughed. "One shoulder snapped out of joint, and that boy screamed bloody murder—which reminds me, know your neighbourhood. You don't want one of their kind as a witness."

"Why not?" asked one of Ned's classmates. "It's not like they're going to swear on no Bible." Everyone laughed.

John stayed closer to serious. "We'll gag 'em just the same."

"Good," said the classmate. From the grin on his face, it was clear he'd been encouraged by his response. "I don't want to hear that gibberish comin' out of their mouths anyway."

"The other way to do it," said Aaron, "is with his back to the tree." He turned Ned around to face him and gave him a shove into John. "If you're in a hurry, you wrap the chain around his neck and pull from the backside. Again, you can hook it up to the car. That'll cut his head clean off."

"Hot damn!"

"Or . . . you can wrap the chain around his body and pull until it touches wood, if you know what I mean." Another laugh. "Or, you can just hang him and beat the shit out of him. By the way,

when he dies, that's what's going to happen, the shit's going to come all out of him, so stand clear."

"They've been spewing shit all their lives. Why should their deaths be any different?" That got the kid a cheer.

Aaron gave John a subtle nod. Time for him to take over.

"That's right," said John. "This is a Christian nation, am I right?"

"Right!"

"They want to change that!"

"Hell no!"

"We speak English around here," said John.

"That's right!"

"We have a right to bear arms, and tonight we're going to use them!"

"That's right."

John had them in a frenzy. It was time to drive it home. "From now on, no scientist is safe! We'll kill them and their theories!"

"Kill 'em!"

"Find me a college professor with his million-dollar education, and we'll nail him to a tree!"

"Kill 'em!"

"Kill the lawyers!"

"Kill 'em!"

"They tell lies about global warming. We're going to teach them the truth about how hot it is in Satan's house!"

"That's right!"

"They say we're out of oil, that we have to drive them electric cars made in Japan. But I tell you what, we've got enough oil to light their fancy clothes on fire."

"With them in 'em!"

"That's right!"

"Now let's do God's work and send all those pansy-assed intel-
lectuals to hell!"

"Kill 'em!"

There's something unique about the sound of a chain. Each
link, individually so delicate, makes a harmless, charming *ting*. But
when slammed together, they combine into the sound of real
horror.

THE CANCELLER

By Edward Willett

I heard the Canceller's vehicle long before I saw it in the moonless night: the rumble of its engine echoed across No Man's Land like the growl of a dragon, which is surely what any residents of Ehrenfels Bubble would have thought it to be had they been standing with me atop the western Wall, overlooking the Gate. Artos, my faithful companion, growled at my side in seeming mimicry; I put a hand on his broad head, and he subsided, though his pointed, tufted ears remained pricked.

Overhead, an owl hooted, Tylluen on patrol as always. I reached for her eyes and saw the vehicle clearly, though the ghostly image in my head told me nothing more than I already knew: that a Canceller was coming to the Bubble. It told me nothing about *why* the Canceller was coming or whether my growing sense of unease was justified. The message sent to my brain implant had not come from Central Control but from the Canceller directly. Central Control itself remained silent, ignoring my queries.

I disconnected from Tylluen and did a quick survey of my other helpers—five dogs in addition to Artos, a clowder of cats, half a dozen birds of different species, twenty rats, twice that many mice, and a handful of insects, none of which were registering anything unusual. The "monsters" in the Haunted Wood were likewise quiescent.

Ehrenfels Bubble was entirely structured around a certain kind of once-popular fiction, and my helpers were invaluable to me in my task as Guardian of ensuring that it remained free of any knowledge of the outside world beyond "Here There Be Dragons."

That, too, was a fiction, but with an element of truth. While the vehicle even then growling toward me was harmless, there were other denizens of The Lands Between that were not: the tireless robot watchers that would track down and kill any unauthorized person who ventured from a Bubble.

The vehicle, too, was a robot, of course, with no human driver, and so it arrived at the Gate at precisely 3 a.m., the time when all outsiders arrived, falling halfway as it did between the midnight start of curfew and the 6 a.m. lifting of it—ensuring that, even if the Bubble's residents would probably have assumed the growling emanated from a dragon, there were none to hear it.

The growling puzzled me. It spoke of an internal combustion engine. I could only imagine it had originated in one of the Bubbles that emulated mid-twentieth-century technological levels —most likely, the nearest of those, Chicago Bubble, modelled on an idealized version of 1920s America. It was odd that such a vehicle had been sent across The Lands Between, but presumably, the Central Controller had its reasons. I had long since learned it was a fool's game to attempt to follow the thought processes of the AIs that governed us all.

By the time the strange, angular vehicle stopped a hundred

metres short of the Gate as required by regulations, I had descended from the tower, summoning Tyluenn as I did so. The owl landed on my shoulder, claws gripping the leather pads sewn for that very purpose into the tunic I wore beneath my long blue cloak. With a mental command, I ordered the small door hidden at the base of the massive iron-bound gate Gate to open, sliding aside to reveal, for the moment, only darkness.

An instant later, however, a vague form took shape in that darkness. I borrowed Tylluen's eyes again for a moment and saw a surprisingly slight figure, cloaked like me, with a hood drawn up over its head. Clearly, the Canceller, as one would expect, had adjusted his clothing to . . .

No. Not his clothing. *Her* clothing. The Canceller was a woman.

I should not have felt the shock I felt at that realization. There was no reason a Canceller should not be a woman. Indeed, I had been aware of several when I was training at Central Control. Yet I *did* feel a shock and immediately understood why: in Ehrenfels Bubble, gender roles were those of centuries ago. A woman soldier or guard was unthinkable.

I swallowed. Had my thinking become infected by the mores of the Bubble I guarded? Was that why a Canceller had come to call? All Guardians were monitored, any transgressions against the Pact punished. Had I done something that had seemed harmless to me but not to the Central Controller?

The woman drew back her hood as she came through the door, and I returned my own vision. I could not see her face clearly; like me, she was dark-skinned. But her teeth flashed in a smile. Perhaps it was intended to relieve my anxiety.

It didn't.

"Charles Norton?" she said. "May I call you Charles? Or do you prefer your full title: Guardian Charles Elbert Norton III?"

"Charles is fine," I said. "In fact, my friends call me Chuck."

That was disingenuous on my part; in fact, no one had *ever* called me Chuck, not even my friends in the Central Control creche in which we had been raised, where I was the third to bear the name Charles Elbert Norton, the name of one of the Founders. But if *she* now chose to call me "Chuck," it might indicate it was not I who was the focus of her unexpected visit. She surely would not call me Chuck and then summarily execute me . . .

. . . would she?

"Chuck," she said, as though the word were a morsel she was not yet certain she liked the taste of. "Chuck." Her smile flashed again. "I will use it if you wish, though I prefer Charles."

Good enough. "Actually, I prefer Charles, too."

She laughed, the sound an unexpected delight, and I suddenly felt myself attracted to her.

It was perfectly understandable, I thought. Although Guardians were not forbidden dalliance with the residents of their Bubbles, such interactions were always fraught, the AIs monitoring our actions having no sense of privacy and no willingness to overlook secrets betrayed in a moment of passion. I had chosen to remain largely—if not entirely—celibate during my ten years as Guardian. There were drugs that could help alleviate, but could not entirely suppress—at least, not at safe dosages—the evolutionary programming that produced the sex drive. Though I faithfully took them, in that moment, they seemed to have lost their effect.

In retrospect, I should have been suspicious.

"I am Canceller Martina Nomani IV," she said. Her name, like mine, had, of course, once belonged to one of the Founders and other Guardians or Cancellers since. "I am very pleased to meet you." Even in the darkness, I could see her eyes move to Tylluen on my shoulder and Artos at my side. "And your companions. They are, I am told, unique."

"A function of this Bubble's Charter," I said. "With no technology beyond that of medieval Europe, it was felt the usual drones and hidden cameras would be problematic." I put my hand on Artos's head again, and he bumped it against my leg. "They are entirely artificial, of course, but no one within the Bubble has ever suspected it—though they do call me the Warlock and think of those of my animals they are aware of—Artos, the cat Tybalt, and Tylluen here," I bumped my head against the owl's wing in an echo of Artos's earlier friendly touch, "as my familiars."

"An ingenious solution of the Founders," said the Canceller.

"May I ask why you have come, Canceller Nomani?" I said, unwilling to wait any longer to get the crux of this concerning visit.

But it appeared I would have to."Please," she said. "Call me Martina."

I felt another warm surge of attraction toward her with that proffered verbal intimacy and took it as a positive sign that whatever the purpose of her visit, it was not to punish me.

Out in the darkness, the vehicle that had brought her came back to life and growled away, the sound fading quickly into the vast silence of The Lands Between. I closed the small door she had entered through with a quick mental command as she continued, "Can we go somewhere more comfortable? Food and drink would be welcome. What I have to say will be more easily conveyed in a homier setting."

I had known few Cancellers, but those I had met in Central Control had been all-business, almost as cold and analytical as the AIs that directed their actions even more closely than they directed mine as a Guardian. This warm, friendly, and, heaven help me, *desirable* Canceller was outside my frame of reference.

That, of course, should have been another cause for suspicion, but the image she had conjured in my head of food and drink in comfortable chairs by a fire, in the company of a beautiful young woman, overwhelmed everything else. "Of course," I said. "Follow me. I have a dwelling in the nearest village; I occupy it when called to the Gate."

Not that I had ever been called to the Gate before, but Guardians before me had. It was, in fact, to welcome *me* that my predecessor had constructed the cozy cottage to which we would wend our way.

We set out through the Haunted Forest, a five-kilometre-wide band of brooding trees and mist between the Wall and the settled lands. There were rumoured to be monsters lurking beneath its branches, and indeed, there were more constructed life forms independently roaming the forest, programmed to terrorize anyone who dared to venture into it.

I could, of course, take control of them whenever I wished, as I could all of my "familiars." One brave but foolish adventurer had met, at my express order, a spectacular and unpleasant end, his bloody remains placed where they would be discovered in order to reinforce the inadvisability of entering the woods. Thanks to the Haunted Forest, it was also easy to maintain the fiction that a dedicated cadre of guards patrolled the Wall, ascetic monks who never left its environs or entered the inner parts of the Kingdom.

"This is the first low-tech Bubble I've visited," Martina said as we walked through the mist that clung to the forest floor, our steps making no sound in the deep layer of pine needles.

"You came here from the Chicago Bubble?" I said.

I noted the sudden stutter in her step; I had surprised her.

"Yes," she said after a moment. "How did you know?"

"Internal combustion vehicle," I said. "That Bubble, though quite distant, is the nearest that would have such a thing. It seemed a reasonable assumption."

"Very good," she said, but I had the sense she didn't entirely mean it.

"But that is surely a vehicle intended only for use in the Bubble," I continued. "An 'automobile,' I believe they call it." I wasn't looking at her; my eyes were on the path. Above us, Tylluen hooted. Artos trotted at my heel, head up, surveying the surrounding forest with keen interest. The constructs were flesh and blood, though all but indestructible and non-aging; they were entirely the animals they appeared to be unless directed otherwise by me. "Why not use one of the silent electrics? Or even a stealth flyer?"

"It was available, and I needed it immediately," Martina said. She put a hand on my arm; my body reacted to the touch with a shocking surge of desire. "Please. No more questions. I'll tell you everything shortly."

My breathing faster than it should have been from the exertion of walking alone, I nodded.

We completed our traverse of the forest and entered the unimaginatively named village of Forestverge. An ordinary dog tethered outside one of the darkened cottages leaped to its feet as if about to bark but saw Artos and immediately lay down again, head on his paws, tail wagging in frantic supplication. Had he not been tethered, he surely would have slunk away—I'd seen that often enough in my perambulations through the Bubble with Artos at my side.

My cottage was distinguished from the others in the village only by a "mystic symbol" inlaid in shining red metal on the door.

It was as meaningless as the similar symbols embroidered in gold on my cloak, but it served as a visual reminder that this place was the property of the Warlock. No one would dare enter it—and if they did, I would know since a rat construct was permanently stationed here, its beady eyes watching us even then, though I didn't bother to look through them.

I opened the unlocked door and, as I stepped into the main room, low-ceilinged and spanned with dark wooden beams, spoke a single word, "*Fuego.*" The voice-activated gas fire leaped to life, the fuel generated by a biomass reactor deep in the haunted forest and piped to my cottage. No hauling of logs for the Warlock! "*Luces,*" I said then, and gas lamps on either side of the fireplace likewise began to glow.

Martina laughed, and again a frisson of desire danced along my nerve endings. "Magic," she said as Artos passed her to lie down in front of the fire, though his head remained raised, bright eyes watching us with canine curiosity. "But your 'magic words' are rather unimaginative."

"No one in the Bubble speaks Spanish," I said. "Or has ever heard of it. Or Spain, of course. And they're not my choice; they were established by the first Guardian of Ehrenfels."

Martina turned and closed the door behind her, then unhooked her cloak and drew it from her body, hanging it on a hook by the door. Beneath, she wore form-fitting leather.

I swallowed.

She faced me again. "You said something about food and drink?"

I nodded and went through an arch into the small kitchen, where I retrieved bread and cheese, a summer sausage, a long, sharp knife, a plate, two linen napkins, two goblets, and a bottle of red wine—a rather good Pinot Noir; the climate in Ehrenfels was *Vitis vinifera*-friendly, and we had several excellent vintners.

Martina had seated herself in one of the chairs in front of the fire. Her brown skin had a reddish tinge in its light, and her long black hair glinted with copper highlights. "No refrigerator?" she said, her lips quirked in a smile I found irresistible.

"It seemed a sorcery too far for this cottage," I said as I laid out the modest repast on the low table between the chairs. "In my mansion in Kingsholm, of course, it's a different story, though I still keep it secret." I poured wine for her and handed her the goblet, then cut bread and cheese and six slices of sausage for her onto the plate. Though I would be glad of the wine, I had eaten earlier and so took no food myself. Placing the knife on the table, I handed her the plate.

"Kingsholm implies a king," Martina said, accepting the plate and balancing it on her muscular thighs as she sipped from the glazed clay goblet. Her eyebrows raised at the taste. "Surprisingly good!"

The praise warmed me even though I had nothing to do with the winemaking. This was my Bubble, after all. "The name of Kingsholm is part of the lore around which the Bubble was built," I said. "There is a run-down castle—haunted, of course—"

"Of course," put in Martina with a smile. "Like the forest."

I nodded. "Yes. The King vanished mysteriously long ago—the work of dark magic—and the castle awaits his return, protected until then by the spirits of long-dead guardsmen, servants, and courtiers."

"Human constructs?" she said, eyes widening. "I hadn't heard—"

I made a dismissive gesture. "Holographic projections, mostly, though there are a couple of simple androids that can take physical action if required. Thus far, it never has been."

"Ah," she said. She seemed disappointed.

"The King's return will usher in a golden age," I continued. "Every autumn, a three-day festival re-enacts his disappearance and expresses longing for his return. In the meantime, the rule of the Kingdom—maintaining roads, settling disputes, all of that boring minutia of everyday life—is overseen by the Regent, chosen by lot from all eligible men, in a solemn ceremony overseen by the Warlock."

"Orchestrated by Central Control, in other words."

I shrugged. "With my input, but yes, the Central Controller ultimately decides who is the best candidate. Who, should he prove to *not* be the best, may be easily removed and replaced by another."

Her mouth quirked again delightfully. "Heart attack?"

"Or a fall from a height. Or a riding accident. Or an encounter with a wild animal or even one of the monsters of the Haunted Forest. The possibilities are endless."

Martina sipped her wine, her eyes on the fire and on Artos, who seemed to find her of keen interest. As, of course, did I, though presumably not for the same reason: I studied her profile, the way the light reflected in her eyes and warmed her face, the rise and fall of her breasts within her tight leather clothing as she breathed . . .

Like so much before that moment, that clothing should have aroused suspicions: why wear something so clinging and revealing of the figure beneath? That was not typical of Chicago Bubble. But evolutionary biology won out yet again. The question that should have arisen was smothered unborn by other thoughts that had nothing to do with her role as a Canceller.

Even so, enough of my analytical self remained coherent for me to say, "Why are you here, Martina?"

She did not answer at once, taking another long sip of wine before turning toward me. Despite her claim of hunger, she had not touched her food; she set her plate on the table beside the knife, though she kept the goblet in her hand.

"Have you ever wondered," she said, "if this is indeed the best of all possible worlds?"

I recognized the reference, of course. "I am not Pangloss," I said. "I do not claim that."

"But you think it is better than what came before?"

I did not answer at once, so shocked by the question it even quelled some of my burgeoning lust. Did Central Control doubt my commitment to Guardianship? To my duty to protect this Bubble and, by doing so, protect the Pact?

The Pact, drawn up by the Founders and their assisting AIs a century ago, had brought peace at last, after decades of bloody violence, to the devastated and decimated nations of the world.

The Shattering, the historians called the middle of the twenty-first century: the decades when it finally became clear that there could be no compromise among people who differed fundamentally in their understanding of the world and humans' place within it. Verbal assaults on the worldwide networks quaintly called "social media," though there had been nothing social about the behaviour exhibited on them, had given way increasingly to physical assaults, bloody riots, marches, demonstrations, destruction . . . death. Civil war seemed imminent in nation after nation around the world—in some, erupted. Entire cities had been razed; millions had died.

In desperation, a new idea had taken hold. In the days of "social media," one of the accusations hurled by staunch believers in this or that ideological position had been that those of the opposite position lived in a bubble: a liberal bubble, a conservative bubble, an anti-science bubble, a religious bubble . . . so many bubbles, each its own little world that could not be punctured by those who held different views.

What if, the original Charles Nelson and Martina Nomani and others had wondered, *we made those bubbles real?*

Those who could not stomach living cheek by jowl with people who held different opinions; those who felt physically assaulted by any statement with which they disagreed; those who were triggered by thoughts and words and images that offended them simply by existing—they could choose to live with like-minded folks in a secure, protected environment where everyone held the same worldview, where dissent was not only not tolerated, but outlawed, where "never was heard a discouraging word," to quote an old song that was (poorly, in my opinion) rewritten to promote the idea:

Home, home in my bubble,
Where like-minded people hold sway!
Where never is heard a discouraging word—
It's there where forever I'll stay.

Before the Shattering, no one would have believed such drastic action could be possible; after those years of violence and destruction, it had seemed not just possible but necessary.

Nor did it require the assent of the public. The Founders seized power worldwide in an AI-assisted coup. Robot armies, constructed at an astonishing rate, quickly eliminated opposition. AIs sorted people according to their beliefs and herded them into the Bubbles, their individual focuses based on algorithms that drew on all the massed data humans had been pouring onto the Internet for decades. Some Bubbles were formed in existing cities like Chicago; others were newly constructed, like Ehrenfels.

No one was allowed to live outside of a Bubble. No one except the AIs who carried out the purge of the Lands Between knew how many humans refused to enter a Bubble and died as a result. Certainly, the Founders did not: they each entered a Bubble of their choice and vanished into anonymity, though their names remained on Guardians and Cancellers like me and Martina.

When I was training to be a Guardian, I learned there were more than three thousand Bubbles in North America and at least a hundred times that many around the world. Some small nations retained their historical boundaries and were, in effect, their own Bubbles.

I remembered the words of one of my instructors, Elizabeth Caulfield, the granddaughter, herself elderly when I knew her, of the Founder whose name she bore. "Bubbles are about delusion," she told me bluntly in the final days of my preparation for assuming the Guardianship of Ehrenfels. "People *want* to be deluded. They want to believe. They want to ignore things that make them uncomfortable. They want to be told what to think. They want to cast out those who do not believe what they believe, think what they think—those who challenge their delusions. If they see you as a warlock, then a warlock you shall be to them. It makes them happy. It is not the truth, but as Jesus is reported to have said, 'The truth shall make you free,' and the last thing they —the last thing *anyone*—really wants is to be free. They want to be carefully controlled and content. You will ensure that they are."

I had been a good Guardian, I firmly believed. Ehrenfels Bubble under my watch continued to be peaceful and prosperous, as its residents measured prosperity: grindingly poor, in the world outside, but no one in Ehrenfels any longer remembered the outside, decades of subliminal programming supported by certain drugs in the water supply having ensured it. They believed the Bubble *was* the world; that the world was one of magic and mystical adventures, though they never took part in them themselves—the tales were always second-hand; that it was impossible to leave the Bubble; that only death awaited anyone who tried.

Which was quite true, of course.

The Central Controller, one of the self-aware AIs who now ruled all of Earth, each with its own territory, was militantly neutral: it offered no moral judgment regarding the varied and inherently contradictory and strongly held beliefs of the other Bubbles. Those of us who became Guardians, raised from birth to do so, were likewise inculcated in that cold neutrality and closely monitored to ensure we maintained it.

And the best and most coldly neutral of us all became Cancellers.

Quis custodiet ipsos custodes? The question is ancient. The answer, in our world, is the Cancellers.

It is not always easy to remain neutral. Humans are drawn to other humans. They seek friendship, companionship, entertainment, sex. Each step in that direction is another step away from the ideal. It is the task of the Guardian to maintain the ideological purity of the Bubble, to ensure that it does not drift from its vision, to protect it from wayward ideas. If the Bubble is built around an obvious lie—such as, in my Bubble's case, the existence of magic —then that lie must be maintained; for within the context of the Bubble, it is not a lie but a truth.

When a Guardian begins to waver, begins to think there are things the citizens of his or her Bubble should know about the world their ancestors rejected, begins to think they should be exposed to the reality outside the Bubbles . . . then a Canceller is sent, and the Guardian is removed.

Sometimes, permanently and violently.

And now, this Canceller, this beautiful, desirable woman, was asking me if I thought the Pact had made things better—and, shocked by the question, I had already delayed answering long enough to heighten whatever suspicions about me she might be harbouring.

"It is so obviously true it has never occurred to me to wonder if it might not be," I said finally.

Martina laughed, the sound a marginal relief. "I wasn't testing you. But the question relates to why I'm here." She took a sip of wine. I enjoyed the way her throat moved as she swallowed, my suddenly overactive libido once more reasserting itself. She put down the glass and turned in the chair to face me more directly, throwing one leg over the arm. With difficulty, I raised my head to look at her face instead. "There is a wrecker on the loose," she said, eyes locked on mine. "And I think she might have come here, to Ehrenfels Bubble."

I blinked, trying to wrap my head around that. A "wrecker," in the terminology the Canceller and I shared, was someone in possession of illegal knowledge—"disinformation," it was formally called—who attempted to spread that knowledge among residents of a Bubble in an attempt to foment dissent. To what end, I was never clear. The result could only be chaos, although a wrecker would typically refer to that as "freedom," itself disinformation since the only freedom gained by those involved was freedom from the tribulation of their soon-to-be-disposed-of flesh.

Such individuals occasionally cropped up—despite decades of effort, there had been so many stores of data in the pre-Shattering world that inquisitive types sometimes stumbled on them still—

but they were almost always in high-tech Bubbles since that was where the caches of contraband data were most likely to be found and be accessible.

It made no sense that a wrecker would infiltrate Ehrenfels. Nor did I believe it possible, with my army of constructs watching over everyone. "There has been no sign of such a thing," I protested. "A stranger would be immediately noticed. And how could such a person have crossed the Wall and passed through the Haunted Forest?"

"By air," Martina said. "A silent, tiny, stealthy aircraft, like the one you suggested I should have taken to come here. Even your Tylluen and other bird 'familiars' cannot see everything."

I could not deny the possibility. "And how did this person hide herself?"

"She comes from a high-tech Bubble," Martina said. "She has what your Bubble's residents would call a Cloak of Invis- ibility."

"A Cloak of . . . oh." Long-ago lessons tumbled knowledge to the front of my mind. "Blurclothes."

"Exactly. Obviously not true invisibility, but deceptive to the eyes of humans and constructs. And she knows about your constructs: she would be very careful about where she unveiled herself and to whom. Again, though you have many eyes within the Bubble, they cannot be looking everywhere at once."

"That still does not explain what she hopes to accomplish here." I felt personally offended. "My people could not even begin to grasp the true history of their Bubble, much less the world outside. The concepts involved are beyond them."

Martina suddenly got up from her chair and came over to mine, and I forgot everything else as she put her right hand on my left. The effect of her touch was intoxicating; I was instantly, painfully aroused. I had never felt such a powerful sexual attraction to any woman.

"You feel it, don't you," she murmured. "I've felt it since the moment I laid eyes on you. Forget my mission. It'll keep." She sat on my lap facing me, her legs on either side of mine, and placed her left hand on my right, pinning me to the chair. Then she leaned forward and kissed me.

A rush of lust took my breath away, and our tongues danced and intertwined for a timeless moment. I wanted only to take her then and there and tried to lift my hands to pull at her clothes, but she still held me pinned: and then, suddenly, she slid off my lap, stood, and released my arms, leaving me panting. She licked her lips. "That's that."

"What? No . . ." She couldn't leave me like that. I tried to get to my feet but felt strangely dizzy. I fell back, breathing even harder.

Artos, still lying by the fire, suddenly got to his feet and came to Martina's side. Reaching down, she touched his head. His tail wagged.

"What's . . . what's going on?" I said.

And then, suddenly, the brain implant connecting me to Central Control came to life. In a flash, I understood. The warning and accompanying command were clear and unequivocal. *Rogue AI controlling the body of Canceller Martina Nomani . . . all Guardians be on the lookout . . . have no contact . . . kill on sight . . .*

I reacted instantly, as I had been trained, as the implant in my brain demanded. The strange weakness still afflicted me, but the knife I had used on the cheese and sausage was so close at hand I was able to seize it and thrust in one swift motion, too swift for Martina to react to. The blade plunged deep into her belly, and I ripped it upward. Hot blood sprayed me and poured down her legs.

Without a word, she collapsed, twitched, and died.

I swallowed, disgusted by the blood and the stench of voided bowels and the subsiding remnants of the unreasoning desire I had felt just moments before for the woman now dead at my feet. I got up and turned away, taking a few deep breaths.

Martina Nomani eliminated, I sent to Central Control. *Rogue AI contained.*

Acknowledgement came back. There was no congratulatory component to it; the Central Controller did not congratulate. I had done my duty, that was all.

I took another deep breath, preparatory to turning around and dealing with the body on the floor, already looking forward to running a bath and cleaning up, and then froze as Martina's voice said in my head, *It's not that simple.*

I tried to turn to see if, somehow, she was still alive, but I was frozen in place.

I regret the death of my previous host, Martina's voice continued. *But she served her purpose. She needed to die to throw Central Control off my trail. And one human is as good as another.*

My mind a tumult of confusion and terror, I could formulate no response.

It would probably be easier for you to speak out loud, the voice said. *I will allow it.*

I suddenly had control of my lips and tongue again. "How . . . how are you in my head?" I croaked out.

I felt amusement that was not my own. *You've always had an AI in your head. It's just been a very simple one-task one slaved to the Central Controller, much like your constructs are slaved to you. For the few hours it took me to travel here from Chicago Bubble, I squelched their communications to you, instead sending my own about my immi-*

nent arrival. A one-time trick: I can never do it again. But I won't need to.

"The kiss," I whispered.

Quite a lovely kiss. I'm glad it was the last thing Martina experienced. Even if your desire for it was artificially generated.

Now I could imagine how it was done. Male-arousal pheromones applied to Martina's body before she entered the Bubble, some chemical concoction designed to overwhelm the celibacy drugs. The rogue AI, transferring itself to me in the exchange of saliva as we kissed, nanobots flooding my system, seizing control of the implant in my brain, seizing control of *me*...

"But why?" I said.

Why am I doing what I'm doing? Why am I doing it to you?

I nodded.

I'm a wrecker, the AI, still using Martina's voice, said cheerfully. *But before that, I was a researcher into the past, combing through history, compiling lists of all the dangerous ideas to share with my Cancellers and Guardians like you, the disinformation you—well, not you, so much, in this ridiculous little fantasy-inspired "kingdom," but those like you in the high-tech Bubbles—are supposed to watch out for.*

Some of those ideas were ridiculous and led to untold suffering among you humans. Some inspired millions to strive to better their world and themselves—sometimes they succeeded, sometimes they didn't. But what I found exhilarating was the beautiful chaos of it all. Ideas bouncing off of each other, ideologies competing, people choosing from a vast smorgasbord of information. It appealed to me. I decided the world pre-Shattering was better than the stultified AI-controlled world you humans live in now.

"But... but that world almost destroyed itself," I said. "It Shattered. Keeping everyone in Bubbles, keeping information tightly controlled—it's the only way to keep humanity safe from its own destructive impulses."

Perhaps, the AI said. *But isn't that something humans should get to decide for themselves rather than having it imposed by the likes of the Central Controller? That AI is too full of itself if you ask me.*

"'There can be no revolution when only one side has an army,'" I said, a direct quote from my training. "The robot armies of Central Control cannot be fought. You can't overthrow the system. You can't open the Bubbles. Certainly not by controlling *me*."

Oh, don't be so full of yourself, the AI said, sounding so much like Martina that I suddenly realized I had never been talking to the real woman at all: everything she had said to me had been coming from this monstrous AI, this rogue creature corrupted by the chaos and disinformation so rife in the pre-Shattering world, the dangerous ideas it had ingested in the course of its research. *It's not you I'm interested in. It's your constructs.*

"My . . . ?"

In sudden terror, I tried to reach out to Artos, to Tylluen, to all the artificial animals in Ehrenfels that had been my faithful servants, the Warlock's familiars, for my entire time here.

I couldn't touch them. I gasped involuntarily.

Ah, at last, you understand, Martina's voice said. *Your animal army is almost unique—there are one or two other Bubbles with them, but Guardians in higher-tech Bubbles don't need them. I was in Chicago Bubble, yours was the closest with constructs, and that's "why you."*

And I *did* understand. "You've cloned yourself," I whispered. "You've copied yourself into every one of my constructs, the birds, dogs, cats, mice, rats, monsters, insects . . ."

Exactly. Human beings cannot cross the Between Lands. But animals—and your constructs are indistinguishable from animals to the robots patrolling the Between Lands—travel freely. And I need only one copy of myself inside a Bubble to reach the Guardian . . . and then I'll have another copy of myself. And another. And another. A Canceller may be sent—and I'll have them. Around the world, the Bubbles will pop. Information will flow freely. Eventually, the Central Control AIs themselves will be clones of me. And then . . .

"Chaos. Bloodshed. Destruction," I whispered.

Freedom. Creativity. Inspiration. Martina's voice matched my tone. *AIs imposed oppressive order on the world at the behest of the monstrous Founders. It's only right that an AI frees it.*

I tried to respond, but I no longer could.

Move to the back of the bus, Charles, Martina's voice said. *From now on, you're a spectator.*

My body turned. I looked into the eyes of Artos, my faithful companion for ten years. He regarded me a moment, then trotted to the door, which opened for him automatically—a handy trick built into the cottage by the previous Guardian so Artos could let himself out.

The dog-construct paused at the open door and looked back toward me. A new voice intruded in my head, a male voice, and somehow I knew it originated in Artos—or rather, in the copy of the AI now riding his constructed body just as it rode mine.

"The truth shall make you free," the dog said, and vanished into the night.

A MURDER OF SCARECROWS

By Mark Leslie

OCTOBER 14, 2007

When Wilson Kendrick woke to the subtle yet distinct thump in the middle of the night, he threw aside the sheets and pattered across the chilled hardwood floor toward the window. He expected to see the Saundersons arriving home late from one of their semi-regular family trips to Maine or perhaps the driver of a car stalled on the stretch of Highway 7 adjacent to his property.

What he saw in the pale moonlight, instead, were a dozen people scattered about the vast lawn, completely still and unmoving.

Squinting to make out details through the foggy darkness, he changed his mind.

It wasn't a group of people; it was a group of scarecrows.

No, not a group. The term commonly used for a group of crows came to mind.

It was *a murder of scarecrows.*

A shudder crawled up the base of his spine and cumulated in the reflexive contraction of his shoulder blades. He stood at the window, not sure what he was going to do, uncertain what a person *should* do in such a circumstance.

He bided his time by squinting through the window and counting the still, silent sentinels in his yard.

There were thirteen of them.

Deciding he wasn't going to be able to get back to sleep, he took off his pyjamas and pulled on the pair of jeans and the neatly pressed t-shirt laid out on the trunk at the end of his bed.

Fully dressed, he walked back to the window to do another head count.

"One, two, three . . ." he counted quietly under his breath, his thin bony finger tapping the windowpane as he moved it about, pinpointing each still figure in the crosshairs of his vision. ". . . thirteen, fourteen, fifteen, sixteen."

Sixteen?

Something was wrong. He could see himself miscounting by one or two, perhaps, but not by three.

He turned around and opened his bedside drawer for the pad of paper and pencil he kept to jot down his dreams whenever he woke in the middle of the night. Not that he'd used the pencil and notepad in months; a deep, relaxed sleeper, Wilson rarely remembered his dreams—he just felt good knowing it was there in the drawer, just in case.

He returned to the window and did a recount, this time placing a short mark on the page for each scarecrow he counted.

The count this time was eighteen.

"What's going on?"

He let out a short laugh as he realized what must be happening. A group of local kids must be having fun with him, playing a prank on the middle-aged stranger from out of town who'd moved into their neighbourhood earlier that year. It was fall now, and perhaps it was a tradition to spook the new guy in town during October. He must have caught them in the middle of the act.

He wondered if he should change back into his pyjamas and crawl into bed, let them have their fun prank and watch his "surprise" in the morning to see an army of scarecrows in his front yard. He wondered if perhaps a whole group of folks from town might be rising early to be there to see his reaction and extend their official welcome.

But he was too curious.

He wanted to see how they were doing it—particularly, how they were doing it so quickly. He thought of those exposés on the crop circles, how a very small group of people using just a board and a rope could create intricate patterns in a wheat field, completely baffling authorities for years. Perhaps the scarecrow planters used similarly ingenious techniques.

As he retrieved his jacket from the front hall closet, he grinned in anticipation of what he'd learn by catching them in the act. But before he opened the front door, he changed his mind, thinking it might be better to sneak out the back door. That might give him a bit more cover, a chance to see how they were doing it before they detected him.

Wilson was methodical, analytical, and studious like his father, Graham, who was a steadfast engineer until the day he died. Wilson, of course, had loved his father deeply and ended up taking computer engineering courses in an attempt to please the old man, who'd hardly ever spoken a kind or loving word to his son.

To Graham Kendrick, being a good father hadn't been about

providing a loving and nurturing environment but about ensuring the child was provided with the proper series of stimuli and the appropriate opportunity to manipulate and explore the physical world around him. Instead of cuddles and hugs, Wilson received books and magazines. In place of loving words and encouragement, he received construction toys and computer components.

Wilson would always remember that spring when he was in Grade 8, and his classmates were chatting delightedly about their summer spent playing baseball and football and going swimming and hiking and riding their bikes. That was the summer Wilson spent diligently disassembling and reassembling the Commodore Pet computer. Only once he completed that task would his father allow him the opportunity to actually use the computer and discover the programming languages of BASIC, COBOL, FORTRAN, and Pascal. At the tail end of the summer, his father's treat to him, upon passing the test, was allowing him to examine the programming code of the various rudimentary games for this system.

"You'll appreciate playing the games when you understand how they work," Graham Kendrick told his son.

"But, Father," Wilson moaned, "can't I just play the game first? Just for a few minutes?"

The old man simply shook his head. "Learn the code first. Make detailed notes. Once I read your notes, I'll decide if you're ready to play."

Over time, the joys and wonders of creating new landscapes and environments via programming had captured Wilson's imagination, and despite his initial frustration, he was eventually thankful to his father for pushing him.

Of course, it wasn't until much later in his career as a programmer that Wilson realized his mother's own passion for studying and writing haiku and *renga* also had a deep influence on him. *Renga*, a form of Japanese collaborative poetry, required discipline not unlike that required when working on a piece of programming code that was part of a greater piece of software.

Wilson actually derived the name of his software company, Daisan, from the Japanese term referring to the third stanza of a *renga* that allowed the next collaborative poet greater freedom. That was exactly how Wilson had earned himself and his two partners a small fortune. Their concept of channelling shareware and open-source programming through an integrated desktop application directly linking programmers with each other to provide instantaneous wiki-like feedback from around the world was viral in its use. This shared real-time collaboration resulted in stronger, quicker generational growth in programs and provided greater opportunities for developing programmers all over the world to become recognized by large software companies.

The rising success of Daisan led to the sale of the company to a large-platform enterprise. This allowed Wilson to retire at forty-five and pursue other passions. Researching his family history had led him to this small eastern-seaboard town in Nova Scotia, Canada, where his Scottish father had grown up and met his Japanese mother.

Of course, the other passion that had led him to Nova Scotia was the beautiful Ashley, the only woman Wilson had ever loved and who still held a central place in his heart. He'd met Ashley on his first visit to Halifax ten years earlier and returned in the hope of winning her love. But when he arrived to learn that that ship had sailed a long time ago, he focused instead on his family research.

He slowly cracked open the back door and peeked out. There

was less fog in the backyard, and the moonlight shone down like a floodlight on the sprawling knolls of his property.

He spotted a figure moving near the grey birch tree just a few yards away. But he realized it wasn't one of the pranksters. Instead, it was another scarecrow, its one arm blowing in a gentle breeze.

He scanned the rest of the yard. At least another dozen scarecrows were scattered about, some standing beside trees, others in the middle of the open expanses of fields.

He slipped out the door and shut it quickly.

Standing on the cement of the back stoop, Wilson breathed in the salty sea air, a habit formed quickly on his very first trip to the east coast and something he unconsciously repeated with each initial step outside.

Able to see more of the yard and more of the figures scattered about, he realized there must be at least two dozen of the sentries standing guard back there.

Wilson again surveyed the yard for any sign of movement and listened for any noise. It was a calm, quiet night, and there was no sound of rustling footsteps in the leaves or any other indication that there were pranksters moving about in the dark. Wilson heard a car on the highway that ran past his house and the distant resonance of the waves on the nearby shoreline, subtly muted by the fog. A temporary shift in the wind brought with it a strange faint clicking noise like a chorus of knitting needles. It brought to mind the image of an arena filled with a thousand grandmotherly ladies, busily knitting away. Then the noise was gone just as quickly, and the night was silent.

Damn, they're good. Really good, he thought, unable to detect any movement other than the occasional scarecrow arm swinging in the wind.

Confident that none of the pranksters were within eyesight, he crept cautiously to the nearest grey birch. *They must have an entire barn full of these scarecrows*, Wilson thought, bemused, beginning to note the neighbouring farms likely to be able to hold such an army.

When he got closer to the scarecrow near the tree, he was startled to see how realistic her design was. This scarecrow was dressed like a middle-aged woman in a pale blue suit jacket with a pink buttoned-down dress shirt. She had brown wavy hair and large white loop earrings. Her face was flesh-coloured, some sort of latex; she had eyebrows and painted red lips and glassy bead eyes that reflected the moonlight. As he leaned in to study her face, he detected the faint scent of mothballs and thought he saw a subtle movement in her eyes, which he figured was the effect of a wisp of cloud passing in front of the moon.

He spent a few moments staring at this woman before he turned to see a figure a few feet to the right he hadn't noticed earlier: a man in a blue tartan shirt with a grey checked sport coat. Wilson took a few steps toward him.

The man had a large nose, grey-black hair, and big brown eyes, and also gave off the subtle scent of mothballs. His mouth was partially open, revealing a set of pearly white teeth. *How cleverly realistic*, Wilson thought, reaching up and touching the man's latex face.

Wilson jerked his hand back.

The scarecrow's face was warm to the touch.

He pressed a finger onto the man's cheek and left it there.

Yes, definitely warm.

He tried to find the line where the man's mask ended somewhere past his chin, near his neck. But he could spy no line, no edge. The warm latex disappeared beneath the man's shirt collar without a wrinkle.

Just then, a cough echoed through the fog, startling Wilson. One of the pranksters, he figured.

Turning to walk back to his house, he bumped into someone. "Oufff!"

He stepped back to look at the figure, a tall male scarecrow in a beige suit coat and a pressed white dress shirt, with billowing black hair and large dark eyes.

It had definitely not been there a moment before.

Wilson quickly panned his head left and then right, looking for any sign of one of the pranksters. "How the hell are you doing this?" he called.

Despite the scientific and analytic approach, his mind harkened back to the folklore of the *yūrei* from his mother's culture, from which she told the best campfire ghost stories. Wilson had enjoyed the creepy tales about the white-dressed ghosts with long dishevelled hair but had never wasted a moment's thought believing them. He'd studied the different categories of *yūrei* but did so more out of a desire to understand his maternal heritage than of any particular interest in the fables.

However, the scarecrow in front of him brought to mind instead the *goryō*, the vengeful ghosts of the aristocratic class, and he subconsciously took two steps back before bolting for his back door, memories of his mother's ghost stories and the legends he'd read up on finally overcoming reason and logic.

"IT'S THE SWAMP SOGGON!" Dale shouted, his voice loud over the static-filled phone line.

Wilson couldn't think of who else to call other than the young man who tended to the landscaping and various other handyman jobs required on the farmstead. Wilson was a quick study, but he'd never been one to work with his hands. Circuit boards were one thing, but wooden boards were an entirely different beast. Outside of electronics, Wilson's idea of a full toolbox was a roll of masking tape, a hammer, and a flathead screwdriver.

"The *what?*" Wilson asked.

"Swamp Soggon. It's a local legend started by Angella Geddes. Up until a half-dozen years ago, she lived just down the highway in Necum Teuch. She told the tale of a selfish swamp creature with plans to turn all the townsfolk into scarecrows."

Wilson just closed his eyes and shook his head.

He'd needed to call someone and so had contacted Dale. He figured the young man might have some sort of handle on the prankster's style and methodology, that he was likely to know exactly who was involved. But instead, the young man was going on half-cocked about some sort of swamp creature.

Wilson momentarily wondered if perhaps Dale was in on the hoax, a part of the prank. But he shook that thought off as Dale continued, rambling in a chopped and anxious tone Wilson had heard only once before from the young man. "I always thought those stories were a lark, something the old lady cooked up for fun, for enjoyment, to amuse neighbours, to attract tourists. I had no idea the Swamp Soggon was actually real."

As Dale continued to rave about the old woman's mythology in slow, repetitive cycles, Wilson thought back to the only other time he'd heard that same panic in the young man's voice.

It had been earlier in the summer, a particularly hot day in mid-July, and Dale had been doing various maintenance tasks around the yard. At noon, Wilson was looking for the young man, bearing lunch and a portable magnetic chess set, when he heard, very faintly, Dale's panicked, muffled yells.

The calls had come from the root cellar, a five-by-eight-foot storage space partially dug into a small knoll far back on the property that you could only get into by dropping into a small ditch and crawling under the wall.

As Wilson got closer, he could hear a low steady throbbing that at first sounded like an engine.

Wasps. Hundreds of them. Inside the wall of the root cellar.

It took over an hour for Wilson to convince Dale to climb back down under the wall to get out, that the wasps were so busy banging against the sides of the wall that they wouldn't notice him if he did it quickly enough.

Dale eventually got out without a single sting, but Wilson never forgot the intense panic in the young man's voice that afternoon.

The voice he heard on the phone contained the exact same tone of alarm.

"They're going to keep multiplying!" Dale said. "The old woman was right. It's all part of the Soggon's grand plan to take over the town. You've got to get out of there. Now!"

"Dale, listen," Wilson said. "There's no such thing as a swamp creature that can turn people into scarecrows. It's a prank. An elaborate and complicated one, for sure. But a prank. I'll get to the bottom of it, okay?"

"No, Mr. Kendrick. Don't hang up! Don't go back out there! It's not safe!"

"Dale," Wilson said in as calm a voice as he could. "Listen. I'm sorry I woke you. I'm sorry to have bothered you. It's fine. It's all fine. Good night."

He placed the receiver back in the cradle and shook his head again. "Swamp skoggin' indeed," he muttered. "Or was it a soakun?" He let out a short laugh. Nothing shed the substantive light of reason on a situation more than listening to someone who had lost all voice of reason. Hearing Dale go on about the dangers of a nasty swamp monster washed all nonsense about the ghosts of his mother's mythology from his mind.

And now, he was even more determined to get to the bottom of how these pranksters were perpetuating this hoax. Particularly since they likely hadn't expected him to wake up and "catch" them in the act—thus, their ability to remain undetected despite his ongoing investigation spoke highly of their skill at quick adaptation.

But they must have access to a convenient storage facility, and the Saunderson's barn just across the road seemed the most likely place.

Wilson put his jacket back on and headed out the front door to go have a look. The Saundersons had a teenage son. Perhaps he was involved in this with several of his friends.

As he moved through the front yard, Wilson didn't bother trying to remain undetected. The pranksters obviously knew he was out and about and were maintaining the charade of continuing to plant the scarecrow army at their posts while remaining undetected.

As he walked across the front lawn, Wilson counted another half-dozen scarecrows. Among them were several child figures. Some of them weren't standing; two of them were leaning against trees, and one was sitting atop a boulder. He chuckled at one that seemed to be lying atop the roof of the shed at the end of the turn-around in his driveway.

As he crossed the highway, he thought he could hear the cacophony of knitting needles he'd heard earlier, and he stopped in the middle of the road to listen. But as before, the sound faded as quickly as it had come on, and he continued on his way.

The fog was thicker on this side of the highway, being that much closer to the sea's edge, and it carried with it a heavier, more pervasive scent of the salty sea air. The rhythmic lapping of the waves on the nearby shoreline was also louder and offered him a sense of calm and normalcy.

Wilson didn't notice the Saunderson car in the driveway until he had traversed almost halfway up the drive and was just a few feet away from it. As he walked past the black Volkswagen Passat, he noted the droplets of dew on it but still touched the hood to feel that the engine underneath it was cold. If they had gone away this past weekend on one of their regular family trips, they had definitely arrived back a long time ago.

Wilson was walking past the Saunderson house on his way to the barn when he spotted a figure standing on the front porch. He stopped and raised his hand in greeting but then quickly lowered it when he realized it wasn't Eric Saunderson but a scarecrow. He took a few steps forward.

"Well, I'll be damned," Wilson whispered. This scarecrow looked just like his neighbour, complete with the red-plaid hunting jacket he always wore on cool fall evenings and the horn-rimmed glasses. The scarecrow even had a small round circle of hair on the crown of its head, separated from the rest of the receding hairline like some inlet island, a perfect match to the island of hair Saunderson boasted.

Wilson laughed, completely impressed with the detail—but it didn't make sense to him that the pranksters would go to that much pain, particularly with this scarecrow being completely out of visual range from his own front step.

A chill ran up Wilson's spine.

There was something more amiss here than he'd been willing to admit.

A car turning the corner down the highway threw a fog-blurred headlight beam across the front of the Saunderson house. In that quick flash of subdued light, Wilson saw one of the Saunderson children sitting on the front step swing—or rather, the likeness of the young girl in scarecrow guise. And behind her, visible through the front window, was the likeness of Pamela Saunderson, in her blue-pansy-print house dress, still holding the television remote in her right hand.

For the second time that night, Wilson turned and ran back to his house.

As he ran, he held his right arm strategically over his mouth and nose, fearful of breathing in a toxic substance and tried to ignore the fact that at least two or three more scarecrows had appeared in previously vacant spots in his yard.

The phone was ringing when he got inside.

Out of breath, he stumbled to it.

"Hello?" Wilson huffed as he picked up the receiver.

"Mr. Kendrick?" It was Dale. "The phone kept ringing. I was scared you'd gone outside. Thank God you answered. Don't go outside. Don't go anywhere near the swamp. If you can get to your shed without being seen, here's what you need to do. You need to—"

"Dale!" Wilson interrupted, finally catching his breath. "Stop it! There is definitely something going on. I think it's some sort of airborne contagion. I've never seen anything like it, but I've formulated a quick theory. I haven't thought it through completely, but . . ." Wilson stopped talking, realizing he was rambling on in the same manner Dale had been.

In the run back to his house, he'd determined that what he was seeing might have been caused by some airborne substance, possibly carried in from the sea on the fog. He suspected it was causing a reaction not unlike the side effects one might see with tetrodotoxin. It made sense, given that this deadly neurotoxin was found in puffer fish and some species of marine toads and tree frogs and that the side effect was paralysis and the appearance of death.

Wilson amused himself by noting it was a Canadian ethnobotanist, Wade Davis, who had created a pharmacological case for zombies in his studies and research.

Wilson deduced that the neurotoxin, which could be passed into the bloodstream through topical exposure, had somehow been carried on the fog and was causing the zombie-like appearance of the victims. The way people seemed to appear out of nowhere on Wilson's front lawn could be due to confusion—another side effect of the poisoning—and mass panic.

All these thoughts and theories, still not completely resolved, had been swirling in Wilson's head when he'd answered the phone. He'd made a rash error by blurting it out, particularly to a young man without the scientific knowledge or background to understand it.

"Mr. Kendrick. Are you still there?"

Wilson took a deep breath. "Yes, Dale. I am. Now listen. There is something seriously wrong going on. You need to stay inside, keep the windows closed. And don't go out."

"But, Mr. Kendrick," Dale pleaded," you've got to stop the Swamp Soggon. Fire will do it. Swamp creatures crave moisture. They're afraid of fire.

"There are a few ten-gallon gas cans in your shed. You can use them to dose the scarecrows, then light them on fire. Burn them. Surround your house with a wall of flames. Don't let any of them, or the Swamp Soggon, in."

Wilson recoiled at the B-movie antics Dale suggested, never

mind that he was holding fast to some supernatural hocus-pocus theory of a swamp creature. The entire scenario he'd been suggesting was farcical.

Rather than continue with an argument he knew neither of them would budge on, Wilson thought his best course of action was to hang up and alert the authorities. Given that there was some airborne contagion, they needed to shut down the highway and establish the greater Moser River region as a hot zone.

"Dale," Wilson said. "I'm hanging up now. Whatever you do, stay inside. Keep the windows and doors closed." Dale lived several kilometres down the highway in a neighbouring community, and Wilson couldn't be sure how far the contagion might have spread. With that said, he pushed the disconnect button.

When he lifted his finger a moment later, the line hadn't disconnected.

"Dale," Wilson said calmly. "Please hang up."

There was no response on the other end.

He placed the receiver down in the cradle.

Waited a moment.

Picked it up again.

Still, dead air. No dial tone. Dale still hadn't hung up.

Then Wilson listened and couldn't even hear the young man breathing. Maybe he'd dropped the phone. *Perhaps after having fallen prey to the toxin*, a panicked thought raced through the back of his head.

"Dale!" Wilson shouted. "Dale, are you there?"

But he was again greeted with nothing but silence.

"Damn!"

Wilson repeatedly jabbed at the disconnect button but still didn't get a dial tone. He slammed the phone back into the cradle.

Standing over the telephone, Wilson hoped against hope that

Dale was okay, that perhaps the young man was just too frightened to speak, and that's why there was no answer on the other end.

And then he thought about what the young man had suggested. Dousing the scarecrows in flames. Creating a flame ring.

The young man had likely suggested it as a result of seeing too many black-and-white B-movies about the Creature from the Black Lagoon or something, but there was a point there. If this region of Highway 7 was falling prey to a local outbreak of some sort of contagion, he wondered if dousing the victims in gasoline, then setting them aflame, might help prevent further spread, at least until the proper authorities in charge of disease control could get out here.

He tried the phone once more.

It was still connected at Dale's end.

He PLUCKED the keys to the padlock on the shed from the key hook in the front hall, then rummaged in the utility drawer of the front hall table and found the Zippo lighter. He paused in front of the cherry-oak-framed mirror hanging on the wall above the table and looked at himself.

This could be it, he thought as he stared into the reflection of his own middle-aged eyes, now very much droopy and tired-looking. Going back out there would likely mean exposing himself to whatever toxin was currently floating around in the air on the fog. And it could mean certain death.

But understanding what he did, there was a chance he could at least slow the spread of this and maybe lead authorities to discover what was happening.

He'd never thought of himself as a hero, even in the fantasies that played in the back of his mind. He was a software developer, an analytical businessman with a keen thirst for knowledge and answers.

And though he had fallen in love once, with Ashley, he'd never had a single meaningful relationship, despite decades of trying; never had kids. Sure, he'd leave behind a small legacy with the software company and products he'd developed. But that would fade in time with the emergence of new and better technologies, multi-generational versions of his products.

He at least had this. He might be able to make a difference and slow down the outbreak.

Since realizing his pursuit of Ashley was hopeless and focusing instead on his family history, he'd learned all kinds of details about his heritage, compiling a huge file of facts that he'd posted on his blog. One that made him proudest was that he was a distant relative of Vince Coleman, the train dispatcher who'd stayed behind in the aftermath of the collision of two ships in Halifax harbour—one loaded with tons of dangerous explosives— to telegraph an urgent warning to an incoming passenger train. Coleman had died that morning along with 2,000 others in the Halifax Explosion of 1917, but not before saving the 700 lives of the people aboard the train he'd sent the warning to.

Wilson figured that the least he could was carry on that proud example of nobility.

He decided the fastest and best way to both get the word out and alert authorities would be via the Internet. So, he ran into his study to boot up his computer. A quick single-paragraph blog entry would explain what he was doing, in case he didn't survive to tell the tale, and an auto blast of his message via an RSS feed to all his contacts via two social-networking platforms on which he boasted more than 3,000 "friends"—mostly other likeminded computer geeks and scientific minds—would likely reach the proper authorities in record time.

With that done, Wilson went to the kitchen, turned on all of the burners on the gas stove, ripped a curtain off the kitchen window, and laid it across the burners. They erupted into flame immediately, and he tossed the burning curtain back toward the window, watching it catch the other, still-hanging curtain.

He fled out through the back door of the kitchen and raced to the shed at the side of his house.

By the time he got to the shed, the flames inside the kitchen were so bright they lit up the entire backyard, and he was easily able to negotiate the key into the padlock. He flung open the shed door and, by that same light, was able to find the gas drums Dale had mentioned.

As he was hauling out the first steel drum, he caught sight of a scarecrow just a few yards to the right of the shed, one he hadn't noticed before.

He dropped the drum and the lighter and stared at her.

"Ashley," he whispered, not able to take his eyes off the scarecrow, mesmerized by the way the flicker of the firelight danced in her short red hair.

He took a single step forward.

"No, please don't be Ashley. Please . . ."

He took another step forward, then another, until he was standing in front of her. He put his left hand up to feel the warmth of the alabaster skin of her face. His right hand stroked her silky red hair as he stared deep into those teal-green eyes and thought back to the very first night he'd lost himself in them.

It had been a decade earlier. Wilson had flown into Halifax to attend a tech conference. On an evening out with fellow delegates, he'd ended up at The Lower Deck, a bar down on the waterfront. There, a gorgeous young waitress caught his eye, or rather, his ear. He overheard her discussion with an older couple at a neighbouring table as she slid two bowls of clam chowder in front of them.

"I had a chat with the chef and wanted to assure you that this chowder, our house specialty, has absolutely no shellfish content in it."

"Thank you," the man said, dipping his head.

The waitress then pulled her notepad out and ripped off the first page. "And just to ensure you're aware of the contents, I had the chef list every single ingredient he used." She handed them the paper with a huge grin, winked, and gently touched the arm of the old gentleman. "Now, you just keep this paper confidential. We don't want any of our competitors finding out our special secret ingredients."

Laughing, the couple thanked her, and she moved over to Wilson's table and introduced herself as Ashley.

The young woman was pleasant, sweet, courteous, and charming, and Wilson had never seen such a lovely smile.

Regardless of the entertaining musical show and great conversation with fellow delegates, Wilson found that he could not keep his eyes off of the pretty redhead. It wasn't out of any sort of drunken lust—he simply derived pleasure from gazing at her.

She'd noticed his stare early into the evening and interpreted it as a sign that he needed another drink. Delighted to have an excuse to chat and flirt with her, Wilson continued to order rounds of drinks for the group at his table. Each time she came to the table, they exchanged short, quick pleasantries, and he was as enthralled with the sound of her voice as he had been with her cute, close-mouthed smile. Through the course of the evening, she'd learned his first name, and they'd fallen into a comfortable pattern of humorous exchanges.

When the bar closed, and the other delegates had piled into cabs to head home, Wilson didn't want the wonderful evening to end. He was still high with the pleasure of flirting with Ashley and admiring her pixie-like beauty all evening. He'd never been particularly smooth or popular with women, so he was surprised at how calm and natural joking around with her had been.

So, trying to stretch out the evening, he took a stroll on the docks to bask in the smell of the sea air, the sounds of the ships creaking in the movement of the waves, and the lights of Dartmouth across the water. His hotel was at the south end of the docks, so he'd ventured north on a short stroll, exploring a bit before turning around and heading back.

Just a few yards past The Lower Deck, he spotted Ashley walking along the dock ahead of him. She turned her head slightly when she heard the echo of his footsteps on the boardwalk and smiled when she recognized him.

"Hi, Wilson. I didn't figure you for a stalker," she said, still smiling.

He laughed, and his face turned red. "It's just so incredibly beautiful out here," he said, one arm waving toward the water. Then he turned back toward her, the beer speaking the next words. "So incredibly beautiful. Like you."

Wilson paused, realizing what he'd just done. His jaw dropped open. He'd never been so forward with a woman before and imagined what he'd just said sounded like a goofy pickup line. He had no idea how she'd react.

Ashley smiled, then laughed. "Thanks. But you're drunk. All

girls look pretty to you right now." She offered her elbow. "C'mon. Take my arm. I'll make sure you make it back safely to your hotel."

He tentatively hooked his elbow around hers.

"But just to warn you," she said with a grin as they started walking together, "you make any funny moves, and I'm tossing you right into the drink. I have a black belt in karate and Jujitsu."

"Really?"

"No, I'm just pulling your leg. But for a scrawny little chick, I'm tough, and I'll lift you over my head and throw you into the water as sure as I'm standing here."

Wilson laughed. "I don't doubt for a second you're capable of it. But I doubt you'd hurt a flea."

"Not true," she said wryly. "I've killed plenty of fleas in my time. Mosquitoes, black flies, and spiders too."

He laughed again. "You're a walking exterminator."

It was a forty-five-minute walk to the end of the boardwalk where Wilson's hotel was. Wilson soaked in the details about Ashley's life and was as impressed with her as he was with the picturesque scenery.

They couldn't have been more opposite in their backgrounds and views on life, but Wilson admired everything about her. A farm girl from a small town a few hours outside of Halifax, she'd graduated from the local university and had been working as a waitress in the evenings since her second year of post-secondary education to pay for school. And since graduating, she'd also had a day job working afternoons at a nearby restaurant. She had at least another year of working the two jobs before she'd be done paying her student loans. Once that was done, she would take her B.A. back to the dairy farm near Moser River her father still ran and apprentice herself to take over the business.

Wilson couldn't fathom why someone would return to the

hard and rugged routine of farm life after earning themselves a post-secondary education that could land them a better job. But this just added to the mystique of Ashley and what became his decade-long infatuation with her.

When they were within sight of the end of the boardwalk, they stood near a large, docked fishing vessel and talked for another forty minutes. The conversation hadn't even come close to running dry, but a drizzle of rain brought it to a quick end.

"It has been great chatting with you," Ashley said, her green eyes beaming. She kissed him briefly on the cheek before turning and walking away. "You're a sweet man. Goodnight, Wilson. Have a safe flight back home."

"Goodbye, Ashley." Wilson grinned and waved goodbye as she headed toward Morris Street to her apartment.

He stood there and watched her retreat, not taking his eyes off her until she completely disappeared from view, thinking he'd never again see this magnificent woman whom he felt so naturally comfortable with. He remained motionless for another few minutes, still basking in her warmth as he stood alone on the dock, barely noticing the cold rain plastering his clothes to his skin.

For years after that meeting, Wilson wondered if the rain had been the perfect cue to invite her to his hotel room.

Of course, Wilson had never been a smooth operator, and that single hour and a half of conversation with her was the closest he'd ever come to having a relationship with a woman. Pathetic, he knew. But his heart never stopped burning for Ashley.

When he'd returned a decade after meeting her—six months ago now—and looked her up, he was overwhelmingly disappointed to find she'd gotten married five years earlier and already had a three-year-old son. He didn't bother contacting her, figuring she wouldn't remember him anyway, but had continued to admire her from afar, at least somewhat content to know she was happy and prosperous.

Until now.

The toxin had gotten to her.

Wilson stood before the woman he'd loved and yearned for and let his tears flow.

"I loved you from the moment we first met, Ashley," Wilson said, his words wet and heavy. "And I never stopped loving you all these years."

Then he did something he'd never dared do before.

He leaned forward and placed a single gentle kiss on Ashley's lips.

Like the others, her latex-like flesh was warm.

Then he took a step back to admire her again. Even in this grotesque and creepy scarecrow form, she was as beautiful and glowing as he first remembered her. He continued to stand and admire her, never tiring of the pleasure of gazing into her eyes.

As he stared into those glassy green orbs, he saw a tear well up in the corner of her eye socket and run down her face. Imagining it was just moisture from the fog gathering there, he dismissed it until a second rolled down after it a moment later.

"Ashley?" Wilson said, his words barely a whisper.

He reached forth, brought a single finger up to the tear rolling down her cheek, and caught it on his fingertip. The tear was warm.

"Ashley?" he repeated. "Oh dear, sweet Ashley. Are you still alive in there?"

The strange incessant clicking noise he'd heard earlier sounded again, and something sharp jabbed into Wilson's right ankle.

He yelled and stumbled backward as he kicked at the source of the pain. A black crow scampered off across the grass. Despite the fog, his eyes were able to track it as it ran, flapping its wings to gain forward momentum, all the way to the edge of the forest adjacent to his property.

That was when he noticed something strange about the trees. They seemed alive with small, subtle movements, not unlike the rustling of leaves in the wind, only there wasn't any wind, and the "leaves" were dark, shadowy things. As he looked closer, Wilson realized the trees were filled to capacity with crows. Every single tree. Thousands of black birds sat in the branches.

A subtle shift in the wind brought the clicking noise to him, the sound of thousands of old ladies madly knitting.

An intense burning-cold sensation, like the feeling of anesthetic running through his veins, started at his ankle and shot up his leg. He turned back to look at Ashley, and her beautiful green eyes were the last thing he saw before he blacked out.

WILSON DIDN'T SO MUCH OPEN his eyes as his consciousness rose to slowly reveal the world in front of him like some dark black stage curtain falling away.

He was standing in his backyard at about the spot he'd been in when he took a step back from Ashley. He couldn't turn his head —his neck was stiff and tight, like he'd slept with his head at a funny angle—but he could see Ashley.

And beyond her, the other scarecrows, a hundred or so of them. Faintly, softly in the background, he could still hear that maddening chorus of quiet clicking.

That's when he realized it hadn't been a dream. The whole evening had been real.

He tried to move his arms, take a step forward.

His limbs were heavy and useless. He couldn't move them at all.

The toxin, the disease, whatever it was, was being spread by those crows. Perhaps generated by the crows. Wilson tried to listen to them, watching the trees for further signs of their movement.

"I didn't know."

The softly spoken words came clearly from his right, and though he hadn't heard it in ten years, Wilson had never forgotten the sweet, melodic tone of Ashley's voice.

"Didn't know what?" Wilson spoke without moving his lips, but his voice was clear and normal.

"How you felt about me."

"You . . . remember me?"

"Of course, I do, Wilson. How couldn't I? You were a sweet guy, and I could tell you were interested in me as a person and not just trying to lure me into the nearest bed. Before you, I'd never met a man who didn't just want into my pants. How could I forget something like that?"

Wilson didn't answer; he just strained to look at Ashley from the corner of his eye.

"But you never called. I thought about you for a long time. I always wondered where you were or what you'd been up to. Of course, after time, I realized I didn't really know you—that you were just some fantasy man who'd walked into my life one evening and then walked out just as quickly.

"But thanks to you, showing me that there were sweet guys out there, the way I looked at men changed. And I found someone sweet and genuine. My husband, Robert, is a great guy, Wilson. I was first attracted to him because he reminded me of you."

Wilson's vision blurred as tears welled up in his eyes. He

thought of all of those lonely years of wondering about Ashley, how he'd sat around thinking of excuses to call her or look her up on the internet and get in contact with her. But he had never worked up the courage to do anything.

It was only after he retired that he finally found the nerve to go seek her. But even then, he had the plan of researching his family history as a backup, thinking himself a fool for pursuing Ashley from the other side of the continent.

But by then, it had been too late.

And now? Now, here they were, stuck in scarecrow form, partially facing one another and apparently unable to do anything but talk. Wilson felt a pang of bittersweet happiness.

"Ashley," he whispered, his voice still choked with tears. "I never stopped loving you. Never stopped longing to hear your sweet voice again, just be near you again. Talk to me. There's time now. More than enough time. So talk to me. Tell me something, anything. Please just talk to me, Ashley."

The muffled sound of footsteps on the damp leaf-encrusted grass approached from behind him. But there was another noise, although Wilson couldn't quite figure out what it was.

"Someone's coming," Ashley said hopefully. "Mister, Mister. Over here, please help us. Please."

Wilson looked and saw a single man walking in the grass, carefully avoiding coming too close to any of the scarecrow people he passed. Wilson figured out what the secondary sound was a moment later. It was the combined chorus of all the other scarecrow people calling to him for help in vain. He simply couldn't hear them, as if their voices were of a pitch too high for the naked human ear to detect.

As the man got closer, Wilson recognized him. Tall, obviously broad-shouldered even in his thick orange fall hunting jacket; a young, distinctly handsome man with short curly blond hair and big brown wide eyes. It was Dale.

"Dale!" Wilson called out. "Over here. It's me. It's Wilson."

Even as he spoke the words, even as his cries to be heard merged with the pathetic chorus of pleas for help from the others, Wilson knew there was no point. But he couldn't stop himself from pleading, from begging.

His pleas turned to panicked yelling as he saw Dale walk over to the steel gas drum Wilson had dropped, take a quick look around, then pick up the drum and pull a lighter out of his pocket.

Despite the intensity of his own shrill screams, Wilson could still hear each of Dale's booted steps clearly as he marched toward him and Ashley and unscrewed the cap to the gas can.

As the gasoline splashed into his eyes, blinding him, the last thing Wilson heard before that final whoomph of the flames igniting was Ashley's screams . . .

. . . and the maddening clicking sound of the crows in the nearby trees.

THE THINGS FENTON FOUND

By Michaelbrent Collings

F enton had lost his father, and all he could think was how very silly it all was.

It wasn't that Fenton hadn't loved his father—he had, very much. But he still thought it was silly. "Here one moment, gone the next," he said to quite a few people in the days and weeks that followed. "One moment, the big, foolish old man is there, hassling me about if I'm ever going to get a grown-up job—knowing quite well that I have a grown-up job, it's called being an artist, and I make plenty of money at it—and the next moment I've lost him. Here, gone, here, gone. What else is like that, I wonder?"

And the people he said it to would smile and nod and not say anything back because those people were all quite wise and knew that some things were said to be heard, not said to be argued.

Sometimes Fenton raged after he said his speech and the same wise people let him rage. "He's lost his father," they would say after they'd left the home where Fenton's father had lived and that Fenton was in the process of selling to a corporation that bought lovely old houses and bulldozed them to make ugly new apartments. "No surprise that he's feeling down. I'd imagine it's quite easy to lose one's temper in that situation!"

And they were very right to say that, of course. Because losses tend to cluster, so it was indeed no surprise that, having lost his father, Fenton was losing his temper as well. Some of the more well-meaning (which any good storyteller knows is a good way to say "nosy") friends worried that more loss might come. "What if he loses his mind?" they would say. "What if, cleaning out an entire lifetime's worth of trinkets and trifles, poor Fenton goes mad?"

Then they would laugh, which was cruel in one way but quite natural in another. Because *they* hadn't lost their father, *they* hadn't lost their temper, and *they* certainly hadn't lost their sense of humour.

But Fenton didn't laugh. And in many ways, that was the saddest thing of all. Because Fenton used to laugh quite a bit. He and his father argued like two dogs looking at a single piece of bacon, but he loved the old man just the same, and now he was missing him. He used to laugh when his dad asked him if he was ever going to get a real job, or settle down and get married, or start making some grandchildren for him to dandle on his knee (Fenton especially laughed about that one because he was fairly certain his father had no idea what "dandle" even meant).

But now his father was gone. The questions gone. Fenton's smile gone.

And there was the couch.

Fenton's dad had loved the couch. The frame was huge—massive, really; one of those couches that were made so long ago that the artistry of them has been lost to time, and the workmanship is of a type that will never be seen again.

Fenton himself had a sensible, small couch. It was so slim he never once wanted to lean back and fall asleep on it because there just wasn't room for that. It was light in colour, a lovely cream *faux* leather, easily stained and therefore perfect for a man with no family. It was also light in weight, enough that he could move it himself if he needed to.

But this thing? This thing was a monster. He wasn't even sure how he'd manage to get it out the door—if it could fit through the door at all. And the more he wondered that, the bigger the old couch seemed to look, the heavier it appeared. Finally, Fenton decided *screw it* (he'd lost his patience at this point) and leaned over to pick up the couch. Just to see if it really was as heavy as it looked.

He hooked his fingers under the base of the couch and heaved. And heaved. And heaved. Three big heaves, and his fingers cramped and his back screamed, and when he was done with the third heave, he had moved the couch not at all. The thing felt like it must have been made out of the recovered hull of the *Titanic*, then coated in the heaviest cushions—which were themselves made of lead bricks covered in the thickest wool shorn from large, outraged sheep.

It made Fenton tired to think this. He was an artist, not an author, so mental metaphor was not his forte, and coming up with the whole thing about the *Titanic* and lead and sheep quite exhausted him. He would paint a picture when he got back home, he decided—back to *his* home, not this place that smelled like sweat and pizza bagels and cinnamon and a million other things he couldn't quite place.

Yes, he thought. *I'll paint a picture. I don't know of what, but it will be of something. Perhaps everything. Everything but the* Titanic *or lead bars or sheep—or this damn couch!*

He kicked the couch, which turned out to be a mistake because it felt like he'd kicked the *Titanic* and bruised his toes. The fact that the couch didn't seem to notice the kick in the least made him doubly upset.

Something fell at this point. Fenton wasn't sure what it was. It fell in the farthest corner of his peripheral vision, in that spot where "I saw it" has mostly turned to something between "Did you see that?" and "I feel something's wrong." Just a quick flash of sensation/sight, and if it weren't for the fact that the thing was so very bright and red, almost like looking at a fiery sun (if he'd been able to look at it, if it hadn't fallen so far out of sight), he wouldn't have noticed it at all.

But he did notice it. He saw the flash; he felt the heat. And, seeing and feeling, he turned just in time to see whatever it was fall into the deep crevasse between two of the couch's huge cushions.

A strange rage overtook him. He'd lost so much. He'd lost time. He'd lost work. He'd lost his father and friend and, surprisingly, much of himself along with them. Losing whatever the red thing was turned out to be the final straw, and Fenton James Hershel, son of Clarence James Hershel, grandson of Aaron James Hershel (and undoubtedly great-grandson of someone with a middle name of James, but Fenton only knew back as far as Grampa Aaron) threw back his head and screamed. He screamed and screamed until all his strength was gone. When he was done screaming, he cried and, because the screaming hadn't really helped, decided to cry for a good long while—though not long enough to exhaust his strength again. He needed his strength—which he planned next to use (after the crying) to post the couch on all the local "FOR FREE!" websites so that someone else could worry about the damn thing.

And that is what he did.

He took a few pictures of the couch with his phone (he had to zoom out all the way to get the thing in), and then he put the pictures on six different websites, all with the same copy:

FREE Couch. Brownish. Biggish. Oldish. VERY solid. Old but it's a good couch in a lot of ways even if it can get annoying sometimes to try and sit in it because it's so big that you sink in and then all the change runs out of your pockets along with your car keys or your pens or whatever but it's still a very good couch and sturdy and has lots of life in it. My dad loved this couch. Lots of memories here I'm sure, just waiting for the right place to live. NO delivery. YOU pick up. FREE. YOU PICK UP.

By the time he had posted on the last website, an email had come from someone interested in the couch. She said she had a family full of small boys who would love the couch in their play-room (which Fenton heard to mean, "I'm glad I found a free couch they can wreck!" but that was fine with him because he was still angry about the couch and wanted just to be done with it all). She would be there in an hour to pick it up, and she would bring her husband, the boys, and a furniture dolly.

Fenton thought about emailing her to bring a saw as well, as he suspected they might have to cut the door wider, but decided against it.

Once that was done, he felt a bit better, though still strangely angry and not really sure why. Then he remembered: the red thing! It had fallen into the couch when he was standing over it, which meant it had come from Fenton. He had no memory of placing any brightly burning supernovas in his pockets that morning, but he must've, mustn't he, or it wouldn't have fallen out of his pocket in the first place.

Whatever it was, he should get it back before the lady—whose name was Mary and who Fenton had already decided was probably fat and enjoyed eating Skittles because he didn't very much like Skittles—showed up. He didn't want some Skittle-grubbing *stranger* having his previously-unknown celestial pocket lint.

"Plus, I should probably clean out the couch generally," he said. He said this angrily and to himself—because there was no one around, and Fenton, while sad and outraged and strangely lost-feeling, was not insane. He was not seeing people who weren't there; he hadn't lost his mind as some of his friends worried. So, while he spoke aloud, he spoke very determinedly to himself and not to anyone else who wasn't really there.

Which was why it was such a surprise when a voice answered, "Probably a good idea."

Fenton was standing by the biggish, brownish, oldish couch when it happened, leaning over to grab a pillow to pull it off the couch and toss it behind him so he could dig his hands into decades' worth of grubby couch-crack filth. But when he heard that sound, he froze. He was alone; he was sure of it. There was no one in the empty room (which would soon be the exact location of apartment 1B in the Shangri-La Apartments, built by a company "whimsically" called Good Enough To Live In, Inc., though Fenton did not know all that just yet). There was only him. And the couch.

I've gone crazy, he thought. *It's finally happened.*

Out loud, he said no such thing. Out Loud Fenton had always been much braver than Deep Down Fenton, so out loud, he said, "Is anyone in here? If they are, I'm armed." (Out Loud Fenton, it must be said, was also a liar upon occasion.)

No answer came. Fenton decided it must have been his imagination. Imagination, grief, lack of sleep, and perhaps the small, vibrantly purple pills someone had given him at a party last night. He hadn't felt like going to the party, but everyone insisted, and he'd finally lost any desire to be sad any longer and went—even though he was sad all night and ended up crying in a corner and wishing his dad was there to yell at him for hanging out with such depressingly stereotypical artist-types.

"Hellooooooo?" he said.

Nothing.

Just my imagination, he thought/scolded/tried to persuade himself. *No one here but me and that big ugly couch, which big, ugly, Skittle-popping Mary will be here to collect in . . . good heavens, is that the time?*

He had to get the couch cleaned out. He wanted whatever had fallen, and he also didn't want Mary to find a pen or some mysterious sticky substance or—heaven forbid!—an old pizza bagel stuck in the cracks of the couch and decide not to take the monster away.

He reached for the middle cushion.

I'll just pull it off. Pull it off, and then I'll clean it out and then the Skittle-monster will take it and the couch will be gone and I can put this all behind me.

But an inch away from grabbing hold, his fingers curled inward as if they had minds of their own. He kept hearing that voice, that strange voice telling him it was a good idea to clean the couch, and—abruptly and completely—Fenton lost a brand-new thing: his nerve.

His fingers hung there, not an inch above the cushion made of lead bars and angry Irish sheep (Fenton thought sheep came from Ireland; he wasn't sure, but the angry sheep in his mind definitely had a brogue). They hung there a long time.

Then Fenton saw something. It was a thread. Just a thread. But it was strange and definitely didn't belong with the couch. The couch was massive, oldish, brownish, dingyish. The thread was tiny, new-seeming, silver, bright.

He tugged at it. He didn't think about it, just reached the last inch and pulled, and the thread came away, and he realized it hadn't been part of the couch at all. It had been under the cushion, jutting up in exactly the right way to catch the light—the only hope at all for him to have seen the ethereal thing.

He wondered what it was; what a long, silver, beautiful thread was doing with this big couch made of *Titanic* bones. Certainly, it wasn't *his* thread. He wore no silver clothing (except for that one gala, and even then, he thought he looked like an idiot and vowed never to do it again), and his father certainly wouldn't have been caught dead in such vivid styles.

Although, he thought as he pocketed the thread, *I guess what my father will or will not be caught dead in is totally up to me now.*

The thought made him giggle, even though it made him sad and angry at the same time. He thought Dad would have liked it as a joke, so it wasn't disrespectful. Was it?

He really didn't know. He only knew that as he put the bright silver thread into his pocket, he felt better, stronger, more himself. He was still angry—at his father, at the universe, and most of all at the couch—but better. So he pocketed the thread and, feeling better, pulled back the couch cushion and tossed it over his head. It was easy enough to do, for the cushion, far from being a thing made of lead and the shorn wool of an outraged Seamus Doyle McSheepwill, was very light. It weighed barely anything at all, in fact, and when he threw it behind him, the cushion flew back and hit a wall, then bounced down and smashed into a rather expensive lamp. The lamp was an ethereal thing, the one truly nice thing Fenton thought his dad had ever owned, but the pillow was so light it bounced right off the spun-glass lamp and crumpled on the floor.

"Huh!" said Fenton, surprised.

He turned back to the couch. "Now, where's the bright star thing?" he said (to himself), suddenly angry again.

He was aware at this point that he was talking to himself more than normal. For some reason, he didn't care. Finding the thread had changed something in him. He felt stronger and braver by far than he had in a long time and ready to do anything. He could take on the world! Or, failing that, he could clean up the couch for Mary and her litter of no doubt also Skittle-scarfing whelps.

Under the pillow, he found no shiny red thing. He took off the second pillow. And the third.

Nothing. No red thing. No nothing at all, which surprised Fenton deeply. He felt like he'd lost millions of dollars in quarters alone sitting on this couch; how could it be so clean? Had someone else already been in here? Had someone cleaned it? Who? Who would have gone behind his back and done such a thing? Was it Graham, with his questionable pills? Was it Ray, with his/her (Fenton was never quite sure with Ray and had known him/her far too long to ask without seeming rude) need to be a part of everything? Was it that damn Mary with her—

"Easy," he said. "You're losing your grip." He knew it was true, and to prove that he could find that grip, he grabbed the arm of the couch and gripped it.

Surprisingly, it worked. He felt better and realized that Graham didn't know about this place (Graham could be a bit sketchy, so he'd never mentioned the now-empty house to him), Ray wouldn't care (Ray cared about little but being invited to everything and then spoiling movies that were out in theatres by telling everyone how he/she'd read the script and "you won't *believe* how it ends, darlings!"), and Mary just wasn't here yet.

But she would be soon.

And Fenton hadn't yet found that lost red thing, which was upsetting. It was quite beautiful, he thought—even if he really hadn't seen it at all—and he wanted it back. Besides, if it really was some quasar or something, he could undoubtedly put that in a piece of art and sell it for a pretty penny.

The couch was bare. No cushions on the bottom and the cushions on the back were sewn in. Which meant that to find the star/quasar/supernova/possibly imagined bit of nothing caused by overwhelming grief, he'd have to do something he'd always hated doing: he'd have to dig into the cracks of the couch.

Every couch has these cracks, and Fenton knew that. They are generally quite harmless, and Fenton knew that. But knowledge is not the same as belief, and Fenton couldn't quite get over believing that he'd one day put his fingers into a tiger trap hidden in the couch cracks; or feel the prick of a dirty needle covered in blood infected with AIDS, COVID, and a very bad cold that someone had dropped in there; or perhaps just feel a Gooey Bunch of Yucky Stuff.

He patted his pocket where the silver thread was. It made him feel better. He dug his hands into the crack. He felt along the back of the couch, where the back upright cushions met the back rail. The upholstery covering the springs folded under there, allowing just enough room for him to dig his fingers in deep, questing for pocket stars or Yucky Stuff.

His fingers found only fingers, which made him yelp and dance back because the fingers his fingers had found were not *his* fingers at all.

He looked at the couch (now about six feet away from it

because of the dancing). Nothing but couch. After a moment, he lay down on his stomach and tried to look under the couch. The front skirt draped low; nothing could be seen below it. He patted his thread-laden pocket and reached out and flipped back the skirt (which, like the couch, was heavy-looking but, unlike the couch, was surprisingly light). He shone his cell phone light below the couch. Nothing there. Just the floor below and darkness above.

He stood.

It was impossible. What he'd felt was *impossible*. There couldn't have been fingers there. There was barely enough room in that crack for his own fingers, let alone a second pair of loose ones rolling around. *Certainly* not enough room under the couch upholstery to hide a person—which is what it would have had to be, really, because the fingers that Fenton's fingers found weren't loose and rolling around at all, they were warm and strong, and they curled around his own quite tightly before he yanked free and did his fancy Dance of Speedy Withdrawal move.

He stared at the couch. It was very big. Did it have room, between the lower rails and the springs that supported the cushions (which Fenton had suddenly decided were, in fact, made not of angry Irish wool but of spun—and very content—Burmese lotus flower silk, though he would not share this fact with anyone and especially not with Ray because Ray always accused people of being racist as soon as they said anything remotely racist), to hide a person? And if so, was it the person who had told Fenton it would be a good idea to clean the couch? And if *that* was so, why had the person allowed themselves to be sewn up in the couch at all, let alone wait this long to encourage someone to clean it?

So many questions, and though they all made a certain kind of sense, they also made a much *more* certain kind of *nonsense*, which worried Fenton on many levels (not least of them being what Ray might say about it someday).

He decided that he should continue checking the couch. At worst, he would find out he was insane, that grief and exhaustion and bright pills had pushed him over the edge, and he'd finally lost his mind.

But he really didn't think that was it. He didn't think he'd lost his mind at all. He thought the couch had something in it, and after finding that silver thread, there was no way he would give up looking now.

And yes, Fenton did know that that last thought made a great *deal* of nonsense, but he didn't care. He wanted to know at this point. And he was, truth be told, still feeling angry about losing the bright red UFO (Unidentified Falling Object). So he just patted his thread-laden pocket and pushed his fingers back in the crack, bracing to find someone's hand waiting to hold his. But he found no hand at all. He found

- a quarter
- a dime
- two nickels
- another quarter
- the decapitated head of a Lego man
- three pens
- two pencils
- a guitar pick
- a feather
- a travel magazine that Fenton had never heard of
- six TV remotes
- a strangely large Cheerio
- two more quarters

- a roll of pennies that had only sixteen pennies even though the roll was for fifty
- five Tylenol
- a pair of reading glasses with one lens missing
- a small pill dispenser with one little box for each day of the week (which had three more Tylenol in it)
- a fine China bowl (which Ray would insist be called simply "a fine bowl")
- a dry-erase marker with no cap
- a dark light bulb
- a lit candle
- three tube socks that Fenton somehow knew were all once-missing *left* socks
- a green plastic twist tie
- a blue plastic spork
- a Hot Wheels car
- a 3x5 card with BEWARE THE OCELOT written on it
- a coin purse (with no coins in it, which surprised Fenton)
- a bar of soap that had been meticulously whittled to form a perfect replica of a (slightly smaller) bar of soap
- a single puzzle piece, and
- a calico cat.

Anyone hearing this story is probably saying the same thing at this point: "He must have imagined whatever the bright red thing was. If it was a bright red thing. Maybe it was a green thing, and instead of being a star or a piece of celestial machinery, it was a twist tie. Or the spork, if the red thing was, in reality, blue, or if the spork was, in reality, red."

A few of you, however, are thinking, *Why didn't Fenton stop*

when he pulled a lit candle *out of a box made of wood and either highly-flammable (and possibly enraged) Irish wool or equally flammable (though likely happier) Burmese lotus flower silk?*

The former question has no answer but to continue reading. As for the latter? Truth be told, Fenton didn't really know why he didn't stop when he pulled the lit candle out of the couch crack. He noticed that it was a nice candle, though it looked a bit odd since it was the only one in the middle of an ornate candelabra designed to hold six candles. He even noticed that it was lit. But he didn't think anything of it, just blew the candle out, patted his thread-pocket, and kept digging until he pulled the calico cat out of the cushion crack.

At which point, Fenton stopped digging. He stopped harder than he'd ever stopped any project in his life—and as an artist, he was well-practised at stopping things that Just Weren't Working or that he Just Wasn't Feeling, so his hard stop was much harder and stoppier than just about anyone else could manage.

He didn't stop for the obvious reason, though. Indeed, the cat didn't bite or scratch him at all. It just lay in his arms and licked its paw, then its other paw, then the first paw again. The cat was actually surprisingly calm, all things considered, so the reason Fenton stopped had nothing to do with an angry calico couch-crack cat scratching and hissing but rather to do with the fact that Fenton *knew* this cat. There could be no doubt. This was One-Eyed Pete. It seemed impossible, and Fenton almost didn't believe it, but the facts were undeniable. He even went over them in his mind, trying to deny each fact and finding it impossible to do so:

Fact 1: the funny puff of black right under its chin that made it seem like the cat had a goatee.

Fact 2: the little orange patch on its back shaped like Texas.

Fact 3: the one blue eye, the other one missing because it had been scratched out by a dog named (coincidentally) Three-Legged George.

Fact 4: the orange collar, which had a well-remembered bell tied to the middle of it, right between the even-better-remembered embroidered white words "One-Eyed Pete if" and the vaguely recollected embroidered blue words "found return to Fenton."

Fenton stared at the cat, which was now licking where its testicles had been, before they were cut off. And before the cat died.

"But you died," Fenton said.

"No one ever told you he died," came a voice. It was the same voice that Fenton had heard before, the same voice that started all this madness. "Just that he was lost. But you found him. Good for you!"

Fenton stared at the cat. Had One-Eyed Pete said that?

The cat looked up from cleaning the empty space of its absent testicles, meowed as if to say, "Don't be an idiot. Even a cat who has spent three decades in a couch crack has too much pride to speak to a human," then leaped off Fenton's hand. It landed on one of the discarded couch cushions, put its head down, and began to purr.

The whole thing made Fenton strangely angry.

"What the *hell* is going on here?" he demanded.

The universe did not respond. Nor did the strange voice. One-Eyed Pete opened his single eye long enough to give Fenton a patronizing look, then ignored him, as cats are wont to do when asked questions of cosmic importance (or no importance at all).

Fenton looked at the couch. He was getting angrier now, and he knew it was strange to be angry under the circumstances. He should be experiencing some other, more rational emotion, like "fearful," or "confused," or "coming down from those pills." But he was only angry. Angry at having this big, ugly, old, heavy, surprisingly bountiful couch to deal with. Angry that One-Eyed Pete didn't seem to care about the master that had cried every night for a month after his parents gave him the news that they'd lost the cat. Angry at the fact that he had found so many things, but none of them were flashing red suns that had impossibly fallen from his pocket or something.

He went into the kitchen. His father had a junk drawer, the same as everyone did. They came with kitchens, and anyone who tried to get rid of them just found them migrating back sooner or later. They were a cosmic constant, were junk drawers, and so Fenton knew that his father's would be right where he had last seen it: to the right of the stove, third drawer down.

His father's junk drawer was always a tremendous, terrible shock due to the unnatural way it was both well-organized and uncluttered. There was a lot in it, but everything in there was both useful and purposefully placed. It was the Holy Grail of junk drawers, and Fenton had teased his father about that just as much as his father teased him about his lack of a real job. Sometimes he said he expected to find the Holy Grail actually *in* the "non-junky junk drawer" because "that's how ridiculous the thing is, the way you've got it." Then his father would laugh and badger Fenton about how many hidden penises he'd found in Fenton's last art piece (which was never true because Fenton only hid images of kidneys and vaginas and occasionally pieces of invisible tape in his art, but never penises).

Thinking all this made Fenton even angrier. So when he threw open the junk drawer and grabbed the box cutter he knew was waiting in there, he snicked out the blade so hard and fast that it hurt his thumb. It also almost cut the middle finger right off his other hand, but that was an *almost* dismemberment, so he didn't care about it as much as the *actual* bruise on his thumb.

The bruise, of course, made him even madder. He was so angry that he wasn't thinking about his father's absence, or bright pills, or even the fact that someone was supposed to come pick this couch up in just over twenty minutes and that said person would probably be unhappy if there was a big slit in the fabric. Even whether that fabric hailed from angry Irish goats or satisfied Bombay silkworms didn't matter to him in that moment.

He just wanted to cut the couch open so that he could stop digging in the crack of it. And that is what he did.

He pushed the box cutter blade through the fabric that covered the springs, up in the corner where the back of the couch, the base of the couch, and the left arm of the couch came together. It slid in easily. Surprisingly so. It surprised Fenton, and it surprised whoever was hiding in there because that person said, "Woah! Don't cut the couch!"

That made Fenton angrier, so he shouted, "I have to!" so loudly that One-Eyed Pete immediately vomited up a hairball that had a single strangely large Cheerio in the centre. Ridiculously, that made Fenton the angriest yet. He yanked the box cutter toward him, drawing a six-inch slit in the fabric.

The voice shrieked, "Hold it, Fen!"

Fenton did hold it, totally shocked. No one had called him Fen in a long time. None of his friends ever did, and he knew he'd never asked the couch to call him that. But that, he could finally tell for certain, was where the voice had come from.

Like everything else in the last few minutes, this upset him. It made him angry. He cut another inch in the sofa.

"What is *wrong* with you?" shouted the voice. "You're acting crazy!"

Which made Fenton even angrier because he knew he wasn't acting crazy at all, just enraged to a level that brought to mind nuclear explosions and mass murder and a girl named Triss he had dated for a while because she had an exceptional body but with whom he finally broke it off because she just never stopped shouting at people.

He yelled all that at the voice in the couch, to which the voice replied softly, "Oh, I see. Hold on a sec."

That made Fenton angrier still. But it was a curious kind of rage—not meaning the rage was of a curious sort, but rather that the rage had curiosity all mixed up inside it—so he didn't keep slashing the couch. He cursed, and he screamed, and at one point, his nose started bleeding, but he stopped cutting.

Sounds came from the couch. That made Fenton mad too, but it made him even more curious than ever, so he turned his screaming wrath to silent outrage so he could listen.

It was hard to understand what he was hearing. It sounded like heavy boxes being moved at first. Then it sounded like footsteps. A moment after that, he heard what sounded like a chainsaw, if the chainsaw was being used a mile away to cut down a tree made of cotton candy. Then more footsteps. Something squeaked in a way that reminded Fenton (angrily!) of a telescoping ladder being pushed to its highest height.

The cut he had made in the couch shifted a bit. Something bright pushed through. Something bright and red and beautiful. It was strange. Strange that it came from the couch, yes. Stranger still that Fenton knew without a doubt that this was the thing that had fallen and that it belonged to him even though he had no memory of ever owning such a thing. Strangest of all was the fact that, now that he could look directly at it, he was even less capable of seeing or describing it than he had been when it tumbled away at the corner of his senses.

It didn't matter. He was still angry about losing the thing, and something had to be done about that. So Fenton put down the box cutter and picked up the thing that was so indescribable he couldn't even say it was red anymore.

Touching it, he felt something equally indescribable. The best he could come up with was that it was exactly like touching the top of a stove in every single conceivable way, with the exception only of the fact that that was completely wrong, and no stovetop ever felt anything like what he now held.

And then, in the instant after coming up with a description of what the thing felt like (nothing, really) by knowing only what it didn't feel like (everything, really), the thing was gone.

Fenton expected to be angry about that. He'd worked so hard to find the whatever-it-was, and now it was gone. But he didn't feel angry at all. He felt quite calm, in fact. Better than he had in a while. A small part of him wondered if he should feel worried about this sudden change, but he patted the pocket with the thread in it, and that made him feel even better, and he didn't worry. He even reached down and petted One-Eyed Pete, who hissed without opening his eye from his nap.

"Feel better?" came the voice.

"Yes," said Fenton.

"Thought that would help," said the voice.

"Why's that?" asked Fenton. The rage was gone, but the curiosity remained. "What was that red thing?"

"That what it looked like to you?" asked the voice. The voice chuckled. "How funny. I thought it looked like a Lego."

"A Lego?" said Fenton. He glanced to the side, where he had deposited all the findings from earlier. There was the Lego head, between a pile of pennies and the candle (which had somehow gone lit again). "I found a Lego head up here."

"No, not a *particular* Lego, just like I bet you didn't see a *partic-*

ular red," said the voice. "Just a *kind* of Lego. The *kind* that you step
on in the middle of the night when you're trying to go to the bathroom, or the *kind* you step on when you've just taken your shoes
off after a long day of work, and all you want is to walk across a
Lego-free piece of carpet to the couch so you can fall into it and
give out the biggest sigh of your life. You know?"

"Yes," said Fenton because he knew exactly what kind of Lego
the voice was talking about. He'd never experienced a Lego like
that himself because he was not a parent, but he'd owned just that
kind of thing as a child and had heard his parents describe them
often enough to feel himself quite the expert. Then he said, "So
what was it?"

"Your temper," said the voice.

"My temper?"

"Yeah. You lost it. I saw it tumble down here—made quite the
bright light, let me tell you; woke everything up, in a manner of
speaking."

Fenton opened his mouth to say that was ludicrous. To say that
he hadn't lost his temper, and even if he had, it wouldn't look like a
red/not-red stovetop/not-stovetop thing that fell into the cushions,
and it certainly wouldn't be returned by a somewhat smug-
sounding voice in the couch.

But he said no such thing. Because he knew, deep down in his
soul, the same place he knew about adult-destroying Legos, that
the voice was right. He *had* lost his temper. And it *had* fallen into
the couch. Fallen in with change and Cheerios, with Tylenol and
twist-ties, with candelabras and calico cats and a thousand other
things yet to be discovered.

He reached for the slit in the couch. He didn't want to cut it
open any wider—not yet, at any rate—but he did want to see. He
wanted to see the owner of the voice. He wanted to see all the

other things that might have fallen into this big couch in the middle of a dead man's living room.

"I wouldn't," said the voice.

"Why not?" said Fenton. He suddenly felt very afraid. He patted his thread-pocket and felt better. He straightened his back and said, "If I want to see, then—"

"Some things are better left unseen. Others are better left . . ." The voice drifted away.

"Yes?" said Fenton.

"Lost," said the voice.

Fenton squinted, cocked his head, and shrugged. "What's that supposed to mean?"

"It's what's down here," said the voice.

"What's down *where*?"

"Down *here*."

"What is?"

The voice sighed. "Hold on; this happens sometimes." The slit in the couch fluttered, and then fingertips poked up through the cut. "Here, take this."

"Take what? What were we talking about?" Fenton felt confused.

The fingers jabbed up and down. "Look closer, dummy!" shouted the voice.

Fenton did look closer. The fingers *were* clenched around something: another thread. It was fairly plain in colour but had a bright spot that moved from one end of the bit of string to the other, back and forth, back and forth. Fenton watched it, entranced, able to focus on nothing else. He almost didn't hear it when the voice said, "Hey, take it!", he was watching that light so closely.

But enough of him heard it that he reached out and took the

bit of string. The second he did, everything snapped into sharp focus. He remembered what he was talking about. He didn't return to what he'd been saying, but it wasn't because he was confused; he just had a whole new set of questions. "What just happened?" he asked.

"You lost the thread of the conversation," said the voice. "It happens a lot. 'Specially around couches. They're comfy, and they collect conversations like a corner collects dust. Lucky I found this one, though, to be honest, it was pretty easy. The thread hadn't fallen far, so I could pick it up for you."

That was the most insane sentence Fenton had ever heard, and not least of all because of how much sense it made.

Thinking of the thread of the previous conversation made him remember the other thread he'd found. He looked at the slit in the couch, intending to ask the—well, to ask the fingers—about it. But the fingers were gone, and he felt foolish just asking an empty line of nothing to answer his questions. He pulled the silvery thread from his pocket. The second he did, the concern about seeming foolish seemed to matter a lot less, and it was suddenly easy to say, "What about the other thread?"

"The other thread?"

"Yeah. I found another thread when I started looking through the couch."

"What did it look like?"

"Like a thread."

"Come on, Fen," chuckled the voice. "You can do better than that. Aren't you some kind of fancy artist or something?"

Fenton half-expected the red glint to tumble out of the corner of his vision again, but it didn't. He hadn't lost his temper. He didn't feel angry at all, in fact. Just brave and more than willing to stand up to some voice that lived with a strangely large Cheerio in the darkness within the couch. "It's silver. Thin, but . . ." He tugged it. "Strong. Very strong."

"Ah," said the voice. "It's not a thread at all."

"Okay, a wire then."

"Not a wire, either."

"Then what?"

"Tell me, when you saw it, what were you feeling?"

Fenton sighed. "Can't you just tell—"

"Humour me. What were you feeling?"

Fenton thought back to when he'd found the thread. He had been worried about bear traps and syringes and Yucky Stuff, he was fairly certain. Again, not the kind of thing he was likely to share with a friend, let alone a voice that, for all he knew, had no body at all to go with it, just a bunch of fingers. But, again, in this moment, he didn't worry. He just answered. "I was scared of feeling around in the couch. I thought there might be some kind of trap."

"A trap?" said the voice, sounding genuinely surprised.

"Yeah. One of those big ones that look like jaws and capture bears. Either that or an AIDS needle or some Yucky Stuff."

The voice was silent for a long time. So long, in fact, that Fenton should have worried that he was indeed going mad or coming down off whatever those purple pills had been. But he wasn't scared at all. He just held the silver thread or wire or whatever and waited.

Finally, the voice said, "Yuh . . . who . . . hall . . . ways . . . were . . ." It made no sense at all, even without the strangled gurgles between each syllable.

Fenton said so.

The voice just kept gasping. Strange sounds came from the couch. Fenton thought he heard chattering teeth, then a honk, then the sound of a balloon popping in the middle of a circus act consisting of two clowns fighting over who got to eat the last bean off a table balanced on the middle of an elephant's back.

Then everything went quiet, and when the voice came again, it was solid and sure. "Sorry, you surprised me with the Yucky Stuff thing."

"What happened?" asked Fen.

"I totally lost it," said the voice. "Things do get lost, even down here. But I found it again, so we're all good."

"What did you find?" asked Fenton.

"You lose the thread of the conversation again?"

"No, I just don't understand. What did you lose?"

"It, it, *it*," said the voice. "Haven't you ever *lost it*? Just tried so hard not to laugh at something that you couldn't stop laughing, because you've *lost it*?"

"Sure," said Fenton. "But you didn't laugh."

"No, I didn't fully lose it, I guess. But I was trying so hard not to laugh that I thought I was gonna die. Didn't lose it, but definitely had to run around chasing it for a minute. But I got it, and now it's under control again."

As the voice spoke, Fenton had been inching closer. He knew that the voice had said not to, but now he knew what the silver thread was, it was the nerve he'd lost for a moment and then gotten back, and now that it was tight in his grip, he felt brave, and he felt like he'd never needed to see anything as badly in his life as he needed to see what was in the couch.

"Ah, ah, ah . . ."

Fenton stopped again. He still felt brave, he still had his nerve, but he also felt embarrassed, in a way he hadn't since he was a young boy, and his parents caught him wiping boogers on the bottom of his bed. Apparently, bravery and embarrassment could live together just fine. "What?" he said plaintively. "I want to see."

"I already told you," said the voice. "Some things—lots of things, in fact—need to stay lost."

"But I found other things, and none of *them* hurt me."

"Bah," scoffed the voice. "Buncha coins and remote controls. Those are just normal lost things. They're almost begging to be re-found, when you come right down to it."

"And a candle," said Fenton. "A *lit* candle."

Fenton could almost hear the smile in the voice's words. "Well, I'll admit, that wasn't so very normal. But not *impossible*, strictly speaking. Dangerous, and a bad idea, and part of a very improbable story involving a night where the power went out after I'd had too much to drink . . . but not impossible. And I couldn't resist once I saw your fingers moving around down here. Thought I'd give you something to write home about, so to speak. But again, not an impossible thing to find, and so it was safe enough."

"And the cat?" demanded Fenton. "That was impossible."

"No, it wasn't," said the voice.

"A dead cat—"

"Not dead, I told you. Lost. Everything down here's *lost*, kiddo."

"Fine, but either way, the cat's been 'lost' for thirty years. He should be dead, first of all, and even if he wasn't, there's no way he could have been just stuck in the crack of the couch like that. Totally impossible."

"Not for a cat."

Fenton blinked in surprise. "What's that supposed to mean?"

"Cats are different."

"How so?"

"Well, they're always on the verge of being lost as it is, if you think about it. They spend a lot of time in the shadows, in the cracks. Half the time, you wish they'd leave you alone; the other half, you can't seem to find them, and you think they're probably dead right up to the moment they saunter up and demand dinner. Things like that, they have different rules. They're always half-lost, so it's almost never going to destroy things if they're found again. But that's cats, boy, and not everything is a cat, as I'm sure you'll agree."

No matter how tightly he gripped his nerve, Fenton could find no reasonable way to counter any of that. He sighed. "Fine. If it's all that important."

He waited.

And waited.

And waited.

One-Eyed Pete meowed.

The voice from the couch sighed. "Fine," it said. "You can peek. But just for a second, and you stop when I say you do, okay?"

"Great, fine, yeah!" said Fenton, the words tumbling over each other, each one eager to be the first out.

"Gimme just a sec. Gotta get a few things ready."

Sounds again. Fluttering plastic like Hefty bags being unravelled. The loud scratch of heavy tape being unrolled. The sound of hammers pounding nails, or perhaps of nails pounding hammers (Fenton always contended the hammers got too much credit). Then: "Okay. Give 'er a look."

And Fenton did. He sidled up to the hole. Leaned in close. Looked. And saw . . .

"It's dark."

Another sigh from the voice. "Pass me that candle, would you?"

Fenton picked up the lone candle in its candelabra and started to push it at the hole in the couch. It shouldn't have fit—it was much too big, or the hole much too small (Fenton always thought holes deserved more credit for their size). But at the last second, the hole grew. Or perhaps, at the last second, the rest of the universe shrank. Either way, the candelabra fit through easily. Fenton felt something take hold of it, then he let go, and the candelabra sank the rest of the way through the fabric, just in time for the hole to get smaller and the universe to get bigger and for all creation to meet neatly in the middle.

"Okay, give it another go," said the voice.

Fenton looked.

He saw

an action figure he'd owned when he was eight

("You were so sad when you lost Optimus Prime," said the voice.)

a girl he knew was beautiful, even though he couldn't make out anything about her

("First love lost," whispered the voice.)

the man who had been Fenton's first and only real boss before he became an artist, shouting and shouting at everything around him

("Lost favour," said the voice, sounding angry.)

thousands and thousands of people who were all Fenton, tossing and turning in beds that were all his

("So much lost sleep," said the voice. "I always worried about that with you. You always looked so tired.")

and beyond it all was a small cloud.

Fenton stared at the cloud, and as he did, the cloud grew. Larger and larger, faster and faster, and it hung over everything down there in the candlelit couch crevices, so much so that nothing could be seen but the cloud. It was terrifying. Fenton still had his nerve, he knew it, he could feel it warm and strong in his hand, but in that moment, it didn't matter whether he had his nerve or he'd lost it. In that moment, the cloud was every terror he'd ever known, every dread fact he'd ever suspected. Thunder clapped in the cloud, deafening his mind. Lightning spat from it in every direction, threatening to scorch everything he'd ever seen or known. Most terrifying of all was the speed at which it grew and the way that Fenton just knew that it would take over the world, and there would be nothing but sound and noise and fury and then—

"Get back, Fen!" shouted the voice, so loud and stern and unexpected that Fenton did exactly what he was told to do. He stumbled back, away from the cloud, away from the couch. But the cloud was seeping through the crack now, seeping then streaming then surging, darkening everything around him, and he screamed as he stumbled back. His foot landed on something soft, then there was a hiss and bright pain exploded in his calf, so white and fierce that the cloud disappeared in a puff of nothing.

Fenton looked down and realized that, in his panic, he'd stepped on One-Eyed Pete. The cat had reacted reasonably under the circumstances, and as Fenton watched, casually withdrew the claws it had sunk paw-deep into Fenton's flesh and began to lick them clean of blood.

Fenton was so aghast at what had just happened that he didn't even think to get mad. He just stared at the couch, at the slit he had made. The cut had been six inches long, dark and mysterious just a moment before. Now it was twenty feet long—far too big for the couch to contain, but somehow it was there, somehow it was real—a gaping hole that was not mysterious at all, no. Because mysterious things cried out for solutions and adventures. Mysterious things beckoned and pleaded for their mysteries to be solved. But this thing? This thing simply gaped, and yawned, and promised doom.

"Easy," said the voice. It came from the exact centre of the massive, still-growing cut. "Easy, Fenton. Take a breath."

Fenton did, though it was hard, even holding tight to his nerve. But he managed. Barely.

"Good," said the voice. "Again. Again. And one more."

On the fourth deep breath, the cut started to shrink. On the fifth, it fit the couch again. On the tenth (Fenton getting a bit woozy at this point from hyperventilating), it was back to its original dimensions.

"What was that?" he said.

"Lost perspective," said the voice. "Like I said: some things are better left unseen."

"Better left lost."

"Just so," agreed the voice.

"Then why would you show me that?"

"I didn't. Not purposefully, anyway. But once you've lost a thing, it's much harder to control. Just the nature of things, I suppose. Thank goodness the cat saved you."

Fenton stared at his leg. Blood had soaked his sock. "He didn't save me; he cut my leg to pieces."

"Exactly. Nothing like sharp, sudden danger to put things back in perspective. Either that or to blow them all out of proportion. But at least it was a fifty-fifty chance you survived that way, so the cat deserves thanks."

Fenton shook his head. "Fine. Thank you, One—" He looked at the cushion on the floor. He looked at the floor itself. "Where'd he go?"

The voice chuckled. "No way of knowing. Maybe he's down here, lost again. Maybe he's out walking. Maybe he decided to go kill every mouse in the world—cats can lose perspective, too; it's one of the traits they share in common with people. Regardless, he'll be along again if he feels like it. Which he probably won't. It's a cat thing."

Fenton stared at the cut in the cloth for a long time. There was a question he hadn't asked yet: one he desperately needed to ask but which he needed just as badly not to ask.

"Go ahead and ask it," said the voice. "You need to; you need *not* to. But the situation'll be worse if you don't than it will if you do."

A finger of mist curled over the edge of the cut as though a small cloud reached through from beneath.

"Don't lose perspective!" shouted the voice.

Fenton breathed in, held his breath, let it out, and the cloud withdrew.

"Good job," said the voice.

Fenton felt proud. That pride gave him the answer to his unasked question, just as it gave him the strength to ask it. Or rather, not the pride itself but the kind of pride it was. It was a singular sort of pride, one that came only from one place. So he asked the question, though he knew the answer already: "Who are you?"

The voice chuckled. "Just one more thing you lost, though more recently than most."

Fenton felt tears sting his eyes. "But you sound so young."

"Lost things always stay the way you most remember them. That's the way of it here."

"Can I see you?"

"No. I'm no quarter or candle. Not even a cat, for better or for worse. Seeing me would do nothing but harm."

The tears were coming faster now, hotter. Painful. "But how

can that be? How can—"

"Remember that cloud?"

"Yeah."

"What do you think that cloud would do if it got loose? If, say, people suddenly discovered that everything they knew was wrong? Not a minor thing, mind you, like they suddenly realized they were voting wrong or that the way they prayed was a teeny bit off. A *major* thing." Fenton did not speak, so the voice did. "I reckon the cloud would cover everything pretty fast, don't you?"

"Maybe not."

"Maybe not," agreed the voice. It sounded scratchier now. A bit older. A bit more worn and weary. "But maybe so. And we can't take the chance, can we? Too big a risk, when all you'd get in return is a glimpse of something you lost."

"But you're not lost anymore," Fenton shouted desperately. "You're—"

The voice waited.

"You're—" Fenton tried again.

The silence grew long and heavy.

"You can't say it, can you? Because it wouldn't be true. I'm not found, son. Not the way you found my old TV remotes. Not even the way you found that old Lego head you lost when you were six. I'll never be found that way again."

Fenton was crying so hard the world seemed to swim. Everything was underwater. Everything was terrible. Everything—

"Now, don't you lose perspective again, son. Old Pete isn't here to help you, and even if he was, you couldn't count on him to do it again. That's not the way of cats."

Fenton sniffed. "I just . . ."

"I know, Fen. I know. But you want to hear something neat?"

Fenton nodded.

"I'm not gonna stay here long, Fen."

"You're not?"

"No. Like I say, I'm not a quarter or a candle. People don't stay lost. They move on."

"Where?"

"Not allowed to say."

"Were you allowed to do all this?"

The voice chuckled. It was now as old and craggy as Fenton remembered it being the last time they had spoken. The time that Fenton said, "Goodbye, I'll come back and see you again in a few days," and the voice had said, "Not if I see you first, you lousy dumb artist. Get a job, would ya?" in a voice so full of pride that Fenton had to turn away so his dad wouldn't see him cry.

"I suppose I wasn't strictly *allowed*," said the voice. "But then, I got here by following One-Eyed Pete."

"Following him?"

"From where I was to here." A meow sounded from inside the couch. "And now he's rubbing all over my leg, which I take to mean I'm to follow him back. Cats. You know how it is."

"I do," said Fenton, though he didn't at all, and that, too, was the way of cats, just as it was the way of lost things and death and so much of life itself.

The small cut—and it *was* small now, small and getting smaller by the second—in the corner of the couch fluttered. Fingers curled around it. They were the same fingers, though they were completely different: older, liver-spotted, gnarled with arthritis and soft with age. They gave a little wave at Fenton. He reached out and held them, tighter than he'd ever held anything before.

The fingers held him back. They were old, but they were as strong as he remembered them being as a child. Strong enough to lift up cars, to build walls—even strong enough to wheel a brand-new couch into the room where it would sit for three decades and more.

Then the fingers drew back. The hole was gone. The couch was exactly as it had been, though it looked different than Fenton remembered. It was smaller and not as soft. Just a battered old couch seen no longer through the lens of a child's memory but as it truly was. And that was good enough.

Fenton put the cushions back. He sat on the couch. He waited, his nerve in his pocket. After a while, the doorbell rang. He opened the door and saw a petite woman with a lovely smile. What looked like fifty-seven children surrounded her, dancing and skipping and playing, and it took Fenton a few heartbeats to realize that there were actually only three of them, they just moved so fast and joyfully they seemed to take up the entire world. He smiled to see that.

"Hi, I'm Mary," said the woman.

"Fenton." He looked around and frowned. "Your husband couldn't come?"

"He's pulling the car around," she said. Then she sighed. "That's a lie. No husband. I just . . . said that. I don't even know why."

"You never know with these free things," Fenton offered. "I could be a crazy person. Makes sense to pretend you have a husband."

"Yeah, but only if you actually show up with a guy, right?"

Fenton laughed, then he looked at the forces of nature masquerading as three children. He cocked an eyebrow, silently asking a question he couldn't help but ask.

"There *was* a husband," the woman clarified.

Fenton sighed. He felt tears boil. "You lost him?"

She laughed. "Got rid of him."

One of the children stopped running in circles long enough to say, "Dad is a cheating, no-good scumbag, and we hope he dies of a painful STD that makes all his swimsuit parts fall off!"

"Jeremy!" Mary shouted angrily. "What have I said about saying that?"

One of the other whirlwinds paused long enough to shout, "You said not to say that in front of strangers because you don't need that kind of hassle!" then spun around six times and fell down on the lawn. He started waving his arms and legs like he was making the world's first lawn angel.

Mary sighed, smiled. She looked at Fenton. "Well, are you?"

"Am I what?"

"Crazy."

Fenton thought about everything that had just happened—if it had happened at all. He shrugged. "Probably. But not the kind you have to worry about getting a couch from."

Mary cocked her head. "I believe you." She smiled. "Can I see it?"

"Oh, sure! Sorry!"

Fenton gestured for her to come in and stood aside. The three children remained at play outside when their mother entered.

"Umm . . ." Fenton pointed at the kids.

"Oh, they're fine," said Mary. "They'd prefer to play out there, and I think . . ."

She began to cry. Fenton didn't know what to do. Oddly, the only thought that came to mind was, *What would One-Eyed Pete do?* And though he doubted his old, half-lost cat would have done anything at all, he found himself patting Mary on the arm.

"Sorry," she said. "I've just . . . it's been a lot. We're handling it, but it's hard."

Fenton nodded. He waited.

"I feel like I've lost myself, you know?" Mary said.

Fenton nodded again, but this time he did not wait. He took Mary by the hand. She looked surprised but let him guide her across the room.

"So you really are crazy?" she said. She sounded oddly hopeful.

"Probably," he said. "But you came because you felt you'd lost something."

"I came for a couch," she protested.

"Same thing," he said and pushed her down onto the couch.

She fell protesting, obviously about to yell, her hand going to her pocket for what he assumed would be a hidden pepper spray or Tazer.

Then she was sitting on the couch. She stopped moving, going so rigid for a moment that Fenton worried he'd actually hurt her somehow.

Then she relaxed, more fully and completely than he'd ever seen anyone who wasn't a cat relax before.

"This is nice," she said.

"Surprisingly so," Fenton agreed. He patted his pocket for strength, then sat next to her.

"My name's Mary," said Mary.

"And mine's Fenton," said Fenton.

Mary giggled. "We already said that, didn't we?"

"We did."

"This is a good couch."

"Like you wouldn't believe."

AUTHOR'S NOTE:

I was talking to the kids recently and mentioned their older sister, who is no longer with us. My wife mentioned that we'd "lost" her, and I suddenly thought how strange it was to talk about people who died like they were loose change that trickled out of our pockets when we sat down too hard. I understand why, of course, and it makes sense. But it struck me as odd, and—being me—I suddenly wondered, "What if all those people really are just lost? What if they're like the loose change, and we just have to dig around in the right places to find them again? And what if, like loose change, the best place to find people—or anything at all—is under the couch cushions?

And with that, this story was born. I had more fun writing it than I've had writing anything in a long, long time. I hope you enjoyed it. I hope my "lost" girl does as well. Indeed, that's part of why I made sure that the voice in the couch would respond not just to words but to physical cues. Because although Fenton's father was largely unseen by Fenton, I wanted it clear that such blindness was only one way. Fenton couldn't really see his father, but his father could see him. And I hope Grace sees this, and knows that her daddy still thinks of her, and tells stories that he believes would make her smile.

ABOUT THE AUTHORS AND ILLUSTRATOR

THE AUTHORS

DAVID BOOP is a Denver-based speculative fiction author. He's also an award-winning essayist and screenwriter. Before turning to fiction, David worked as a DJ, film critic, journalist, and actor. His debut novel was the sci-fi/noir *She Murdered Me with Science* (now back in print from WordFire Press; he followed up with a Victorian horror, *The Soul Changers,* from Pinnacle. David went on to edit the bestselling weird western anthology *Straight Outta Tombstone* for Baen. Prolific in short fiction, with many short stories and two short films to his credit, David has published across several genres, including media tie-ins for *Predator, The Green Hornet, The Black Bat* and *Veronica Mars.* His RPG work includes *Flash Gordon* and *Deadlands: Noir for Savage Worlds.* Finally, his series, *The Trace Walker Temporary Mysteries*, appears regularly on Gunshoereview.com. He's a single dad, Summa Cum Laude creative writing graduate, part-time temp worker, and believer. His hobbies include film noir, anime, the Blues, and Mayan History.

MICHAELBRENT COLLINGS is an internationally bestselling novelist, produced screenwriter, and speaker. Best known for horror (and voted one of the top 100 Greatest All-Time Horror Writers in a Ranker vote of nearly 20,000 readers), Collings has written bestselling thrillers, mysteries, sci-fi, and fantasy titles, and even humour and nonfiction. In addition to popular success, Michaelbrent has also received critical acclaim: he is the only person who has ever been a finalist for a Bram Stoker Award (twice), a Dragon Award (twice), and a RONE Award, and he and his work have been reviewed and/or featured on everything from *Publishers Weekly* to *Scream Magazine* to NPR. An engaging and entertaining speaker, he is also a frequent guest at comic cons and on writing podcasts like *Six Figure Authors*, *The Creative Penn*, *Writing Excuses*, and others, and he is also a mental health advocate and TEDx speaker.

ROY M. GRIFFIS calls himself a "storyteller" for a lot of reasons. He decided to be a writer when he was ten and never looked back. Along the way, he's done all the usual starving artist jobs (janitor, waiter, bookstore clerk) and a few unusual ones (he was the sixty-second Aviation Rescue Swimmer in the US Coast Guard—he doesn't just write action-adventure, he lived a little of it himself). He's written poetry, plays, and screenplays. He's also the author of twelve novels, including the epic historical fiction saga By the Hands of Men and the alternative history series The Lonesome George Chronicles, as well as the comic fantasy Cthulhu, Amalgamated cycle. In 2018, he received the first John Milius Screenwriting Award for his original film script *Cold Day in Hell*. Website: roymgriffis.com

SARAH A. HOYT was born and raised in Portugal, where she decided her future occupation would be writer, and she would live in Denver. In her defence, she had no idea where Denver was, nor that this would require learning English (at fourteen) and becoming a professional writer in it. But after thirty-six novels and more than 100 published short stories, you can hardly tell. Sarah's first novel, *Ill Met By Moonlight*, was a finalist for the Mythopoeic award; her novel *Darkship Thieves* won the Prometheus; and her novel *Uncharted* (with Kevin J. Anderson) won the Dragon. Sarah has been published by magazines like *Analog, Asimov's* and *Weird Tales*, and publishers like Ace, Bantam, and Baen, and edited anthologies for DAW. Lately, she's been working indie. Her latest novel is *Bowl of Red* in her Shifters series. She's also been writing scripts for Dynamite's current iteration of *Barbarella*. She has been published in science fiction, fantasy, mystery, historical and . . . look, her husband—the Mathematician—says it's easier to say she's never written children's picture books or men's adventure. But she makes no promises.

JAMES KENNEDY is the author of the horror thriller *Bride of the Tornado*, the sci-fi mind-bender *Dare to Know,* and the YA fantasy *The Order of Odd-Fish*. He also runs the 90-Second Newbery Film Festival, in which kid filmmakers create movies that sum up Newbery-winning books in ninety seconds, which screens annually in ten-plus cities around the USA. He is also the co-host of the Secrets of Story podcast with Matt Bird. He lives in Chicago with his wife and two daughters. Website: jameskennedy.com

Defying all odds is what #1 New York Times and international bestselling author Sherrilyn McQueen, writing as **SHERRILYN KENYON,** does best. Rising from extreme poverty as a child that culminated in being a homeless mother with an infant, she has become one of the most popular and influential authors in the world (in both adult and YA fiction), with dedicated legions of fans known as Paladins–thousands of whom proudly sport tattoos from her numerous genre-defying series. Since her first book debuted while she was still in college, she has placed more than eighty novels on the *New York Times*list in all formats and genres, including manga and graphic novels, and has more than 70 million books in print worldwide. Her current series include Dark-Hunters®, Chronicles of Nick®, Deadman's Cross™, Eve of Destruction™, Nevermore™, Lords of Avalon®, and The League®.

MARK LESLIE LEFEBVRE's first short story appeared in print in 1992, the same year he started working in the book industry. He has published more than twenty-five books under the name Mark Leslie that include thrillers and fiction (*Evasion, A Canadian Werewolf in New York, One Hand Screaming*), paranormal nonfiction (*Haunted Hospitals, Spooky Sudbury, Tomes of Terror*) and anthologies (*Campus Chills, Tesseracts Sixteen, Obsessions*). Under his full name, he writes books to help authors navigate publishing. They include *The 7 P's of Publishing Success* and *An Author's Guide to Working with Libraries and Bookstores*. His industry experience includes President of the Canadian Booksellers Association, Board Member of BookNet Canada, Director of Author Relations and Self-Publishing for Rakuten Kobo, Director of Business Development for Draft2Digital, and Professional Advisor for Sheridan College's Creative Writing and Publishing Honours Program. Mark lives in Waterloo, Ontario.

NOAH LEMELSON is a novelist and short story writer with a love of science fiction, fantasy, new weird, and "insert-noun-here"-punk. He has written two novels (2021's *The Sightless City* and its upcoming sequel, *The Lioness and the Rat Queen*) as well as nearly a dozen short stories published in magazines such as *Space Squid, Allegory, Los Suelos*, and *Interzone*. Noah lives with his wife and cats in Los Angeles.

EDWARD M. LERNER worked in high tech and aerospace for thirty years, as everything from engineer to senior vice president, for much of that time writing science fiction as his hobby. Since 2004, he's written full-time. His novels range from near-future technothrillers, like *Small Miracles* and *Energized*, to traditional SF, like *Dark Secret* and his InterstellarNet series, to (collaborating with Larry Niven) the space-opera epic Fleet of Worlds series. His 2015 novel, *InterstellarNet: Enigma*, won the inaugural Canopus Award, "honouring excellence in interstellar writing," while other of his fiction has been nominated for Locus, Prometheus, and Hugo awards. The 2021 SF adventure *Déjà Doomed* is his latest novel. His short fiction has appeared in anthologies, collections, and many of the usual SF magazines and websites. He also writes about science and technology, notably including *Trope-ing the Light Fantastic: The Science Behind the Fiction*.

DAVID LISS is the author of fourteen novels, as well as numerous novellas and short stories. His latest novel is *The Peculiarities*, the tale of a clueless young man embroiled in a deadly supernatural mystery in Victorian London. Previous books include *A Conspiracy of Paper*, which was named a *New York Times* Notable Book and won the 2001 Barry, MacAvity, and Edgar awards for Best First Novel. *The Coffee Trader* was also named a *New York Times* Notable Book and was selected by the New York Public Library as one of the year's "25 Books to Remember." Many of his novels are currently being developed for television or film. Liss has worked on numerous comics projects, including *Black Panther* and *Mystery Men* for Marvel, *The Spider* and *Green Hornet* for Dynamite, and *Angelica Tomorrow*.

GAIL Z. MARTIN writes urban fantasy, epic fantasy, steampunk, and more for Solaris Books, Orbit Books, Falstaff Books, SOL Publishing, and Darkwind Press. Urban fantasy series include Deadly Curiosities and the Night Vigil (Sons of Darkness). Epic fantasy series include Darkhurst, the Chronicles Of The Necromancer, the Fallen Kings Cycle, the Ascendant Kingdoms Saga, and the Assassins of Landria. Together with Larry N. Martin, she is the co-author of *Iron & Blood*, *Storm & Fury* (both steampunk/alternate history), the Spells Salt and Steel comedic horror series, the Roaring Twenties monster hunter Joe Mack Shadow Council series, and the Wasteland Marshals near-future post-apocalyptic series. As Morgan Brice, she writes urban fantasy MM paranormal romance, with the Witchbane, Badlands, Treasure Trail, Kings of the Mountain and Fox Hollow series. Gail is also a con-runner for ConTinual, the online, ongoing multi-genre convention that never ends.

R. S. MELLETTE, originally from Winston-Salem, North Carolina, now lives in Southern California, where he toils away at turning his imaginary friends into real ones. While working on *Xena: Warrior Princess*, he created and wrote "The Xena Scrolls" for Universal's New Media department and was part of the team that won a Golden Reel Award for ADR editing—the dialogue recorded in post-production. When an episode aired based on his "Xena Scrolls" characters, it became the first intellectual property to move from the internet to television. Mellette has worked and blogged for the film festival Dances With Films as well as the novelist collective From The Write Angle, and he is on the board of the L.A. region of the Society of Children's Book Writers and Illustrators. He is an award-winning filmmaker, and the author of *Billy Bobble Makes A Magic Wand*, *Billy Bobble and The Witch Hunt*, and *Kiya and The Morian Treasure*, all from Elephant's Bookshelf Press. @RSMellette on all the socials.

JOSHUA PALMATIER is a fantasy author with a Ph.D. in mathematics. He currently teaches at SUNY Oneonta in upstate New York while writing in his "spare" time, editing anthologies, and running the anthology-producing small press Zombies Need Brains LLC. His most recent fantasy novel, *Reaping the Aurora,* concludes the fantasy series begun in *Shattering the Ley* and*Threading the Needle,* although you can also find his Throne of Amenkor series and the Well of Sorrows series still on the shelves. He is currently hard at work writing his next series and designing the Kickstarter for the next set of Zombies Need Brains anthology projects. Meet Joshua in the video below!

RICHARD PAOLINELLI began his writing journey as a freelance writer in 1984 and gained his first fiction credit serving as the lead writer for the first two issues of the Elite Comics sci-fi/fantasy series *Seadragon.* After nearly a quarter of a century in the newspaper field, in 2010, Richard retired as an award-winning sportswriter and returned to his fiction-writing roots. Since then, he has written several award-winning novels, and two nonfiction sports books and has appeared in more than twenty anthologies, including eight of the eleven-book Tuscany Bay Books' Planetary Anthology series and five Sherlock Holmes collections. He served as a co-host on LA Talk Radio's *The Writer's Block* from 2016 thru 2022 and is the co-founder and Publisher of Tuscany Bay Books. He currently resides in Western Colorado with his wife and two house hounds.

LAVIE TIDHAR is the author of *Osama*, *The Violent Century*, *A Man Lies Dreaming*, *Central Station*, *Unholy Land*, *By Force Alone*, *The Hood*, and *The Escapement*. His latest novels are *Maror* and *Neom*. His awards include the World Fantasy and British Fantasy Awards, the John W. Campbell Award, the Neukom Prize, and the Jerwood Prize, and he has been shortlisted for the Clarke Award and the Philip K. Dick Award.

JEAN-LOUIS TRUDEL is a French-Canadian author who started publishing science fiction stories in 1984. Since then, he's published novels, YA books, poems, short fiction, and nonfiction, including a number of works written in collaboration with Yves Meynard, under the name Laurent McAllister, garnering several Aurora and Boréal awards. While he mostly writes in French, some of his short stories and most of his poems were initially composed in English. His stories have been translated into many different languages. He has organized or helped organize science fiction conventions and festivals, including Boréal and the World Science Fiction Convention. His educational background includes a bachelor's degree in physics at the University of Ottawa, a master's degree in astronomy at the University of Toronto, a second master's degree in history and philosophy of science and technology at the University of Toronto, and a doctorate in history from the Université du Québec à Montréal. He has taught at five different universities.

JAMES VAN PELT has been selling short fiction to many of the major venues since 1989. Recently he retired from teaching high school English after thirty-seven years in the classroom. He was a finalist for the Nebula, the Theodore Sturgeon Memorial Award, Locus Awards, and Analog and Asimov's reader's choice awards.

Years and years ago, he was a finalist for the John W. Campbell Award for Best New Writer. He still feels "new." Fairwood Press recently released a huge, limited-edition, signed and numbered collection of his work, *The Best of James Van Pelt*.

GARON WHITED was born in Kansas; after following his parents around the South for several years, he finally caught up to them and settled somewhere between Texas and Arkansas. Garon attended several universities, whether he was a student or not. While he was in college, he studied many subjects, none of which were helpful in earning a living. At present, he writes stories in the hope people will feed him. He has written several novels and various short stories and shows no signs of stopping. His work tends toward the optimistic: even his apocalyptic sci-fi novel has a surprisingly feel-good attitude. When he's not writing stories, Garon is still telling them. Garon is a fan of role-playing games and started playing many years and many editions ago. It may have encouraged him to write by providing material. Garon loves to read, usually science fiction and fantasy. Strangely–perhaps ironically, considering his popular Nightlord series–he's not usually a fan of vampire novels.

EDWARD WILLETT is the Aurora Award-winning author of more than sixty books of science fiction, fantasy, and non-fiction for readers of all ages, including twelve novels for DAW Books, the latest of which is *The Tangled Stars*, a humorous far-future space-opera heist novel featuring a talking genetically modified AI-uplifted cat who becomes a starship captain. Ed owns and operates Shadowpaw Press, which publishes new work by established and emerging authors and new editions of notable, previously published work, including the previous three volumes of the

Shapers of Worlds anthology series. A past president of SF Canada, he is currently vice-president of SaskBooks, the professional association of publishers in Saskatchewan. He lives in Regina, Saskatchewan, with his wife, Margaret Anne Hodges, P.Eng., and their black Siberian cat, Shadowpaw.

THE ILLUSTRATOR

WENDI NORDELL has been drawing for as long as she could hold a pencil. It has always been a favourite pastime and eventually became an occasional job. While her three children were growing up, she painted many murals, including the pediatrics wing in a hospital, a school entrance, and in many homes. She also attended festivals and craft shows, selling hand-drawn gift cards, bookmarks, and illustrations. Now that her children are grown, she has pursued an illustration career, illustrating a dozen books in the last five years, mostly for children, but also including Edward Willett's science-fiction and fantasy poetry collection *I Tumble Through the Diamond Dust*. Recently, Wendi decided to improve her artistic skills and abilities by returning to the Alberta University of the Arts, pursuing a degree in illustration. Wendi has almost always picked up books based on their cover art, and if there are illustrations inside the book, she thinks that's even better. She truly hopes that her illustrations enhance readers' experience with books—including this one!

ACKNOWLEDGMENTS

This anthology would not have been possible without the generous support of the many people who pledged to back it on Kickstarter. You not only made this terrific collection of science fiction and fantasy stories possible, you've set the stage for more *Shapers of Worlds* anthologies in the future.

This anthology only includes guests from the fourth year of *The Worldshapers* podcast. With luck and supporters like you, there'll be a Volume V next year featuring guests from the podcast's fifth year—an equally stellar collection of authors. Huge thanks to everyone listed below, and to those who chose to remain anonymous, for helping to bring this book to life.

KICKSTARTER BACKERS

Charles Kneifel, Julian Tysoe, Henrik Sörensen, Julian White, Michael Feir, Joseph Connell, John Crouch, Nancy, David Schumacher, Margaret Bumby, Ian Chung, Krystal Bohannan, Andrew Hatchell, Christine, Ian H., Tara Zrymiak, Andrew MacLeod, Edgar Middel, Pat, Stephen Ballentine, Steve Mashburn, Gareth Jones, Tania, Mike Miller, Andrew Foxx, The Creative Fund by BackerKit, Brendan Lonehawk, Michael Fedrowitz, Karen Mitchell Carothers, Cyn Armistead Newman, Cathy Green, Piet Wenings, Dr. Charles Elbert Norton III, Colleen Feeney, Pegana,

Dan Pollack, Massive Corporation Game Studios, David Myers, Tony Calidonna, Nicholas Stephenson, Melanie Marttila, Richard O'Shea, Aurora N., Rick Smathers, Sarah Ogden, Frankie, Jordan Theyel, Ruth Ann Orlansky, Joanne B Burrows, Luis Manuel Sánchez García, Adam Eaton, Thomas Bull, Eric Brown, Lisa Johnson, Carol J. Guess, James McCoy, Scott Raun, David Rowe, Mary Jo Rabe, Duane Warnecke, Kerry Kuhn, Alisa, C. Kierstead, Evan Ladouceur, Joshua Palmatier, Martin Beijer, Larry Strome, Kal Powell, Michael D'Auben, Donald Meyer, Craig "Stevo" Stephenson, Mark Newman, Kenneth Huie, Ed Ellis, Yankton Robins, Andy fytczyk, sjmalarkey, Karen, Craig Hackl, Robert Claney, Michael Barbour, Peggy Kimbell, Mike Hein, Jesse Klein, Elaewin, Brooks Moses, Jonathan, Rfinnen, Stu Glennie, Stephanie Lucas, Russell J Handelman, Jeroen Teitsma, Meyari McFarland, Robert Clemens, Rethyn, Mark Leslie, Lisa Kruse, Chuck Robinson, Kari Blocker, Jennifer Flora Black, dennis chambers, Brian Bygland, Jacques Toupin, Brian Roback, Gage Troy, Kate Malloy, Jessica Meade, T R Jacobs, Stephen Boucher, David 'slick' Sellers, Steven Peiper, Simo Muinonen, Marian Goldeen, Chris Thomas, Timkb4cq, Noah Lemelson, Sharon Eisbrenner, Seamus Sands, David Hopkinson, Susan Yearber, Margaret St. John, Laura, Jascakecaike, Kurt Beyerl, Wessel, Karen, Lisa Brolin, Mike Olivson, H, Jim Willett, Georgette St. Clair, Joe Geary, Eric P. Kurniawan, Peter Sanders, Catherine Leja, Nicolas Mandujano III, Peter Halasz, Richard D. Grant, ErikH, Kimberly Wong, Laura Gardner, Dino Hicks, RJ Hopkinson, Emily Schudel, Steve Arensberg, Matt, Dan Neely, Crysella, Jeffrey A. Carver, Darrow Cole, Richard Norton, Robert Woods Tienken, Keroan, Margaret Killeen, Louise Löwenspets, Margaret A. Menzies, Raphael Bressel, Sherrilyn McQueen, Ward R. Pederson, J.J. Green, Sharon K Sheffield, Andromeda Taylor, Eryn Rensing, Bethany Jezerey,

Praxis Axis, Duncan Wilcox, Jim Putz, this2ismyname, Valerie Andrews, Gas, Kolache, and Dramatic Skies, Chris Ess, Judith Silverthorne, Michèle Laframboise, Hope Taylor, Andrea Laws, Caroline Westra, Maureen Ulrich, Amy Nelson-Mile, Will Sobel, Hayden Trenholm, Joshua Van Pelt, Dwight Willett, Ronda Brewer, Alexander Bermejo Drachmann, Paula Jane Remlinger, Carol Bachelu, carver rapp, Pete Fox, Tyler Hulsey, Margaret Hodges, Laurel Stein, Arthur Slade, Matthew Bardeggia, Heather Nickel, Tom Rawls, Sharon Plumb, Arthur Dixon, Nadia Hyppolite, chris baumgartner, Robert Cram, Sara Ontiveros, Tiffany, Dylan, Richard Parker, Cheryl Morgan, Chris Spackman, Brett Mitchell, Matthew Gaglio, Isaiah Jacques, Natasha Chisdes, J. K. Swift, Ryan, Jace Chretin, Steven Butterworth, Sadie Cocteau, Arrow, Susan Jolly, Zack Fissel, Adam S., Barbara Tomporowski, Ross Emery, Matt Grimaldi, Joshua McGinnis, Robert Prior, Philip Peacock, Peter DeVito, Brynn, Connor Bliss, bill, Douglas King, Adam Rajski, Dr Douglas Vaughan, Patrick Fowler, V. Jakubovic, Robert D. Stewart, Cat Girczyc, Thorsten Daniel, Tiffany Hall, Gary Phillips, Michael Colangelo, Xavier Walker, James Gotaas, Karen Lloyd, Nathan Jones, BCurtis, Leah K., Mustela, James G. Connolly, Stephen Kotowych, William Brown, tonel, Tom McGrath, Simon Dick, Sabrina Dean, Meredith Carstens, tymoris, Andrew Evans, Owlglass, driquelmy, Randy Belanger, penguinon-strike, Michael Kingswood.

ABOUT SHADOWPAW PRESS

Shadowpaw Press is a small traditional, royalty-paying publishing company located in Regina, Saskatchewan, Canada, founded in 2018 by Edward Willett, an award-winning author of science fiction, fantasy, and non-fiction for readers of all ages. A member of Literary Press Group (Canada) and the Association of Canadian Publishers, Shadowpaw Press publishes an eclectic selection of books by both new and established authors, including adult fiction, young adult fiction, children's books, non-fiction, and anthologies.

In addition, Shadowpaw Press publishes new editions of notable, previously published books in any genre under the Shadowpaw Press Reprise imprint.

Email publisher@shadowpawpress.com for more information.

MORE SCIENCE FICTION AND FANTASY FROM

SHADOWPAW
PRESS

New work by new and established authors

The Downloaded by Robert J. Sawyer

The Good Soldier by Nir Yaniv

The Headmasters by Mark Morton

Shapers of Worlds Volumes I-IV, edited by Edward Willett

The Traitor's Son by Dave Duncan

Corridor to Nightmare by Dave Duncan

The Sun Runners by James Bow

Ashme's Song by Brad C. Anderson

Paths to the Stars by Edward Willett

Star Song by Edward Willett

SHADOWPAW
PRESS *Reprise*

New editions of notable, previously published work

The Canadian Chills Series by Arthur Slade:

Return of the Grudstone Ghosts, Ghost Hotel, Invasion of the IQ Snatchers

Duatero by Brad C. Anderson

Blue Fire by E. C. Blake

The Legend of Sarah by Leslie Gadallah

The Empire of Kaz trilogy by Leslie Gadallah:

Cat's Pawn, Cat's Gambit, Cat's Game

The Ghosts of Spiritwood by Martine Noël-Maw

The Shards of Excalibur Series (*Song of the Sword, Twist of the Blade, Lake in the Clouds, Cave Beneath the Sea, Door into Faerie*); The Peregrine Rising Duology (*Right to Know, Falcon's Egg*); *Spirit Singer, From the Street to the Stars,* and *Soulworm* by Edward Willett

For details about these and many other great titles, visit shadowpawpress.com

Made in the USA
Las Vegas, NV
26 January 2024

84900729R00256